# VOYAGE OF THE HEART

# OTHER TITLES BY SORAYA LANE

# VOYAGE OF THE HEART

Soraya Lane

Published by Lake Union Publishing, Seattle

www.apub.com

Amazon, the Amazon logo, and Lake Union Publishing are trademarks of Amazon. com, Inc., or its affiliates.

ISBN-13: 9781477826553
ISBN-10: 1477826556

Cover design by bürosüd° München, www.buerosued.de

Library of Congress Control Number: 2014942831

Printed in the United States of America

*For Mackenzie & Hunter. I love being an author,*
*but nothing beats being mum to my two gorgeous boys.*

# FOREWORD

By the end of World War II, more than 100,000 British women had married American soldiers. These women, some with children, were desperate to travel to America to be with their husbands, and in 1945 the United States Embassy in London was picketed with war brides demanding ships.

On December 29, 1945, the War Brides Act was passed by the United States Congress, which allowed war brides and minor children of American citizens entry into America.

The War Department commenced Project "Diaper Run," an operation to reunite husbands with their foreign brides and children in America. The first ship set sail on January 26, 1946, arriving in New York Harbor to the sounds of "Here Comes the Bride."

# PART ONE

# CHAPTER 1
## FEBRUARY 1946

Madeline Parker clutched her hat to her chest and waved goodbye to her parents. The ship groaned and heaved beneath her feet, as if straining beneath the weight of so many women. Heels cascaded over timber, the decibels of high-pitched female voices assaulting her eardrums, but nothing could quell the excitement beating a steady drum in her stomach. *This was it.*

A ship that had once transported soldiers to war was now taking them across the ocean to their husbands. To a new life so far from London they could have been traveling to another world.

A shriek made Madeline turn. She watched a young woman fall to her knees, sobbing as the ship pulled away. Madeline looked back to catch a final glimpse of her own mother, of her father bravely holding his wife against him. Tears fell down her cheeks, but she held her head high, and gave herself an internal talking-to. *She was leaving home for the man she loved.* It was time to start her own adventure, and she needed to count her blessings and get on with it.

All around her, women cried, giggled, screamed, and chatted. It was incredible. All these girls fleeing their families, leaving everything they'd ever known, to be with their handsome GIs.

"America," whispered Madeline. America. It sounded so exotic, so unknown, so decadent.

Her heart skipped its rhythm just thinking of her husband—a mix of love, excitement, and a strange fear, too, which she tried her best to ignore. Three weeks they had known one another—three exhilarating, exciting weeks they had spent together in total—and now she was finally going to be with him. All those months of waiting, hoping, and the day had finally come. She swallowed down a lump in her throat. Leaving her family was so hard, but it had to be worth it. It just had to be.

Madeline lifted her bag and moved away from the ship's edge, the people on the dock now dots in the distance. She wiped the tears from her eyes with quick, determined movements. There was no turning back. She just had to get on with what the future held now.

She was surrounded by women, although she knew no one. But she didn't feel alone. They were all leaving England with the same purpose; all wives who had patiently waited to be transported to their new homeland.

Signs had already started to be pinned up to boards, with different states scribbled across the top. Madeline watched as a group of women scrambled to add their names to a list. At the entrance to the ship's lounge was a huge poster—a map of the United States of America. She could see painted fingernails tracing every inch of it, working out exactly where they were going.

The flutter of identity cards pinned to jackets made her look down, then finger her own. Each color represented the state they were destined to live in, and right now hers made her feel like a refugee or cargo being shipped to the other side of the world.

"Great idea, don't you think?"

Madeline turned. The voice belonged to a pretty blonde, her hair a shimmer of tight curls falling almost to her shoulders. A sweep of red lipstick adorned full lips that were set in a wide smile.

"Ah, yes, it's clever."

"Alice Jones," said the other girl, extending a petite hand. She turned her shoulder to reveal another woman, standing behind her. "And this is June West."

"Madeline," Madeline replied.

They shook hands and smiled, before a shyer June stepped forward. Her hair was set in soft waves, hazel eyes hidden by her dark lashes as she glanced up, only briefly making eye contact.

"Where are you headed?" asked Alice. "Besides into your husband's arms, of course!"

Madeline couldn't help the smile that tugged at her lips. She held up her red identity card.

"New York."

"Oh my goodness. Us too!"

Alice clutched Madeline's hand and linked arms with June, before marching them off in the direction of the lists.

"We *must* sign up now. Imagine who else we could meet!" she said, sweeping them along with her.

"Are we assigned to rooms?" asked Madeline.

Alice shrugged. "I don't know, but we'll bribe whomever we have to so we can all room together, don't you think?"

Madeline nodded and hurried to keep up with her new friends. She guessed from the still-shy expression on June's face that she was a new recruit of Alice's too.

She was relieved. It was going to be a long journey and having someone fun to pass the time with was precisely what she needed— it was no good being alone with your thoughts for too long. Alice was confident and beautiful, and while that might have intimidated her at home, being under Alice's wing on a ship full of strangers was strangely comforting.

The beat of heels on the wooden deck was deafening, the sway of the ship as it moved out into deeper ocean already sending unwelcome rumbles through her stomach. Betty Olliver pressed one hand to her belly and tried to focus on breathing. In and out, she reminded herself, but it wasn't as easy as that. She had forced her oversized stomach in tightly under her blouse with the help of a corset, terrified one of the authorities would notice her pregnancy, and while she was pretty sure she'd gotten away undetected, it was making her feel faint. So faint she had a feeling she was about to keel overboard.

Betty grasped a nearby railing and wished she could just let her waist out from its restraints. She'd been determined not to wait around at home and give birth without her husband nearby, but now she was starting to feel differently. Very differently indeed.

When the letter had arrived telling her it was time to depart, there was no chance she was going to be left behind. *But now . . .*

"Oh dear, are you okay?"

She looked up and into the kindest blue eyes she'd seen in a long time. Betty just nodded, squeezing her own eyes shut for a second as if the act itself would give her strength.

"Oh no you're not," said the self-assured voice again. "I shall call an official over." Her tone was so bright and confident that Betty was sure she would do exactly as she said.

"No!" Betty expelled the word with all her might, reaching for the woman's wrist. "No."

The blue eyes turned from kindly to uncertain. Betty released her grip. She noticed two other women standing slightly to the left, and wished she hadn't spoken so rudely.

"I'm sorry, it's just, well," she dropped her voice an octave. "I'm in the family way."

The three women looked at one another. Betty felt dread shiver down her spine. Had she been too quick to voice her condition? Too trusting?

"Alice," said the first woman, her expression turning from serious to kind again, "and this is Madeline and June."

Betty smiled back at them, grateful they were being so kind. June's smile reached her eyes, her compassion clearly genuine as she worried her bottom lip with her top teeth. Madeline nodded to her. She was more reserved than the other two, and Betty felt a little scrutinized by her gaze, although there was undoubtedly a warmth to her brown eyes. They might be strangers, but they were looking at her like they were already friends.

"Betty Olliver." She regained her composure and straightened her shoulders. "I'll be fine in just a moment."

"Do you need to sit down?"

She didn't need to think that one over. She'd never been so in need of a seat. "Yes. Oh yes."

Alice wound her arm around her and took her weight. Betty didn't want to be a charity case, but she wasn't above admitting she needed help.

"I really owe you," she managed, feeling a sharp pain with every step despite the help. "I just . . ."

"You're not wearing a corset under there, are you?" Madeline hissed, pulling at the back of her cardigan. "Ooohh, you are, aren't you?" Her eyes narrowed, hands on her hips as she scolded her.

They all stopped. Betty knew she looked guilty, but what could she say? It was wait around alone or get on the first ship to find her husband. The first plan wasn't an option she could have ever entertained. Not when she had no family at home in London. In one way, Madeline was right in being angry with her. Women as heavily pregnant as she was weren't meant to be traveling, but she'd made a decision that she knew she wouldn't regret.

"I might not know a lot, but medical matters are what I *do* know something about. You could hurt the baby, not to mention yourself. And what if it brought the labor on before you're both ready?" Madeline looked angry, face flushed from telling her off, and Betty didn't have the will to fight. Maybe it had been a silly plan, but she was on board now and there was no going back.

"Quickly, let's undo these laces and you can throw this shawl over yourself." Madeline put an arm around Betty to help shield her from view. "No one will notice, not with everything going on." Her tone was kindly now, her anger replaced with a softness that sent a wave of relief through Betty. She spoke so authoritatively—she probably knew more about pregnancy than Betty knew herself.

"Thank you." It was all she could say. "Thank you, thank you so much."

Madeline tsked, and Alice just smiled kindly. So did June. Betty was on the verge of bursting into tears. It was nice not to feel so alone, to have company after so long without it. Madeline might be bossy, but there was a kindness and capability to her that settled Betty's racing heart. "There are medics on board," said June, her voice whisper-soft. "If something does happen, there'll be someone to care for you."

"Come on, let's find a cabin," announced Alice, holding out a hand. "I've heard there are eight hammocks in each, but the ship's not full and I'm sure we can get one together."

࿇

The girls huddled around Betty when they reached the cabin as she attempted to catch her breath. Lying down without the corset was helping. Her lungs still felt like they were heaving; even now her breathing had slowed, and she was grateful for the help. With her parents dead and no siblings, and a husband overseas, she'd been alone for her whole pregnancy. For once it was nice to be cared for.

"How many months are you?" asked Madeline.

Betty gulped. This was not a question she wanted to answer. Madeline seemed to know a lot about pregnancy, which meant she'd probably think even less of her once she knew.

"It's okay, we won't tell."

Betty smiled at Alice who, she'd decided, was perhaps the prettiest girl she'd ever met. All smiles and dimples, with a face that couldn't be called anything other than beautiful.

She noticed that Madeline was pursing her lips. She had a feeling she was the one who *would* tell. Or judge her. But maybe she just knew the most about babies. *And dangers.*

Betty felt all eyes on her. There had been times she'd wondered what it would feel like to be interrogated, to be a prisoner of war like she'd feared her husband could have been, and now she had an inkling of what it might be like.

"Betty?" asked Madeline again.

They deserved to know. She knew that. They had shown her kindness, helped her, when she needed it most. But could she risk it?

The faces around her were smiling, but also looked worried and tense.

She blew out a deep breath. There wasn't an easy way to say it. "Eight months."

"Oh my goodness, and you were trying to wear a corset?" Madeline gasped.

Betty's face flushed burning hot, her breath caught in her throat, but a warm hand thrust into hers helped to steady her. It was Alice's face she braved a look at first, followed by June—who was looking upset but not angry, and then finally Madeline. She knew she was only trying to help, but there was also something about Madeline's bossy attitude that made her want to square her shoulders and make her understand why she'd had no choice but to board the ship pregnant.

9

Betty swallowed her emotion and thrust her chin up, looking first Madeline in the eye, then the others.

"I just didn't want to do this alone. I wanted to be with my husband. I've no one else."

The nodding of heads around her made her realize she wasn't alone.

"And you felt like you'd waited long enough?" asked June, to more nodding from all of them.

"Well, I suppose there are lots of pregnant women on board," said Madeline, her voice softer now. "It's not like being pregnant or having a child with you is forbidden."

Betty shrugged and glanced at the girls. "They would have wanted a doctor to examine me first, and I'm too far along to be allowed on the ship." She rubbed her belly. "There's more than a chance I'll have this baby on board. Once we're out at sea there's nothing they can do, but they could have stopped me getting on in the first place."

They looked at her, a combination of smiles and frowns. She guessed they all understood, in a way. As would the women divided into the other side of the ship with their children. What had the paper called them? *The floating nursery?*

It was a feeling they all knew well, that desperation to be with their men. It wasn't every day you were surrounded by women who felt the same way, who were in love and desperate to see, *to feel*, their husbands in their arms again.

"So how did you meet yours?" Betty asked.

Alice laughed, a gentle, sparkling noise that made even Betty, with her still-aching stomach, grin.

"You do realize we've all got different answers to that question," Alice pointed out.

"And we probably all have really *long* answers to that question," chimed in June.

"Just so happens I've got all night," said Betty, wryly.

"I think what we need is something to eat, then we can yap all afternoon," said Madeline, ever practical.

Betty smiled at Madeline. "I'm all for eating," she said, rubbing her belly. "But I think I'll stay put here for a bit longer."

Madeline stretched and stood. "I'll go investigate. Anyone else want to come?"

Alice jumped up and joined Madeline, leaving Betty to stay reclined, with June tucking up in the adjoining hammock bed beside her for company. June might have been quieter than the others, but there was something very reassuring about having her near.

Betty watched as June patted her hair, absently tucking a few loose strands behind her ear on one side. Her skin was so pale it was almost porcelain, her lips painted a soft shade of pink. When she looked up and smiled, her gaze was shy but pure and genuine, too. There was not a bad bone in June's body; the kindness in her smile was like a reassuring hand against Betty's skin.

⌒◟◞

It seemed odd lying next to a pregnant woman who she'd only known for an hour, June thought, but somehow it felt right. They both lay in silence—the sort of silence that wasn't empty, that didn't need to be filled.

"So how long have you been married?"

That made Betty smile. "Guess?"

"Don't tell me. Eight months?"

They both laughed.

"I got pregnant on our honeymoon. We spent a weekend together at a little guest house, and I've only seen him once since."

June nodded. "I haven't seen my man since he left after our wedding. We were married in July, so I haven't seen him for months."

"Are you nervous about seeing him again?" Betty asked. "All I've heard of my Charlie has been by letters and telegram, and they're often so delayed in getting to me. But, he's promised to meet me at the docks—I sent word as soon as I heard what ship I was on and I just have to hope he gets it. Oh, the idea of seeing him again after so many months sets my heart thumping!"

Their eyes met, warily at first, but June recognized her feelings reflected in her new friend's gaze. It was a hard emotion to describe, one that only another war bride could ever share, but still June had worried that she was the only one nervous about seeing her husband again. They had met and fallen in love so quickly, faster than would ever have been allowed if the war hadn't been breathing down their necks. But fallen in love she had, and now she'd left everything she had ever known behind. Forever.

"So tell me about him. Your man. What's he like?" asked June.

Betty had looked exhausted, but the question about her husband seemed to revive her.

"I need a few more minutes to catch my breath." Betty smiled and changed position. "You go first."

June reached over to plump the two pillows behind Betty's back and wriggled to sit cross-legged on the hammock beside her, thankful it was sturdier than it looked. It was like sitting with her sister, like they'd always done at night, gabbing away about what they had seen that day, who they had talked to, and of course who they'd fallen in love with.

A pang of sadness made June ache, but she did her best to ignore it. She'd agonized for months about leaving her family, about never seeing her sister again or her mother and father. For all twenty-one years of her life, they'd meant the world to her, and now she'd left them forever to follow a handsome soldier she hardly knew. But then she had known that when she'd married him, that if he survived the war she would have to travel to be with him, and besides, she'd made a promise before God.

"You want the short version or the long version?"

Betty rubbed her hands together and smiled. "I want every last detail," she said, resting her hands on her belly. "I'm a hopeless romantic, in case you hadn't already figured out."

The clatter of heels made them both turn to look, and Alice and Madeline appeared in the doorway. They'd managed to smuggle four cups of something steaming, and what appeared to be some tomato sandwiches.

"You're just in time," announced Betty.

"For what?"

Madeline passed two cups to Betty and climbed onto the edge of the facing sling. Alice did the same for June.

"June's about to tell me how she met her man."

All eyes turned to June, and suddenly she wasn't sure if her story was even interesting enough to tell three other women. Alice was so confident, and with all the attention focused on her, she could feel heat slowly spreading up her neck and across her cheeks.

"It's really not that interesting."

"Don't be silly!" Madeline exclaimed, hands pressed together as if she couldn't wait to hear it.

"Nonsense," insisted Betty at the same time. "Now settle back down and get talking."

Alice might be larger than life, but the eager look in her eyes as she leaned forward to listen told June that she genuinely wanted to hear her story.

So she began. With three pairs of eyes on her and a cup of sweet tea in her hands, June let her mind drift back to almost eighteen months ago, when she'd first met the man of her dreams.

# CHAPTER 2
## APRIL 1945

Wind echoed through the trees and pulled her along in its embrace. June felt lucky today—there had been no bombs, no explosions to hinder the warmth of the sun. For once it was high in the sky and not hidden behind grimy clouds and belching smoke-filled air.

That was when she saw him. Sitting on a park bench, his head lolled back as if his neck could snap with the weight of it. It wasn't like she hadn't seen a soldier before. Almost all of the boys she'd grown up with or known from the neighborhood were off fighting in the war; indeed, the *only* young men she'd seen of late had been soldiers. But he was different.

June had heard talk of the American soldiers, even seen a few of them, or heard them wolf-whistling out to the girls when they passed. They wore uniforms that looked clean and crisp, not quite freshly laundered, but close. They would stand on street corners chewing gum, talking in their drawling accents.

This young man looked just like them, in his five-button uniform jacket, but he wasn't moving an inch and he was all alone.

June didn't know what to do. It was only a few minutes' walk to her house, but she didn't want to just leave him there. *Couldn't* just leave him there. He was a soldier, from an allied country, so it wouldn't be right to just ignore him. *Would it?*

"Huh-hmm." June cleared her throat with as much force as she could, almost starting a coughing fit. "Excuse me, sir."

She wondered if he was injured. There was no blood or wound she could see, but he seemed to be in a very heavy slumber.

She took a step forward, then another, inching slowly closer to him. She went to open her mouth then gulped back the air already in her lungs. He stunk. The pungent stench of alcohol seemed to seep from him.

"Yoo-hoo," she muttered. When there was still no response she kicked him firmly in the lower leg. "Soldier, wake up!"

A snort of a snore emitted from him and then his head snapped straight up. June jumped at least a foot backward, eyeing him cautiously.

"Soldier, you must have fallen asleep." The confidence in her voice surprised her when she was usually never so bold.

He blinked a few times before dropping his head in his open palms and rubbing at his face.

June waited. She quickly smoothed her hair, then folded her hands in front of her.

"Are you okay?" she asked.

The soldier shook his head and squinted one eye at her, as if the sun was simply too bright for his pupils, then cleared his throat.

"I think I'm drunk."

She tried not to giggle. His accent was funny enough without a drunken slur attached to it.

"I think," she said, "that you might be correct."

He tried to stand up and sat back down again with a thump.

"Yup." He hiccupped.

June went against her better judgment and, balancing her bag of groceries in one hand, moved forward to offer him the other.

15

How had a simple trip to the store ended in a rescue mission of a stranger?

"Here, take my arm." She surprised herself with her confidence, felt as if she was acting a role in front of the handsome soldier. "Can I help you back to where you're staying?"

"I can't go back," he mumbled. "Not in this state."

She pursed her lips, fidgeting on the spot as she tried to think what to do.

"Can't you take me home with you?"

"Home?" she squeaked. "With me?"

"Please?" His eyes were pleading, his smile making her heart thump far too hard.

"I, well," she hesitated, uncertain. "I guess I could take you back, but only to clean you up then send you on your way."

"You would?"

He stumbled as she helped him, his face falling only inches away from her own. Even smelling like a pub and unable to stand on his own feet, June couldn't help but notice how handsome he was. He had dark brown hair that was short at the sides but flopped ever so slightly over his forehead at the front. Eyes the color of a hazelnut stared back at her—even slightly glassy and alcohol-enhanced, they were the most honest, deep eyes she had ever looked into. Maybe that's why she was acting so out of character. Somehow, she instantly felt connected to this man.

"Hi," he said, looking like a puppy dog as he watched her watching him.

"Come on." June forced herself to look away, feeling a blush rise to her cheeks. "Just put one foot in front of the other."

And so they walked, she assisting a soldier, and he gazing back at her as if he'd never in his life seen a woman before.

June took a deep lungful of air before pushing open the door to her house.

"Hello. Anyone here?" she called down the hallway.

There was no reply. She didn't exactly want to be alone with a strange man—she'd never caused her parents alarm before and she didn't want to start now. And yet, another part of her wanted nothing more than some extra time with him just to herself.

"Ma!" she hollered this time.

When there was no response, June went against her better judgment again and hauled the soldier in with her. She still couldn't believe she was acting like this, but she was overwhelmed by the effect he was having on her. This despite the fact he'd hardly uttered a word the entire way, with the exception of the odd hiccup or apology for stumbling.

"Come on now, sit here," she instructed him.

The soldier did as he was told, thumping down in a seat at the table. June looked out the window and saw her mother wrestling with wash on the line. That gave June a few moments to compose herself before she had to go out and explain that they had company. Their home was tidy but modest. Her mother kept everything scrubbed clean and looking immaculate, whether they were expecting visitors or not. She glanced at the soldier, wondering if he was used to a house like hers or something more extravagant in America.

"What's your name?" she asked, busying herself with putting the kettle on to boil.

He gazed up at her, a goofy smile on his face.

"Edward West," he told her. "My friends call me Eddie."

She smiled over at him as she poured them tea. "Well, it's nice to meet you, Edward. My name's June."

He took the cup happily, holding on to it while she spooned some sugar and gave the liquid a stir.

"Now, Edward . . ."

He interrupted her.

"Eddie," he said, narrowly avoiding swishing his tea over the floor. "You can call me Eddie."

"Eddie, my mother will be inside soon, and I need you to sober up. She doesn't take kindly to men that drink."

"I don't usually drink," he said, his dark eyes wide with honesty. "It's just my friends got me drunk, we were out all night, then they left me."

June nodded. For some reason she thought she could trust him, but it was her parents he was going to have to convince.

"Either way, just drink that tea then I'll show you where you can wash up."

Eddie gulped down the last of the hot tea, the cup lost to his big paw of a hand, and stood up. He was still slightly unbalanced, she noted, but getting better.

"Come on, quick," she said, eyes on her mother as she followed the path back in, dry laundry in her arms.

June led him to the washroom, passed him a towel and face cloth, and closed the door.

"Is that you home, dear?"

June leaned against the timber frame and counted to ten. Her mother might frown upon her spending time alone with a young man, but she'd never turn him away. Her father would have done the same thing in June's place. The Americans were going to help them win the war, and that meant showing gratitude and kindness in their direction whenever possible. So why was she so worried about facing her mother?

"June?"

"Coming, Ma," she called back.

A bang in the room behind her made June's heart jump, but she ignored it. He could make all the noise he wanted, so long as he came out smelling of soap with his hair combed.

"You okay, love?" her mother asked as she joined her in the kitchen. "You're very flushed."

Another bang echoed, louder this time.

"Is that your father home early?"

June felt her face flush even hotter. "Ah, no, it's not Father," she said.

Her mother pressed her lips together, her eyebrows knotting in the middle. "Well what's all that noise, then?"

June hesitated. "I'll make you a cuppa and tell you all about it."

⟅⟆

To say her mother had been taken by surprise would have been an understatement. But being the type of woman she was, she'd simply dealt with having a strange American in her home, and gone about making a larger dinner. Although she still wasn't convinced about how they'd met.

"You sure you've never seen him before?"

June glared at her mother. "I've told you, I have never set eyes upon him before. *Ever.*"

Her mother raised an eyebrow again, gave her *the* look.

"Ma! I've never even met an American before."

A door down the hall banged shut. June gulped. Her mother put down the wooden spoon she'd been using to stir the stew and wiped her hands over her apron.

Eddie appeared in the kitchen, and June nearly lost her balance. She gripped the old wooden chair. She'd expected him to come back out looking no better than when she'd left him.

*How wrong she'd been.*

Eddie had combed his hair back off his face, scrubbed his skin clean, and his cheeks were soft from being freshly shaved. She guessed he'd found her father's razor. His eyes were still bloodshot,

19

but he was quite possibly the most handsome man she had ever encountered.

"Well, I take it you're our soldier?"

Her mother asked as if he was a pet her daughter had just brought home rather than a man serving his country.

"Yes Ma'am," he replied, his voice lacking the slur it had had earlier.

June guessed he had been splashing a lot of cold water on his face.

"I'm Edward West." He held out his hand.

June's mother nodded and, looking slightly flustered, took Eddie's hand and gave it an awkward shake.

"Well, Edward West, you're very lucky our June here found you." She turned back to stirring. "I'm hoping you like stew. I'll be serving dinner soon."

June glanced up at Eddie and he gave her a wink in reply. She felt yet another blush start at her toes and work its way up every square inch of her body.

"Is there anything I can do, Mrs. . . ."

"Mrs. Smith," she replied.

"Mrs. Smith," he said, smiling at June as her mother kept herself busy. "Is there anything I can do for you?"

Madge Smith turned around and waved her spoon at him.

"Now why would I let a guest help me in the kitchen, and a man at that?"

He shrugged. "My mother always told me to keep myself useful. She'd give me a clip around the ears for taking liberties."

June stifled her laugh as her mother muttered away to herself about men in the kitchen, before catching Eddie's eyes again.

"Why don't you show me around?" suggested Eddie.

She glanced at her mother, who didn't respond, and picked up her shawl, which was resting on the table.

"All right."

"So where is it you come from, Eddie?" He'd complimented her on their home after taking a look around and she was proud. It might not be flashy, but it was home and she loved it.

He stretched back on the seat outside, his long legs crossed at the ankle. June was trying hard not to stare at him, but it wasn't easy. The olive skin on the planes of his cheeks, the dark lashes that framed those hazel eyes, even the way his hands moved in expression as he talked. She was fascinated by him.

"Home is a long, long way away," he said, his face turned up toward the sky. "I come from a place called New York. We've got a farm there, with fields stretching for miles, cows milling around, even a few horses and a wooden stable block beside the house."

He looked at her, his eyes searching hers, as if worried she wasn't interested. Her lips turned up into a smile.

"We've lived there all my life," he said, taking her smile as an invitation to continue. "It's two story, built from wood with my father and grandfather's own hands. We have a big porch where we eat in summer, there are trail rides nearby for taking the horses out, and a lake where I fish with my dad. Just me and my sister, our parents, and a whole lot of animals."

"It sounds incredible," she said, almost seeing the picture in her imagination. He spoke with such enthusiasm, such love, that it was hard not to imagine it along with him.

"It is," he said, turning back to face her. "I really miss it, and my family. My sister would like you."

She wondered how he knew that, when they hadn't even known each other more than a couple of hours, but she believed him. Her worry was that her own sister might like him too, and that was not a thought she wanted to entertain.

He watched her then, his eyes locked on hers. She hadn't been attracted to a man before, not like this. She was only nineteen.

There had been no romances in her life before the war, and for the last couple of years all the young men she might have met had been away fighting. And now here was Eddie, this dashing soldier in an American uniform, looking at her as she imagined a sweetheart would. His eyes on hers, his body a little too close, and her breath catching in her throat as if she'd just run a mile.

"Dinner's ready!"

Her mother's voice jolted her from the little fantasy she was lost in. She couldn't believe it was already five; she'd found him early afternoon and the time had flown past.

Eddie stood and held out a hand.

"I'm starved," he said with a grin. "Been a long time since I've had a home cooked meal."

June took his hand to rise then walked ahead of him, conscious of his presence behind her. She knew it was silly, but she wondered if it was possible to fall in love with someone so quickly. She may have led a sheltered life, but she'd never felt like this. *Ever.*

Eddie reached in front of her to open the door and she walked through. But not before the side of her body brushed past his arm. She didn't dare look up at him, sure he must be able to hear the pounding of her heart.

Her illusions abruptly ended when she saw her father already seated at the table. She cleared her throat and composed herself and moved another step away from Eddie.

"I'm told we're in the presence of a soldier," her father said, smiling as he stood.

She glided the few steps between them and kissed her father's cheek.

"We are, Daddy. This is Edward. Eddie West."

"How do you do, Sir," said Eddie, gripping her father's hand as he offered it. "It's an honor to be in your home."

Her father shook his head. "It's nice to have a soldier for dinner. Especially an ally."

Eddie moved to assist her mother as she clutched a large pot of heavy stew, taking it from her hands and ferrying it safely to the table.

"You're not a deserter though, are you son?"

June could have laughed at her father. He must have been beside himself, worried they could be harboring a coward.

"No Sir," said Eddie, looking unfazed by the question. "I'm on four days leave, then back with my unit."

"Very well." Her father sat back down.

June smiled shyly at Eddie as he watched her from across the table, then tried to concentrate on her dinner. She'd gone from feeling unfortunate for stumbling across him in the street to feeling very, very lucky. Not for the first time since the war had started, she thought about how being in the right place at the right time sometimes meant everything in life.

Thank goodness her sister was at a nurses' meeting. She wouldn't have stood a chance otherwise if Lilly was here.

Eddie grinned at her and she tried to avoid his gaze.

Or maybe she would have stood a chance still. *Maybe.*

"How about I take you to a dance tomorrow night?"

June tried not to smile too brightly, instead wrapping her hands one over the other and squeezing hard, not wanting to seem too keen. They were sitting outside, just the two of them, and she was trying to behave how she imagined her sister would.

"That would be lovely."

Eddie grinned at her, looking wolfish in the almost darkness. A ray of light illuminated only part of his face and it made his mouth look lopsided, white teeth glinting.

"And then the night after that the pictures?"

June couldn't stop her smile that time. He wasn't still drunk, was he? Could he really be as attracted to her as she was to him?

"What do you say?"

She swallowed her fears and looked up at him.

"I say that sounds like a nice idea."

He took one of her hands in his, his skin rough against the softness of her own. Manly, like hands that had known real work.

"You English girls are so restrained."

She almost pulled her hand away. What did he mean by that?

He responded by dropping a kiss filled with laughter to her palm.

"Nice?" he repeated. "I was hoping you would say that a night or two with me sounded smashing, but you just think it would be *nice*."

She giggled and swatted at him.

"Eddie . . ."

"What?" His eyes were glinting.

A noise nearby made June leap away from him.

"Is that your mother?" he whispered.

June nodded. "Uh-huh."

"It's been a lovely evening, but I really must be off now." His loud voice belied the humor in his face.

All she could do was nod. She knew her mother would be listening. It seemed Eddie did too.

"I'll just thank your mother for tea and ask your father's permission to escort you to the dance tomorrow evening, then I'd best be off."

The soft bang of a door closing signaled her mother disappearing back inside, probably to sit down with her feet up and pretend that she'd been there all along.

Eddie stood first, then pulled her up to her feet. He leaned in and stole a kiss to her cheek—a firm press of his lips that lingered slightly too long, and that had blood pumping so fast through her body that she almost keeled over right there on the spot.

It wasn't even on the lips, but it still felt like her first real kiss.

❦

June waited, her breath crowding her face as she lay with the blankets tucked up to her forehead. It seemed like she'd been lying there forever, listening to her sister bang about as she came in, talk to their mother as she ate leftover stew, and finally traipse down the hall to the room they shared.

She continued to stay still, silent, as a sliver of light spilt into the room from the hallway.

"Lilly!" she hissed, flinging the covers back as her sister appeared, making Lilly jump.

"June," Lilly scolded, throwing her cardigan at her. "You scared the blinkin' life out of me!"

"Just scoot in here, would you!"

Lilly ignored her for a moment, pulling off her clothes and getting into her flannel nightdress. June wriggled over in the small bed so her sister could fit in beside her. They both had their own beds, but since they were little girls they had tucked in beside one another to talk, sometimes long into the night, before parting ways to sleep.

"Okay, spill," said Lilly as she snuggled beneath the covers and they wriggled together for warmth. "What do I hear about you entertaining soldiers while I'm away doing my duty?"

June blushed, her cheeks igniting as if fire had kissed them. She was pleased the dark hid her excitement, so her sister couldn't tease her about her naivety and inexperience with boys.

"Before you say anything, don't get any fancy ideas about your date tomorrow night." Lilly dug her in the ribs with a sharp elbow as she teased. "Mother has appointed me your chaperone, so he had better have some nice friends."

June stayed silent. It wasn't because she was disappointed about not going alone. Her sister was older than her by two years, and knew about things like boys and dances and how to impress. But she was used to being overlooked when her sister was nearby.

"So? Come on. What was he like, how did you find him, and how did you get him to ask you out?"

ᕫ

The faint light in the living room wasn't helping June feel any less nervous. They had black-outs over the windows and her father preferred a dim light to sit and talk in. But she wanted a bright light under which to scrutinize her appearance.

"You look fine, June," announced Lilly, gracing the room with her presence, and looking stunning as usual.

She did an impromptu twirl, encouraging her calf length dress to flit out around her. Her blonde hair was pulled half-up, back from her face, eyes made up and lips pouting in a hard-to-find pink. Her sister had had enough dates for the both of them, and June guessed one of them must have been American for her to end up with such a decadent new lip shade.

"Are you sure about this dress?" June had a feeling it was too much. Too girly. Too . . . She glanced down at her borrowed green dress covered in black polka dots, worrying she didn't look as good as Lilly had when she'd worn it. The waist was nipped in, her legs on show from just below the knee.

Lilly grabbed her and swung her around. "You look gorgeous, little sister, just gorgeous."

26

Their father looked between them and chuckled before standing and kissing each of them on the cheek.

"Lilly, beautiful as ever," he said, reaching for his eldest. "But June, you look lovely tonight. Belle of the ball."

She had a feeling her father was trying to make her feel better, but her mother was nodding her head too and dabbing at her eyes. Heavens! It was as if she was off on her honeymoon, not just going out with her sister to a dance.

A tap at the door made June freeze. If it hadn't been for Lilly grabbing her hand, she'd have run to her bedroom and locked the door.

"For heaven's sake, you're nineteen!" scolded her sister. "And you'll be fine," she added with a whisper, dragging her along. "If he liked you yesterday, then he'll love you tonight."

June hoped so. Oh, she hoped so!

She sucked back a deep breath and opened the door, Lilly standing behind her, eager to get a look at this man.

"Hi June." Eddie thrust a handful of daisies at her and placed a clumsy kiss on her cheek.

"Ah, thank you," June said softly.

Lilly pried the flowers from her and passed them to her mother.

"They're beautiful, Eddie, they're . . ." June looked over at them then back at him.

"From your neighbor's garden." He said it with a touch of regret, and she liked that he was at least honest.

She also liked that he didn't so much as glance at her sister.

"This is Lilly. My sister," she said, waving back in her direction.

"Eddie," he said, taking Lilly's hand for a polite moment before touching June's elbow and leading her out of the door.

"Like a lovesick puppy, this one," she heard Lilly laugh to her mother before following them down the street.

But she couldn't have cared less. She was the luckiest girl in the world as far as she was concerned. And right now, that was all that mattered.

୬୬

June was thankful to have her sister walking with them. Aside from his initial welcome, Eddie had seemed even shyer than her and although she found that oddly reassuring, she was glad to have Lilly there to break the silence. June and Eddie were walking side-by-side, arms bumping every few steps, and she felt every touch. Lost her breath every time he glanced at her and didn't know how she could possibly cope with dancing in his arms.

"So Eddie, our June tells me you live on a farm."

Lilly winked at June and she wished it was dark. That night would fall and conceal her face.

"Country born and bred," he answered.

"And you're not married or promised to a lass back home?"

"Lilly!" June couldn't believe she'd even thought to ask something like that.

"No ma'am," said Eddie, his voice overlapping with June's.

He stopped walking and faced her sister. Had he taken great offense to her question? Was he going to put an end to their night here and now? June bit hard on the inside of her mouth.

"I wouldn't have asked your sister out if I was promised."

The look on his face was so serious June might have laughed if she wasn't so embarrassed.

Lilly nodded. "Fair enough."

"I love her," he blurted. "I fell in love with her from the moment she found me."

Heat rushed through June's body. He loved her?

28

"Love?" repeated Lilly, waving her hand dismissively in the air. "Only an American would waffle on about love. You've only known her a day!"

But though she couldn't muster the energy to look at him, was too embarrassed to even think of responding, a warmth that she couldn't describe filled June's heart.

Eddie took her hand and squeezed it tightly. She squeezed his in return. And as they walked, palms pressed together, for the first time in her life she started to believe in the idea of love at first sight. She might have despaired at finding him when she'd first seen him, but one look into those dark hazel eyes had been all she'd needed. The realization had taken the breath from her lungs. She also knew, from that day forward, that she'd follow Eddie to the end of the earth, if it meant never having to let go of his hand.

# CHAPTER 3

June wiped a tear as it trickled a path down her cheek. Just thinking about Eddie had her heart racing. Would it still be the same? Would he be waiting for her as he'd promised? And her sister. Her mother. Her father. *Would she truly be able to live a happy life without them?* Writing letters had been lovely, but it wasn't like being with him, like having him near. They'd only had one week together since their wedding, and in the months that had passed since, she'd worried between each letter she'd received about how he might be feeling.

"You'll be okay, luv. It'll all be fine," Betty said gently, jolting June from her thoughts.

She squeezed Betty's hand and turned to face her. The other two girls had already fallen asleep in their hammocks once she'd told her story, tired from the excitement of the day and soothed by the rocking of the ship. But June had decided to stay awake with Betty, who was struggling to get comfortable and still had cramps in her stomach.

"June?"

She reached to pull a blanket over herself and made out Betty's face in the fading light, looking concerned. She realized she hadn't responded to her yet.

"You're right, it'll all be fine," June sighed. "It just feels like there's a long road ahead."

"You never did say what happened to your sister. Did she find her own prince charming?"

That made her laugh. "Our Lilly had plenty of suitors, but she went and fell for a Yank too."

Betty was suddenly upright. "Oooh, please, you *have* to tell me!"

June shook her head. "I've done enough talking for today. Let's just say that Lilly met a man that night at the dance who managed to knock the cynicism out of her. But she was never going to be manhandled off to America."

Betty reached out to June with one hand, the other rubbing in large circles on her belly.

"Did they marry?"

"Yes. But only once she'd made him swear that he'd never ask her to move to Big Sky Country. Once the war ended, he came back and they rented a little cottage down the road from our parents' house."

"You're going to miss her terribly. But I guess you know that, don't you?" said Betty.

June blinked as tears filled her eyes again. "Let's just hope these men are worth it, huh?"

"They will be, won't they?"

June could hear the sincerity in Betty's voice. There wasn't a doubt that Betty had a kind heart. She'd taken a leap of faith in telling them about her pregnancy, and she'd listened so intently to June's story, tears swimming in her chocolate brown eyes when she'd told her about the dance.

❦

It was a hard thing to do, leave the world you knew behind and as good as go to live on the moon. Because that's how far away they were going to be from their families. They came from decent people who worked hard, but would likely never be able to afford to visit their daughters abroad.

"Betty, even if they're not, we've got to make the most of it," June said, trying to be braver than she felt.

She did her best to ignore the sob threatening to strangle her throat. Betty squeezed her hand harder, and June felt comforted.

At least she had someone who understood, who was in the same situation. Someone who could be her friend now and in America. Or at least she hoped.

⚬⚬

"So, what do you know about New York?" Madeline asked.

Alice smiled and placed one hand dramatically over her forehead. "Why, it's the place movie stars and moguls live, ain't it?"

Her American accent had them all giggling.

"I think you're thinking of Hollywood," corrected June.

Betty wriggled beneath a wool blanket as Madeline and June sat down with a paper bag full of chocolate chip cookies. They'd all managed to get a good night's sleep the night before, and they'd wanted to get out of the cabin even though it was still cold out. They felt cozy and protected in each other's company, but they'd all been craving fresh air. Up on deck, the air was salty and a breeze was blowing, but that hadn't stopped plenty of passengers from getting out in the open.

"Where did you get those?"

Alice wiggled her fingers in delight and Betty smiled.

"The canteen has food like you've never seen," said June. She passed the packet around. "And stockings, and pretty writing paper and pens."

Betty giggled before taking a biscuit for herself. "I was more interested when you were talking about the food," she said, rubbing her stomach, "but it all does sound rather incredible."

"How much money do you have?" Madeline asked.

June blushed before whispering. "I tucked a little extra away in my knickers."

Alice put out her hand for another treat. "You'll have to give us all another one then to stay quiet."

"£10 won't go very far. I think that was a bit mean, not letting us bring any more. I mean, what if something happened and we had to live off our own means for a while?" Madeline said, her eyebrows drawn together, clearly worried.

They sat and ate, nibbling the chocolate and licking at their fingers. There was no land on the horizon, just water stretching out for miles all around them, the sun glinting off the blue-green ocean.

"Do you think they let you do this in America?" asked Alice.

Betty giggled at her. "What? Lick our fingers?"

She nodded.

June reached for her bag and pulled out a magazine. "Haven't you girls been reading up on our new country?"

That made them all laugh.

"My mother bought this for me the week before I left. Thought it would help me, you know, prepare," June told them, no longer feeling so shy in the company of the other girls now that she'd opened up to them about Eddie.

Madeline wiped her fingers on a napkin then sat back in the sun. "You'd better start sharing then."

"How about a quiz?" June waggled her eyebrows.

"Oooh, I love a good game," said Betty.

June waited for the other two. They nodded, reluctantly.

"Don't make it too hard," moaned Alice.

"Let's start with names," June said, beginning to enjoy herself.

"Names?" They all answered in unison.

"You know, like what the American word is for things."

"I thought they spoke English?" Alice groaned.

June leaned over and placed an arm around Alice's shoulders. "Well, they might not speak Chinese, but there are a few differences."

June giggled as the girls sat like school children, crowded around her. "No peeking," she instructed. She held the magazine high against her chest. "All right, an easy one to start with. What's the name for a sweet biscuit?"

Betty thrust her hand into the air. "Cookie."

"Well done, Miss Betty."

Alice groaned again and shut her eyes. The other two clapped politely.

"How about lavatory?"

"As in I'd rather be in a lavatory right now?" said Alice cheekily.

"No, Alice! What's the word? No one in America will know what you mean if you ask where the lavatory is."

They all looked back at her like they had no idea what she was talking about.

"Toilet."

"Oh, I knew that one!" Betty sat up straighter. "Come on, more."

"What is a scone?"

"Biscuit!" yelled Madeline.

A sharp look from an official made them drop their voices.

"Verandah?"

They all stayed silent.

"Porch," Madeline whispered.

"How about you read to us and we'll just listen?" suggested Alice, leaning back with her ankles elegantly crossed, gazing out toward the ocean.

June flicked through the pages and then dumped the magazine on the table. "I think you all need to read it anyway. I've done enough talking for the day."

A plop of rain hit Alice on the forehead and she squealed. "Quick, to the cabin!"

June helped Betty to her feet, then linked arms with her and Madeline. They followed Alice as she fled, heels starting to skid on the deck as rain fell with fury from the clouds above.

⁊

Alice grimaced as she peeled her wet cardigan from her body and strung it up on the line hanging across the room. She re-tucked in her camisole and reached for a woolen top.

"I guess we're stuck here until dinner?"

Alice looked up as Betty spoke.

"We could go to the lounge," she suggested.

June shook her head and tucked up under the covers. "I think we should stay right here."

"While you read us out passages from *Good Housekeeping*?" teased Madeline.

"No, while one of you tells us your story."

They all looked in opposite directions.

"Come on! You made me tell mine, so now it's someone else's turn." June glared at them all.

Betty pointed at Alice. "Make her do it," she said. "I just get all emotional talking about my Charlie." She rubbed her belly, eyes downcast.

Alice straightened her shoulders and stretched her back, before slipping a scarf around her neck to combat the cold and sitting on the center hammock. Their surroundings were bare, with nothing but hammocks hanging around the room. If it hadn't been for their bright clothes and things strewn everywhere, the cabin would have been depressing at best. "You really want to hear my story?"

"Yes," affirmed June.

"How long do I have?"

"Until dinner," said Betty.

Alice gave a dramatic, arms spread wide pose, then lay on her stomach, elbows propping her up. She blocked out the murky cream walls and peeling paint, and let her mind wander. It wasn't hard, she thought about her man constantly, remembered everything about him. Every moment they had spent together. Writing letters these past five months hadn't been the same as having him near, but she knew how lucky she'd been to see him after the war had ended when so many others hadn't seen their husbands for a year or more now.

"My father always said that to sit idle during the war was to not make an effort at all," she began, in her clear, confident voice. "If you believed in your country, no matter how old you were or what your standing then you had to do something. So I joined up with the Red Cross, trained as a nurse, and started to look after our men as they came home. Or any men really, any soldiers who needed medical assistance."

She cupped her chin with her palms and closed her eyes. It still felt like just yesterday . . .

❦

Alice would never forget the day Ralph Jones grabbed hold of her wrist. She was walking between the beds, refilling waters and checking temperatures, when a strong hand closed over her skin and didn't let go.

"Don't leave me." An American voice croaked, tight, as if it hadn't spoken in days.

"It's okay, soldier, you're not alone here."

He still didn't let go of her wrist.

"Please."

Alice scanned the room. The battle-axe who passed for head nurse was nowhere to be seen.

"Would you like water?" she asked.

His head moved, only just, side to side. "No."

Alice looked again but saw no one. "If you let go of my wrist I'll pull out a seat and sit with you."

"Promise?" he asked.

"Promise."

She reached beneath the bed and slid a seat out. She knew there was one there because she'd stored it there herself before the bed was filled. Alice leaned over to get his charts and had a quick scan.

"Well, Captain Jones, it seems you're lucky to be here."

There was no response. His eyes were closed. She put the chart back and pushed back the seat to stand.

He touched her wrist again. Not the strong hold like before, but a skim of his hand against hers. She stopped. "Please."

Alice sat down again. She'd lost plenty of soldiers since she'd started working as a nurse, men she'd cared for as best she could when they'd arrived at the hospital injured, but who still hadn't survived. She'd even had some propose to her—even fancied the odd one. But this man was different from anyone she'd ever encountered before. Even with the bandage disguising half his face, the leg suspended in a cast, and blankets covering almost all of his body, there was something about him, a strength, a power that his injuries couldn't disguise.

She reached for the water and tucked her arm beneath his pillow. "Take a sip."

The captain leaned forward, his lips parting softly as she tipped the water for him.

"Thank you."

It was then Alice felt a peculiar sensation trace her arm. She placed the cup back on the side table and took up her seat again. The soldier kept his hand on hers, his fingers caught against her own. The sensation kept crawling against her skin. Tickling her. Making her aware of him.

He opened his eyes, turned his head slightly, and looked straight at her. She swallowed, not breaking their gaze.

"You can call me Ralph."

"Alice," she whispered.

"Alice," he repeated. "Thank you, Alice." He relaxed back into the pillow, closing his eyes.

Alice stood, worried about being caught. She watched him for a while, listened to his breathing, and decided he was asleep.

She ran her fingers over his palm, said a little prayer that he'd still be alive when her shift started in the morning, then left.

∽

Every day that Alice saw Ralph Jones was a good one. Even when she wasn't assigned to look after him, Alice found an excuse to visit him, to sit beside his bed and read to him. The paper, poems, anything really, just so she could spend time in his company. He told her stories of America, talked about friends he hoped to see again one day, and every day he told her that once he could walk, they'd go dancing.

"But I'm your nurse, that wouldn't be proper!" she told him when he asked her out.

"Sweetheart, I'm a Captain in the United States Army. No one's gonna tell me off for taking you for a spin."

"How about that sweetheart of yours back home? I'll bet she'll care!"

"I don't have a sweetheart back home, Alice. Would I be talking to you like this if I did?"

And then she'd done what she did every day. Pressed a kiss to his forehead, squeezed his hand, and walked away. She didn't want to get too attached, and besides, she liked to keep a man hanging. It was all about the thrill of the chase for her, the glamor of meeting a man who wanted to wine and dine her, and she had no intention of settling for just any man.

But the day she arrived at work, rushing to spend time with Ralph before her shift started, and he wasn't there, she regretted playing hard to get. It was all she could do not to sob and crawl into a ball on his bed. She might have, had his bed not already been filled.

She'd rushed into the nurses' station, hands shaking, to find a note pinned to the board. A messy "Alice" was scrawled on an envelope.

Alice reached a finger out to trace the smudged writing, before pulling it from the board. It didn't say much. No words of love or misery. But in all her life she would never forget what he'd written.

*I'll find you.*

Every day after, for two months, she'd wished those words would come true.

Alice was so tired, her head so heavy it felt as if it belonged to a giant. Part of her wanted to ignore the knock at the door now that she was finally home and desperate to crawl into bed, but she was too polite to hide. Her shift had gone on hours longer than expected, and she'd seen more blood than she could ever have imagined witnessing in her pre-war life, when every day had been simple, easy, unlike the endless hours that stretched out as a nurse. Before the war she'd been pampered, her father indulging her and wanting the best for his only daughter. Her family wasn't particularly wealthy, but her father always seemed to find a little bit extra to treat her with. But all that had changed and she'd had to get used to going without.

Another bang echoed down the hall. She cringed. Company had not been part of her plan. The empty house had suited her mood just fine.

She hauled back the timber door.

Her eyes locked on a uniformed body, on piercing grey eyes that didn't blink. *It couldn't be, could it?*

Alice looked him up and down again before braving another glimpse at his face.

"Remember me?" he asked.

She couldn't have stopped her smile if she'd tried.

"Ralph!" Alice flung her arms about his shoulders. "Oh, Ralph."

"I said I'd find you, didn't I?"

It had been months since he'd disappeared. Months since she'd last held his hand, whispered a kiss against his cheek, watched him sleep.

*And now he'd found her.*

"Are you going to let me in?"

Alice moved aside and let him enter. She didn't even bother to close the door. She touched her fingers against his and took the hand he offered.

*Ralph was back.* That was all that mattered.

She could inspect his old wounds later. *He was here.*

"I was called away, love, as soon as they discharged me. But I always knew I'd find you."

Deep down in her heart, Alice had known that too.

Before the war, Alice had been used to the high life. And even since times had become tougher, she'd always managed to find nice men who liked to indulge her and still had the means to do so. She liked being made a fuss of, and if she was asked out to dinner or a show she always said yes.

Ralph? He was a cut above the London men she'd once been impressed with. Now that he was back, he was intent on making up for lost time—he showered her with gifts, found things that just weren't possible to locate in wartime rationing, and made her heart race like no man before.

The stockings, squares of chocolate, even ridiculous luxuries like legs of turkey, only made her love him more.

It was the official uniform, pressed and distinguished, and the way even her senior nurse looked the other way if Ralph wanted to see her at work that really made her excited, though. The power made her giddy, although she never let him take charge of her like he did his men.

But she still didn't know how much longer she'd have him for. Or what was to become of them. He could be called away at a moment's notice from his posting in London, and he was always telling her that the day would come when he'd be needed elsewhere.

And only a few weeks later, her fears came true. Now she was facing life alone, again, without him now that he'd been called away again. Would he ever come back to her? Could he even make that promise again and know in his heart he'd be able to keep it? A fresh wave of tears threatened to spill again and she dabbed at her eyes, not wanting to ruin her make-up before her nursing shift started. It was one thing to plan a future pre-war, but he could just as easily be killed the moment he left London. And what if he never proposed? If they never even had the chance to get married?

"Alice?"

Ralph's voice rang out in the crisp London air. She had purposely chosen a quiet spot to sit; a seat hidden by the breadth of a large oak tree, in the little clearing near the hospital. It had once been a private garden, now it was a park of sorts for injured men to be wheeled about in.

She stood, revealing herself. Her eyes drank in the outline of his figure, the cut of his uniform.

"Alice!"

Ralph lengthened his stride until he reached her. His smooth cheek touched hers as his kiss lingered.

"You're going today, aren't you?" she asked him.

The solemn depth of his eyes told her she was right. Alice bit the inside of her lip until her tears passed, then cleared her throat.

"How long do we have?"

Ralph pulled her against him. She inhaled the smell of him, the feel of his body beneath her hands. *She was in love.* So desperately in love. *How would she survive without him?*

"I fly out at 2200 hours."

It was just before noon now. That gave them less than twelve hours and she'd have to get another nurse to cover for her.

He was coming back, Alice told herself. He wasn't on the front line. He'd be fine. This wasn't the end. He hadn't made it to captain without being good at whatever it was he had to do.

"Alice, you know I don't want to be unromantic, but . . ."

Her heart thumped.

"We need to get married today."

Alice squeezed her eyes shut. A war time marriage was never going to give her the wedding she'd dreamed of as a girl, but if it meant their union would be recognized, that she could legally become his wife, then she wasn't going to say no.

"I have a priest organized."

He liked taking charge. That's what made him so well respected. *Of course he had a priest.*

"Alice?"

She nodded. It was all she could do. Of course she'd marry him, if it was their only chance; what other choice did she have?

Ralph pulled her back down to the seat. She complied. There was nothing he could ask of her right now, with him on the cusp of leaving, that she wouldn't do.

"I have something for you," he said.

Ralph reached into his breast pocket. Alice held her breath.

"Here."

He opened his palm to reveal a gold heart on a fine chain. Alice bit her lip again.

"You like it?"

"I love it."

Ralph touched her shoulder and she turned, just slightly, as he fixed the necklace. The light touch of it against her skin was cool, calming.

"It looks beautiful on you."

She smiled. Tears filled her eyes, but she didn't give in to them. Tomorrow she could let them out, but today was about being together and being happy. Giving him happy memories to take with him.

"The day I saw you in that hospital, Alice, well, you did something to me. You mesmerized me."

She fingered the heart. She wished she could tell him how much it meant to her, but she couldn't get the words out.

"Ralph, I . . ." her voice faltered.

"Come on, kitten. Let's get you home to tell your parents."

Alice imprinted the weight of his hand in hers in her memory. Squeezed tight to make sure he was real.

He was the man she'd dreamed of. She just hoped by the time she finally made it to America that he would be right behind her. Or already there. *Anything so long as he wasn't only known by a white cross pushed into the earth somewhere in Europe.*

# CHAPTER 4

A whistle blew and alerted them it was time to rise. Madeline stretched and rubbed at her eyes. She felt like a soldier forced to stick to a constant schedule, but she wasn't complaining. No lolling about and wishing for home, or time to worry too much about what would happen when they arrived in America. It was only day five and they had another ten to go.

What she did have time to worry about was how to be a good American housewife, the kind that made sure her home was always welcoming for her husband, a happy place to raise their children. There was the odd list of instructions floating around, but she'd heard their new families would have reams of notes prepared for them. Maybe it was a silly rumor. But the magazine *Good Housekeeping* had dedicated entire issues to foreign brides. It was like all the Yanks were expecting untrained native women to arrive in their country.

Surely being a good wife in America was the same as in their home country? If you could cook, sew, and run a household, what more was there to know?

"Come on Mads, I don't want to miss breakfast." Betty's voice cut across her thoughts.

Madeline grinned at Betty, who stood with one hand wrapped around her stomach and the other rubbing at her back. Her friend was definitely eating for two.

"You go ahead, I just need a few moments," Madeline said.

The other girls might think her silly, considering there were only other women on the ship, but she didn't want to go down without making at least a small fuss over her appearance. Looking well groomed had always been important to her. Something her mother had insisted upon since she was a little girl. It wasn't about wearing a lot of make-up, it was about being well presented, being proud.

Her mother had been the most well-kept woman on their street. She never left the house without a sweep of lipstick, a carefully styled hair-do, and pressed clothes. They didn't have a lot of money, but her mother sure liked to appear as if they did. *To succeed in life you have to believe in yourself, Madeline. And to succeed you have to look the part.* They were words she knew she'd never forget, no matter the time that passed away from her family. They hadn't had a lot, but they'd always been a family proud of who they were.

"You ready, Madeline?" Alice called out as she passed and Madeline nodded.

She placed the last pin into her hair, checked her skirt for creases, and followed her friend.

"Alice," she called, catching her up.

Alice stopped to wait for her.

"We will stay in touch when we get to America, won't we?" Madeline asked her.

Alice grabbed hold of her arm and squeezed it tight. "There's no chance I'm giving up you lot when we get off this damn boat."

"Promise?" Madeline asked.

"Promise!" Alice exclaimed.

Madeline sighed and let her head rest on Alice's shoulder before they walked off, arm in arm.

"I'm glad we found each other." Madeline's voice was so soft she wondered if she'd even spoken out loud. It wasn't like her to be so sentimental, but these were strange times they were living through.

"Me too, Mads, me too," Alice reassured her.

∽

The dining hall was crammed full of women. Wafts of perfume and fatty foods cooking added to Madeline's nausea as the ship rocked back and forth, but the crew were strict about the girls eating. *Their plates had to be empty.*

Madeline giggled as she thought of the most recent letter Alice had entertained them with. She'd been writing letters to her family almost every day—letters she was going to send in one big bundle to her family as soon as they arrived in America.

*We have four meals a day, us girls.* Madeline could still hear her reciting it, having them all in stitches of laughter after dark. *Two down, one up! We eat a hearty meal, then we're generous enough to give it to the ocean for dessert.*

The food had been a shock to the system—eggs, meat, cheese— all the wonderful, delicious things they'd missed while every type of food in London was rationed. Madeline knew she'd never stomach a powdered egg again. But, coupled with the swaying of the boat, the rich food wasn't so easy to digest either. She hadn't been too bad, but some of the girls had taken to wearing big belts around their skirts just to hold them up around their disappearing waists. Keeping food down was the main topic of conversation, besides gabbing about their husbands.

The din of so many women eating had been unbearable at first, but now she found it comforting. She loved that they were all trying their hardest despite the conditions, but she was jumpy and she couldn't help it. The others seemed so confident about their husbands, yet she couldn't help the gnawing doubt in her stomach sometimes. It wasn't her nature to take such a big leap of faith when she was usually so cautious, and leaving her family behind worried her terribly.

"The first issue of *Sailing Wives* is out today," said Alice, piling scrambled eggs on top of a piece of hard toast. "Think there might be some good tips for us in there?" She raised her eyebrows archly, and made them all laugh.

"The official publication for the sailing brides of American men," said June, mimicking the clipped voice of the onboard official.

"In America, your husband will expect you to sing the national anthem every morning before you leave the marital bed," announced Betty, her voice shrill and fake.

They roared with laughter. Madeline had tears streaming down her face.

"He will expect you to forego tea for coffee, and paint pictures of the American flag to be pinned around the house," Betty continued.

They all giggled as they picked at their food.

"I think we should brave a stroll up on the deck in our swimsuits," whispered Alice, voice lowered as an official passed.

"Huh! I don't think they let elephants out in swimsuits," said Betty, her hands disappearing to rest on her stomach.

She was keeping it mostly concealed—a huge shawl wrapped around her body had kept away any unwanted attention. There were plenty of women with children onboard, the odd pregnant one, but no one was as far along as Betty.

"What do you say?" Alice directed the question to June and Maddy.

Madeline shook her head along with June. "Not a chance! Imagine getting sent back home just for a spot of sunbathing."

"They wouldn't really send us home, would they? Not just for foregoing modesty?" asked Alice.

Madeline got up, her plate still half full. "How about a game of cards instead? I'll go back and get them and maybe we can show our ankles to the sun and not get in trouble."

"What are we playing for?"

Madeline rolled her eyes at Alice. If there was one thing for sure, it was that Alice would keep them entertained until this darn ship docked. There was nothing better than enjoying a glorious day on deck, the ocean twinkling back at them as they all chatted and laughed.

"Oooh, I know!"

Betty's excited voice made them all look up.

"I know what you're going to say," said Alice, reclining back, her legs crossed at the ankles as she posed. "Silk stockings from the shop."

Betty burst into laughter before showing off her own ankles. "No silk stockings are going to do these legs any good at the moment."

June tut-tutted before placing her cards out in a fan and dropping them, face up, on the table.

"I win ladies. Tell me what the prize is."

"Chocolate," said Betty, her voice animated. "Chocolate from the shop."

Madeline had plenty of money left, but she'd been careful with it ever since they'd left home. No amounts of sweets, gum, stockings, or anything else that had been forbidden during the war were going to tempt her to spend. What if she needed it for transport? For food? What if no one was there to meet her and she had to survive on her own until she found her new family? She'd been told of the ship's departure only days before it sailed, and hadn't had time to confirm details with her new family. She'd sent word but she had no idea whether they'd be waiting for her or not, or whether she'd have to make her own way to her new family's address. Roy's correspondence to her had been brief and intermittent, but she guessed that was just because he was busy back home.

The what-ifs were making it hard to sleep at night. Although she had an independent spirit, she'd never truly had to fend for herself, and yet here she was with only herself to rely on. She'd always been so close to her family: her parents and sisters meant the world to her and to even think of being without them made her want to burst into tears. Doing all this without their support seemed impossible.

"Madeline?" asked Alice.

She looked up.

"Not tempted by the illicit treats?"

She smiled. "No, Alice. Not tempted at all."

Alice wasn't going to let her get away with it—Madeline could tell by the smirk on her face.

"Oh go on, let's play for chocolate!" Betty was practically salivating.

Alice spoke again. "I've a better idea, and it won't cost us. Losers have to tell a secret."

"Guess you girls need to spill, since I won and all."

Now it was June sitting back, one hand shielding her face from the sun.

"I don't know . . ." Madeline wasn't convinced.

"I'll go first," offered Betty.

They all placed their cards on the table.

"It's naughty, though."

Alice squealed with excitement at Betty's words.

"Calm down or you'll get us sent back below," Madeline hissed.

"We're having a boy," she said, her eyes dancing.

"Not such a great secret," said Alice, unimpressed. "Not by the size of that belly."

"Oh yes it is," giggled Betty. "Want to know how I know?"

That kept Alice quiet.

"The night I fell pregnant was on our honeymoon. They say you make a boy by, you know, being on top." She paused, cheeks flushed crimson. "All I know is that I was on top of my husband most of the evening, so there was no chance for a little girl to be made!"

Madeline blushed, June laughed, and Alice stomped her feet with glee like a child after her first taste of a sweet. Betty looked embarrassed, but her eyes were shining.

"Alice, your turn," she said. "If you think you can beat that."

"That old wives tale? Of course I can." Alice wriggled around before giving them all a wicked grin. "Prepare to gasp, ladies."

Madeline held her breath.

"It can't be any more naughty than Betty's story."

Betty giggled, her cheeks still flushed. "We're all married women. There's no harm in a little chitter chatter."

Alice batted her eyelids dramatically and leaned forward.

"Before the war, I was propositioned by a married man." They gasped collectively. Alice dropped her voice an octave. "He had a Rolls Royce, a moustache, and a tailor-made suit."

"Did you . . . take him up on his offer?" June's voice came out as a gasp.

Alice shook her head. "I was so young, and he was so, so handsome." She paused and looked down at her hands. "So I went for dinner with him. He even kissed me." She giggled. "His moustache tickled my lips."

They all sat silently, waiting to hear what happened next. Alice's life before marriage had been nothing like the rest of theirs.

"He offered me a life as his mistress, with lots of money, and an apartment of my own. But every time I looked at him I thought about his wife, and his wedding ring seemed to glint at me under the light every time I looked up."

"So what did you do?"

Alice grinned. "I was a little tipsy from the wine, but I excused myself to go to the rest room, and then I slipped out the back door and found my way home."

Madeline gave Alice a push, but from the serious expression on her face, the story was true.

"You just left him there?" Madeline knew she would never have the nerve to do that, but then she'd probably never have had the nerve to meet him in the first place.

Alice shrugged. "He was a very rich man, and very rich men are hard to say no to." The other girls gasped and giggled, caught somewhere between shock and amusement.

Eagar to shift the attention, Alice swiveled to watch Madeline. The other two did the same.

She felt uncomfortable. It was her turn and she didn't know what to say. Or she did, but she didn't want to say it aloud.

"Come on, Mads!" said Alice.

"My secret?" she said, gulping a lump of . . . what? Fear? "I don't have anything much to call a secret, but, well, I guess there's something I'm keeping to myself at the moment, if that counts?"

She looked up as silence surrounded her. The smiles were wavering, unsure of what she was going to say. She could have cut the air with her mother's cheese knife.

"I'm scared that I'll get off the ship that you'll all run into the arms of your husbands, and there'll be no one waiting for me." She sighed, playing with the fabric of her dress against her thumb. "It's just been such a long time since I've seen him. What if he doesn't want me after not seeing me for so many months?"

"Oh Madeline! Don't say that." Alice switched seats to put her arm around her and June came to her aid too.

"He'll be waiting for you, Mads, don't even think that. All our husbands will be there and none of us have seen them for months, so if that was the problem none of us would have men waiting for us."

"It's just that I haven't heard from him about whether or not he'll be waiting, and I just keep worrying."

"There, there," said Betty, hands on her stomach. "I'd give you a hug, too, but my ankles are too swollen to get up. And besides, I haven't heard from my Charlie in a month now. It doesn't mean anything, and sometimes those letters just go astray or arrive all out of sequence. And remember, we know the most important thing—that they all survived the war and got safely home."

"I know," said Alice, fingers tickling along Madeline's arm. "How about you tell us all about your man, Miss Secretive, and we'll help you decide if he'll be waiting or not."

Madeline wanted to open up to the girls, to be as honest with them as they'd be with her, but something was worrying her. Something she couldn't put her finger on that was sending her stomach into a flurry of knots.

꩜

There was a reason Madeline was attracted to Roy. He wasn't the most handsome man, he wasn't the most charming, but he was the first who'd asked her to dance. And he was the first to come to her door with flowers. The first to ask her father if it was acceptable to take her out on a date. And then the first to ask for her hand in marriage.

She knew she was attractive—the smiles and attention directed her way at church every Sunday weren't just because her father was the local butcher. Maybe no one had ever had the courage to ask her out—she knew she could come across as bossy sometimes, and maybe men didn't like that. Or maybe no one in the village thought of her that way. She was only seventeen, so it wasn't as if she'd been available for very long.

But when Roy had made his interest clear, a butterfly in her stomach that she'd never felt before had started to beat its wings with fury.

She loved her family, but it was like the touch of Roy's skin, the drowsiness of his kisses, had spellbound her. Even seeing her father with tears in his eyes when he knew she was going to accept Roy's offer of marriage hadn't changed her mind. Her strong, manly father who never showed his sadness, nor his fear, only his happiness.

Sometimes she wondered if she'd been drugged. For her to say yes to leaving her parents, her sisters, even her little nieces and nephews . . . it was such a huge decision it was a wonder she had ever been able to make it.

Sometimes she hadn't been sure. Sometimes she thought all she wanted was a nice local boy, so she could move into a home nearby and raise a family like her sisters had. To be grown up like them so she didn't have to feel like the baby sister still. But when he'd asked her, she'd forgotten all that with the excitement of a man like Roy showing such interest in her. Then suddenly they were married, and there was no backing out. Not even when the reality of what she'd committed to had sunk in. He'd left to go back to war after their wedding and she'd seen him just once since the war ended. That was five months ago now, and it felt like a lifetime had passed since then.

∽

The night air sent a chill across her shoulders and Madeline wished for Roy's warm coat. She had a cardigan slung over her, buttoned under her bust, but it was no match for the cold that had swept in with the dark as they sat outside her house on the big chair that her father had made before the war.

"You still haven't told me about your home," she said to him. Madeline could count how many times she'd asked Roy about America, but he always seemed reluctant to talk about it.

"I've told you, Maddy, I come from a farm in New York."

She fought to wrap the cardigan even tighter around her. His reticence to talk about his home life was like a tiny fly constantly landing on her leg, a niggle that just kept persisting. Every time she brought up his home, they went from happy-go-lucky and fun to quiet. *Silent.* Did it hurt him that much to recall the home he'd left behind?

"But what's it like? What is your house like? What is your family like?"

A look she couldn't identify passed over his face, but it disappeared so fast she almost wondered if it had ever been there at all.

"Honey, what do you need to know?" He took her hand and dropped a kiss to it. "We live in a farm house in a little New York town, where hens mill about and there are endless fields and long sunny days."

She smiled. How could she not? When he put it like that it sounded, well, wonderful.

"And your family?"

"You know I have a sister. She's unmarried, or at least she was when I left, and my parents are just usual Americans. There's really nothing to tell."

"So your sister lives at home too? How many bedrooms does your house have?"

"What is this? Twenty questions? Enough already." Roy stood abruptly and stalked a few steps away.

She bit back a response. Most of the time he was so kind and loving, so sweet, other times he got annoyed and rude with her, like she had no right to ask him personal questions. It was like they lived in a bubble, where everything was wonderful until she spoke out of turn. Sometimes, after they'd said goodbye, she'd worry if what she'd said might have spoiled everything.

But her father had told her that Roy had come over to see him and that he'd asked for her hand in marriage. And now it was all she could think about. She needed to know what kind of life to expect if the question was put to her.

Could she really leave everything she knew behind? Leave her family for good? It was something that worried her every night before dark, because she'd thought about marrying him plenty of times before now. She did want to marry him, but she had no idea where New York even was on the map. Didn't she have a right to know a little about where she might be moving if she said yes to him?

"Roy, I'm sorry, I just . . ."

He turned to face her, a smile just noticeable from where he stood in the half light. She felt that now-familiar tickle in her stomach, the one that reminded her she was in love.

"Maddy, it's me who's sorry." He knelt in front of the seat, taking both her hands in his own.

*Oh God.* Was he going to ask her now? Did she have to decide tonight? Her heart started racing, pulse thundering at her neck and in her wrists. It was a wonder he couldn't see it pounding beneath her cardigan.

"You can ask all you like." He leaned forward to kiss her nose. "I'm just thinking about the war. About leaving. About . . ."

She pulled his hands into her lap. "You can tell me."

He shook his head. "I just think we need to live in the now, not waste time talking about America or what might be. Are you cold?"

She nodded. He pulled off his coat and tugged it around her shoulders.

"Why didn't you tell me?"

Madeline felt warmth spread through her, inhaled the smell of cologne on his jacket and looked into his eyes. Maybe she was supposed to ask for his coat? She had no experience and she'd just guessed a man would offer it. Her thoughts made her feel bad for doubting him. He was a good man. A kind man. She just had all types of romantic ideas flitting through her imagination. It wasn't good for her.

"Let's get you home before your father comes looking for us."

She leaned into him as he slung an arm around her. Every now and again she questioned him, worried about whether he was right for her, and then at times like this, she wondered why she was so silly.

But then again, she'd only known him for such a short time. He'd be gone soon and yet she had to make a decision that in pre-war times would never have had to be made so fast.

"Tell me about the farm again," she asked him.

This time he was relaxed. This time he pulled her closer rather than push her away.

Roy dropped a kiss to her head. "Every morning someone goes down to collect all the eggs and let the hens out. They roam free across the fields, until they're called in for a dinner of hot mash."

"You feed chickens mash?"

"Hens, baby, hens," he drawled, slowing down their walk.

She giggled.

"You got a lot to learn about being a farmer's wife."

Madeline's heart started to thud again. It seemed like a question, like a hint, but she wasn't going to acknowledge it, not until he asked her outright.

Because she wasn't ready to make a decision, not yet.

"Have you given that boy an answer?"

Madeline turned her eyes back into the house. She had been gnawing on a piece of toast and gazing out the window.

Her father looked up over his glasses, newspaper held down so he could see her.

"I haven't been asked."

She'd always been honest with her father, but it was awkward talking about Roy. They normally chatted about books and happenings, about her friends, about the butcher shop, but never about boys. She'd never had a boy to talk about.

"He'll be asking you soon."

Her father went back to reading the paper, but she didn't look away. Was he saying it was all right to say yes? Did he *want* her to say yes? She was the last of his four daughters to be at home. The youngest, but still the last, and she'd always been a daddy's girl. Her sisters had married young, had children of their own already.

She watched her mother fuss in the kitchen as she always did, listened to the shuffle of paper as her father turned the page. It was all so familiar, yet one day she'd have to leave it behind. But to think about not hearing or seeing them go about their daily routine scared her.

"You're not still thinking about him, are you?"

Her father hadn't even dropped the paper this time. She glared at the newsprint but it was hard not to smile.

"Of course not, Daddy."

She heard him chuckle.

"I'll bring you home," he said.

Her mother dropped something metal into the sink. The clang echoed.

He folded up the paper and placed both hands on the table, before stretching to stand up.

"If you marry the boy and it's that bad over there, I'll bring you home."

"Harold!" Her mother's face was bright red. "We haven't the money to bring her home if she takes a fancy on coming back."

He swatted behind him without even looking—a wave of the hand as if to silence her. Madeline kept her eyes on him, trying to stop the tears in her own.

"She's my youngest daughter, Sylvia. If Madeline roughs it out over there and the boy doesn't treat her right, or something happens, I'd sell everything we have if need be to bring her home."

He walked the two steps around the table and stamped a kiss on her head.

"I don't want you to go, girl. But if you love him, you say yes to the boy when he asks."

Tears tickled her eyes, but she fought to keep the smile on her face until her father had turned away. She loved her mother, but she adored her father. And if she had his blessing, and Roy asked her, she would go.

She wouldn't want her father spending all his pennies on bringing her home, but if it was that bad over there, at least she knew she was wanted here. Even if it did mean coming home a woman no one else would ever be interested in.

Her father loved her and that was what counted. If he thought she should go ahead and marry Roy if he asked her, then she would.

~

The days seemed to drag by. Every time she saw another couple holding hands, every time she listened to her friends talking about their sweethearts, every time she so much as breathed, her heart felt like it could burst and explode into hundreds of tiny shards. The weight that seemed to press down her chest made her feel like she was suffocating. And the thought of what she was going to leave behind made her want to retch.

She kept seeing Roy's face. His dark brown eyes swam in front of her. She could almost feel his sandy blond hair beneath her fingers. Fingertips that itched to touch him.

She saw the farm as he'd described it. Plump hens strutted about, the fields were full of thigh-high grass, and a horse gazed from over the post and rail fence, just like the ranches she'd read about.

She dreamed of the babies they would have, of toddlers barefoot and perhaps even riding ponies. But then that only reminded her that any babies born would probably never see their grandparents, and that made her want to be sick all over again.

The night he asked her should have felt so right, but the worry that had turned her stomach had been genuine, her anxiousness almost too much to bear. It had been nothing over the top, nothing contrived; just the two of them sitting on the wooden seat in her family's back garden, the light from the moon illuminating the ring he'd pulled from his pocket.

"You know I love you, Madeline."

She had simply nodded her head. Mute.

"I know you love your family, but I want to make our own family together." He had dropped to his knees, pulled out the ring, and was staring straight in to her eyes. "I don't want to leave tomorrow and not know that you'll marry me. I want you to be my wife, Madeline."

Tears had trickled down each cheek, words dying in her throat. But somehow she had managed a smile as he pushed the ring on her finger.

"You will marry me, Madeline, won't you?"

"Yes," she had whispered. "Yes, Roy. I'll marry you."

He had pulled her in for a kiss. Hugged her tight until she'd stopped crying. She held her hand up to squint at the ring. A simple, thin band that said she was promised.

"Let's go tell your parents, okay?"

She followed him inside, aware of her hand clasped in his, and nearly burst into tears again when she saw her parents waiting, sitting at the table.

Their reaction had been happy. Her family had pulled out a bottle of sherry that was tucked away for an occasion, and Madeline had sipped at her glass. Still unsure. Still fighting with the emotions that battled her daily.

And then she was left, waiting.

Her fiancé went back to war, like most of the other young men on the continent. He had been promised leave to marry her, now that their permission had come through. But then, after that, she'd be lucky to see him again before she arrived in America. Unless he came back injured and needed recovery.

She didn't let herself think about the possibility of him coming home a corpse rather than a fiancé.

# CHAPTER 5

I think it's fair to say he loves you," said Betty. "After all, he *did* come back from the war and married you! You're just worrying because you've not seen him, like all of us."

Madeline gave Betty a tight smile. It was odd talking about her feelings, opening up. But the other girls had and there was something nice about being honest.

"And it's not that you don't think he's fond of you, is it?"

She turned as June spoke. They all did.

"It's that you don't think you'll love being with him as much as you loved being at home with your family. And maybe you're worried he won't be the same when you arrive."

Madeline brushed at the tears collecting on her cheeks. She nodded.

"We've all had those thoughts," June continued. "Or at least I've had them. Will he still love me after all this time? Will his family like me? Will I wish I'd stayed at home and married a local boy?" June sighed. "I used to have thoughts like that every night. Now I just pretend to myself it will be perfect, and leave it at that."

"At least none of you are pregnant," moaned Betty. She managed to lift the mood as always. "If he didn't love me then, he ain't gonna love me with this big belly."

Madeline laughed, her tears starting to disappear. "He'll love you, Betty. If one of us is going to be loved, then I'll put my money on you."

Betty rubbed her stomach the way she always did when they spoke about her. Only Alice looked indignant.

"I'll have you know that my man loves me," said Alice with a theatrical pout. "Or at least he better. I'll give him the flick for another if he doesn't."

Her joke made them all giggle.

A whistle blew.

"That'll be lunch," announced Betty triumphantly, extending a hand.

"Food, it's all she thinks about," muttered Alice.

"You wait until you're eating for two. This fella's got an appetite."

"What do you say we hit the shop after? We can share a block of chocolate between us later?" June said.

Alice nodded her agreement and Betty licked her lips.

"You coming?" June asked.

Madeline smiled and watched them. They were all grinning at her, their excitement contagious, but she needed a moment to herself. It wasn't that she didn't love their company. Making friends with the girls had made the voyage an incredible experience already. She just wanted a little time to think.

"I'm going to stay sitting a while. Save me a sandwich."

"You sure?" asked June. "I don't mind staying."

"Go have lunch." Madeline swatted at the air. "I just need a minute to catch my breath."

She didn't let the smile fade until they'd disappeared, not wanting them to think something was wrong. It didn't matter that she'd told them, although it did feel good to get it off her chest. But she needed to relive it for herself. Needed to just think about her marriage. About her family. Thank goodness the girls understood that she needed time to herself every now and again.

Besides, she hadn't told them everything. Would their reaction have been the same if she'd been completely truthful? She loved Roy dearly, couldn't wait to see him, but that didn't mean she wasn't worried about the man she'd married, and what life with him was going to be like.

~~~

Their wedding day brought with it a steady trickle of rain, before the clouds parted and allowed a light blue sky to appear. Roy had arrived the day before. She'd been bursting with excitement about seeing him, desperate to hold him and talk with him again, but something had been wrong.

His eyes had shown none of the love she'd expected. But maybe she expected too much? She needed to stop being all romantic and just get on with things. Goodness only knew her mother had made it clear that marriages didn't need romance to be happy.

He had sat with her only briefly, in her family's kitchen, before turning in for the night. Her mother had set up a bed in their sunroom, and once he was asleep, they continued the wedding preparations. They were to be married in the little church down the road, the one she had visited every Sunday since she was a girl. Neighbors had kindly pooled rations to see to it there was a cake, and her mother was mixing the icing as one of her sisters sat and fiddled with Madeline's dress.

"Concentrate," her sister said.

Madeline stopped wriggling.

"If you weren't so tiny I wouldn't still be here," she grumbled, a pin between her lips, but Madeline knew her sister was happy to alter the dress and see it worn again. It was only a few years ago she'd worn it down the aisle herself.

Madeline just shook her head and smiled, but inside her stomach was churning. She'd lost weight with the worry, with the anticipation. But now that he was here, the knot of worry had wound even tighter, her fears clawing at her like hands tightening around her throat.

"Madeline?"

Her sister's voice startled her.

"You're not having second thoughts, are you? You're away with the fairies today."

She braved a smile. "No. It's just, well, I kind of thought he'd be more pleased to see me."

Her sister threw her hands in the air. It put a stop to her tears before they fell.

"He's a man who has just arrived back after being on the front line. *War*, Madeline. Goodness only knows what the poor man's seen." She wagged her finger for effect. "These are hard times and you need to be patient with men at the best of them."

Her mother looked slightly more sympathetic. "How about you take yourself off to get ready for bed and we'll finish up here. You've just got a lot on your mind. Start fixing your hair and I'll come to help soon."

She reasoned with herself that they were right. It was the stress of not having seen her groom for so long, of wondering what he was thinking. Not to mention their honeymoon, a night away at a little cottage on their own, or going to live abroad.

That scared her more than anything.

She undressed, sucked in a big breath of air, and came to the conclusion that the only way she was going to survive the wedding day was to turn off the thinking part of her brain.

Then her eye caught the little pile of things on her dresser. It made her breath catch in her throat. A frilly garter that she'd never seen before was propped against a baby blue corsage that she recognized from her sister's wedding. Something borrowed, something blue. It sent a trill of excitement down her spine. Did it count for old too?

Madeline reached for the garter to feel the soft lace, and her hands skimmed over a string of white pearls hidden beneath. *Her mother's.* She would have recognized them anywhere. When they were children, she used to finger them around her mother's neck before her parents went out for dinner . . .

Now they were waiting for her to wear. Her something old. Or maybe something borrowed too.

Was Roy waiting for her to wear the garter?

She swallowed a lump of fear, almost too afraid to find out.

- ᠙

The only thing Madeline was sure of about her marriage was that Roy took his conjugal rights very seriously. She had become a married woman with little other than fear of her wedding night. Not an all-consuming fear, just a worry that she might not know exactly what was expected.

*She needn't have worried.*

After Roy's leave was unexpectedly extended, she had come to know precisely what was expected of her. It wasn't that she didn't like it, but the fact it was a nightly routine had started to become exhausting.

Two weeks after their wedding, she sat in her room, brushing out her hair. If Roy wasn't here, she would have simply crawled into bed and fallen into a much-needed sleep. But she knew he would stay up for another drink, long after everyone else had retired to bed, and then he'd expect her to be waiting.

A creak made her place the brush back on the dresser. She looked around and met eyes with her husband.

"Hello, wife."

She felt a familiar flutter, that tickle that tore her between love and uncertainty. She was also worried about telling him that tonight was not going to go as he expected.

He started to take off his clothes. She swallowed away her worry and tried to think of herself as a grown, married woman who shouldn't have to worry about talking to her own husband about delicate matters.

"Roy, I . . ."

He watched her, his impatience obvious as she stuttered.

Madeline cleared her throat. "I'm experiencing my monthly, ah, course."

He finished taking off his clothes and got into bed. "So?"

"Well, I just wanted to explain why I'll have to refuse you tonight. I didn't want you to think I . . ."

"I'm not going without just because of, well, because of a little blood."

A crawl of embarrassment made its way from her stomach all the way up her neck and to her face. Her skin felt like it was burning.

"Come on, it's our last night. Don't give me any more excuses."

She felt sick. Physically sick. Was that what it meant to be a wife? To not have a choice in the matter, even at a time like this?

During the day, when they were together, even at night when they were in one another's company, she loved him. So much she could burst sometimes. But this? Something about it just didn't feel right. But then she was the inexperienced one, so maybe it was just normal? If only she was brave enough to broach the subject with her mother, or one of her sisters to ask.

"Madeline?"

"Give me a moment," she said, forcing a smile. "I'll be back in a second."

She ran to the bathroom, toes light to avoid waking anyone. She clicked the door closed behind her and sunk to the floor. Humiliation suffocated her.

All she had ever wanted was to be married. But right now, her husband was acting like an unfeeling monster.

*Was she being immature?* She let her tears fall, staying as silent as she could, then rose to press a cold cloth to her face. She didn't want to disappoint him, but . . .

She almost wished he was back on the battlefields already.

Madeline touched a dab of perfume behind her ear, took a towel with her, and decided to be braver. If this was what marriage was all about, then she'd just have to get used to it. Besides, he was a man about to return to war. Her mother would tell her simply get on with things and fulfill her wedding vows, and that's exactly what she had to do.

∽

"Madeline!"

She raised her eyes from surveying the ocean and pushed up on her elbows, pleased to put her memories at bay again.

"You don't have to get that excited over my sandwich," she said, smiling as June came flapping toward her. Then the smile died on her face as she saw June's expression. "What is it? What's happened?"

June was puffing and stopped to catch her breath before pushing out the words. "It's, it's Betty. We think she's in labor, but she doesn't want us to call the doctor."

Madeline jumped up and scrambled for her shoes. "Where is she now?"

June's eyes were wild. "Alice is taking her back to the cabin. She's a nurse but," June squeezed her hand hard. "I'm pretty sure she knows about nursing soldiers and nothing about childbirth."

They started hurrying toward the door.

"Do you know anything about babies?" June asked.

Madeline laughed. She knew more about babies than she cared to. That was one thing she wasn't naïve about. "I have three sisters, and they've all got children. I helped deliver one before we left, and I've been at most of the births."

June looked ready to pass out. Madeline grabbed her arm tight and marched her faster.

"I can deliver this baby, with some help," she told her. "So long as nothing goes wrong I know what to do. Babies enter the world every single day all over the world, June, so stop looking like she's about to die on us."

June nodded, the color slowly inching its way back into her face.

Madeline shook her head. "I still say she's a silly girl saying no to the medics though."

But she wasn't going to tell her off. Betty could get in trouble for lying to the authorities, and now was not the time for her to worry. All they had to do was make sure this baby came into the world kicking and screaming, with no complications. They could deal with any trouble later.

"Isn't she rather early?"

June eyes widened. "Three weeks or more, she thinks."

Madeline didn't even think about it. If the baby was ready to come out, there was nothing they could do to stop it. She picked up the pace. "Come on, June. Hurry!"

# CHAPTER 6

Water hit the deck as the ship swayed from side to side, and Betty tried to focus on the movement and the sounds rather than the next wave of pain. She listened to the insistent drum of rain as it intensified, bracing herself for the next contraction. The pain was explosive, unlike anything she could have ever imagined before—her pain and the raging storm conspiring against her in rough waves that she feared might kill her before the night was over. Just as the pain subsided it built again with such intensity she would have done anything to make it stop. She had been in labor for several hours now, and was getting exhausted.

"You're going to have to push this time," instructed Madeline. "Take a deep breath, and then push hard."

Her friend's face was stretched into a determined grimace as she knelt at the end of the bed, much like the other two women crowded around her.

"No!" she wailed, delirious with pain. "It's too early. I can't. Make it stop!"

"Betty, you don't have a choice. This baby is coming now!"

The pain built so fast she cried out, but suddenly she had to push, the intensity so strong it was the only thing she could do.

"Push, Betty. Push!" Madeline encouraged. "Keep going, I can just see the head!" She couldn't take it anymore. She couldn't . . . another contraction hit, the pain searing this time.

"Push!"

A hand slipped into hers and she squeezed it tight, holding on as hard as she could. Another hand pressed a cold cloth to her forehead, but there was only one thing she was focused on now, the pain subsiding now she had something to focus on.

*Push.*

As the next contraction bore down on her, Betty fought for oxygen, sucking in sharp bursts of air. It built with all the fury of Neptune in the sea below her, and this time she tried to weather the storm. To push with all her might and force this baby out once and for all, because she knew she wasn't strong enough to ride out the pain any longer.

"Ooohhh . . ." She cried out, gritting her teeth as she kept pushing, a sob escaping from deep in her throat.

"You can do it," soothed Madeline, her voice softer, kinder now. "You can, honey, just pant, keep breathing, he'll be out on the next contraction."

"I can see the head, too!"

The excited squeal from one of the other girls gave Betty the confidence she needed. Maybe she should have called for the doctors, but right now she felt safe, knowing that the people around her would look after her.

"Come on honey, come on," Madeline soothed.

Betty waited the seconds until the next spasm hit and then pushed as hard as she could, holding her breath as she fought.

A burst of noise filled the room, like a kitten meowing, and suddenly she couldn't feel the pain, the hurt, not even the worry she'd felt only seconds before. She could hear her baby!

"Oh Betty, it's a little boy!" June had been waiting with towels and warm water, and was now wiping down a bloody, messy little scrap of a child.

Tears of joy fell in cold drops against Betty's hot skin. She had done it. She'd done it! Charlie's face swam before her, and she let her eyes drop shut to hold him there in her mind, imagining the look on his face when he saw his little boy for the first time. She could picture him holding their son, the smile on his face, how proud he would be of her.

"We're not quite done yet," said Madeline. "You should feel another contraction and then . . ."

Betty hadn't been prepared for any pain to continue, but Madeline seemed to know what she was doing. She focused on her baby as another contraction hit and pushed as Madeline put pressure on her abdomen and guided her.

"Done." Madeline smiled. She looked relieved. "Now we need to get you cleaned up."

"Here, Mummy."

Betty looked up as June spoke. The pure joy of seeing her little bundle, wrapped in a soft towel, brought on a fresh wave of tears as June placed him against her chest.

Betty wrapped her arms around him, kissing his damp little head. The girls were all cooing and smiling, weeping and giggling as he squirmed then let out a giant wail.

"Good set of lungs," said Alice with a laugh. "That's what we like to hear."

"Your dad will be proud, little one," murmured June, tucking one finger against the baby's cheek. "What will he say when he sees you getting off the ship, huh? A son already."

They all stood in silence, united as only women can be. Betty swallowed her modesty as Madeline checked her down below one last time then slipped her nightgown down to cover her. The baby squawked indignantly as she tried to guide him to the breast, before latching on and sucking hard on her nipple.

"Ooh, he's a fighter, this one," said Madeline, as they all laughed at his balled fists and determined action. "Tiny as a bird, but a fighter all right."

"Like he's at the milk bar!" Betty said with a slow smile, looking down. She was exhausted, but she loved watching the enthusiastic way he suckled, even if it was a little painful.

"So what are you going to call him?" asked June.

"I think I'll name him after my father. William. I lost both my parents to a virus before the war, and I miss them so much still. Always, even after all this time."

They all smiled at her.

"William," said June. "He looks just like a William, I reckon."

Madeline nodded then quietly clapped her hands together. "Let's give them some time to get to know one another," she instructed. "Have a little sleep and then we'll come back with something for you to eat." She leaned in close to her. "Let me know if you want some privacy to wash. I can help if you need me to, or take the baby so you can tend to yourself."

Betty nodded her thanks, conscious of how weary she was. She glanced down at her wee man and saw that his eyes had fallen shut, although his mouth was still sucking every now and again, like he was hungry even in sleep.

"Good night, my love," she whispered.

And as the ship continued to sway from side to side, the storm still beating on the deck, Betty let herself fall into the beginnings of slumber, lulling her into its embrace. She tried to forget about the pain, about the aches and tenderness she was experiencing, and think only of baby's little face, and Charlie's. *Her darling Charlie.*

The dance hall was crowded with young people. Betty played with a loose piece of cotton on her dress and shifted from foot to foot. Since her parents had died she'd spent a lot of time on her own, and as much as she wanted to be out having fun she would have been more comfortable staying in for the night. It had been a long time since she'd said yes to a dance, and she would have felt more confident if she hadn't been standing on her own.

She'd walked for five miles with her best friend Lucy to get here. The night air had been warm on their arms, shoulders bare except for their shawls. Her friend's mother had rolled her hair into a chignon, and she did feel wonderful, even if she was dreadfully nervous. But she needed to get on with her life. Forget the war and blackouts and food rations and what she'd lost, *and just be young.*

If she'd thought about it properly she would have realized that Lucy wouldn't be by her side all night. The whole reason they'd gone was because a young American had invited Lucy to join him. And sure enough, they hadn't been there fifteen minutes before she was whisked away to dance.

Betty surveyed the room again and smiled. She could just make Lucy out, lost in the arms of the handsome Yank she'd been jabbering about for days. Other young people looked wildly in love, wrapped together as the song slowed its beat.

It was silly worrying about standing alone, she knew that. There were men and women dying all over the world in this war, so standing alone while her friend fell head over heels in love was a predicament she should relish. She took a seat, deciding to simply enjoy watching the couples dance.

"Excuse me."

Betty turned at a deep drawl. Was someone talking to her? Her eyes fell on a man standing less than two feet away. His wide brown eyes shone as he looked back at her.

"Is this seat taken?"

*He was talking to her.* She looked over one shoulder just to make sure there wasn't a woman behind her before she made a fool of herself.

"Ah, no. Please go ahead."

The young man sat down. She squirmed in her seat, not sure what to do. Should she introduce herself? She knew what she *shouldn't* be doing and that was ogling him, but it was hard not to.

He had sun-kissed skin and light brown hair. It was parted but slightly unruly. His uniform, not to mention his accent, made it clear that he was an American, like almost all the men here.

Had he sat down to rest his legs, or had he come over to see her? She didn't consider herself a complete fool when it came to men, but she just didn't know what to do with herself right now.

She saw him look across the room and she followed his eyes. A group of guys were nudging and elbowing one another. Were they laughing at her?

"Would you like to dance?"

Betty's face burnt hot. She didn't like to be made fun of and she was back to wishing she hadn't come at all.

"You can tell your friends that I'm not interested in being the butt of some joke!"

Now it was his turn to look embarrassed. He turned his flushed cheeks to her, eyes pleading, and shook his head fervently.

"Oh, please, no. You aren't a joke, it's just . . ."

She glared at him. She'd heard these Yanks' sweet talk was a dime a dozen, but she wasn't going to be fooled. She crossed her legs delicately and turned her shoulders away.

Betty saw him slump back in the chair. She was still curious, but she wasn't going to be swayed.

"I've been watching you since you arrived with your friend, and they've been trying to get me to come over to you, that's all. Honest."

That made her turn slightly. Maybe she'd overreacted. Still, she wasn't going to let down her guard just yet. Betty kept herself angled away from him.

To her surprise he got up and walked away. Walked away! If that didn't make a girl feel rejected then . . . Betty fumed inside. If she hadn't promised Lucy she'd go home with her, she would have walked straight out the door. She stood up and looked for her friend again, intending to beckon with her head that she wanted to go.

"Huh-hmm."

Betty turned. What the . . .

"Hi, I'm Charlie Olliver." He held out a drink to her. "Two L's," he told her with a laugh, "just in case you're interested."

She didn't know what to say. *What was he playing at?*

"I'm sorry about before, can we start over?" he asked.

Betty searched the crowd for Lucy again and couldn't locate her, so she reached for the drink he was holding out and gingerly extended her right for him to shake.

"Betty Sanders," she said. She sighed as he looked rather pleadingly at her. "And yes, we can start over if you'd like."

Charlie grinned at her, and she knew that she'd been wrong to judge him. He might be cheeky, but he had an honest face. That's what her mother would have said, if she were still alive.

"So Betty, what on earth are you doing sitting at a dance alone?"

She laughed and shrugged. She wasn't going to point out that she had hardly ever danced before, let alone been faced with men desperate to ask her.

"The other guys are just too scared to ask you. Pretty girl like you should be dancing 'till her shoes wear out."

Now she knew what Lucy's mother had been on about, warning them about the charm of an American.

*They have silver tongues*, she'd said, waving her finger at them before they'd left. *They don't call a spade a spade like our local boys, and it doesn't mean you should believe what they say.*

Betty and Lucy had giggled on their walk here, taking turns to mimic her mother, but she suddenly understood. American boys *were* different, and she knew exactly why so many girls were falling in love with them.

Betty sipped on the punch and felt a brief rush to her head. The last thing she wanted was to meet a dashing young man then swoon at his feet. Or worse, be taken advantage of. She put the cup down.

"So how about that dance?" he asked.

Charlie grinned at her before standing and extending a hand to her. She took it.

"I'm not much of a dancer . . ."

"Nonsense," he insisted, keeping hold of her hand and walking closer to her than she'd expected. "A girl that looks as good as you has got to be good on the dance floor."

Betty tried not to laugh.

*Oh yes*, she understood how easy it would be to fall for an American's charm.

The band burst into a rendition of the Glenn Miller orchestra as the singers belted out The Andrews Sisters, and Charlie tugged at her wrist so insistently she thought it might actually fall off.

"Come on girl, let's get dancing!"

Betty thought of resisting, of digging her heels into the floor and not trying something new. She was used to always letting Lucy be in the limelight when they were out, to standing back for her. But Charlie was so persuasive. He didn't even need to say anything. The flash of his eyes, his smile, the pull of his body as he stood waiting for her.

She sucked in a deep breath of air, filled her lungs with enough oxygen to make herself light-headed, and swallowed her fears. She had wished for her very own prince charming for years; *imagine if this was him and she let fear stop her from finding him?*

Once her arms were pressed against his, she felt a burst of excitement. She straightened her shoulders, followed his lead, and felt as if her feet were moving so fast they weren't even touching the ground.

Charlie had a smile on his face like she'd never seen before. Perhaps it was the war making the good times seem happier than ever. Maybe it was the heat in the room, the swill of the crowd, the thrum of adrenalin caused by the band, but Betty found herself lost to Charlie.

Only moments earlier she'd thought of ignoring his advances.

Only moments earlier, she hadn't even known he existed.

And now here she was, twirling, swirling, and falling into his embrace, acting as if they'd been sweethearts for months.

As the band wound down, belting out the last tunes of a song, Charlie spun her out then pulled her in tight against him. She was cocooned between his arms and his chest. Like an insect in a web with no chance of escape.

If he'd let her, she would have looked away. But his eyes weren't letting her off that easily.

"You're beautiful, you know that?" he said.

She listened to his drawl and tried to push the words away. She wasn't used to compliments.

"You are, Betty." He paused and looked at her, ignoring the fact the band had started another tune. A slow tune. It felt as if the room was spinning away from them, the other couples a blur in the far distance. "You're the most beautiful girl here."

He kept his eyes on hers, his arms looped around her body. She'd never in her life been this close to a man, never before felt the excitement of being held in a man's arms or hearing such flattering words.

Charlie brought his lips slowly toward hers. She raised her chin, fighting a tremble as he moved even closer. It felt like an age before his lips actually touched hers; before their skin met. Her mouth parted ever so slightly as they kissed. A soft press that lasted forever yet was over too quickly.

As Charlie pulled away, a whoop made her turn. Charlie tugged her back against him, glaring at his friends. They were all clapping and catcalling. He hadn't just kissed her to show-off to them, had he?

"Charlie . . ."

"Ignore them, sweetheart," he said, drawing her close. They swayed together to the soft, slow lull of music. "They're just jealous."

She believed him. Not the jealousy part, but the fact that he wanted her in his arms.

The spicy scent of his aftershave filled her nostrils, the breadth of his shoulders felt endless beneath her palms. And the feel of his hands as they skimmed her waist made her forget that there was anyone else in the room.

"I am going to see you again, Betty, aren't I?"

He held her away from him for a heartbeat and she gazed into his eyes. Her voice felt as if it had been stolen away from her, so she just nodded in response.

Charlie let her nestle back against him.

"You know what I said to my friends when you walked in tonight?"

She shook her head against his chest, her forehead tucking under his collarbone.

"I said, *that's the girl I'm gonna marry*, and you know what they said?"

She fought a laugh and swallowed her worries. He might be exaggerating, but she didn't mind.

"They said you haven't got a chance in heck of getting that girl to fall in love with you, Charlie. She's way out of your league."

Betty was pleased the music was still playing and she had an excuse to stay tucked into his arms.

She had a feeling that falling in love with Charlie Olliver wouldn't be so very hard at all.

∞

"I think we should just leave her be."

Betty awoke to the whisper of voices in the room. She sat up in the near-darkness and blinked, trying to clear her sleepy eyes. Where was she?

A pain in her lower regions made her shut her eyes tight again. William. Her baby.

*Charlie.*

The dream echoed in her memory still and she fought to hold on to it. Being in Charlie's arms, feeling him, tasting him.

"Honey, are you okay?"

"I think she needs something to drink. And some food."

A light flicked on and Betty was forced to open her eyes. She recognized the faces of her friends crowded around her. The dull cream color of the room, the other hammocks.

*But not William.* "Where is he?" She could hear the panic rising in her voice.

Madeline pushed her back down with a firm hand and soothed stray hairs from her face.

"William's fine. June swaddled him and took him for a little walk to settle him."

Alice handed her a glass of water and she took it gratefully.

"And you'll be needing something to eat, too," said Madeline, moving away from the bed. "The little blighter will have a big appetite, so you'll need your strength."

Betty nodded and reached beneath the bed clothes to rearrange herself. She was aching, but it was bearable. Especially given the gift she'd just been blessed with.

"He is all right, isn't he?" She still couldn't believe that he'd come so early.

"He's just fine," said Madeline as if she knew exactly what she was talking about, settling herself down beside the hammock with a bowl of soup. "Now eat this and you'll be ready to feed him again."

Betty took the spoon and sat up, happy to comply. She was hungry and she needed to regain some strength.

She still ached for her husband. For Charlie. She would have done anything to have him here right now. To have his arms wrapped protectively around her, holding their baby. To know that he was safe, and that they could finally be together.

Ever since her parents had died, she'd had no family, except for her friend Lucy's. It was why she'd taken such a risk by getting on the ship pregnant: she hadn't wanted to burden them with having her *and* a baby living under their roof. She'd stayed with them ever since her father had passed, but she couldn't expect them to look after her forever. And besides, she couldn't wait to be with Charlie any longer.

Charlie and William were her life now. All that she had. There was no going back and she didn't want to.

Unlike the other girls, she had no fear. Charlie would be waiting for her, waving his cap at her as the ship pulled into dock, running toward her to fold her in his arms. He'd promised in all of his letters that he'd be waiting when the ship docked, she just had to let him know when it was due to come in, and she didn't doubt him for a second.

"Come on Betty, you're away with the fairies, you are."

Betty popped her eyes open and refocused on Madeline.

She could do this. They were almost there. *She was almost with Charlie.*

80

# PART TWO

# CHAPTER 7

Alice wrapped her jacket tighter around her body. She tilted her chin and squared her shoulders, gazing out at the blue sea as they slowly made their way closer to the harbor.

The others looked scared, worried, but she was fine. She didn't have anything to be concerned about. There was no doubt in her mind that she was going to love America, love the whirlwind glamour of it all.

The siren echoed, loud and clear, just like the officials had said it would. She couldn't help smiling—this was it. She'd made it.

*They were finally in America.*

She was finally going to be with Ralph again. In his arms. Part of his family. *As his wife.* And what fun they would have together!

"Alice! Quick, come and see it."

She smiled as June called out excitedly, Madeline holding her skirts and running alongside. But Alice didn't move.

*America was close.* So close she could almost smell it on the air. New York was within view, the captain could see it himself.

She didn't need to push up against the other women for the view. Alice just closed her eyes and saw Ralph. Watched him in her mind as he smiled, so dapper in his uniform.

When the others started to part ways, then she would walk to the edge of the ship and hold the handrail. She was in no hurry to push her way to the front.

"Alice! Alice, what are you doing?"

That voice did make her turn.

Betty was standing behind her, baby tucked under one arm, scarf draped around them both. Alice laughed. They looked so at ease and yet such a mess, all at the same time. But they looked happy.

"I'm just watching," she said, taking a step back so they were side by side. "Can't see the point in elbowing my way up there."

Betty held William out. "Want a hold?"

Alice shook her head. "I'm sorry, it's just . . ."

Betty pulled him back in against her and started to rock him.

"Don't worry, Willy, the other girls love you," she cooed. "Aunty Alice just doesn't want to get her pretty jacket all covered in sick."

"It's not that."

Betty gave her a nudge before dropping a kiss to William's head.

"It's okay, Alice, I'm just so used to the other two wanting to grab him all the time."

Alice felt awkward, which wasn't something she was used to.

"I'm just not . . ."

"I know, I know." Betty smiled at her then cooed at the baby again. "You're a good friend, Alice. You don't need to hold my baby to prove that. You were there when it counted and I'll never forget that."

"I've seen it! I've seen it with my own eyes!" Madeline exclaimed, appearing alongside them suddenly.

Alice was pleased to be distracted. She didn't like the tears in her eyes. Or how it was making her feel talking to Betty like it was the end. They were so different, yet they'd become so close on the ship, all of them like sisters now.

Madeline was jumping around like she'd just won the lottery and June wasn't acting much different.

"We're here. We're actually here." Madeline breathed the words like she was whispering a secret. "I've seen the Statue of Liberty, the actual statue!"

They all stood, staring at one another and then out at the horizon. At the tiny block of land that was New York, and the giant statue holding a torch up high, to the sky.

"We are all going to keep in touch, aren't we girls?" Alice had to ask. She might be the confident one, the one who was sure about how her life was going to pan out. But she didn't want to go it alone. Not when she'd made friends like these three on her voyage over. "We need to swap addresses now before we dock."

"You bet." June leaned into her, the American phrase sounding a little uncertain in her English accent. They'd all picked up bits of slang from their husbands and the magazines they were reading.

"I don't ever want to lose you girls, not ever." Betty held William tight against her as she shuffled closer.

"So that's settled then," said Alice.

"We're to keep in touch, no matter what," said Madeline. "Our friendship is forever." They all looked at one another and suddenly Alice couldn't help it. She started to cry. Big, fat dollops of tears started falling, and no matter how hard she tried to choke them back or look glamorous, there was no way to stop it.

Betty, June, and Madeline were the same. Tears falling, sobs escaping, like someone had just died.

Only William's sharp cry made them all sniffle back their emotions.

"Look at us!" Alice tried to be the brave one again. "Crying like a bunch of old ladies."

"I love you girls," said Betty, rocking her baby back and forth.

Alice didn't need to say it back. She loved them too—there was something between them that would never die. Aside from her husband, friendship was more important to her than anything. Especially here, all the way on the other side of the world.

Friendship meant everything. It was all they had had for the past weeks. She'd been dreading the voyage when in actual fact, it had been the most fun she'd had since before the war. They'd had nothing to do other than enjoy one another's company, to become so close and confide all their hopes and dreams. And no matter what happened, she would never forget the girls. *Not ever.*

"New York can't be that big, can it?" Betty asked. The other girls were bustling round, scribbling notes on scraps of paper and swapping them round.

Madeline shrugged. "All I know is that we live a bit of a drive away, in the countryside. I'll write it down for you."

"Me too," said June. "But you're right, the place can't be that big. We'll find each other, don't any of you worry about that."

Alice and Betty both nodded. There was no chance they'd lose touch, not after all they'd been through together.

# CHAPTER 8

Betty had that sinking feeling, like the one she'd had the day of her labor. A tremor snaked through her body and left a dull ache in the base of her spine.

For the first time since leaving London, she was starting to worry that Charlie wouldn't be waiting for her. There was an emptiness within her. A thud that was trying to tell her he wasn't there, which was silly—he'd promised he would be and Charlie would never let her down. But the feeling had built all through the hustle and bustle of disembarking, the scores of women sweeping off the ship. She'd told the other girls to go on ahead, and she'd catch up with them once they were through the immigration office. But that was looking difficult.

The crowd was a thriving, moving mass of people. It was overwhelming, especially when she'd been used to the close company of only the girls for weeks. The same song played over and over again, blaring loudly through jittery speakers as she waited for her papers to be stamped in the crowded office. *Here Comes the Bride*. If she heard the beat once again she would scream.

William made his little bleat, whimpering against her.

"It's okay, darling. Shush now." She pulled him tighter against her.

Betty's other arm felt dead, but she didn't let go of her suitcase.

She shouldn't have let the other girls go on without her. Charlie had promised that the day she arrived he would be waiting at the dock, standing closer than any other person dared and flapping his cap in the air so she could see him. *Waiting to spin her around and around and welcome her to America.*

But he wasn't. She'd looked and looked, and she hadn't seen him yet.

*Charlie, where are you?*

She gave William a little jiggle as he whimpered again. He was hungry, but she didn't want to feed him in such a public place.

"Come on, then." She forced a smile and used her best singsong voice. "Let's find somewhere quiet, shall we?"

Charlie would find her. He would come for her. She had never doubted him before and she had no good reason to start now. There could be any number of reasons that he was delayed, and the worst thing she could do for her marriage's sake was to put blame on him before it was warranted.

She could see the size of the crowd with her own eyes. He could be stuck in traffic, a delayed train . . . she wasn't going to doubt him. Not yet.

"Betty!"

She turned. June was battling through the crowd.

"Betty! Oh, thank goodness I found you."

She smiled at her friend. "I'm just looking for somewhere to feed William."

"Where's your Charlie?"

Betty felt the tears threaten again.

But before she could answer, a tall, brown-haired man appeared behind June. He slung his arm around her waist and Betty watched as June giggled, wishing all the while that Charlie was standing with his arm around her.

"Betty, this is my husband, Eddie. Eddie West."

"How do you do?" he said to her.

Betty held out her hand as he spoke. "I've heard a lot about you, Eddie. Pleased to meet you."

"Your husband is meeting you here?"

June reached for William and Betty passed him to her. Willy loved the girls—they had held and coddled him almost as much as she had on the voyage.

"I haven't found him yet." Betty spoke with as much bravery as she could muster. "I'm going to feed my son and then keep a look out."

"Here, let me take that." Eddie reached for her case. "How about you settle over there." He pointed. "We'll help you over."

June passed William back to her and they all walked side by side.

"He was going to meet you here, wasn't he? I'm sure you could travel with us if you need to," June said.

Betty shook her head. "I'll be fine, he'll be here soon."

Eddie put her case down and gestured for her to sit. "We can wait if you'd like."

"Please, Betty, come with us. I can't leave you here alone," pleaded June.

"Go," said Betty. She gave June her bravest smile. She wasn't going to ruin their day, too, with her silly fears. "You two need to get on your way."

June looked unconvinced, but she bent to give William and then Betty a kiss anyway as Eddie took her hand. "Eddie's mother and sister are waiting, so I suppose we should."

Betty felt a lick of jealousy and quickly wished it away. She would have loved to be greeted by her new family. To have found them straight away and be ushered into their care. June deserved it, but it still hurt.

Eddie pulled a card from his pocket and passed it to her.

"If you need us, just phone the number on here, any time. A friend of June's is a friend of mine."

Betty took it and tucked it into her bag. The embossed cream card did at least give her a back-up plan if something serious had delayed Charlie.

"Have a good trip," she said. Eddie had to drag June away but Betty was fine. All she wanted was to feed her baby, then find Charlie. The crowd was slowly thinning out already, and surely it would be easier to find him once there were less people about?

∾

Betty was alone. The dock was still busy, but it felt as if she'd been waiting hours. She had no idea how long it had actually been, but it felt like too long. The majority of people had left, reunited finally with their loved ones. Her hair curled, damp against the base of her neck.

William was starting to fuss again and she was trying hard not to cry herself, a rising panic fighting in her throat. She had no idea what to do. If he didn't come soon would she have to try to find her own way to his house?

"Betty Olliver?"

Her head shot up. A middle-aged woman with a tired face stood before her. She was clutching a photo in one hand.

Betty squinted up at her, eyes burning from the tears she'd been trying to hold back. "I'm Betty," she confirmed.

"Oh, thank goodness." The woman reached for her case and extended her other hand to help her up. "I thought I was never going to find you."

Betty held William tighter and kept an eye on her luggage. She didn't trust strangers.

"I'm sorry, are you Charlie's mother?"

"We weren't expecting a baby yet," the woman said. "Luke said you were in the family way but . . ."

"Luke?"

"The other Mr. Olliver, Charlie's brother," she said, pulling at Betty's arm as she started walking.

Betty dug her heels down and stopped. "I was expecting Charlie to meet me. I think I'll wait if you don't mind."

*Who was this woman?*

The lady stopped. Betty sensed that something was wrong, but the woman smiled. The type of smile that made Betty's toes tingle with worry. What was going on?

"I'm sorry dear, I should have introduced myself properly. It's been a long day." She put the case down. "I'm Ivy. Luke's house-keeper. He asked me to meet you and take you home to him."

"But . . ."

"My dear, you did receive the telegram before you left, didn't you? We weren't sure you'd still come, but when we had no word back Luke said I'd better come down to meet you, just in case. We were already prepared for you, after all."

Betty's head started to thump. She squeezed William, hard against her.

"Where is Charlie?" Betty was starting to panic, ready to scream for her husband.

Ivy reached for her, eyes suddenly damp with tears. She gave her a tiny smile, followed by a big sigh. The way she held her body, the slump of her shoulders, told her something was wrong. *That this kind-looking woman didn't want the burden of sharing something with her.*

Betty shuddered as her heart pounded harder and faster until she thought it might actually beat right out from her jersey.

"Betty, I'm so sorry, I didn't think I'd be the one to have to break it to you . . ."

"Where is he?" the voice she heard didn't even sound like her own. It was strangled, pained. Heartbroken. She could almost taste what was coming next, but she knew she didn't want to hear what this Ivy had to say. *She needed her husband.* "Where is my Charlie? Tell me where he is!"

Betty let the woman take William as he started to scream. Her hands were shaking too hard to hold him herself.

"I'm sorry, my love. Charlie's dead."

❦

June tried to sit still. After so long at sea, she was desperate to stamp her feet, walk about on the firm ground, but she was soon travelling again, this time by train. Eddie had gone off in search of refreshments, leaving her with his mother and sister.

"We're so excited to finally have you here, June." Eddie's sister, Patricia, grabbed hold of her hand and squeezed.

Tears pricked June's eyes, but she blinked them away. Having another girl, a sister-in-law beside her, was making her nostalgic. Would she ever hold her own sister's hand again? See Lilly, or her mother and father?

She braved a smile as she saw Patricia and her mother-in-law trade glances.

"Are we not what you expected?" Patricia asked.

"Oh, heavens no! I mean yes," she laughed at her fumbled words. "It's just you remind me of my own sister so much. It makes it hard, knowing I might never see her again."

Patricia slung an arm around her shoulders. "You'll love it here. We know you will."

Eddie appeared in the carriage door. They had a private compartment to themselves with four large seats.

"What's going on here?" he passed around coffee from a tray and set it down on the table. "You're not scaring my wife are you?"

June couldn't help but smile back at him. His grin was infectious. From that first day when she'd struggled home with him, helping him despite his drunken stupor, she'd not been able to take her eyes off that smile. Even though she was a million miles away from where she'd grown up, being with Eddie felt like coming home.

"We like her just fine, Eddie. We just don't know what she sees in you." Patricia thumped him on the arm as he tried to manhandle her out of the way.

Eddie winked at June as he managed to dislodge his sister and steal her seat. He put his arm around her.

"We call her Patty," he said, indicating with a thumb at his sister. "She landed in a cow pat as a kid and the name stuck."

Patty squealed. "I did not!"

Their mother put her hand up to stall their playful squabbling. Eddie pulled June against him and planted a kiss on her head.

"Didn't I tell you she was the best?"

The two women laughed. June felt her cheeks flush, heat flooding them.

"You must miss your family terribly, June."

She looked up and met her mother-in-law's eyes. "Yes."

"Will they come and visit?"

June gulped. Her family weren't exactly poor, but coming all the way to America was too extravagant for them to ever consider.

"One day, maybe. But it wouldn't be easy for them to, well, afford to do so."

Her mother-in-law smiled and looked at Eddie. "Well, I'm sure we can help them make a visit one day, can't we, Eddie?"

He echoed his mother's kind smile. It made June feel . . . content. She'd been so worried about meeting his family, tied in knots over the idea that they might not like her, and here they were doing their best to be kind. To welcome her.

Eddie pulled her even tighter to him.

"Oh, and June?"

She looked from the window back to Eddie's mother.

"You're part of this family now. Call me Mother, or Irene. Whatever you feel most comfortable with."

June snuggled closer into Eddie. For the first time since she'd stepped foot on the ship to leave home, she felt truly happy. There was not a doubt in her mind that she'd done the right thing.

Eddie was her husband. She had a wonderful new family. And if Irene kept her word, one day her family would come to see her.

"Have a sleep, darling," Eddie whispered into her ear, brushing her hair back with his thumb and index finger. "Just relax."

She was so tired that she didn't argue. Instead she just lay her head against his shoulder and let her eyes flutter shut.

She'd spent all those days at sea worrying. Staying awake at night and torturing herself with visions of what might happen when she arrived. Some of the other girls had been full of dreams and fancy ideas, but her only hope had been that Eddie's family would accept her.

*For once in her life it seemed her modesty had been rewarded.*

June's heart thudded with excitement. Patty and Irene were waving frantically to a man with a moustache, who was pulling to the side of the road in a car with no roof.

"Eddie. Eddie!" June called to him as he lugged her case over.

He gave her one of his big grins. "Thought you'd like Dad's car."

"It has no roof!"

June ran over to him and clung on to his forearm.

94

"Don't need a roof in New York. Not in summer."

She followed her husband to the car. The other two women were already sitting in the back seat. June watched shyly as the man kissed Irene on the cheek, before walking around to greet her.

His stomach protruded over his trousers in a well-fed kind of way. Her mother would have said it was evidence that a woman loved him and labored in the kitchen for him. He ran one hand over his thick moustache as he neared her, before taking the hat off his head.

"Well, if it isn't my new daughter-in-law, huh?" he said warmly.

She crossed her ankles awkwardly on the spot, not sure what to do.

"We've heard a lot about you, my girl. Eddie's talked of nothing else since he arrived home."

She nervously took a step forward, then wondered why she was being so silly. Eddie's father pulled her in for a big bear hug, before planting a kiss on each of her cheeks.

"Welcome to the family, my love."

She knew her cheeks were flushing but she couldn't help it.

"Thank you for having me," she stammered.

He gave Eddie a slap on the back and took her case.

"You were right about her, eh? What a girl."

It made her heart sing. Made her skin come alive with excitement.

"Wait 'till you've seen the new house," continued Eddie's father. "We've been . . ."

"Dad!" Eddie scolded.

His father put his hand over his mouth and gave her an apologetic look.

"What house?" she asked.

"It's a surprise," said Eddie. "Come on."

He took her hand and helped her into the car. She sat beside Patty, the three women all tucked into the back. Eddie took the front passenger's seat and his father drove.

"Hold on to your hats, ladies," warned Eddie as they set off.

They all laughed, June louder than any of them.

Life couldn't get any better than this.

❧

*Or could it?*

June hated being in the dark, but she dared not peek. The scarf was tied tightly over her eyes. Eddie was leading her, and she held tightly on to his arm.

The others had mysteriously stayed up at the house, refusing to show her what room she was to call her own. Their home was beautiful, statuesque, and elegant. Full of lovely furniture, framed photos, delicate cushions that she was sure were handmade.

The entire property had stolen her heart from the moment the car had ascended the drive. Up the slight incline of a hill, and flanked by endless fields full of cows and others full with crops. A real-life ranch if ever she'd seen one.

"Almost there."

"Eddie, please! Let me take it off," she begged.

He stayed silent for a few steps, not offering her any words. Then he stopped.

"Okay, if you must."

She tugged the knot at the back of her head. The handkerchief slipped away.

*Oh.* It was a house.

She looked at him. Why were they here? Who lived here?

"Eddie, where are we?" she asked.

"Home." He said the word simply.

"But . . ."

His smile couldn't stretch any wider if he tried. "Let's have a look, shall we?"

She was puzzled. Why would they look inside the house? And why had he called it *home*? They'd just been at his home.

It was large and built from wood—cream weatherboards that had obviously been freshly painted. Two chimneys stood proud on the roof, large windows looked out over fields. It was settled high on the land, looking down to the contours of the fields below.

Eddie was almost at the front door. She hurried over to join him.

"Stop," he called out.

Her foot froze mid-air. He'd opened the door but halted her with his hand before she could walk inside.

"Eddie . . ."

He scooped her up into his arms and carried her over the threshold, before kissing her softly on the lips.

"I've been back almost four months," he told her, placing her down on polished timber floorboards. "I've worked with my father and his builder every day on this house to have it ready for us."

June gulped. "This is *our* house?"

Eddie grinned at her. It was a smile that lit his eyes and made them crinkle in the corners. "All ours."

"Oh, Eddie. Oh my goodness!"

She walked through the lounge and into the kitchen. She touched her palm to the solid timber counter before skimming her fingers across it. She took in the new stove, the appliances, before walking back into the lounge. The fire was set with kindling, despite the warm weather.

"Is this really ours?"

He nodded. "Do you like it?"

She ran into his arms and squealed like she'd never done before. "I love it! Oh Eddie, I can't believe it's ours. Truly ours!"

"We need to get some more furniture, but it'll do for now."

"Do? Eddie, it's *perfect*." She exhaled the word with a sigh. "I don't ever want to leave."

He took her hand to lead her up the stairs. "I'll show you around then we'll go get your things. Everyone's waiting to hear what you think."

"I can't believe they would help you to do this for me. Have you been living here?"

He shook his head. "We only finished it last week." Eddie paused mischievously. "And I wanted us to spend our first night here together."

He moved away from her and disappeared through one of the doors.

"Where are you?" she called out.

June looked in. He was lying propped up by one elbow on a large bed. June didn't know where to look, not with the way he was watching her.

"Want to try it out?" he asked.

"Eddie! We can't."

He sat up and grabbed her hands, pulling her down on to the bed, too. He rolled on top of her and sat astride, holding her down playfully.

"Eddie!"

He leant down and kissed her neck, teasing her.

"Eddie, please! Stop!" But she couldn't stop giggling and he wasn't taking her seriously.

He released her arms and kissed her mouth instead, but he didn't stop.

"I love you, June." He paused and looked down at her, his eyes searching hers.

She smiled straight back at him. "I'm glad I found you that day, Eddie West."

He rolled off her and tugged her into the crook of his arm.

"As much as I'd like to stay here, mother will have half the neighborhood at the main house by now. She's throwing you a party."

June jumped up. "Oh no! They can't see me like this."

She fingered her hair, unwashed and in need of styling. Her clothes were embarrassingly crumpled and she had no idea what they'd expect her to wear.

Eddie bent to kiss her then straightened his trousers.

"Stay here. The bathroom is down the hall, and the hot water's on. Mother put towels in there already. I'll run back and get your things."

Eddie took off and she lay back down on the bed, stretched out like a starfish.

She couldn't wait to write to her family.

She'd worried about her husband, whether he would have regretted marrying her on a whim in London. She'd expected his family to be cautious, distant even. Thought she might have set her hopes too high on what their home, what the farm would be.

*But she'd underestimated.*

It was like her every dream, every wish had been answered.

If her family could see her, could be here with her for even one moment, it would make her the happiest girl in the world.

# CHAPTER 9

Betty pressed her head against the cool glass of the window. The car lurched forward before coming to a crawl in the traffic again. She heard William cry, but her heart ached so much that she couldn't even muster the energy to turn to him. She wanted to ask about Charlie, but didn't want to admit to the truth of it. *Couldn't.*

"I think Master William needs a feed," said Ivy.

She lifted her head and the thump of pain hit her between the ears all over again.

*William.* Her baby's name was like a wave of relief. *William.*

Betty reached for him, taking him from Ivy, who was seated beside her. He gurgled as she cradled him.

Ivy passed her a blanket and she draped it over herself for modesty and let her little boy drink. Tears stung at her eyes, but she wouldn't let them fall. Crying would be admitting that Charlie was gone. Crying would mean that it was real. *And she wasn't ready for real.* She didn't want to know any details, nothing; she just wanted her Charlie back.

"Do you need something to eat? I brought a sandwich for you just in case."

She didn't look at Ivy, just shook her head. Besides, the choke of emotion in her throat wouldn't have let her answer back.

"Oh love, I'm so sorry. I just, well, I think you'll feel better once you've spoken to Luke," Ivy went on, watching her anxiously.

Betty heard the kindness in her voice, knew this woman was trying her best to comfort her, but she didn't want to hear it. How could Charlie's brother make things better?

"He wants you here, Betty. Luke will care for you. He won't let you or young William go without."

Betty turned her eyes back out to the landscape, to the farmland whizzing by outside the window. She had hoped to enjoy the surroundings on this journey. To absorb the countryside of the place that was to be her home.

She didn't want Luke to look after her. She just wanted Charlie. How could he have made it home from the war and died in America? Memories of him crowded her mind, painful and beautiful at the same time.

⁓

His hands encircled her waist. Betty laughed, she couldn't help it. Being around Charlie was like having a comedian on hand, telling her jokes, making her laugh.

"Can't we just pretend you've injured yourself?"

Now it was Charlie who was laughing. "Oh, sergeant, I've got a broken heart. I can't fly! Let me stay."

She shook her head at his drawl. They might be making fun, but the anxiety was real. She'd already waited for him while he did his last stint away, and he hadn't exactly hidden the fact that less than half of his crew had made it back.

*They didn't call them widow-makers for nothing.*

"But Charlie . . ."

"Baby, let's forget about the war. Come on, let's get something to eat."

He didn't even seem the least bit scared. *But she was, more than she'd ever like to admit.*

"They reckon it'll be over soon enough, you know that, right?" he said, hugging her tightly again.

"Who's they?" she asked, but as usual he'd bounded on to his next thought.

"Come on baby, let's catch up with the others."

She still didn't know who *they* were, but she was going to take his word on it. Once this war was over, they had their whole lives ahead of them—so long as he made it back in one piece.

She slipped away from him slightly and caught his hand.

"What're your family like, Charlie?" Ever since she'd lost her parents, she always wanted to know about other people's families. It wasn't until she'd lost hers that she'd realized how precious they'd been.

He stopped and pulled her in close, pressing a kiss to her lips.

"Charlie!"

"What?" He bent for another. She tried to pull away, but he didn't let her go. "We're married, who's gonna care about us necking?"

Betty swiped him across the shoulder with her handbag.

"So?" she asked, wanting to hear about the family he'd left behind in America.

He started walking again and swung her hand in the air, back and forth. "I've got an uptight brother who can be a pain in the neck, but he's a good man, the best, a mother who would be able to run this war if she set her mind to it and stopped thinking about herself, and a father who spends most of his day reading the paper and snoozing in his chair."

She pictured them all, hoping they'd be as kind as Charlie.

"Oooh." Suddenly heat flooded her body, making her go clammy all over.

"You all right?"

Charlie's steady hand supported her.

"I think I'm going to be sick." She leaned against him and took a few deep breaths.

Charlie guided her to rest against a little stone wall off the road. She sat down. Then up again. She was sick on the grass.

"I'm sorry, oh Charlie, I'm sorry. I . . ."

He held her hair off her face and rubbed her back. "You'll be fine. Take some deep breaths." Betty wiped at her mouth delicately with a handkerchief then tucked it back into her bag. She knew it wasn't every day you married a man who would hold your hair back while you vomited.

He sat down and pulled her on to his lap.

"Charlie, I . . ."

"What is it, are you ill? I can take you home if you want to lie down."

She smiled and touched her open palm to his cheek.

"I'm not sick, Charlie, I'm pregnant."

He stared at her, shaking his head. "Are you sure?"

She nodded.

"Woo-hoo!" Charlie took hold of her and flung her in the air, twirling around and around.

"We're having a baby!" he shouted.

"Charlie, I'm not feeling that great."

He dropped her to the ground before wrapping her in the most tender embrace she'd ever experienced.

"We're having a baby," he whispered.

*Yes*, she said silently. *So make sure you make it home safely. Because I can't do this alone.*

༄

The dream made her wake with a smile on her face, but the cold sting of reality hit her the moment she opened her eyes. The worst thing was that he *had* made it home safely. She'd been so anxious all through his last missions and journey home, but he'd come through. What cruel twist of fate had happened? She simply couldn't accept it. She didn't want to know.

She glanced down at William, still asleep in her arms, tucked into her body like he was part of her.

"We're almost there," said Ivy gently.

Betty blinked to help her eyes focus and looked up. She still felt numb. Her body was moving, but her brain was sluggish. She didn't trust her voice to cooperate. Thank goodness for the comfortable leather seats in the car, which she could just slump against for support.

"Luke will be at the house soon after we get there. He planned to finish work early."

Betty nodded. "And their parents?"

Ivy smiled. "The boys never did see a lot of their folks. Kept to themselves, mostly. Mrs. Olliver can be, well, let's just say I worked for the family for years and I was mighty pleased when Luke asked me to run his home instead."

Betty nodded again. Just saying those few words had left her throat dry and aching.

"Shall I take the baby for you? I'm happy to hold him again."

Betty changed her position and rearranged William in the blanket. "I'll be fine."

She was grateful for Ivy helping her, but she wasn't going to give up William. He was all she had now, all she had to live for, and she wasn't letting him out of her arms again.

She wondered what this Ivy thought of her. What Charlie's family would think? They'd not even really expected her to arrive, and certainly not with a baby in tow.

William gurgled, but she didn't feed him. She hadn't even had anything to eat on the journey, her stomach flipping into a web of knots instead. She doubted there was anything there to give him.

But she vowed to make herself drink and eat when they got to the house. She needed to feed him, needed to care for him. *Her life was William.* Without him, she had nobody. And of course, Charlie was a part of him and that made her love him all the more.

"Not far to go now." Ivy patted her kindly on the leg.

Betty looked up. She couldn't help it. She had waited for this moment for so long, only she'd expected to be seated next to Charlie, gabbing away about her trip across the sea, snuggling into him, stealing kisses. Not seated beside the housekeeper, hoping her brother-in-law wouldn't turn her out or insist she go back to London. *And certainly not a widow.*

The car turned. She listened as gravel crunched beneath the thick tires. The driveway was wide, flanked by trees that were yet to have their leaves returned to them for summer.

A house loomed in the distance. In London, they would call it a mansion. She couldn't remember what the *Woman's Guide* would have called it, in American parlance. But it was impressive. A little too big, too cold looking for her liking, but beautiful. Charlie had said they had a lovely home but she'd never known his family had this kind of money. He'd never acted like he came from a privileged background and she'd never thought to ask.

Another car was already outside, taking first place at the foot of the entrance.

"Luke's home already."

Betty took a deep breath. William let out a muffled cry.

"Shoosh now, shoosh William." She gave him a jiggle. "It's time to meet your uncle."

He opened his eyes to watch her. Betty's heart wanted to shatter into a million shards, but she stuck her chin up and sniffed back the tears.

William was about to meet his uncle. If he couldn't have his father, at least he had someone who might care about his well-being, other than her. *Family.*

∽

Luke wasn't waiting at the door for them. Something about that fact meant Betty knew instinctively that he wasn't like his younger brother. Charlie had been like an over-excited puppy. *He would have been waiting at the front door.*

She told herself off. *Never judge a book by its cover.* Well, she wasn't so much judging as summarizing. She had to hope that this Luke had something of his brother's warmth and kindness—she and William were completely dependent on him for help. She looked round again at the big triple brick house, the servants in his employ, the fancy car. Betty gulped. She hadn't hoped for a wealthy husband or cared about status—all she'd cared about was Charlie. Yet here she was in the fanciest house she'd ever seen.

"Why don't I show you to your quarters," said Ivy, nudging her along.

Betty looked back to see the driver taking her case from the trunk.

"Your things will be brought in. Now let's get you upstairs, then you can come down to meet Luke once you're freshened up."

She could see the anxious look on Ivy's face. Was she worried how Luke would react to the baby? Had he been hoping she had stayed behind in London? Her body shuddered. Tears burned against the back of her eyes again. Surely Charlie would be in there waiting for her? It had to be some kind of a mistake, some kind of silly joke.

Betty followed Ivy and kept her head down, her focus on holding William. But she couldn't help but notice the expensive antiques and lavish rugs, the polished wood of the floor as she passed, the elegant swirl of the staircase as they ascended it.

She wished Charlie had mentioned how well off his family was. At least she would have known what to expect.

A deep male voice carried up the stairs from another room, and Ivy was quick to hurry her along.

"You know, Master William looks just like the boys when they were babies. Spitting image."

Betty gave her a tight smile. She knew what Ivy was trying to do; wanting to make her feel okay about the baby coming early, but she had no shame. This was Charlie's baby. She'd never been with another man before, and she'd hoped to never be. And her feelings hadn't changed.

"Here we go."

Betty looked into the room as Ivy swung back the door.

"This was to be your room to share with Charlie. We expected you both to live here for at least the first few months."

Betty changed her grip on William and let him face the room too, his back firm against her chest. The room was enormous. She wriggled off her shoes and felt the plush carpet beneath her toes. The drapes were heavyset and dramatic, swept back from the windows by what looked like gold claws at each side. The walls were painted a deep cream, and a door on the far wall opened into what she presumed was a nursery.

Ivy waved her hand toward it. "He can sleep in here with you if you'd prefer. We can bring the bassinet in. Otherwise the nursery is all set up."

Betty walked toward it. Tears caught in her throat as she looked in.

A tiny bassinet was set beneath the window, a cot for when William grew older against the other wall. There was a changing table, shelves for his clothes and large wicker baskets that she guessed would be for toys. There was even a delicate looking wooden play pen that he would be able to use once he was bigger.

If she'd had Charlie with her, seeing such a room would have been a joy, but alone she just felt like a fraud.

"Betty?"

She didn't turn. Instead she placed William in the basinet, smiling through her tears and tucking the blanket over him. He whimpered, but she ignored it. She needed a moment. He'd barely left her arms, or those of her friends, since he'd been born, but she needed to put him down.

Betty turned slowly. Ivy was still standing inside the door. Her face was like that of a mother's, of a grandmother's—the type of face that knew what it was to deal with heartache, to help heal someone's wounds. Betty could see that now. It had been a long time since she'd had her mother to hold her, to guide her, but right now, she wished for it more than ever.

Ivy took a few hesitant steps toward her. When she held out her arms, Betty fled into them. Her sobs racked her entire body, tears falling like raindrops down her cheeks.

"Oh, Betty. My dear, it's going to be okay," Ivy soothed her, rubbing her back as if she was a child.

She squeezed her eyes shut. She wished she could believe her, but her life was not going to be any more okay than if she'd stayed in London.

"There, there. It's all right my dear."

Betty held on tight. Her sobs were starting to ease, but the desperation in her heart was only becoming worse.

Ivy pulled back slightly and wiped stray hairs back from her face.

"I'm going to leave you for a moment and tell Luke that you're not up to meeting him today. I'll draw you a bath and then you can both have an early night."

Betty shook her head. She wiped at her eyes and braved a tiny smile. "I'll be fine, I just need a moment."

Ivy looked unsure.

"I need to thank him for allowing us into his home. I want to meet him."

Ivy gave her a stern look then sighed. "How about that bath though? You can take an hour to yourself, soak for a while, and I'll look after William. Then you can have dinner with Luke."

She nodded her acceptance.

Betty didn't mind the compromise. A bath sounded like exactly what she needed. So long as Luke didn't think it was rude to draw a bath first, she was grateful. But she was determined to meet him today and get it over and done with. She was going to make her brother-in-law like her, no matter what it took.

She was an orphan and a widow. There was no one in her life besides William and now the boy's uncle. She had nowhere else to go, no one to return home to.

This was her life now. Charlie or no Charlie, America was her home, and she had to do the best she could. There was no other choice.

There was a tap at the door.

The driver appeared with her one large case and her duffel bag. "Thank you."

The man gave her a smile and touched his hat. She'd been so numb earlier that she'd hardly noticed him, but now she saw the same kindness in his face that she'd recognized in Ivy's.

"It's nice to have Charlie's wife here, Ma'am."

He held his cap in his hands.

Betty nodded. "I just wish he was here, too." She was proud of herself for getting the words out.

"Me too, Ma'am. We all wish things had turned out differently."

Betty gave him a quick smile then turned away. She wasn't going to cry again. There was a time for grieving, and that was when she was alone—she needed to remember how lucky she was not to be turned out on the street. She'd faced that before, when her parents had died, but her friend's family had opened their doors to her. She'd never considered that it might happen to her all over again one day.

She was sure not all American families would welcome foreign brides, *widows*, with as much concern.

William started to fuss.

"Don't touch that baby!" She heard Ivy's bossy command the moment she went to step toward him, and was reminded of Madeline's practical, caring manner. "The bathroom is straight across the hall and the water is running."

Betty hesitated.

"Off, young lady!" Ivy disappeared into William's room. "Before I have to march you in there myself."

๛

The water was almost cold. Betty eyed the towel, draped less than a few feet away from her hands, and could barely summon the energy to reach for it. Her body was starting to chill, but the water had been such a luxury that she hadn't been able to resist staying in it until the end.

She'd listened to William cry then whimper, and then fall silent, and he hadn't made a noise since. Neither had Ivy. But she was missing him, and so was her body. It was time to feed her baby.

Betty stood up in the bath and cocooned herself with the thick towel. She rubbed at her skin, still awed at the luxury of being in a real bathroom. There were tiles on the floor, and the faucets were all gold plated. It was like something she'd never even dreamed of before.

She wrapped the towel tighter around herself and stepped out before reaching back in to pull the plug. Water gurgled as she turned to face the mirror. Her own reflection surprised her. Last time she'd looked at herself properly, her face had been full, not to mention her belly. Now her cheeks looked less like those of a chipmunk and more like the Betty she'd been when Charlie had first danced in to her life.

Her fingers traced over her hair, wet from washing and fragrant from the delicate shampoo that had been resting on the edge of the bath. It was already springing into loose curls. Thanks to the days she'd spent above deck with the other girls, her skin was less pale than it usually was, a smatter of freckles tickling over the bridge of her nose.

Betty sighed. She hardly had any decent clothes with her— when she'd left London, her stomach had been huge and she'd disguised her body beneath over-size garments. Hopefully Ivy had some cotton, because she might need to get darning, not to mention knitting some clothes for William.

"You all right in there, Betty?"

She smiled at Ivy's voice and pulled her eyes from her reflection. Betty tightened the big fluffy towel around her body and pulled the door open.

"Sorry, it was just so good in there."

Ivy didn't look worried. "The wee man's still asleep."

"Thank you."

"Let's get you dressed and down to see Luke, then, shall we? He's waiting for you."

Betty gulped. This was it.

"I don't have many good clothes to wear," she confessed.

Ivy patted her arm and guided her across the hall and into her room. "Let's find something for now, and when you're more settled I'll take you to the dressmaker. She'll put some nice things together for you in no time."

Ivy must have seen the look cross her face. Betty couldn't disguise it. She hardly had a penny left, not after her cravings on board the ship for chocolate and buying some things for the baby. There was very little left, let alone enough for new dresses. She hadn't even had close to the £10 limit imposed on traveling brides.

"My dear, you don't need to worry. Luke is a wealthy man and you're the mother of his only nephew."

She looked up and met Ivy's eyes. There was honesty there, and compassion, but she didn't expect charity.

"Ivy, I . . ."

"Come on, love, let's get you dressed. We can talk about all this in the morning, once you've settled in."

Betty held her tongue. She wasn't going to argue. This woman was her only ally right now, the only person she could trust. It could be weeks, if not longer, before she saw the other girls from the boat. What she had to do now was make a good impression and take care of her son.

❧

Betty let her hand glide along the polished timber of the banister. Her heart hammered in her throat. Nausea bubbled in her stomach, but she kept her teeth gritted and rehearsed words in her mind.

*Thank you for having me in your home. William is fortunate to have an uncle like you. Please accept my condolences. Charlie was a wonderful man. We are so grateful that you have opened your doors to us.*

She only hoped her voice would comply.

William cooed in her arms. She looked down at him. His dark eyes twinkled at her, a funny smile taking over his mouth.

"We're going to be fine, my wee man. He's going to love us."

Betty almost tripped over her own feet at a deep cough. She stopped. A tall man stood there, a glass in his hand. He was watching her.

There was no doubting he was Charlie's brother. He was younger than she'd expected, but he looked years older than Charlie. Where Charlie's hair had been longish and flopped over his forehead sometimes, Luke's was cut closer, more businesslike. He had the same tanned skin, although his was lighter than Charlie's. Strong shoulders, tall, commanding—just like his brother. Only where Charlie had always been grinning and joking around, even with strangers, Luke looked far more serious.

Worry ran like a shiver down her spine. Her mouth felt as if it was stuck together with glue. William's hand fisted around a curl of her hair, but she didn't have the energy to scold him.

Luke spoke first. He placed his glass on a sideboard and walked slowly toward the foot of the stairs.

"You must be Betty."

He extended his hand. She walked the last few steps and reached out with her own. It was an effort to make a smile appear, but she did it. This was the man who was keeping a roof over her head, after all.

"I'm sorry, you just look so like Charlie," her voice was soft, low. "It took me by surprise."

She watched as something passed over his face. A darkness, a sadness, perhaps.

"And this is my nephew?"

She took a last step towards him and propped William up in the crook of her arm.

"This is William Charles Olliver," she said proudly. "I named him for my father, and for his own father too."

Luke nodded. She noticed that he kept snatching looks at her face, but she tried not to let it bother her. He was probably as unsure of her as she was of him.

"Let's have dinner, shall we? Then you can tell me all about your voyage."

He took up his glass. She walked beside him, keeping his pace.

"I want to thank you for taking us in, Luke. I am so grateful. Without Charlie . . ."

He cut her off. Abruptly. "William is my only nephew and you are my sister-in-law. There are too many unfilled rooms in this house as it is."

His expression had gone from serious to solemn, his mouth turned down into a frown. Had she said something to offend him? She hoped not.

"Ivy has dinner waiting," he told her.

Betty wished Charlie was by her side, wished he was joking and prodding at her, teasing his brother, introducing them himself. Talking about their plans, their future. Instead she was embarrassed about being a charity case.

Luke might bear a resemblance to his little brother, but she had a feeling that was where the similarities ended.

"Shall we let Ivy take William while we eat?"

It was a simple question, but Betty couldn't help the quiver in her bottom lip. Charlie would have wanted William at the table, in her lap or his.

"Of course."

He dropped his now empty whiskey glass on a low table as they passed and led her to the dining table. It was ridiculously large, but she was pleased to see they didn't have to sit at opposite ends.

Ivy appeared. She had a younger woman by her side who carried a tray of food. Ivy gave her an encouraging smile.

"Thank you, Ivy. Are you sure you'll be okay with him?" Betty asked.

She hated to put the woman out. Looking after William twice in less than two hours!

"My dear, that's why I'm here." She reached for William and tucked him against her body. "He'll be fine. Enjoy your meal."

Luke stood at her chair, pulling it out and waiting for her to be seated. She complied and watched as he folded himself into the seat to her left. She found it hard to meet his dark gaze.

He'd probably formed a picture in his mind of what she'd be like, how she'd look. She was embarrassed to say she'd thought very little about him; it was Charlie who had always been on her mind. She'd often thought of where they might live, but other than looking forward to meeting his family, they hadn't often filled her thoughts.

Betty tried not to wriggle nervously in her seat. In the center of the table were pepper and salt, and in front of her was a steaming bowl of soup. Growing up, soup had always been accompanied by her mother's own crusty loaf of bread, used to mop up every splash of soup. But dunking bread didn't seem fitting given her surroundings.

Luke smiled and dipped his spoon into the velvety soup, signaling that they were beginning their meal. She'd eaten well enough on the ship, but the constant motion had made her feel queasy. Not that sitting with Luke was helping her nerves any.

"Ivy tells me you didn't receive the telegram."

She stifled a choke and placed her spoon down. She'd hoped they wouldn't cover anything so serious so soon.

"I'm sorry if you weren't expecting me." She kept her eyes down. Where could she look? Was this his way of telling her he wished she'd stayed behind?

Luke's eyes drilled a hole into her. She had to look up. He was waiting for her to make eye contact, she could feel it, like he was silently commanding her.

"I'm sorry, Luke." She barely recognized her own voice. "I'm sorry for Charlie, and I'm sorry for not staying behind."

She wanted to flee. To run so fast up those stairs, gather her things and go. But she didn't. There was nowhere else *to* go.

Luke picked up his spoon again and started to eat. As if nothing had happened. She did the same. Swallowing was hard, but she forced each mouthful down.

When there was no soup left in his bowl, he put down the spoon again, wiped at the corners of his mouth, and folded his arms, chair pushed back from the table ever so slightly.

Betty hadn't finished, but she did the same. She doubted she could force any more down if she tried.

The young maid scurried over and took their bowls, leaving the room as quickly as she'd appeared. Betty wished she wasn't alone with Luke.

"It's not that I don't want you here, Betty." Luke looked thoughtful. She saw a flicker of something that reminded her of Charlie, just briefly, in his eyes. "It's just an awkward situation. I'm sure you agree."

She nodded, but inside she was furious, her heart pounding. What had happened to her wasn't *awkward*, it was devastating, as if her heart had just been ripped out

He smoothed a hand over the tablecloth, long fingers tracing a rhythm over the surface. "Charlie was my only brother, and he would have wanted me to look after you. I'm unmarried, so there are no heirs to our family's property and interests, and William is my nephew. He will want for nothing, I can promise you that."

Betty felt a shadow fall over her—a whisper of cool air that told her she deserved better than what sounded like a business arrangement to ensure the family had a successor.

"I love him," she said, forcing the words out. "He's my husband, and I love him." She couldn't bring herself to use the past tense about her darling Charlie.

The young girl appeared again then, with two plates, one in each hand. She placed them down. Betty could feel anger burning in her veins, threatening to explode, but she held her feelings tight.

"Roast duck, with an orange Cointreau sauce, candied yams, and green beans," said the girl, before departing.

"I've no doubt you loved him," Luke said in a low voice once the maid had disappeared again. "Charlie wrote home about you frequently and when he returned he spoke of you constantly. He was very pleased you were expecting."

"He's Charlie's son." She spat out the words, forgetting her manners.

Luke smiled tightly at her and picked up his cutlery.

"He looks very much like an Olliver. I never doubted it, not once I saw him."

Betty took her anger out on her food, cutting violently at the meat.

His words hung stale in the air. Was she to presume he had doubted it *until* he saw William? Her hands started to shake, but she wasn't going to flounce off.

Luke was a strong man, but she was strong too. You didn't survive losing your parents and being newly married in wartime London without being a fighter. *So long as they didn't have to talk about how Charlie died, she'd be fine. She wasn't ready to know the details now, and she doubted she'd ever be, because at least not knowing meant she could pretend he wasn't truly gone.*

# CHAPTER 10

Madeline stared at her hands. She could see every line, every crevice. They were red and raw from hours working in the fields, and the incessant scrubbing afterwards to remove the embedded dirt.

They told a story of their own.

A thud echoed down the hall, and she cringed fearfully.

"Hurry up, girl!"

Madeline didn't bother with a response. She hated her mother-in-law's voice more than any other sound. Loathed hearing the coarse, grating accent of a woman who treated her like the dirt beneath her boot. They might loathe her for being a foreigner, but she despised everything about them, too.

"You not hear me, girl?" came the harsh tones once again.

*And she hated being called girl.*

"I heard you just fine, and no, I'm not finished, as you can well see," Madeline replied tartly.

She wished she'd bitten her tongue, but it wasn't in her nature. She'd grown up with parents who treated their children and those around them with kindness. She had no problem pulling her weight, just like she'd been expected to do at home, only at home she'd been treated with respect and love, working alongside her mother and siblings to make their house a happy one.

Here, she was no better than a slave, working to the point of exhaustion in a house that was meant to be her marital home. She had to work her fingers to the bone just to keep a roof over her head and food in her belly. From the moment they'd arrived at the farm, her heart had sunk. When Roy had met her at the docks, the atmosphere had been awkward, stiff, between them, but she'd hoped that it would become easier once they were at his home. But when they arrived, she knew instantly that everything he'd told her about his home life had been a lie.

The house was ramshackle at best, the tin roof looking like it wouldn't even weather a light storm, the inside cold even when it was warm outside. Her own house in London hadn't been over the top, but she was used to homes full of love and happiness. But Roy's family were surly and unfriendly and their house was no different. His father was either in the field, eating dinner, or asleep; although the few times he'd actually seemed to notice her he'd been just as hostile as Roy's mother and sister.

Her mother-in-law, Sarah, gave her a look of disgust and inspected a plate from the pile Madeline had almost finished washing, turning it over contemptuously in gnarled, tobacco-stained fingers.

Dropping the plate back into the water, Sarah gave her a cruel smile.

"Wash it again. Didn't your mother teach you how to be a wife? Or are English women always this filthy?"

Madeline struggled to breathe. The plate was spotlessly clean. She managed not to scream, held the words in check, but she wasn't going to put up with this any longer. Had to say *something*.

"If it's not to your liking, then perhaps you should attend to them yourself," she said.

The older woman glared at her, spittle forming at the edges of her mouth as she flustered.

"I'm not feeling myself. Please excuse me." Madeline turned sharply on her heel and walked away. Calmly. Shoulders squared, with dignity, moving gracefully and fighting the urge to run away from Sarah as fast as she could.

"Don't you walk away when I'm talking to you! An American wife would know what's expected of her, you hear me?"

Madeline squeezed her eyes shut for a heartbeat, but kept moving.

Her room appeared in front of her. She was at least grateful that it had a door: the room her sister-in-law slept in was separated from the living area by only a curtain, hanging crudely from a low pole protruding from the wall. The small privacy afforded by the thin door was her savior.

Madeline jammed a chair beneath the door handle as a make-shift lock and flopped down on the bed. Springs assaulted her spine but for once she didn't care.

She half expected banging on the door, for Sarah to come in and demand she get back to the dishes. Then pull vegetables from the garden or hoe weeds. Or worse, wring the neck of a hen for dinner.

Madeline shuddered. She had no idea what to do, how to deal with the situation she'd ended up in. It wasn't that she objected to some hard work—indeed, she'd expected to put in some graft to get their new home in order. But the amount she was expected to do was horrendous, and the sneering cruelty and bullying of her new family made it all the more unbearable.

Her beloved father kept appearing in her head, his kind face swimming in front of her eyes. She could hear his words, over and over. *I'll bring you home, Madeline.* She needed to keep thinking it, to remind herself that what he'd said was real. *If it's that bad over there, I'll do whatever it takes to bring you home.*

Could she ask that of him? Would he still want to help her if she truly told them what it was like here? What her new family expected of her? How they treated her?

When she'd first met Roy's mother at the house, it had been a shock. A stooped lady who had once been very tall, with a mouth set in the meanest of lines, not to mention her grey hair and sharp eyes. *Like a witch.*

Since she'd arrived, there had been times when Sarah had smiled. Or been kind. But never to her. Sometimes to her daughter, but most often to her son. It was as if she thought Madeline inferior, and not good enough for him. She was mildly better in her behavior towards Madeline when Roy was around, but she made up for it when he wasn't.

She had never been one to compare, but it was she who felt superior in this house. Not from a monetary point of view, but certainly when it came to manners and status, and the basic rules of how to decently treat other human beings.

But the biggest shock had been her new sister-in-law, Carolyn. She'd hoped for the friendship of another woman her age, but Carolyn was as mean as her mother, if not more so, with a look on her face that read of nothing but disgust.

They treated Roy like he was something special, as if she wasn't at all good enough for him, and it drove her mad.

Where was the man she'd met in London? Where was the strong, assertive young soldier who had made her believe in him? Impressed her family and made her want to leave them behind just to be married to him? No wonder he'd avoided her questions about his home and family. The man he was now was a spineless rodent, hardly even able to look her in the eye, and scuttling off at the first signs of his family's bad behavior towards Madeline. He knew he'd deceived her, yet not once had he said sorry or tried to explain himself. He worked quite hard himself, though he often sloped off into town for hours, under the pretense of meetings or selling their goods, arriving back late with little to show for his supposed labors. But that didn't stop his mother lavishing praise on him for his mediocre efforts.

The doorknob rattled. "Madeline, open up right now!"

*Speak of the devil.*

She rose and pulled the chair away. Roy burst through. He ran one hand wildly through his hair, the other hanging limply at his side as if he didn't know what to do with it.

"*Mother* had to run and tell on me, did she?" Madeline said acidly, sitting back on the bed. Every inch of Roy's face showed his anger.

"I had to come up from the field, Madeline. You better have a good reason for disobeying . . ."

"Disobeying? For goodness sake, Roy, she's supposed to be my mother-in-law, not my master!"

He glared at her. "All she asks of you is a few chores."

Madeline laughed. Out loud. If she didn't laugh she would have started bawling her eyes out, and showing Roy she was anything but strong wasn't going to help her cause.

"I work *hours* every day, Roy. *Hours*. That's hardly helping out around the house."

"While you're a guest in this house . . ."

She stood, eye to eye with him. Far braver than she felt. Braver than she'd ever known she could be.

"I am *not* a guest, Roy. You married me and brought me here. I should not have to feel grateful, it should be my right. Isn't a husband expected to provide a home for his wife?"

His throat pulsed with anger. She could even see a tic in his eye, face burning red.

"So when *are* we going to move to our own place?" she pushed on. "Because I'm sure as heck not going to put up with this any longer."

"Or what?" he spat.

"Or I shame your entire family by filing for divorce and going home," she told him. She wasn't going to be meek and mild when it came to Roy or his family, not after how he'd lied to her or how they were treating her. She only had herself to count on, and that meant being brave even when she was scared inside.

"You wouldn't."

She didn't miss the hesitation in his voice. The way his voice stuttered and caught in his throat.

"One message home and I'm on the next ship out of here."

They stared at one another. Madeline knew she only had another few minutes before she couldn't pretend any longer. But she was determined to stay strong for as long as she could.

"I would have to take a job in town if we left here. You don't expect me to just leave my parents, do you? Who would help them here?" He sighed heavily. "I'm a farmer, Madeline, this is where I belong."

She glared at him.

"One month, Roy. Otherwise I'm gone."

Madeline lay in bed, dead still. Too frightened to move.

Tonight, she'd walked into the kitchen, her back straight, and reached into the fridge. She'd taken a block of cheese, plunged a knife into it to retrieve a few slices, before returning it and helping herself to a slice of bread. Then she'd turned on her heel and retreated to her bedroom.

They'd all been watching her. Their eyes had been like the devil on her skin, following her every move. But no one spoke. They rarely ever did at the dinner table.

It was so unlike her own home that it made Madeline feel sick. She could imagine her family now, Harold laughing and entertaining his daughters, her mother trying to purse her lips and swat at him, but giving in to his jokes in the end. His grandchildren would be huddled around him as he told them a story from his rocking chair, in the lounge beside the fire.

Madeline let the door fall away from her fingers with a bang, and she sat down to eat her cheese and bread. They would have made a mental note of what she'd taken, to write on the chit they kept, to record how much it was costing them to keep the newly married couple.

But she knew better than to let them outsmart her on these terms. She'd never taken what wasn't hers. And the work she did here every day accounted for a whole lot more than the food and board they gave her in exchange. If she had to hear one more time that she must have had it darn easy back in London she'd scream! What she didn't understand was why Roy wanted to stay here so badly? Why wouldn't he want them to have their own farm? She would gladly work hard alongside him if he wanted to make a go of things. All she knew for sure was that his mother's influence was set in stone—she was an expert at controlling her son, and Roy either didn't want to acknowledge it, or didn't even realize it was happening.

But she had a plan. Tomorrow, she was going to start walking into town. Someone passing would give her a ride. The other farmers seemed kind enough, no different than the farmers her father had dealt with at his butcher shop. They were no doubt nice people who would be hard pressed to drive past a young woman and not offer her a seat in their car or cart.

Madeline swallowed her final mouthful as Roy swung open the door.

"This is ridiculous," he bellowed.

She smiled sweetly at him. "You're right. This hell hole *is* ridiculous."

The words didn't come easily to her, but she forced them.

"Madeline, you are being unreasonable."

She liked that he was so agitated. Part of her had come to loathe him already; in just four weeks, she'd started to despise him. For lying to her about his home, for allowing his family to treat her as they did. For everything.

But most of all for deceiving her, for telling her he loved her, and bringing her here. She didn't doubt that he had *some* feelings for her—perhaps he even had fallen in love with her in London; she just couldn't be sure of anything anymore. But if he loved her here and now, he wouldn't let her family treat her this way—he would stand up for her and what she needed.

He sighed. "I'll have a word with them. Ask them to go a bit easier on you."

She looked at his face—at the premature lines that had embedded themselves in his forehead, at the dark tinge around his eyes.

A flicker ignited within her, but she stomped it out.

She couldn't feel sorry for him, but she almost did. The brave man she'd met in London had disappeared, swept firmly back under the thumb of his mother. But she sensed his vulnerability at that moment. She needed to stand up for herself, assert her rights.

Roy sat on the bed beside her, his head dropped into his hands.

"We can't afford to move out," he told her. "And I don't want to anyway."

She nodded. She'd been expecting him to say that. *His mother had clearly done her work in telling him what to think.* She touched her fingers lightly to his hand.

"I'm going to get a job."

His head lifted. "You're what?"

"A job. I'm more than capable."

"They won't let you. Don't be ridiculous!"

"Who, Roy? Who won't let me?" She knew exactly who he meant, but she needed him to say it.

"It would shame my family. Everyone in town would think we couldn't make enough money from the land to feed one more mouth."

She smiled. "More so than if I left you?"

His face was tortured.

"I'm going to get a job, and so are you. Or they can pay you what you're worth. Either way, we *will* find a house of our own.'

Roy stood up and left the room. She didn't call him back.

Slowly she undressed, stepping into her nightgown, and lay beneath the covers. Finally now, she could let herself be weak for a moment. Tears stung her eyes and fled her lashes as if they fell from a waterfall. She hiccupped softly, swallowing what she could, not wanting to be heard.

A footstep sounded nearby. Madeline turned her head and cried silently into her pillow.

She was going to look for a job, but what she hadn't told Roy was that she wouldn't be able to hold anything for long.

If her suspicions were correct, she was pregnant already.

She touched her belly and the tears began to fall harder.

All her life she'd wanted to be a mother. Now she was stuck over here, as good as alone, and suddenly a mother was the last thing in the world she wanted to be. She couldn't possibly bring a child into this situation.

*She wanted to go home.*

When Roy came to her tonight, slipped beneath the sheets in their bed, she intended on refusing him. Every night until they moved out, she would refuse him the one thing he wanted from her.

He was going to be like an angry bear with a thorn in its paw, but she didn't care.

It was either her rules or a ship back to London. The decision was his. She'd give him a chance, because if she even glimpsed the man she'd fallen for it would be worth trying to save her marriage, but she wasn't going to be treated like this for the rest of her life. And she certainly wasn't going to allow children to be born into an unhappy family.

Home was like a mirage, disappearing into the distance of her memories. It called her, pulled her like a magnetic current, but it was slipping from her grasp. Fast. And that scared her more than anything.

# CHAPTER 11

Alice felt like there was a hand around her throat. Tight, squeezing the breath from her windpipes, suffocating her. She woke with a start. She was hot and clammy, her hair slick against her forehead.

Only the noise of snoring made her realize she was safe. Or at least she was as safe as she could be, *for here.*

She lay her head back down on the pillow and listened to the now familiar rumble of her husband as he slept. Sometimes she kicked him and then stayed deathly still, pretending to be asleep in case he caught her out, but it never helped. He would stop, fidget, then start the bear-like breathing all over again. Her only relief came in falling asleep first, but waking up like this from a nightmare left her awake for hours.

*And left her thinking.*

Her life here was nothing like she'd hoped. Not even a shell of the life she had imagined as they'd sailed across the ocean.

Where was her husband? Where was the man, the soldier, who she'd fallen in love with? Where was the in-control, strong, devilishly handsome man who had looked so dapper in his uniform, so kind and dignified even when he lay helpless on a hospital bed?

Who had courted her so diligently? Who had progressed through the ranks in the United States Army to become a captain before his 25th birthday? From the moment she'd seen him waiting for her, she'd known something was wrong. It was like the light had gone out in his eyes—he was the same man on the outside but her darling Ralph, the dashing, confident man she'd fallen for, was gone.

Alice rose from their bed and wrapped her shawl tight around her shoulders. The house was cool, the sweat drying quickly to chill her skin. She was exhausted from work, tired of worrying, and sick to death of missing home. But most of all she was annoyed at having to watch every penny they spent.

She'd expected lavish parties, a handsome townhouse, never having to lift a finger herself unless it came to the odd spot of housework.

*How wrong she'd been.*

Here, she worked long hours, cooked for her husband, cleaned, washed, managed the household. And worried each week about the bills they had stacking up on the counter.

Not to mention watching as her husband used every spare penny they had to buy whiskey. Then he'd drink himself senseless, before passing out on his chair, or ranting at the wireless, or worse, yelling at her. But when he refused to speak to her for days on end was as bad as it could get.

She desperately wanted to go home. She wanted to step back in time and turn down Ralph's advances. But she knew if it happened over again, she would still marry him. No girl would have turned him down, not the way he had been then.

But that didn't help her cope with the disappointment. Her husband was a loser. A man who'd been important once, in the army, but who was nothing in the real world.

A man who had lost everything and given up. What had happened? What had changed since she'd last seen him? Every time she tried to bring it up, tried to talk to him, he just shut down and became more withdrawn than he'd been beforehand.

Tears prickled her eyes and she blinked them back. And as she often did in the wee early hours of the morning, she boiled the kettle and made herself a sweet cup of hot chocolate, like she always had back home, and let big juicy tears roll into her cup as she bravely took each sip.

She was a lonely, miserable excuse for a married woman. She hated her job, she hated her home, and worst of all, she hated her husband like she'd never hated a human being before.

She thought of the soldier whose eyes had caught hers when she was on duty as a nurse. Of the strong, tall man who had so gallantly proposed to her, searching her out and knocking on her door.

And then she listened to the repetitive, snarling snore from the other room.

*What had she ever done to deserve this?*

❦

Alice didn't want to argue today. Not again. Every time they were together they either argued or he ignored her, and today she didn't have the energy. She found herself hoping for the silent treatment.

She stared at her complexion in the mirror and fought against the frown that was hovering over her mouth. Her lips seemed to be in a constant fight with gravity these days, whereas before she'd found it hard to wipe a smile from her face. She was exhausted from yet another bad night's sleep, and it showed.

Alice smoothed powder over her skin, gently sweeping the blush over her cheeks. Then she picked up her lip brush and fought the shake of her hand, trembling as she painted red across her mouth. But it didn't help. She could see how lifeless her eyes appeared, dull instead of radiant, and there was no glow to her face.

She forced herself to smile and pulled on her panty hose, the last pair she owned that weren't peppered with holes or runs. Just because she was unhappy didn't mean she was going to let her standards drop. It was all that kept her going that reminded her of who she had once been. Keeping up appearances was the only reason she was able to brave the world each day with her chin tilted, head held high.

The sun shone with such ferocity outside that Alice wondered if it was trying to cheer her up. She decided that she would try and feel better, that she wouldn't feel sorry for herself any longer. They would get through this. Ralph would come right. She could get him help. It couldn't stay like this forever. Surely someone could help her, someone who knew about soldiers with problems like this. She'd read something somewhere about men who came home traumatized from the war—was that what was wrong with him?

She straightened her skirt, wishing she had something slightly shorter to match the new fashions. But she still looked good. The clothes she did have were expensive, tasteful, even if they weren't the latest designs. She heard the other girls snicker about her at work, whispering as she passed, refusing to let her become part of the group. But she didn't care. Women had gossiped about her, her entire life. Hated her because men always turned their heads when she walked by.

She didn't need friends, she told herself. Well, she didn't need new ones. The only friends she cared about were the girls from the ship. Girls who were probably having the time of their life as newlyweds, while she suffered through each day with her man. She'd do anything to see them all, to confide what she was going through, but as much as she'd love them to talk to, her pride wouldn't let her. They were no doubt busy living the dream while she was stuck in some kind of married hell. She'd been so self-assured about her new life, and yet here she was miserable and wishing she'd never married her man.

Alice thrust her chin up and walked out of the bedroom. She grimaced at the mess in their tiny lounge but kept on moving. She walked past her husband, who was staring into space on the porch, his big frame dwarfing the rickety chair. She paused, fiddling with the hem of her skirt for something to do, then bent to touch the edge of a lone flower. For the first time in her life she didn't know what to say; all she wanted was for Ralph to notice her. For that spark to reignite between them, to see that old, familiar look he'd always had when he clapped eyes on her.

Alice waited, watched him, pressed her hands down her skirt hoping he'd notice her. But he didn't so much as smile, just kept staring ahead like she wasn't there at all.

Alice squared her shoulders and left. She cringed as she headed down the street, hating that she could leave home without him even acknowledging her, or caring, but she didn't stop or give in to the tears. There was no room for emotion in her life, at least not in public.

It took her half an hour to walk to work, but it would do her good. The sunshine on her skin felt pleasant, uplifting almost, and it beat catching the bus.

༄

Alice didn't so much hate her work as she hated *having* to work. She'd never expected to do more than cook and clean her home, care for children when the time came, all with help of course. But work? It hadn't really ever been part of her life's plan.

And she especially hadn't ever considered that she'd be the only one working.

"Mrs. Jones?"

She looked up, her fingers hovering over the typewriter.

"Mr. Roberts has called a full staff meeting. We are to meet promptly at ten-thirty in the boardroom."

Alice nodded. Mrs. Perkins, the old tart who ran the office team, had never been particularly friendly. She'd hardly cracked a smile once since Alice had started.

She went back to typing. Her fingers moved surely over the keys, not as fast as most of the others, but neatly and without error. Alice smiled as she tapped. Her teacher never would have believed that her worst student would end up typing for a living, but something about her years at school had stayed with her.

A whisper of cologne wafted past her, making her head snap up. *Oh.*

Her eyes followed her nose and fixed on a handsome man as he glided through the office. He smelled and looked expensive. His black hair was swept back, grey inching past his temple. He was tall, had a neatly trimmed moustache that followed his mouth, and the watch on his wrist was made from thick gold.

Alice darted her eyes back to her work as he looked her way.

*Oh Lord!* He'd caught her staring.

She didn't dare peek at him again, but the heat creeping up her cheeks and flushing her face would have given her away if he was still watching.

He had to be Mr. Roberts.

*Her new boss.*

Alice hadn't been invited into the boardroom before. Only the senior assistants were asked to sit in on meetings and take notes.

It was as elegant as a meeting room could be. A large mahogany table was flanked by numerous chairs, and the windows looked out over the city.

She hesitated by the door before taking her place alongside the far wall, leaving the chairs for those higher up the chain than her.

The room filled within minutes. A low hum descended as the employees spoke in hushed tones, but no one spoke to Alice. She was used to it.

Then one of the men cleared his throat. She looked up.

Mr. Roberts appeared, walking through the door and taking his position at the head of the table. The energy in the room became more charged with his powerful presence. She watched as he smiled, completely at ease with so many people's attention focused on him.

"Thank you all for gathering so promptly," he began, in a deep, assured voice.

"I wanted to take this opportunity to introduce myself, and let you all know that I anticipate the change of leadership will not cause any disruption."

Mr. Roberts paused and coughed.

"Would someone be so kind as to fetch me a glass of water?"

Alice felt a painful stab in her ribs, followed by Mrs. Perkins' snappy voice in her ear.

"Get to it, Alice."

Alice wasn't about to argue about jumping to attention, not when she was the newest employee. If anyone was going to get the boot, it would be her, especially given how frosty the other girls were to her. She moved slowly through the crowd of women at the back, who didn't seem interested in moving out of her way, and slipped out of the door.

Alice hurried down the corridor, poured a glass then walked back to the boardroom. She glared at those in her way this time, not wanting to spill the glass.

Her pace slowed when she neared the new boss, though. When he looked up, he met her gaze.

It felt like the whole room was watching her. Her hand quivered as she set the glass down on the table before him.

"Thank you," he said, fixing his eyes intently on hers.

She smiled. "You're welcome."

He laughed. He actually laughed at her. She could have died right there on the spot.

"An English girl, huh? Well, fancy that. Your name?"

Alice swallowed. "Alice Jones, sir."

"Mrs. Jones," he said. He held up the glass and downed half of the water. "Thank you."

Then he continued on, like nothing had passed between them. Like it had been only the two of them in the room and now they were suddenly surrounded by others.

She ignored her burning cheeks and took her place at the back of the room again, hoping the meeting would be over fast. She couldn't fail to miss the scowls directed her way.

Alice didn't look up again until the meeting was over. The women around her were already shuffling off, so she forced her feet to obey and followed them.

Until she heard a clear, deep male voice ring out across the room.

"Mrs. Jones."

Oh, no. She froze. *Please don't fire me today. Please.* He hadn't mentioned anything about employee cuts, had he? Had she missed it while she'd been daydreaming about him? Alice waited until the remaining employees had left, then walked toward him. Her body felt numb, her feet heavy as she met his stare.

"What can I do for you, sir?"

"Please take a seat," he beckoned for her to sit across from him with one hand. "And call me Matthew, at least when we're alone."

He winked at her. Her boss actually winked at her.

Alice just nodded. She couldn't make her tongue form words. She'd forgotten what this felt like. Talking to a man like this, being in a man's company—it used to come so naturally to her.

"Alice. May I call you Alice?"

She nodded again.

"Well, Alice, I'm in need of a personal assistant, and I think you'd be perfect." What? She shook her head. "What about Mrs. Perkins?"

He smiled wryly, and raised his eyebrows for an instant.

"Mrs. Perkins is, well, not exactly what I'd hoped for. You'd do the job much better, I'm sure."

He was attracted to her, she could sense it. This powerful man was actually attracted to her. Why else would he ask her when he could have had any of the ladies in the office assisting him? *He knew nothing about her.*

"So, will you accept my offer?"

She took a deep breath and forced her eyes to meet his. It would make the others only hate her more, but what did she care? She had nothing to lose and everything to gain.

"I'd be honored, Mr. Roberts."

"Matthew," he reminded her, before giving her another wink.

Alice tried to keep the smile on her face, but inside she was in knots. The old her would have flirted and bantered with him, but it no longer came as second nature.

"When do I start?" she asked, feigning confidence.

He grinned, folding his arms over his chest as he appraised her.

"Just let me offer Mrs. Perkins an early retirement package first, then you'll be my right-hand lady."

Alice stood up, standing straight, shoulders back, smile firmly in place still.

"Until then, *Matthew.*"

He stood too, his eyes never leaving her face.

"Until then."

Alice's only regret was that he wore a wedding band.

She ignored the niggle of guilt as it wound its way through her. She'd turned down a married man once before, and now she was married herself.

But Matthew had only asked her to be his assistant.

*For now.*

# CHAPTER 12

June still couldn't believe it. Every time she looked around, every time she stepped foot inside a room, she couldn't believe the house was hers. *Theirs*. Built with her husband's own hands, with the land gifted to them by his family. She loved it, loved what they had done for her to give her the most wonderful start imaginable in a new country, and she'd settled in well.

A knock echoed at the door.

June fiddled one last time with the stem of a flower, pushing it further into the bunch, then wiped her hands on her apron.

"Come in!"

She loved the sound of her voice ringing out clear down the hallway. Her family home had been modest. Lovely, but not large, whereas this house was big enough to accommodate an entire brood of children.

"June, what are you doing?"

Patricia appeared.

"Just fiddling with things," June replied.

Her new sister laughed and waved her hand at the window. "Haven't you noticed what a nice day it is?"

Of course she had; the sun had been beaming through the windows. "I just want to get the house right. Nice for Eddie."

That elicited an even louder laugh. "He built the darn house, and he's got you in it, so come on. You could have it looking like a dump and he'd still smile when he arrived home."

June blushed. She couldn't help it. Eddie was like her own personal ray of sunshine. Every time he looked at her, touched her, laughed with her, it made her feel alive. *Happy.* So incredibly happy.

"So do you want to come?"

"Where?" she asked.

Patricia followed her into the kitchen.

"No time for a *cuppa*, 'luv,'" Patricia said in her best British impersonation. "Mother's taking us both into town for lunch."

June smiled. She was so lucky to have a nice sister-in-law, not to mention a mother-in-law who was determined to march her about in an attempt to show her off. "What's the occasion? Have I missed a birthday? Eddie never mentioned anything this morning . . ."

"We don't need an occasion, silly." Patricia laughed, pulling the kettle from her hand and marching her back down the hall and toward the stairs. "We just want to show you around. Make sure everyone in town knows who you are."

June felt her face flush. "Me? Oh, I don't know. Really, I think I'd . . ."

Patricia gave her a firm push on the rear end.

"Put something nice on. You've got fifteen minutes."

"Fifteen, but . . ."

"Get a wriggle on, girl."

She took one look at Patricia, hands on her hips, and went up the stairs. Maybe it would be nice to go out, to have a look around and be pampered by her new family. But she didn't like to be made a fuss of, certainly not the center of attention.

Although it would mean she could post her letters and try to find the other girls. Time had flown past and she was sure they felt the same, busy enjoying their new lives in the months since they'd parted ways. Sometimes their time on the ship together felt like a dream, but she was still keen to get back in touch.

She smiled just thinking about her friends, then her thoughts quickly turned to where she was heading. Maybe they could drop in and see Eddie at work while they were out.

That made her move faster. Any excuse to see her husband.

⁓

The sun beat down on June's skin and made her smile all over again. It was hard not to. She'd worried about not fitting in here, of being so homesick that she'd be miserable, but it couldn't have been further from the truth.

Patricia had her arm slung firmly in hers as they sauntered down the street, and June was glad she'd come out. Being in town for the day was much more enjoyable than she'd expected.

"So where are we going for lunch?" she asked.

"Mother wants to take you to The Ridges," Patricia told her.

It sounded fancy. *Far too fancy for her.*

"Aren't we meeting Eddie?" she asked.

Patricia swatted at her. "Don't you get sick of seeing him all the time? I mean really, he's nice and all, but you don't have to pretend you're *that* crazy about him."

June stopped dead. They thought she was pretending?

Her sister-in-law must have seen the look on her face.

"Kidding, June. Kidding." Patricia held her hands up like a criminal who'd just surrendered. "Geez, you Brits take things so seriously."

June smiled and sighed in relief. She wasn't used to the way Americans joked. Especially not about things like that! Besides, how could she ever tire of her Eddie?

"Anything you want to do?" Patricia asked.

They went back to walking, arm in arm.

"Post some letters back home, that's all."

"Don't need to stop and look at baby clothes?" her sister-in-law teased.

June felt her eyebrows begin to frown, but she tried not to react. "Another American attempt at humor?"

This time it was Patricia who pretended to look horrified.

"Well, kind of . . . but you being a newlywed, not to mention you and my brother being holed up in that new house of yours every night just made me wonder, that's all."

June couldn't help the blush that stung her cheeks. She'd never get used to how brash women were over here. No topic seemed off limits, even the most intimate ones.

"So?" Patricia asked.

June glanced at her sideways. "Can I call you Patty?"

"Of course."

June kept walking. She hadn't known if Patty was just the nickname Eddie called his sister and she had kept forgetting to ask.

"But that still doesn't answer my question. Baby clothes or not? I'm ready to be an aunt!"

"No baby clothes yet." June was surprised with how firm her voice was. It wasn't that she didn't want to be pregnant—heavens, she wanted nothing more! But she hadn't been blessed yet, and she wasn't about to jinx herself by buying clothes before she needed them.

"Oh look, there's Mother."

June followed Patty's gaze and they walked off together. Patty was already busy chatting about something else, but June was still stuck on the baby thoughts.

Eddie was as desperate for a family as she was, but all they could do was hope and pray.

She suppressed a giggle.

*And keep trying.* They still couldn't keep their hands off one another.

# CHAPTER 13

Madeline sat, back ram-rod straight, on a small sofa outside a polished mahogany door. Her palms were damp and clammy, like she'd been out too long in the sun. But it wasn't the heat. It was because this interview could change her life. This job, and the money she'd earn, could end up being the one place where she could seek refuge and start to find a way out of the awful situation she'd found herself in.

*If they gave her the job.*

After what seemed an age, she heard the creak of the door and jumped to her feet. A man appeared. He was a little older than her own father, with a thick bushy moustache and small spectacles. She was relieved that he looked kind, almost friendly, and certainly not the stern man she'd been expecting.

"Mrs. Parker?"

She nodded and braved a smile, holding out her hand just like she'd practiced in the mirror at home.

"Yes. Pleased to meet you, sir."

He nodded and ushered her into his office.

Madeline took a deep breath and walked forward. The office was neat and orderly. A large desk, with a formidable leather chair seated behind it, sat in the center of the room. She waited until he was standing in front of it, and only sat when he beckoned for her to do so.

Right now, her manners were the only thing she was sure of.

"So, Mrs. Parker, you seem to have impressed my secretary."

Relief hit her in a great rush. "Mrs. Ronson seems like a lovely woman. It would be a pleasure to work with her," she replied.

He smiled and rubbed one hand over his moustache, as if in contemplation.

"We've had many applicants. However I like to keep my staff happy, and it's Mrs. Ronson who you will be working alongside, after all."

Madeline just nodded and waited. She didn't want to ruin her chances by saying anything foolish. It wasn't like she'd ever applied for a job before—school and then her father's butcher shop were all she'd ever known.

"So tell me why I should hire you, Mrs. Parker. What makes you special?"

Madeline forced herself to unfold her hands. She placed them on her lap, and began speaking.

"Mr. Curtis, I appreciate you have a tough decision to make here, however I know you'd be very happy with me. I managed my father's shop alongside him for many years, and assisted with all the accounts. I like to get a job done well."

His smile was kind when he looked up from his notes.

"I have heard that you British girls have a good work ethic," Mr. Curtis said. "And, judging from what you say, I think the rumors might well be true."

"Yes, sir. I wouldn't let you down. My father liked to say that if you can't do a job well, you shouldn't do it at all, and I believe that statement to be true."

He studied her. Looked her over and then cast his eyes down to his papers. She'd first been interviewed by Mrs. Ronson, and she guessed he was studying the notes she'd made.

He looked up again, a serious expression on his face as he considered her. "Well, I think I've had enough time to make my decision."

Madeline hung her head, and felt her heart sink. *She wasn't good enough.* He liked her, but there had been too many other candidates to select from. She should have known. It wasn't as if she'd specifically trained for this type of role.

"Thank you for your time, sir. I certainly appreciate it," Madeline said.

She stood up, handbag clasped between her fingers, and began to walk dejectedly towards the door.

"Mrs. Parker?"

She turned back to him. "Yes?"

"Please don't make me change my mind."

He was smiling again. Was this some strange American humor that she didn't understand?

"I beg your pardon?" she asked.

"What I was about to say, was that I've made my decision and you may have the job. That's if you still want it?"

*He what?*

"Oh, my. Golly. You do?" she stuttered.

He chuckled again. "We might need to get Mrs. Ronson to work on some of the words you use, but yes, you have the job. Congratulations."

If she were braver she would have run around the desk and kissed his cheek. But she didn't. Instead Madeline just stood still, unable to wipe the smile from her face.

"When shall I start?"

"How about Monday? Report in at eight-thirty, and your duties will be assigned then," he told her.

Madeline left his office walking on air. She'd done it. She had secured a job, without anyone's help. All on her own she'd impressed two people who wanted to hire her, *and she had gotten the position.*

The first face she saw at the end of the corridor was Mrs. Ronson. Madeline guessed she was only a couple of years older than her at most, but she exuded competence and professionalism. Her hair was severely pulled back in a tight bun, but her friendly smile was the complete opposite of her style.

"Well?"

The other woman had a worried look on her face, her hands clasped against her pretty spotted dress.

"I'm to be here Monday morning!" Madeline told her, hands shaking with excitement.

The broad smile she received in return mirrored her own.

"Well, you'd better start calling me Lauren then, if we're going to be working together every day," said Mrs. Ronson.

"Madeline," she replied. "You may call me Madeline."

They shook hands, lightly squeezing one another's.

"I've waited a long time to have someone like you working here," Lauren said.

Madeline smiled so hard that her cheeks hurt. She had no one in her life here except for Roy and her in-laws, and Lauren was like a breath of fresh air. She couldn't wait to get stuck into a proper job, where her hard work would be appreciated. It seemed like forever since she'd just grinned from happiness. She knew she should have tried to contact the girls from the boat, but she just couldn't. Couldn't stand the thought of confessing how miserable she was, or of pretending that everything was fine when they were all probably so blissfully happy.

And now she only had five days to move into town so she could start work on Monday, and her husband didn't even have a job yet. She knew he wouldn't take the news well, to say the least, but she had to keep going with her plan to escape the farm.

❦

"I don't care, Roy. I've already taken the position."

She'd never seen him so angry.

"You should have asked me first!" he shouted, slamming his fist against the wall in frustration.

But Madeline wasn't going to back down. Not now. She needed to get out of this house and earn some money of her own. Needed to do whatever she could to get into a better situation before she found out for certain about the baby.

Deep down, she already knew. She'd missed her courses twice and she was feeling queasy in the mornings, but right now that wasn't her focus. Moving out of here and forging a life, with her husband, was all she wanted to do. It was the only thing she could do. Because if that didn't work, she was all out of options.

"Madeline, I cannot do this to my family. You know that."

"Do what, Roy? Stand up to them? Be a man?" He glared at her, but it didn't slow her words, didn't stop her saying what she really thought about him. "You disgust me."

The words hissed from her mouth. She barely recognized her own voice, it was so savage.

"I've done my time here. You hear me? I'm done," she told him. "Now you either come with me this weekend and look at the houses I've inquired about, or I'll go on my own."

She had no doubt his family was listening on the other side of the door. There was no privacy in this place. But she was beyond caring. She might dislike him, but she was going to try to bully him

147

into moving. Once it was just the two of them, maybe things would get better?

"And what will I do? Huh? What work will I find in town?" he came back at her.

"My wage will keep us going for a short while. You'll find something, or else you can commute back and forth to the farm."

They stared at one another, both furious. The only difference was that Madeline had made her mind up and she had no intention of changing it.

"You said you've made appointments?" said Roy, finally, in a quieter tone.

The slump of his shoulders and downturn of his mouth told her she'd won this first battle.

"Yes. Saturday morning," she told him.

"And you won't reconsider this job offer?"

"It is not an offer, Roy. I've accepted the position, they'll pay me fortnightly, and I start first thing next week."

He turned to leave the room. She stayed put.

It didn't matter what she heard once he walked out, how much of a fuss his family made, she was going to let him deal with it.

Sometimes she felt sorry for him. *Sometimes.* She knew he was caught between the pressures and manipulation of his family, and what she wanted. But he'd made his own choice, bringing her here. He'd lied to her about what their life in America would hold, and he had refused to stand up for her, to protect her, *to love her*, as he'd promised.

Maybe he'd married her because he *had* loved her then, or at least liked her. Maybe he'd thought the war would take his life, and that they'd never actually end up here. Maybe that's why he'd pretended his life in America was something it wasn't. Or maybe things had just been different during the war.

But whatever his reasons, she deserved better. And she wasn't backing down.

Madeline placed a hand on her stomach and rubbed it, softly.

If she was pregnant, she wanted a real home for their child. Enough money to buy a crib, pretty clothes, and a handful of toys.

She didn't want much, but she did want to be comfortable.

*But more than anything, she wanted to be home.*

⤳

Madeline was starving. She'd stayed in her room all night, except for sneaking out late to use the toilet, but she couldn't hide any longer.

She'd heard everyone else have breakfast, listened to the clang of the dishes, and heard the back door swing shut a handful of times.

Now, it seemed, the house was quiet.

How she was going to put up with four more days of it, she didn't know. Right now, all she wanted was some bread to fill her belly.

The coast was clear. She tiptoed out to the kitchen, scanned the room and the large window, and started to relax.

She picked up the butter knife and reached for the loaf. Then heard the creak of a floorboard behind her.

Her heart felt as if it leaped to her throat.

"You heartless little bitch."

The words were laced with evil.

Tiny hairs prickled on the back of Madeline's neck, but she continued to spread butter on the bread.

"Did you hear me?" Carolyn, Roy's twisted, bitter sister went on, her voice getting louder.

"How dare you come here and ruin my family! You disgust me. Turning a man against his own flesh and blood."

Madeline placed the knife down. Biting her tongue was no longer an option.

"I don't want to have this conversation, Carolyn. I have done no such thing and I think you need to apologize to me."

Carolyn's eyes flashed.

"Don't use your haughty words with me, miss. We know you want to poison him against us, but you won't. You're no better than a stinking pig, you filthy English tart."

That was enough. A burning heat hit Madeline's chest, flushed up her neck.

"Had you made even a hint of effort, *just tried*, to accept me into this family, it never would have come to this. I came here expecting love, expecting a family to call my own, and look what I ended up with." She glared at her sister-in-law with disgust. She'd kept her words to herself for long enough; her rage made her strong. "A bitter spinster with a nasty mother, and nothing better to do than treat me like a human slave!"

For a moment she thought she was going to be slapped or clawed at by this wild-eyed woman. But instead Carolyn just glared at her, then stalked away. Her silence was almost more chilling.

It was then she saw Roy standing in the doorway that led outside. He looked stunned. He didn't say a word.

But Madeline was on a roll. She wasn't about to let him defend his family, not now.

She turned to unleash her anger on him instead, no longer able to keep her cool.

"It's true, Roy. Every word of it. You painted this beautiful picture of what it would be like here. Now I know why you resisted for so long when I used to ask you about home and your family. You waited just long enough, until you'd concocted the story you thought I wanted to hear."

He hung his head. Finally, she hoped, he was ashamed. *Finally* he might realize what he'd done to her. How he'd robbed her of her family. Taken everything from her with a lie.

"I loved you, Roy. And I married you because I thought you loved me too. Because I thought you'd stick up for me. Because I thought your family would love me as their own."

"I'm sorry," he said, quietly but firmly. She was surprised.

For the first time since she'd arrived, his voice sounded like the man she'd met in London.

"So you should be." But she wasn't letting him off the hook so easily. He should have said this weeks ago. Maybe she should have forced him to see what things were like for her sooner, but he should have been more attentive—he couldn't have failed to notice how miserable she was. So, no matter how sincere he sounded, he didn't deserve forgiveness, not yet. "You snatched me away from my family, pretended to be something you weren't. I won't ever forgive you, Roy. Not unless you make things right. And fast." It wasn't her fault that his family obviously didn't want a foreign wife in their house; he was her husband and it was his duty to look after her and protect her.

They stood, staring at one another, an uneasy truce between them. The look on his face almost made her think he cared.

She no longer wanted her breakfast. The growling in her stomach had gone, only to be replaced by a deep thud, an emptiness. Her entire body felt like it was pulsing from the adrenalin of the arguments.

But she had to eat. Had to keep her strength up, so she covered the toast with jam, hand shaking, and turned to go back to their bedroom.

"Madeline?"

She looked over her shoulder. Saw that Roy had moved into the kitchen and had his cap folded in his hands.

"Yes?"

"I'll take a job in town."

She nodded. It felt like a win but she knew they had a long way to go before she'd ever respect or care deeply for him again. Besides, she didn't know if she'd simply put enough pressure on him to make him give in—for now—or if he was actually, finally seeing her point of view.

She walked away. There were no words left to say. It was time for action.

Maybe they did have a chance. Maybe they could make things work once they moved away.

She hoped so.

Because being sad, alone, and miserable had not been part of her plan when she agreed to come here.

His words echoed in her mind.

*I'm sorry.*

Well, she was sorry too.

*For ever thinking she could be happy in a country without her family. For ever coming here at all.*

# CHAPTER 14

The bed was soft, luxurious. The house was silent, except for the odd scratch of a bird on the roof. William hadn't made a noise since before midnight. And still Betty couldn't sleep.

Closing her eyes made her see Charlie. Keeping them open made her think of Charlie. Everything about where she was, the house she was in, the reason she was here. *It was all Charlie. It had been two months since they'd arrived, but it felt like only yesterday that she'd found out Charlie was gone.*

She still had so many questions. How had he died? Why had he died? Would she be able to stay here long term? Would Charlie want her to stay here, to be with his family? There was still so much she didn't know. So many questions she'd been too afraid to ask for fear of the answers, words she'd refused to hear from anyone. But now she needed to know. She couldn't stay in her little daydream-like bubble any longer, pretending somehow that Charlie was going to come back. She couldn't shy away from the truth any more, devastating as it was.

When she'd lost her parents, she'd thought it was the worst thing imaginable. But now . . . she only had to look at William to see all they had both lost. It struck at her heart to think that he would never know his father.

Betty rose. She padded into the adjoining nursery and watched William in the half-light as he slept. His tiny mouth was puckered, head turned slightly to the side. He looked so tiny, so vulnerable. She resisted the urge to pick him up.

William was all she had now. The only reason she had for living. For staying on at the house. Would Luke have even welcomed her into his home had William not been born? She didn't want to think.

She tiptoed out of the nursery and pulled her shawl around her. The house was cool as she stepped into the hall. It felt almost wrong, creeping through the house, but she couldn't lie awake in bed any longer. She needed to do something, drink something warm and comforting, to calm her mind.

The memory of her mother's chamomile tea haunted her still. The aromatic scent of it as it sat in a pot on a table, then watching as her mother sipped at it so delicately. And then taking the first sip for herself and feeling how it calmed her with every tip of the tea cup. It was so long ago, yet being here had brought back so many memories of her mother—she missed her so intensely.

"Are you all right, my dear?"

Betty's hand flew to her chest. "Ivy!"

The other woman smiled at her, standing near the foot of the stairs. Her grey hair was like a loose halo, her skin pale in the half-light.

"You scared me half to death," Betty whispered. "I didn't expect anyone to be up."

Ivy smiled and rubbed at her eyes. "I'm a light sleeper, always have been. I heard you."

"Oh, I'm sorry. I . . ."

"You've nothing to be sorry for. I don't sleep well either. Would you like a hot drink?"

Betty nodded and followed Ivy.

"Chocolate or coffee?"

She tried her hardest to smile. She was in America now. The land of coffee, not tea.

They both walked into the kitchen and Ivy flicked a light.

"While I'm here I'll have to teach you how to make a good cup of tea, you know," she told Ivy.

"A cup of tay," mimicked Ivy, long hair falling over one shoulder as she laughed. She filled the jug and set it to boil.

Betty laughed, too. She couldn't help it.

"Our Charlie wrote home and told me I'd have to learn to make a cup of tay, as he called it, before I'd win you over."

At the mention of his name Betty felt a frown tug her lips down. She fought to pull them back up. She'd been moping around here too long and it wasn't doing anyone any good, least of all her. She'd felt unable to engage with anyone except William for the past weeks, often keeping to her room to avoid the others. Luke was barely at the house anyway, and since their first dinner, they had only fleetingly greeted each other in passing. Ivy had been on hand helping her with practicalities, but Betty had closed down if the conversation veered onto more emotional territory—namely Charlie. Now it was time to try and change that.

"Charlie liked a good sweet cup of tea. Or at least he did a good job of pretending he did when I made him one," Betty said, with some difficulty.

Ivy placed the two cups down.

"From what he told me in his letters, there was nothing about you that he didn't love, my dear." Ivy spooned dark black granules into a fancy looking pot. "Now I'm going to make you a coffee just like he would have made you. Strong, with cream and sugar."

Betty blinked back the tears and sat down at the table. It felt good, being here with Ivy. They might not have gotten off to the best start, when Ivy had broken the news, but she'd shown herself to be a kind, caring woman. The type Betty could trust. Confide in, even. She'd been there at her side to help her with William since day one, but it was only now that her deep grieving was over, that she'd realized how impossible it would have been to cope alone, without Ivy by her side.

"Ivy, I need to know how, well . . ." she gulped in a big breath. She needed to be brave, finally give in and listen. "Ivy, I'm ready to know how Charlie died."

Betty watched as Ivy poured the coffee, spooned in sugar, then reached for the cream. She was acting like Betty finally asking was no big deal, but she was sure the other woman's calmness was for her benefit.

"From what I gather, and I'm only going from the details I know for sure, Charlie was asked to fly for a company near where he'd been stationed."

Betty wrapped both hands around the mug Ivy passed her, to still their trembling.

"You see, Luke has always been the successful one, in the financial sense that is. Charlie told him that he wanted to save enough money to make a deposit on a house. Said he wanted to make you proud. Have a home for you and the baby."

Betty sipped at the coffee. Even though it was sweet, the taste was strong and unfamiliar to her. This was nothing like the calming brews of tea she was used to.

"And something went wrong?" her voice wobbled, a weak edge to it, but Ivy just continued calmly.

"He had a contract to work for a month. Said that would mean he could save money and still get back before you were due to arrive. If they let you on the boat pregnant, that was."

Betty nodded, it was all she could do. She didn't trust her voice again, but she needed to hear this.

"He had a week left on the job, and it seems there were complications. There was a fault, with the engine they believe, and his plane went down."

"Where?" Betty was numb, empty inside. She'd known Charlie had a flying job, he'd told her in their last letter just before she'd found out when the ship was leaving, but she hadn't known it could be dangerous—not like flying in the war had been dangerous.

"Over the ocean. His body was never retrieved, but they received a mayday, and they found the wreckage shortly after."

Betty gulped, and nodded some more. She forced the burning hot coffee down her throat. It wasn't until Ivy reached for her hand that the tears fell, like a wave that couldn't be stopped. She'd thought the worst of her grieving was over, but this was hard. Knowing was harder than wondering—it made everything so final.

"I'm sorry, Betty, I truly am. I've known these boys since they were in diapers. Charlie was like a son to me. He would have been a great father, I just know it."

"He was a great husband." Betty choked out the words. "He was the best man I'll ever meet."

"All you can do is make him proud, my dear." Ivy scooted her chair around and placed an arm about Betty. The weight of it comforted her. Settled her. Helped ease the tears. "You need to be the best mother you can be. Honor his memory and enjoy living here. It's what he would have wanted."

"Really?" Betty asked.

"I've no doubt he loved you, Betty. And I can see why. Now come on back up to bed and let's see if you can get some sleep before Master William starts to fuss."

Betty allowed Ivy to lead her back to the bedroom. She was still exhausted, drained, but at least she finally knew.

Charlie had died wanting to be the best father and husband he could be. He'd died trying to please her. Being the Charlie she'd fallen in love with. Perhaps now it was time to try being the Betty he'd fallen in love with again.

When her mother had died, Betty's father had said that it was better to have loved once and lost, than to never have loved at all. Then she'd lost her dad to the same illness just weeks later, and now Charlie. All people she'd loved who she'd never see again. How could her heart take it? Little William was her lifeline.

She didn't feel it now, but she knew one day, sometime in the future, she'd might agree with her father's sentiment.

But she'd never stop wishing Charlie was still with her. *Never.*

∽

The morning dawned bright and sunny. Betty had slept late, much later than she'd expected. She stretched, lazily got out of bed and strolled into the nursery. William wasn't there.

She smiled. Ivy to the rescue again. She'd gone to bed feeling numb and sad, but this morning she'd woken feeling refreshed. There was a dull ache deep within her, still yearning for her Charlie, but she was almost glad that she hadn't known the truth until now. She wouldn't have been able to face it. But now that she did know, she felt like the healing could start.

She dressed quickly and ran a brush through her hair.

Betty heard William before she saw him. He was making the little whimper that she knew so well. Hungry. Ivy looked up gratefully but kept walking him, William slung over her shoulder as she patted firmly on his back.

"I wanted to let you sleep, but this little beggar wasn't going to take a bottle!"

Betty reached for him, cooing as his little mouth formed a smile at seeing her.

"Hello, little one." She kissed his forehead. "I've missed you."

Ivy touched the small of her back and propelled her forward.

"You come and feed him in here and I'll fix you your breakfast."

"Sorry I slept so long, I didn't realize how tired I was."

"You had a lot to take in last night." Ivy set about boiling the kettle and cracking eggs. "You've missed Luke for the morning, but you'll be seeing him tonight."

Betty was pleased she hadn't seen him. The months since she'd arrived had been awkward and tense, and she'd tried to stay out of his way as much as possible to avoid any awkward conversations. She wasn't really up for company, except for Ivy's, and she'd been relieved that he'd mostly been away on business for the past few weeks.

"You like them scrambled or over easy?"

Betty laughed. "I would have said fried if you'd given me the option. What in the lord's name is over easy?"

Ivy's entire body shook. The laughter rumbled deep from her belly, and when she turned her eyes were twinkling.

"Believe me, if the Lord was eating eggs for breakfast he'd choose over easy, I'm sure of it."

Betty settled William in for his feed, enjoying being in this woman's kitchen, laughing over breakfast. "Over easy it is then." It was the first time she'd felt genuinely happy since she'd first arrived, and it was a feeling she'd missed.

"Betty?"

She looked up from watching William suckle.

"We're going to get on fine, you and me. Just fine."

Betty forced herself to smile. She was not going to allow herself to wallow in any self-pity or sadness any longer. "You're right, Ivy. We are."

"So how about you and I head into town and get you some pretty dresses today? Just what you need as a pick me up, now that you look ready to brave the world again."

"Sounds good to me." She had to make an effort, there was no other way forward. Besides, they'd been meaning to go shopping since the first week she arrived, so she couldn't exactly put it off any longer. She'd been slopping around in her old dresses for months now, and she'd lost a lot of weight since she'd arrived.

Charlie's smiling face passed through her mind, like a hazy dream that was fading into the distance. He wanted her to be happy. She knew that he wouldn't want anything else.

She was going to make a go of life in America. She was going to make him proud.

And besides, it was the only choice she had. It wasn't like she could afford the fare back to England, and even if she could, who would she go to there?

"I learned a lot of funny American words on my trip over here, Ivy, but I'm thinking I might need some lessons."

"Why don't you start by telling me the words you *do* know," said Ivy, putting a full plate in front of her and sitting down herself with a mug of coffee, "and I'll tell you what sounds funny."

Betty passed William to her so she could eat.

"Well, what I do know is that what we call the lavatory you unofficially call the John."

Ivy nodded, laughter shining in her eyes again.

"Don't think I'll get used to that one, though," Betty said. "My uncle was called John and he'd be mighty offended."

Both women started to laugh again and William joined in, squealing with all his might.

"Let's just stick with lavatory then and move on to the next word."

◌◦

New York City was nothing like Betty had imagined. The hustle and bustle reminded her of London, but it was so much more exciting. Some of the women they passed seemed so glamorous, but at the same time more brash than what she was used to. But the shop

160

windows looked amazing, and she tried to focus on that instead of how dowdy she felt in comparison.

"This way."

Betty kept her eyes trained on Ivy. She had a feeling that if she so much as blinked she'd lose such a little woman in this huge place. She held William close, tucked tightly against her chest.

A beautiful store appeared before them. The windows shone with beautiful clothes, dresses elegantly placed on stationary models, shoes beneath them, fashionable hats hanging nearby.

"Are you sure?" Betty asked.

Ivy just gave her a look and dragged her by the elbow.

A bell tinkled overhead to announce their presence. Betty felt like a fraud. Her scruffy, over-worn dress showed her to be less than their usual clientele. After losing her family, saving and scrimping for baby items and paying her own way before she set sail, she had no extra time or money to invest in her appearance. And they'd only been allowed to bring a very small number of items with them on the ship.

A beautifully groomed woman appeared. Her stockinged legs, polished leather shoes, and sweep of red lipstick reminded her of Alice. *Darling Alice who had kept them all entertained every day of their journey.* Alice who was no doubt living in the lap of luxury with her man, Betty thought. She'd been so deep in her grief for the past few months that getting into contact with the girls had only fleetingly crossed her mind—she just couldn't face it. And anyway, the last thing she needed was to tell them all how terribly things had ended for her and ruin their happiness. She'd tell them about it one day, but for now she was going to let them enjoy their no doubt idyllic lives.

Betty was relieved when the assistant didn't so much as sweep her eyes over her shabby attire. But she was pleased that the lady directed her questions at Ivy. Betty wouldn't have known what to say.

"How may I help you today, ladies?"

Ivy stood tall and proud. Betty wished she could do the same, but she simply didn't have the energy.

"We would like a collection of new dresses for Mrs. Olliver here," Ivy replied.

Betty was sure she detected a raised eyebrow from the saleswoman. No doubt the gossip would start about who she was married to, and why she was here. The thought made her feel nauseous. Maybe she had over-stretched herself by heading into New York so soon. She was still so emotionally fragile.

"Any particular occasion?"

This time, the question was sent her way but she didn't know what to say.

Ivy stepped in again. "Just a nice collection of day dresses, everyday wear to start with, please. Along with suitable footwear."

"Of course. Come this way."

Betty felt like she was totally out of her depth, but she followed the saleswoman's tapping shoes anyway. Ivy had made it very clear before they left home that she was not to make a fuss, to just try the clothes on and select some new outfits.

"Do you like pastels or more neutral tones?"

She couldn't help but think she should be wearing black. *Widow's black*. But she didn't dare say it.

"Whatever colors you think would suit me will be fine."

The shop assistant smiled. "Well, if it were up to me I'd make the most of those lovely blue eyes and go for pastels."

Ivy gave her a prod in the back and reached for William.

Betty reluctantly passed him over and let herself be ushered into the fitting room. *There was no backing out now.*

They left with bags full to overflowing. Betty was nervous more than embarrassed. It didn't seem right, pretending like nothing had happened, like she was meant to be here. Would others think she was the new wife of Luke Olliver? Surely not, when she had a baby in tow.

"You all right, my dear?"

She braved a smile at Ivy. "Just thinking."

"Of Charlie?"

She nodded. When wasn't she thinking about Charlie?

"He would have wanted you to be happy. For Luke to look after you."

Would he? "It just doesn't feel right, carrying on, shopping, like nothing has happened. Like he's just going to arrive one day and things will be normal. Like they were supposed to be."

Ivy took her elbow and steered her across the road. It was busy, too many people for Betty's liking.

"Come on, let's get back home and you can have a lie down. Or take William for a walk around the gardens."

That sounded better than being in town. She was getting that terrible feeling like she couldn't breathe, just like when Ivy had told her the news. Like a hand at her throat, slowly squeezing all the air from her lungs.

They got in the car. She smiled gratefully as their driver put the bags in the trunk and closed her door. The sounds of the city were drowned out, and the relative silence was a relief.

"Do you wish you were back home?" Ivy asked her softly.

Betty shook her head and focused on William. On his round little face, fists balled, one in front of his mouth.

"You don't wish you were back with your family?"

She turned to Ivy. "I don't have any family, Ivy. That's why I had to come. Why I couldn't wait and risk having my baby alone. I'd long since outstayed my welcome at my friend's home."

Ivy moved closer, put an arm around her, and held her tight.

"I've a daughter your age. I think you'd like her. She has some little ones of her own, too."

Betty snuffled, trying to stop the heave of her chest as tears welled in her eyes again.

"Whenever she was feeling down, or something bad had happened, we always cooked. Baked up a storm, we did. Would you have done that with your mother, do you think?"

It sounded perfect. "I think that's just what I need," Betty told her.

"I also used to say that baking wasn't a cure for a broken heart, but it sure was a good start."

Betty settled William against her and let her head rest on the back of the seat. Whatever would she have done without Ivy?

"Is it proper, for me to be in the kitchen with you?" she asked. "In England it can cause a fuss."

Ivy patted her hand. "We don't fuss so much here. Besides, when Luke was a boy he spent hours in the kitchen with me, he and Charlie both did, always under my feet or standing on a chair to help. He's not going to mind. His mother might, but not Luke."

That relieved her. As much as she wanted Ivy's support, she didn't want to upset Luke.

"Do you think he likes me, Ivy?" Betty asked.

"Who?"

She closed her eyes and focused on the movement of the car. "Luke."

"Luke's a good man. He likes you just fine. But Betty, you've seen so little of him—he can't be expected to really know you yet."

Betty nodded in agreement. Ivy was right. The familiar worries began to circle round her head. How long could Luke be expected to provide for his sister-in-law and nephew? It was fine while there was no lady of the house, but she wasn't so sure what would happen if there ever was one.

# CHAPTER 15

Rain tapped on the roof as incessantly as a drummer in a marching band. But Madeline didn't care.

It could snow, hail, or howl with wind. So long as she was here, in her own home, and not with her in-laws, she was happy.

She was exhausted from working every day, but she'd rather be exhausted from working where she was appreciated than being on the farm. At least she was being paid. And soon, once they received Roy's first paycheck, she would have money enough of her own to start saving.

*For the baby, or for her fare home.* So long as she had an emergency fund to fall back on, for whatever reason, she'd feel more secure.

Roy hated working at the grocery store, unloading boxes and carting produce, but she didn't care. She didn't care that they hardly had a penny to rub together, that they had only a bed, an old sofa, and an upside-down wooden grocery crate as a coffee table. That they had only one pot and a few mismatched plates and cups.

All she cared about was that they weren't on the farm any longer. That she was never going to have to even visit again if she didn't want to.

Roy was glum, often depressed and dull about moving, but it was worth it. Surely he would come around to the idea soon. She still couldn't work out why he had wanted to stay there. Was it because he believed he could make something of the place one day when it was left to him? She'd tried to bring it up with him but he wouldn't discuss it. All she knew was that it was his home and he liked being on the land, although she sometimes suspected it was due to the amount of slack they gave him here.

They were questions she couldn't answer. Questions that continued to circle in her mind, but at least they were fading.

The only thing that wasn't fading was her stomach. It was still small, but it now had a slightly rounded edge to it, a hint of a curve where before it had been flat.

Next month she would go to the doctor. For now, she just wanted to enjoy having a place of her own, her job, and the fact that she wasn't feeling such a deep dislike for her husband any longer.

She heard a shuffle at the door. *Roy.*

What was he doing home early? She'd had the day off, in lieu of the overtime she'd done for Lauren earlier in the week. But Roy should have a few hours more away from home.

She listened to the noise of him jangling his keys on the porch, but she didn't go to open it. Instead she went back into the kitchen and put the kettle on. Ordinarily, or at least when her father had arrived home from work, either she or her sister had poured him a drink. Usually a small brandy, to help him unwind, but Madeline didn't have enough money yet for the privilege of alcohol. Besides, she hadn't noticed Roy or his family drink a drop since she'd arrived.

"Madeline?"

She turned at the sound of her name. He hadn't called out to her like that since before they were married.

"Madeline?"

"In here," she called back.

166

Her husband appeared. He held a modest bunch of flowers in one hand.

"Oh my, are they for me?" she asked.

Roy smiled at her and set them on the bench.

"Sure are."

She didn't want to point out that they couldn't afford them. He'd bought them now, so what good was moaning going to do? And it was an unusually sweet gesture from him.

"We don't have a vase but a glass will suffice," she told him, smiling before turning away and taking their only not-chipped glass from the cabinet.

"I was promoted today."

She spun around. *Promoted?* He'd only had the job two weeks. "Promoted?"

He grinned at her as she picked up the flowers and put them in the glass.

"The produce manager had a heart attack this morning at work. He's recovering in the hospital but there's no way he can come back. Can you believe it?"

The man had been pretty old, so she didn't find that so unbelievable. The fact they'd chosen Roy for the promotion so quickly was a different story. And as manager?

"They just asked you? Like that?"

"Yep."

Madeline poured them coffee and walked both cups into the tiny lounge.

"Does it mean more pay?"

"More money, same hours, more responsibility."

"That's great, Roy. I'm really very proud of you." She smiled politely at him, as if talking to a colleague instead of to a man who was her husband. A man whose bed she shared every night. "And thank you for the flowers."

"I got to thinking, Mads." He looked down at his coffee cup, then back at her. As if he were shy. "When we were in England, I had so many dreams. So many hopes. I thought we'd be so happy. Then I realized I hadn't ever even bought you flowers before. What kind of husband does that make me?"

His words touched her. Things had been different between them back then, but it wasn't she who had changed. It was he who had pretended to be something he wasn't.

"I'm sorry, Madeline. I wanted you to marry me, and I thought if I told you the truth about my life here, you wouldn't be interested."

She swallowed the emotion choking in her throat. It wasn't that she wouldn't have been interested in him—she would still have been attracted to him. But, in another way he was right. She never would have considered leaving her family to trade for this. Not if he'd said she'd be going to a farmhouse with no indoor lavatory and only a tiny room to themselves, with no intention of ever moving to a new house, or renting somewhere, for just them. And certainly not if he'd said how much his family would resent a foreign wife, or how they would want to work her to the bone like she was a slave.

"Can we try to make it work, Madeline? Really try?" he asked.

She smiled at him. The first real, genuine smile she had wanted to send his way since she'd arrived.

"I hope so, Roy. I really hope so."

Since the day she'd made up her mind that it was either they moved out or she went home to England, she'd refused him night after night. Unlike when they were first married and he'd as good as demanded his right to her body, now she was in charge. Maybe it was time she stopped resisting him, stopped pushing him away.

"Why don't we have a meal out to celebrate?"

"Can we afford it?" She hated being the practical money counter, but finances were the one thing she couldn't turn a blind eye to right now.

"Just this once. I get paid tomorrow."

He stood up and took a hesitant step, then another, toward her. She was almost nervous.

Roy stopped in front of her. Held out his hands and smiled, inviting her to stand up. She did.

They stood like that, so close, staring at one another. Madeline felt an intimacy with her husband that she'd hoped for so many times.

He bent down, slowly, and touched his lips over hers. Just briefly. A press of his lips that made her sigh.

"I don't want us to argue all the time, Madeline."

When he put his arms around her, all the bad memories seemed to fade away. They shivered down her spine and disappeared.

She couldn't hold it inside any longer. Couldn't keep the secret to herself. If this was going to work, if they could truly get their marriage back on track, then she needed to be honest with him.

"Roy, I think I'm pregnant."

She blurted it out. The words just tumbled from her mouth.

He took a step back, arms still loosely around her, then forward again. And blinked a few times in fast succession.

"Pregnant?"

"I don't know for sure, but I'd say there's a fairly good chance."

"All the more reason to celebrate," he said with a smile on his face. "How about a steak dinner?"

She laughed, laughed like she hadn't in a long time.

"I'd like that."

He let her go and she walked toward their bedroom to get changed. Roy followed.

"When will we know for sure?"

She shrugged. "As soon as we have enough money for a doctor's appointment."

He grinned at her, and she grinned back.

Maybe this baby was exactly what they needed to make things right between them.

Now that she'd told Roy, she had to write and tell her family. They would be so excited for her.

Being pregnant finally felt real.

All she needed now was to find her friends from the boat and then life might start to feel like normal. Maybe seeing them again, being with them, would help her to settle. Now that she had a place of her own and a job, she'd be proud to tell them about her life. They'd hardly believe she'd fallen pregnant almost the moment they'd landed on American soil.

"Will you be long?"

She looked up to find Roy watching her as she slipped into a dress.

Madeline shook her head.

"Great, 'cos I'm starving."

# CHAPTER 16

Alice slipped from the house with a spring to her stride. It was about to rain, the air thick with the muggy smell of a storm headed toward the city, but she didn't care.

Most mornings she escaped her house, happy in the knowledge that she wouldn't have to face her husband or the ugly, dimly lit interior of their home for at least eight hours. But today, she had another reason to be sunny. Mr. Roberts had finally sorted a retirement package out for Mrs. Perkins, and she was starting her position as his assistant.

Along with the prestige, she was going to get a pay raise, a small office of her own with a desk large enough to spread out at, and a window glimpsing the city below.

And she was going to be reporting directly to Matthew.

*Matthew.* Just saying his name made her tingle all over.

There was something between them. Something that she wished wasn't so forbidden.

Comparing him to her husband was like pairing a box of shiny apples beside a handful of rotting plums. Back in London, choosing between the men might have been more difficult. Now, her husband would be unlikely to appeal to any respectable woman.

*But Matthew?* Matthew was something else entirely.

And married, she reminded herself. A mean-faced Mrs. Perkins had been sure to emphasize that piece of information as she'd strutted from the office last night.

But Alice didn't care. All she cared about was the extra money in her paycheck each week. Although it would be a nice change to take orders from a man who looked like a screen actor and smelled so wealthy it literally oozed from his skin.

༄

Alice was trying hard to wipe the smile from her face. He'd already called her into his office twice. Twice in one morning! It shouldn't have, but it made her body sing. Made her want to dance about the office and bask in the delight of feeling wanted, of knowing a man was interested in her.

Like she used to feel as a single girl in London. It was a feeling she hadn't experienced in so long.

"Alice?"

She jumped. Her fingers hit the typewriter keys by mistake.

"Yes?" She sat to attention, head poised to one side.

Matthew was leaning around the door of his office, his mouth stretched into a smile. She couldn't help but grin back.

"I might need you to work late tonight. I have some clients coming in at five and I'll need you to sit in on the meeting."

Alice nodded. "Of course."

He winked. *She loved that wink.*

"That's my girl. Take a longer lunch break if you like to make up for it."

He disappeared and closed the door behind him again. Alice felt her heart thud to a stop. Then start up again.

Staying late would mean Ralph wouldn't have any dinner, not until much later anyway, but she wasn't going to worry. If he was the husband she'd expected, hoped for, then she would have scurried home on her lunch break and told him. Hurried home to fix something basic.

But then, if she was in the marriage she'd expected, she wouldn't be working. She'd be at home fluffing about, making their home beautiful, preparing delicious meals and preserving fruits. And of course, a bit of shopping and pampering for herself, too.

No, she wasn't going to feel guilty about working hard.

Besides, by the time she got home he'd either be asleep, so drunk he wouldn't care, or in one of his silent, morose moods that meant he wouldn't eat what she put in front of him anyway.

She pulled the piece of paper from her typewriter and let it fall into the trash can. She hated making mistakes.

Her fingers started to glide across the keys again as she worked on the letter.

The office was starting to empty out, and Alice was getting nervous. She was starting to wonder if the meeting was just a ploy to keep her here alone. And she hadn't decided if that would be a good thing or not.

Thinking about being unfaithful was one thing. Wanting to fall into another man's arms and be swept away was passable. But actually acting on it? With another woman's husband? She wasn't so sure.

Alice rose from her seat, uncomfortable from sitting in the same position for so many hours, and glanced at her boss's door. It was still firmly shut. She hadn't seen him since early afternoon.

Alice reached for her bag and moved quickly down the corridor. She didn't bother making eye contact with any of the others who were leaving, just focused on the door to the restroom.

It was cool and silent in the ladies' room. She made her way to the mirror, listening to her heels as they clicked on the tiles. Alice dug around in her purse for a tissue, wiped her lipstick off, then powdered her face and started again with her lip brush. She swept some more mascara over her lashes then fiddled with her hair. She had it in a soft roll, keeping her blonde hair off her face, and she wondered about letting it loose instead.

Would that be too obvious?

She didn't have time to wonder. The thud of approaching footfalls made her gather her things and head for the cubicle. The last thing she needed was to be caught out fixing her appearance when she ought to be on her way home like the others.

Alice straightened her skirt, fiddled with the buttons on her blouse, then dug out her tiny bottle of perfume and dabbed a little to each wrist. On second thought, she dabbed some to her neck too.

She took a deep breath, before deciding she was so nervous she did actually need to relieve herself.

Alice waited for the other toilet to flush before she let herself out. Then she washed her hands and took one last look at her complexion.

*Guilty*. She looked guilty. But she did look attractive, too. More so than she'd felt since arriving here.

Alice hurried back down the hall, then stopped. The office had completely emptied out now, except for two men in suits who were standing talking to her boss.

Matthew seemed to sense her presence. He turned and smiled, before waving her over to join them.

Part of her was relieved, but a lot of her was disappointed. She'd hoped that it was her he wanted to see. That there was no meeting at all.

Now she just felt a fool for bothering with her appearance.

❧

The men had been talking for an hour. Alice had diligently been taking notes, but her hand was starting to cramp. And now they'd stopped talking purely business and were chatting.

She had no formal training, so she didn't know if she should excuse herself, keep writing, or sit back and smile politely as they spoke.

"Well gents, I think it's time we called it a day."

*Finally.* Alice set her pen on the table and folded her hands in her lap, waiting to be dismissed.

"How about a drink?" one of the men suggested. His ruddy face and portly belly made Alice think he was probably always first to suggest alcohol or food. "A drink or two at the Club?"

Alice hadn't heard of *the club* before. She guessed it was a place for wealthy men to socialize, given the businessmen before her. It was probably full of beautiful woman, which made her feel stupid all over again for trying to impress her boss.

She watched as Matthew nodded. "Good idea. How about you two head over there and I'll catch you up shortly? I just need to make a few phone calls."

The man stood, hands on his stomach. "No need, we'll wait."

Alice stood too, then promptly wondered if she should have stayed seated.

"Don't let me hold you up," insisted Matthew, walking around the table to slap each man on the back. "I'll see you there before you've downed your first whiskey."

That made them all laugh.

Alice stood still. She wasn't much enjoying the leery looks she was receiving from either of his clients. She hoped they'd leave now instead of hanging around while she readied herself to go home.

And she was feeling rejected. Matthew hadn't so much as glanced at her the entire meeting, except to clarify a matter he wanted her to take down.

"See you there, then," he said.

She watched as he escorted them out. Alice bent to gather her notes and Matthew's belongings. She moved back into the adjoining room, placing his things on his desk.

"Sorry to keep you so long."

Alice turned at his voice. Matthew was behind her, his hand hovering over the door handle.

She gulped. He was closing the door. Her heart began to race.

They were alone, no one else was in the office, and he was slowly but surely shutting the door.

"Oh, I didn't mind at all," she managed.

He smiled. Like a fox with a hen within its sights, she thought suddenly. His lips parted, showing his white teeth, and she wondered if he was actually going to pounce upon her.

"Your husband must be wondering where you are."

Alice shook her head. "I doubt he'll even notice I'm late."

That made him laugh. He stepped toward her, his movement predatory.

"I find that hard to believe."

Alice wanted to reply but couldn't. She'd stuttered over her last words, now she was mute.

Matthew stopped a few feet away. Close enough to make her blush, to make her eyes flit across his, but far enough away that he wasn't making an advance.

*Yet.*

"They'll be expecting me shortly," he told her.

She swallowed again. It was like a stone had lodged itself in her throat and she couldn't push it down.

"I'll, ah, let you make that phone call then."

He moved even closer. Now he was in her space. Staring down at her. The heat from his body reaching out to her.

"There's no phone call, Alice."

Her heart pounded so fast it frightened her.

The meeting might have been real, but his excuse for staying behind had been phony. *Deliberate.*

Alice closed her eyes as his hand moved toward her face. She felt his fingertips graze her cheek, before stopping at her mouth.

"Alice?"

She opened her eyes and found his trained on hers. She looked at his neatly clipped moustache, his lips, then back up to his eyes again.

"I'm going to kiss you," he told her.

She nodded. She couldn't speak.

Matthew's mouth pressed against hers. His moustache tickled her, his soft lips sweeping back and forth across hers.

Then he stopped. Alice moaned. She couldn't help it. Why was he stopping?

"We're both married, you realize that, don't you?"

She nodded again. It was the only response she was capable of. His deep, husky voice did something to her senses, not to mention his touch.

This time he spoke low, directly into her ear.

"This is just for now. Just for here. You understand that, Alice, don't you?"

She didn't care. She should, but she didn't.

This time when she nodded he took her in his arms, and forcefully bent her back over the desk. His lips crushed hers, his tongue made her legs buckle, hard body straining against hers. She held on to him, desperate, like she'd never be able to get enough of him, no matter how hard she tried.

*It was the best kiss of her life.*

Alice took a deep breath before walking through her front door. She refused to think about what had happened at work; she needed to get through the evening at home first, and then figure out her feelings. She felt guilty. Should she make still more of an effort to save their marriage? But then she'd tried so hard—maybe it was too broken.

"I'm home Ralph," she called out, putting her handbag down and walking down the hall and into the kitchen.

He was sitting on the same chair she always found him in, an empty cup on the table beside him. The sight of him brought out such a mix of emotions—pity, sadness, anger, and an echo of love. She dropped a kiss to the top of his head, lingering, hoping he'd say something, *anything* to her, but he didn't make a noise.

"How was your day?" she asked, trying hard to keep the smile on her face as she surveyed the room.

Alice crossed the room and opened the fridge, taking out some ingredients since she could start dinner. He was here all day alone, but he'd never once had a meal made for her, never thanked her for the long hours she worked to pay their bills.

"I was busy from first thing this morning," she continued, pretending like he'd already answered her. "I hardly even had time for my lunch break."

Ralph was staring at nothing, his gaze empty. Alice blinked away tears, wanting nothing more than to just collapse into a heap and give up. But she couldn't, because where could she go? What could she do?

"Ralph?" she asked, putting down the knife she was using. "Please talk to me."

He looked up but it was if there was no one home behind his eyes.

"I miss you," she whispered. "Please just tell me you want me here."

His expression never changed, but he did pat her hand when she came close, pressed his palm against hers and squeezed her fingers before letting go and staring off at nothing again.

Alice silently walked away, forgetting her dinner preparation and going into the bedroom. Her tears were impossible to control then, a flood of emotion that bubbled from deep inside. Her Ralph was gone. *He was gone.* And as guilty as she felt at what had happened at the office earlier, it was better than the gut-wrenching sadness she felt about the state of her marriage.

# CHAPTER 17

"So is it different here?"

Madeline sat with Lauren on the back steps of their office building. It was flooded with sun, and they had their legs stretched out as they ate their sandwiches. Lauren was keen to know what Madeline thought of her new country.

"You mean aside from the funny accents and names for things?"

Lauren gave her a nudge with her shoulder and rolled her eyes skyward.

"You know what I mean."

Madeline thought about it. There were ways in which it was different that she had no idea how to describe. Ways that she'd never imagined.

"It's not really different." She didn't know how else to answer. "I mean, Americans talk more, you know, about things and to one another than we do back home. More forthright, I think that's what the book said."

"What book?" Lauren took a bite of her sandwich and then leaned back heavily on her palms to turn her face to the sun.

"*Good Housekeeping.* They made a book for foreign brides, to, well, to teach us how to be good American wives."

Lauren laughed. "Maybe they should have given Roy's parents a copy to help them be good in-laws."

Madeline liked that she could talk to Lauren. She still hadn't been in touch with the girls from the ship so it was nice having someone. They ate lunch together most days, and between them, got their workload completed quickly. It wasn't that she didn't want to see her other friends—part of her was desperate to be with them—but admitting what her husband was like wouldn't be easy. They'd all be asking each other questions, expecting to know everything about one another's lives, and she just wasn't ready to admit the truth yet.

"When are you going to tell Mr. Curtis that you're pregnant?"

Her hand fell to her stomach. "I guess soon. I just don't want him to fire me."

"He won't fire you, silly. You're far too good."

A shiver shook her body. "I don't want to upset him. It's not like I've been here long." She paused. "You won't tell him, will you?"

Lauren rolled her eyes before scanning her watch. "You don't even have to ask me that. But he'll fire us both first anyway if we don't get back soon. It's already five past one."

They both stood up and walked back inside.

"Why don't you and Roy come for dinner this weekend? Unless you already have plans?"

"That would be great."

They hadn't been to a friend's house for dinner since they'd been married. It felt like a huge step forward in the right direction.

"Should I bring dessert?" Madeline asked.

Lauren grabbed her hand and squeezed it. "Oh, yes! Do one of those cream cake things you told me about. You know, the ones you said your mother does."

Madeline nodded and retrieved her hand. She didn't want Lauren to see the tears in her eyes.

What she wouldn't give right now to sit down for a cup of tea with her mother and ask her how to make the dessert properly. To smell the morning's baking still lingering in the kitchen, to watch her father kiss her mother on the cheek and drop his cup into the sink as he passed. To hear the squeal of her nieces as her sister chased them about the house and threatened punishment.

"Are you all right?"

Lauren *had* noticed. She wiped at her tears, gave her friend a smile, and walked back off to her office. Missing her family never got any easier. And she doubted it ever would.

҂

Being in Lauren's kitchen was like being in her eldest sister's back in London. It was clean and tidy, but tiny. And obviously well loved.

She got the same feeling about her new friend. Her husband seemed to dote on her and Madeline secretly hoped that some of it might rub off on Roy. The two men were chatting in the living room and seemed to be getting on well.

"The lads seem to be hitting it off."

Lauren looked at her as if she was speaking another language. "The who?"

Madeline laughed. "Lads. That's what we call men back home."

"You and your funny sayings."

"Believe me, there's plenty more where that came from," Madeline told her.

Sam, Lauren's husband, burst through the kitchen door then and made a beeline for the fridge.

"Two more beers for the boys."

He dropped a kiss to his wife's cheek before reaching into the refrigerator for the drinks. Lauren didn't take her eyes off him, and

Madeline watched them. Saw the way they looked at one another. Laughed along with them when Sam nibbled at Lauren's neck, before pressing the cold bottles against the bare skin of her arms to make her squeal.

Madeline hated to admit it, but it made her jealous. She and Roy had been getting on fine together, been companionable ever since he'd got the promotion, but it was nothing like this. *And she doubted it ever would be.*

"Let's get this food on the table so we can sit down."

Madeline helped her carry the plates, straight from the warming drawer, then the main dish. She'd only tasted meat loaf once before, and this looked great.

The men were seated as soon as the aroma wafted into the sitting room.

Roy sat next to her and she smiled at him. Really smiled.

Maybe she needed to make more of an effort. Seeing Lauren and Sam together had made her want that, too. She wasn't afraid of hard work, and that extended to her marriage. If there was a chance she could make things work between them then she was prepared to do anything to make it happen.

"Need to make the most of nice quiet dinners like these before children come along and take over, huh?"

Madeline smiled at Sam's words. It was so true.

"You two want children, then?" she asked.

"Whenever the good Lord decides we're ready." Lauren looked embarrassed at the topic but Madeline noticed how Sam's hand brushed her own when she spoke. "We've been hoping for a while now."

"I suppose Madeline's told you our good news?" asked Roy.

She turned wild eyes on him. It was inappropriate given Lauren's words, and it was supposed to be a secret!

"Roy, I don't think we need to . . ."

"You're pregnant?" Sam had a huge smile on his face. "That's great news."

She appreciated that Lauren had kept it to herself, but why did Roy have to blurt it out? If she hadn't told Lauren already, it would have been a very difficult situation given that they worked together.

"Honey, who else have you told?" Madeline asked.

"No one, but we're with friends here. What's the problem?"

Lauren looked sympathetic, but she could tell that Roy genuinely couldn't see what the problem was. Madeline wasn't going to cause a scene. Not here.

"It's fine, I'm just not sure about telling everybody yet. You know, until I'm a little further along." She hesitated. "Until my boss knows at least."

"So Roy, tell us about your family's farm?" Sam asked.

Lauren threw her an apologetic glance.

"We have mostly crops. Run some cattle there too."

"Sounds nice."

She watched Roy as he nodded. "It is. Great place."

"Roy, Madeline tells me you're enjoying your job," Lauren interrupted.

Sam smiled at his wife, but he wasn't about to let her change the topic. "Honey, Roy was just telling me about his farm."

Madeline started to feel clammy. Her palms, the back of her neck, even her face. Just talking about the place, as if it were some pretty, happy ranch, made her feel sick. As if it was in fact the fairy tale she'd been promised.

"You visit there often?"

She heard Sam's question despite the ringing in her ears.

"Ah, no." She didn't look up when she felt Roy's gaze over her. Watching her. She concentrated on pushing meat on to her fork and then forcing it to her mouth. "Not since we moved into town."

"I have thought about moving back there once the baby is born. Great place to grow up," Roy said, like it was something they'd talked about before, something they both wanted. "It was fine staying in town when it was just the two of us, but it's not where I want to raise a family."

Madeline almost spat her mouthful out on to the table. Her entire body went cold.

Move back there? There wasn't a chance. *No! Over her dead body would she take a child back to that awful place.*

She started to cough, like she was choking. Why had he never said any of this to her before? Had this been his plan all along? To get her pregnant and then insist they go back? Had his mother told him to bide his time until she was in the family way?

"Are you okay? Do you want a glass of water?" Lauren looked concerned.

Madeline rose, unable to look at Roy, and hurried into the kitchen. Lauren was hot on her heels.

"It's okay. Here, have this."

Lauren passed her the water. She drank it down, quickly.

"I need to go to the bathroom. Where is it?" Madeline asked.

She held the kitchen bench for strength, wanting nothing more than to double over. This couldn't be happening. She must have misheard him.

"I'm sure he didn't mean it, Mads. It was just conversation. You know, him thinking out loud."

Madeline knew better. Last weekend he'd gone to visit them, without her, but she hadn't minded. They were his family and if he wanted to see them that was his decision. But he must have told them they were expecting. Now they wanted the baby. Not her, she knew that already. But the baby. They wanted her baby!

"Bathroom?" Now she was in danger of fainting.

"Down the hall, first door on your right."

She ran. Just made the bathroom before she started vomiting, over and over, into the toilet.

She wasn't going back there. *She couldn't.*

"It was just an idea, Madeline. Something I've been thinking about."

She was on the verge of hysteria. After managing to get through the rest of dinner, making small talk, and then finally leaving, they were back home.

"It is not an idea, Roy. Because for it to be an idea there would actually have to be a possibility of it happening."

He sighed and pulled back the blankets, before getting into bed.

"Would it be that bad, really?" He sighed. "I think you need to give it a chance, especially once you become a mother."

"Do you not remember how they treated me? What it was like for me there? Do you not recall why and how we left?"

He sat up, propped by the pillows. She stood, bewildered, in the center of the room.

"It would be different if we had a child."

"Different?" Now she was feeling like a nut case. "Different because they'd not only have me to be awful to but a child too? I'd be stuck in that house day after day, Roy. Absolutely not."

He groaned. Right now, she didn't know how serious he was. *Whether it was just him testing the waters or if he actually intended on pushing the point.*

"How are we going to get on once you stop working? It's not exactly cheap living here, and we need to get more furniture, things for the baby. Besides, mother was fine with us leaving for a short time, but she made it clear that when we had a family they expected us back home."

"We'll cope, Roy. Lots of couples have to do without. We'll be just the same as them." She took a deep breath. "Your mother should have no say in what we do or don't do." She knew now what had happened, that he'd been under his mother's influence all this time, without her even realizing. Was that why he'd gone along with the move into town? With his mother's instructions that it would be fine simply as a short-term measure?

He shook his head. "I just don't see why we can't give it another go. That's all I'm saying. I never wanted to live in town, I did it for you. You just need to give the farm another go. You'll grow to like it, I'm sure."

"So long as we're married, we won't be living in that house again. Ever."

His reaction was to lie down as if to go to sleep. "I'm tired, we can talk about this another day."

She wasn't even remotely sleepy.

"Aren't you coming to bed?" he asked.

"No."

Madeline went to the kitchen, flicked the switch on, and picked up her pen. She needed to write to her family. She had tried so hard not to burden them with her problems, even thrown letters out she had penned before making it to the store to post them.

But tonight she needed to talk to someone. And she was alone. She should have searched for Betty, Alice, and June as soon as they'd moved into town. At least then she'd have friends to confide in. Why had they not all realized how tricky it would be to get in touch? They should have named somewhere to meet, set a date, instead of all these months passing without contact. If she'd realized how massive New York was, she'd have made sure they gave each other more exact details.

Madeline started to write to her mother and father. *About her fears for the future. About her mixed feelings for her husband. About her concern for her job, money, and her unborn baby.*

But mostly she described why she missed them. Why she would do anything to be back home, as part of her family, instead of on the other side of the world. This time she didn't try to gloss over what was wrong.

She remembered the way her father had looked at her when she'd been torn about accepting Roy's offer of marriage. The kindness in his eyes when he'd promised to bring her home if it was that bad in America. She didn't want to tell him, not yet, that it was worse than the most hideous nightmare a child could have, or more correctly, that it would be if she had to move back to the farm.

But she did tell them that she missed them. That she would do anything to come home. She needed them to know that.

She'd wait until after the baby was born before asking her father for help. See if Roy insisted on going back to the farm. She wanted them to know the truth, but she didn't want to take that step yet—not until she knew for sure what Roy would be like as a father. To see if it changed him.

Just when they'd been getting on, when things had seemed okay, it was like he'd thrown a grenade at her. She was completely bewildered, couldn't believe that his mother had such control over him. She knew he enjoyed working on the farm, and for some godforsaken reason he wanted to be near his family, but to move back there? Madeline shuddered. She thought he'd been happy with the life they'd started to build.

If she couldn't stand it any longer, if he forced her to move, she was going to run. She was going to send a telegram to her father and beg him to help her.

Not yet. But she would do it if she had to.

Madeline folded the letter and placed it in her pocket, deciding not to send it just yet. She wanted her family to know what she was going through so she didn't feel so alone, but she also didn't want them to worry about her, not until she knew more about what her future held.

❦

"I hope Sam didn't upset you last night." Lauren looked worried as they sat together eating lunch the next day.

Madeline tried to be brave, when all she wanted was to curl up into a ball and cry. She didn't trust her own voice, so she just attempted to smile.

"Oh, I'm sorry!" Lauren put her arm around her. "I knew it upset you. I should have told him off then and there."

"It wasn't Sam's fault. It was Roy." She started to cry. "I just can't believe he actually suggested us going back there."

She'd told Lauren bits and pieces about what it had been like for her on the farm. Not the complete truth, but enough for her to paint a fairly vivid picture.

It had been . . . a long, long time since she'd let anybody see her cry. Since she'd been this honest about her feelings.

"It'll be all right, I promise." Lauren still had an arm slung over her shoulders. "Once the baby comes you'll be just fine. You'll see."

She hoped so.

But something told her she was going to need to do a lot more than hope to get through what her future held.

# CHAPTER 18

June sucked in a deep breath and focused on the bathroom ceiling. She was not going to cry.

Each month that passed without her getting pregnant was a heartache like she'd never known before. It made her feel so incapable, so pathetic. So *barren*. It hadn't been long, but still. *She was ready to be a mother.* It had been five months now and every month she hoped and prayed, then ended up disappointed.

She forced the thoughts from her mind as she listened to Eddie's cheerful whistle. The clop of his shoes up the staircase made her feel better, but she knew he'd be disappointed too.

"Where are you, darling?"

June cleared her throat and flushed the toilet.

"Just a moment."

He continued to whistle the tune. When she opened the door and walked to their bedroom, he was sitting on the bed, waiting.

"Ready to go?"

June smiled, but when her eyes met his she lost control. A sob escaped from her mouth, her body shaking. Eddie was by her side in less than a heartbeat.

"June, sweetheart." He pulled her tight into his arms, rocking her back and forth. "June, what is it?"

She squeezed her eyes shut and wished the tears away, before pulling away slightly so she could look up at him.

"Why can't we have a baby, Eddie? What have we done to deserve this?"

He sighed, before pulling her tight again and dropping a kiss to her head.

"We have to be patient," he whispered, his voice soothing in her ear. "You are going to be a wonderful mother one day, just you wait and see."

That only made her want to cry more.

"You've given me this beautiful home, you're so kind and wonderful and . . ." her voice was barely a murmur.

"Sssshhhhh," he whispered. "Don't say that."

"But it's true!" This time she pushed hard away from him. "You've given me so much and I can't even manage to get pregnant."

Eddie shook his head, a smile twisting his mouth. "Well I'm pleased I'm kind and wonderful, but you're not exactly a bad catch yourself."

June tried to keep her mouth straight but she couldn't help the smile that started tugging at her lips. He always managed to do this to her, make her feel good when she should be miserable.

"I just really want a baby, Eddie. Is that so much to ask?"

He closed the distance between them again and kissed her forehead this time, then her cheek, then her mouth.

"I'm enjoying just having you, there's no rush. When the time's right, it will happen. Okay?"

She leaned into him, his tall frame bracing hers.

"Okay, June?" he asked.

"Okay."

She didn't want to wait, she wanted to be pregnant now, but when he put it like that . . . It wasn't like there was any great hurry. They were having a lovely time together. She couldn't have asked for more in a husband. It was silly to get so upset when they were still only in their first year of marriage. *But still, she wanted a family of her own, and she didn't want to wait.*

"Shall we go?"

June smiled up at him, stood on tiptoe to kiss him again then walked back to the bathroom.

"I don't know what I did to deserve you, Eddie West."

She grinned as his laugh echoed out behind her.

"My family's still trying to figure out how I tricked you into marrying me. They're sure I did something to fool you."

"Oh really?" She suddenly felt lighter, happier. He was always able to joke her from a mood. It was right to share her concerns with him, he'd made her feel better in no time. "And what do you think?"

June jumped as he appeared in the mirror behind her, arms wrapping around her waist as she tried to fix her lipstick and wipe the tear tracks from her cheeks.

"I think," he said, lifting her hair to kiss the back of her neck, "that I'm the luckiest guy in the *world.*"

She wriggled but he held tight.

"Anything else?"

"Yeah. I think we should skip dinner and stay home."

She gave him a soft shove with one hand.

"Absolutely not."

He pouted, eyes like a puppy that had been locked out in the rain.

"Why not?"

She powdered her nose one last time then twirled around to face him.

"Because, Eddie, we spend every night home alone together. Your family is probably starting to think we're weird."

※

Every single time June set foot inside her in-laws home, she smiled. Not just a polite smile—the kind of wide, hurt-your-cheeks, show-your-teeth kind of grin that could only come with great pleasure.

Patty wiggled her fingers in greeting from her spot on the sofa, while her mother-in-law rushed over to kiss her on the cheek.

"How's my favorite daughter-in-law?"

June kissed her back. "Great."

Eddie leaned over to kiss his mother, too, before disappearing over by his father, who was opening a bottle of sherry.

"Sorry we're late," June said.

She knew they wouldn't mind. It was like walking into a stage for the perfect home. It was so warm, even at night when the sun had tucked itself away for the day. Large rugs adorned the floors, oversize sofas and chairs filled the room, and a large table was set for dinner, without looking austere. It was a real home. The kind of relaxed, happy home she could imagine Eddie and Patty growing up in.

"Glass of sherry, June?" offered Eddie's father.

She snapped out of her dream. "I'd love one."

Eddie walked a glass over to her. She smiled at him, trying not to giggle at his wink. He looked so funny doing things like that—he wasn't exactly the suave ladies' man that he would like to pretend he was.

"We've got some gossip," Patty declared proudly, stretching then standing as her father brought her drink over.

"Patty, that's enough!" June suppressed a laugh as her sister-in-law was scolded by her mother. "You shouldn't talk like that about people behind their backs. Not to mention finding entertainment in the misfortune of others."

Now June was dying to know the gossip.

Patty grinned and skipped over, almost spilling her drink.

"Do you remember the posh lady we saw in town a few weeks back? The one who was making a fuss about the food in the restaurant?"

Oh yes, she remembered her. Women like that always stood out.

"What about her?" June asked.

Patty leaned closer, as if she was about to divulge something of the greatest importance.

"Well, her *unmarried* sixteen-year-old daughter is pregnant. *Pregnant!*"

June didn't feel like laughing along with Patty at all. It just wasn't fair! How could a young girl with no interest in getting pregnant do so with ease, and here she was still trying with no success.

"Did you hear me? *Sixteen*," Patty hissed.

"The poor girl," said June, starting to feel hot all over, like she might faint. "It's just not fair."

"Not fair!" her sister-in-law scoffed. "She should have thought about that before she started rolling in the hay with the butcher's son."

"Patricia! That's enough."

June dropped her head. She shouldn't have encouraged her. Patty bit her lip and looked apologetic as her father glared at her.

"What will she do?" June whispered.

Patty snuggled in closer against her.

"They'll probably send her away, then arrange for the child to be adopted. You know, some nice couple who can't have one of their own will take the baby."

June nodded. *Someone like her and Eddie.*

"Come on, dinner's on the table."

June turned as Eddie took her elbow. She let him steer her over to the table.

*Adopt*. Was that something they could do? "Sweetheart, are you okay?"

Eddie's concerned voice shook her from her thoughts.

"Oh, of course!" She smiled at the anxious faces directed her way. "Never felt better. Just daydreaming."

Eddie didn't look convinced, but she squeezed his thigh gently beneath the table and leaned into him.

If they couldn't have a baby, they could adopt one.

She would love any child, whether it was hers or not. So if they couldn't conceive all was not lost. There was still hope. Even if they adopted now and had their own later when the time was right.

"June, we've been thinking about your family," Eddie's father said.

So had she, every day without fail.

"I would love you to meet them one day," she beamed at her father in-law. "They'd just love you. All of you."

June passed her plate over and watched as roast beef, potatoes, and vegetables were piled high.

"Well, that's what we've been talking about," her father-in-law said.

June wasn't quite sure she understood.

"I doubt they'll be visiting anytime soon, unfortunately," she told them.

She watched as the three of them all looked at one another and smiled. Like they knew something she didn't.

"We're going to bring them out here to stay."

Eddie must have noticed her mouth gaping open. To *stay*? They would actually do that for her?

"I told you we'd consider it, didn't I, June?"

She couldn't believe it.

"You shouldn't feel obligated, I mean . . ."

"Nonsense!" Now it was her mother-in-law speaking. "You're part of our family, June. It won't be for a little while, maybe in six months, but we'd like to start making some arrangements. See when might be most convenient for them."

June couldn't even pick up her knife and fork, she was so stunned. Tears filled her eyes, happy tears that she managed to smile through.

"You all mean so much to me. I'll never be able to thank you enough," she said, choked up.

Eddie put his arm around her and kissed her cheek, while his father raised his glass in a toast.

"To June, our newest and most treasured family member."

# CHAPTER 19

W e just can't stay here."

Madeline was determined not to cry. One hand fell to her stomach, and found comfort there. Some days, it was all she had: the feeling of her palm connecting with her belly.

She certainly found no comfort in her husband's arms.

"I am *not* going back there."

He glared at her. "We're not having this conversation again."

"No, Roy, we're not."

She looked around at their home. Still bare, sparse, but it was *hers*. Every day she loved the fact that it was her own space, that it was their own house.

*It held hope.*

Moving back to the farm held nothing but unhappiness. No bright future. Nothing for her to look forward to. And nowhere she wanted to be with her baby.

Here, she could hold onto a dream that they might one day be a real family. That her husband would be more like the man she'd met in England, more like the man she'd seen glimpses of when they'd first moved into town, that their marriage could evolve into a loving one like Lauren and Sam's.

"Roy," her voice was strong, firm. "I'm not moving back to the farm."

He didn't look impressed. "I've already handed my notice in at work."

Pain exploded through her body, like fire tearing through her brain.

She sat down. No. *No, no, no!*

"You what?" Her voice had lost its strength. It sounded like that of a child's.

He smiled at her, a knowing smile that almost made her heart stop, but not in a good way.

"I'm your husband, Madeline, and I have made the decision that we are moving back to live with my family." He folded his arms across his chest. "I indulged you for a while, but Mother didn't expect you to last so long working. And now that you're in the family way, it's time I started to make the decisions about what's best for us. And besides, I think you were overreacting a little before. The farm's very different to what you're used to, but you need to adjust to the way of life there."

"You can't . . ." the words choked in her mouth, "you can't just make that kind of decision on your own."

She knew now. His mother had been working on him. Forcing him. Telling him what to do. She groaned. Each week when he'd gone there for dinner, when she'd stayed home so she didn't have to see them, they'd been figuring it out. Waiting until she was helpless, until she didn't have a choice in the matter. How could she have been so stupid!

"And where will we live there?" Her words were stuttered.

He smiled again. It disturbed her how calm he was being. "In the room we shared last time. It's plenty big enough for the baby too, until I build an extra room on the house."

She was numb. Her entire body felt cold. She started to rub her stomach again, trying to draw strength again. She'd walked straight into a trap she'd had no idea was even set.

"I'm not going, Roy. I told you before, I will not live in that house again."

He sighed wearily. It was like he'd known what she was going to say, she thought. Like he had prepared his answers. This was the most decisive she'd seen him since she'd arrived in the States. Her arguments held no sway with him.

"You're not going to leave me." His tone was cool. "I know you think you're better than us, that my parents' farm isn't good enough for you, but we're going to be a family, Madeline."

She gulped. Air seemed to be in short supply.

"I will leave," she affirmed. "If you force me to go, I'll leave you."

"How?"

She didn't want to have this conversation with him. She still wanted to give their child a chance at a family. At a mother and father who loved him. A mother and father who had tried to make it work.

"I don't want to leave you, Roy, but if you keep siding with your mother and letting her interfere in our marriage, I'll have no choice."

"Madeline, you have no money to leave me. I won't let you go." He paused. "And you won't be taking our child anywhere."

"We don't have to be like this, Roy. Please, let's just give this a go. Being here together. Living in our own home."

He gave her a cold look, a controlled, slow-burning anger in his gaze she hadn't seen before. "It's all been organized. I'll be giving notice on the lease here as soon as my job is filled, which shouldn't take too long."

Tears started a steady pelt down her face. Her body started to shake. This could not be happening. Surely not now. Not when she was pregnant. Not when she had no options until after the baby was born.

"I will leave you, Roy. I will. One message back home and I'm gone."

"We'll see."

It was like he knew something she didn't. She knew it was stupid, but the smug look on his face told her there was something going on. Something his mother was no doubt a part of. Her body shook, hands trembling. She'd expected to be close to her mother-in-law, to have a loving relationship with her husband's mother, and instead she hated her more than she'd ever hated anything or anyone in her life before.

Roy walked out and left her sitting there, rocking in her chair. She felt her baby move inside her belly, but she couldn't focus on it.

All she knew was that she wasn't going back to that farm. She just couldn't.

It was time to ask her father.

*It was time to go home.*

# CHAPTER 20

Alice stood in the doorway and watched her husband. She had spent so many weeks, months, hating him, but now she just felt sorry for him. Every time she'd tried to connect with him it was like he hadn't even noticed her, like he'd forgotten he even had a wife.

She didn't know what to do. What she could have done differently, if there was anything she could do to help him.

His mother obviously felt differently, but she wasn't going to dwell on that. At least she lived halfway across the country, so it wasn't like Alice had to deal with her on a regular basis. There was the odd phone call when she was unlucky enough to answer it, but that was all. But then his mother obviously knew more about what had happened and Alice didn't. All she knew was that they were broke and the man she had known, had disappeared.

"Where are you going?"

Alice turned. It was the first time Ralph had taken notice of her in as long as she could remember.

"Just a work thing, I won't be long."

Ralph studied her. Despite the drunken haze over his eyes, he was watching her, considering her.

She should have felt guilty, but she didn't.

"What about my dinner?" He slurred the words and it made her snarl. The only thing worse than being ignored by him was when he was drunk and finally spoke to her.

Just listening to him like that, hearing his voice and seeing him so slovenly, it made her sick. All he cared about was filling his belly with food and alcohol.

"There's a casserole in the oven. Take it out when you want it."

She could hear the clipped tone of her voice as she acted out the part she wanted to play. He had a distant look back on his face, eyes glazed over as he stared at the wall. He wasn't even listening to the wireless, wasn't even looking out of the window.

"Goodbye, Ralph," she said the words, but they held no warmth.

She only wished she was saying goodbye for good.

Alice collected her purse and slipped out the door. She only had to walk a block before she saw the sleek car she was looking for.

He didn't get out, but then she hadn't expected him to. It was risky enough him picking her up, and she didn't need anybody seeing them together, not so close to home. They'd never been so brazen before with their meetings.

"Hello, darling." Matthew seemed to purr the words.

She snuggled deeper into the seat and enjoyed the feel of his hand on her thigh. Alice wanted to press close to him and kiss him, but she knew he liked to be discreet.

"Hard to slip away?" he asked.

She shook her head. "Not at all."

"Good."

Alice looked ahead and wondered where they were headed to.

"I hope we're eating, I'm starving."

Matthew responded by taking his eyes off the road to grin at her, and throw her one of his winks. "I was expecting you to have an appetite."

Alice suddenly wasn't hungry any longer. *She was terrified.*

They'd kissed passionately, gotten close to going further, but they hadn't been intimate yet. No wonder he'd been so insistent about tonight.

He'd planned it.

This was the night she was to become her boss's lover.

After tonight, they weren't just playing, they would be having a full-blown affair. She would be the other woman. She would be committing the most serious act of adultery.

But she couldn't say no. They'd been secretly seeing each other after hours in the office and on lunch dates for weeks now.

Alice looked at Matthew. Took in the smooth fall of his hair, his strong jaw, his immaculate clothes. She would never tire of the sight of him.

"I've got a present in the back for you," he said.

"For me?"

He nodded. "Reach over and take a look."

The lid had fallen off a large black box. Alice wriggled to push it off further.

"Oh my!"

She wanted to squeal with delight.

Matthew was smiling.

"You like it?"

Alice let her fingers trace over the soft, luxurious fur. Her own fur coat! She'd longed for one all her life, had imagined her husband would buy her one when she'd arrived here.

Enough, she reminded herself. When she was with Matthew she was forbidden to even think about Ralph.

She made herself calm down. Pushed the bubbling worries aside. Her husband didn't care what she did or where she was, so he was hardly going to notice a fur coat. And it was he who should be feeling guilty about his behavior, not her. Being unfaithful wasn't something she wanted to do, and she *did* feel a pang of guilt, but she just wanted someone to love her. To feel wanted instead of taken for granted, to not be alone anymore.

"Alice, you haven't answered my question?" Matthew took his eyes off the road to watch her. "Do you like it?"

"You're the best, Matthew. Thank you so much!"

She leaned over and pressed a kiss to his cheek, nearly bursting with the pleasure of his gift, her worries cast aside.

"I want you in that fur coat and nothing else." He kept his eyes on the road now but his smile was wicked.

A shiver of excitement tickled her skin.

"Yes, boss."

⁓

Alice slipped into the coat the moment she stepped from the car. It seemed to envelope her, caress her, made her feel desired. She'd imagined Ralph would want to treat her like this. Spoil her. Worship her.

How wrong she'd been.

Matthew's warm hand clasped hers, firmly. Like they were meant to be connected.

"You look beautiful."

She smiled at his words.

Alice wiggled her fingers against his, then snatched them back. "Alice?"

She shook the feeling away and forced her feet to keep moving, forced her mind to go back to the happy place it had been before.

But the cool indent of his wedding band grazed against her fingers again as he reclaimed her hand, reminding her that what she was doing was wrong. He would never leave his wife for her. Never think of her as anything more than a good time. He was betraying another woman to be here. The odd kiss and giggle and stolen moment before hadn't concerned her too much, but this felt different. More dangerous. More serious.

"You do realize I'm going to peel your clothes off and kiss every inch of your body tonight, don't you?"

His smile was infectious. She was nervous, yes, but excited too. She just wanted to feel *wanted*. Wanted to be his for the night. Wasn't that enough? If he didn't want to think about his wife then why did she have to?

"I might play hard to get," she murmured, trying to fall back into role again.

He chuckled, before grabbing her wrist tight and raising her hand to kiss it, his lips wet as they trailed across her skin.

"But I like to play."

Part of Alice's brain told her to run, to scurry back home to her husband before she ruined her marriage completely. She might have had plenty of fun in her past, but she'd never been unfaithful; for all her talk all she wanted was a loving relationship. Committing adultery had certainly never been something she'd expected to do, especially not given the way she'd fallen so head over heels for Ralph.

But the other part of her? The part that was making her press tighter into Matthew and wish they could stay out all night? That part kept reminding her that the Ralph she loved, the Ralph she'd married, was long gone.

Alice tried her hardest to smile, when all she really wanted was to hide her face, her body, in shame. To cover her nakedness and curl into a ball like she had as a little girl. To cry and cry until she had no more tears left to shed.

"You need anything?" Matthew asked.

Alice shook her head. Like what? A second chance? If she'd known it would feel like this, so dirty and distasteful, she would never have gone through with it. *This wasn't what she wanted. This wasn't what she'd expected.*

"I'm fine, Matthew. Thank you."

He leaned over her, his undone belt buckle falling against her skin, cold to the touch. She tried so hard not to grimace as his moustache brushed her face, his wet lips over hers. *Before it had felt exciting, now it just seemed . . . disturbing.*

"I'm thinking lunch tomorrow? What do you say?" he asked, hands falling to her hair then to casually cup her breast.

She wanted to scream, to slap his hand away and tell him not to treat her like that. But she couldn't. *Because she'd known why he wanted to bring her here, and had followed him with her eyes wide open.*

"Alice?" he asked, groping her now. "Another rendezvous like this when we should be drinking coffee and eating lunch is just what I'd like to look forward to."

Alice felt like a cheap whore. Revolting. *Betrayed.*

"Darling, I need a few moments to tidy up. Do you mind awfully?" She did her best to purr, but talking to him like that, like he was her lover, no longer felt natural. It hadn't from the moment he'd pulled her clothes off and flopped down on top of her. It had taken him a minute or so to find pleasure, with no thought to her needs, to making her feel good too.

She bit down hard on her lip. She'd only been intimate with Ralph once, when he'd been drunk, and he'd never shown her any interest again. It was one of the things that had made her feel hollow, a shell of the woman she'd once been back in England. But even that was preferable to the guilt she was feeling now.

"Of course." He finished buttoning his trousers and pulled on his shirt. "I'll have a drink in the foyer while I wait."

Alice watched him go. She waited for the final click of the door, then stood, naked, in front of the mirror. She looked at herself, eyes touching over every inch of her reflection.

She was trim. Curvaceous. Attractive.

Only her face looked like a painted doll's, make-up hiding the person beneath. Hair so bright and brassy she no longer recognized it.

The woman she saw looking back wasn't the woman she'd known all her life. That woman had had morals. That woman had turned down a married man when she was single herself. That woman would have made an effort to make her marriage work. She'd been fun, yes, but she'd also known right from wrong. All the money and pretty clothes in the world couldn't make up for what she'd done.

The woman she'd just been was cheap. She'd just given herself to her boss like some sort of tramp. And for what? She could never be anything more than a mistress to him. One gift and a handful of flattering words and she'd fallen at his feet.

Alice turned away and reached for her clothes.

The only thing she knew right now was that she was never, ever going to do this again.

She was never going to feel like this, so disgusted by her own behavior, ever again.

She was going to give her marriage one more chance. If she could live with this guilt, the weight of it pressing down on her chest, then she would try her best to make amends with Ralph. Otherwise she'd leave him, but she wasn't going to be anyone's mistress, not now, and not ever again. *Not now she knew how it felt.*

Could she ever make her marriage work now, though? Because she knew men. And no man would ever forgive his wife this type of sin.

*If he ever found out.*

# CHAPTER 21

Madeline's hand shook as she reached over the counter. Her boss had said that there was a telegram waiting for her, and she had that sinking feeling that it was bad news. She'd sent word to her family after they'd moved to tell them that they were to send letters to her at work. But she'd not heard from them in a long while, and being notified of a telegram worried her.

Would her family send a telegram instead of a letter if her sister had had her baby? To celebrate a milestone?

She could think of no good reason other than tragedy. Goose pimples tickled her forearms. She needed her family right now, especially since Roy had made his announcement they were moving back to the farm.

The lady behind the counter smiled. A soft smile which only made her feel worse.

There was a bench outside the store and Madeline sunk to it with relief. Her feet ached from standing in the bank, filling in for a teller all morning.

The paper was folded crisply. She slipped her finger in between the fold and pushed it open, but shut her eyes at the same time.

She'd been waiting to send a telegram herself. Ready to tell her family that she wanted to come home. Ready to give in. *To renounce her marriage and flee.* She'd been saving for weeks to get the money together, without Roy realizing. He'd taken over tight control of their finances since his decision they were moving back to the farm.

Madeline gulped, opened her eyes and scanned the page.

Her entire body seemed to falter, like she'd received an electric shock capable of paralyzing her.

No! *Please, no!*

This was worse than moving back to the farm. This was . . . it couldn't be true!

"No!" she wailed. "Please Lord, no."

Madeline ripped the paper into pieces, over and over and over. It couldn't be.

Not him. *Not her father.*

But no matter how hard she tore, the printed words remained in her brain. Imprinted, ingrained in her memory.

MY DARLING MADELINE STOP YOUR FATHER HAS DIED STOP HE SUFFERED A HEART ATTACK IN THE SHOP STOP PLEASE KNOW HE LOVED YOU AND MISSED YOU STOP

Her father was gone.

And so was any chance of her leaving this hell hole.

She was going back to the farm.

# CHAPTER 22

**B**etty heard Luke arrive home. It was late. She'd already eaten her dinner with Ivy, and now she was in bed. The rumble of the car as it had pulled up the gravel driveway, the depth of his footfalls, the bang of the door—she heard it all. After so many months she felt she was finally ready to be part of the world again, to connect with someone other than her baby or Ivy.

Part of her was intrigued by him. Desperate to find out more about him and understand what, if anything, about him was like her Charlie; he was a living link to him, after all.

She'd been trying so hard to fit in and be discreet, that she still didn't know him well at all. Between his travels away for business and the hours he spent at work, she hardly saw him.

William was sound asleep beside her. She had felt sad and lonely tonight, and when he'd fallen into a deep slumber in her arms, she hadn't the heart to put him in the nursery. Instead, she'd tucked him into the crook of her arm and snuggled up beside him.

She inhaled the smell of him. The tangy soap from his bath, the sweetness of his little breath as he exhaled.

She might have lost Charlie, but she was not going to lose this wee man. He was her future. Everything she did from this step forward was as his mother. She had to keep Charlie in her heart, and in her memory, and be strong.

She heard the muffled noise of Luke's words to Ivy. It soothed her, knowing she wasn't alone in the house, even if it felt like it sometimes. It was almost like Luke was an irregular visitor here, and she and Ivy were the only residents of the house.

Talking to Ivy, spending time in the kitchen with her each day, had revealed more about the type of man Luke was. He was the serious brother, had made a financial success of himself, and he'd somehow managed to avoid military service. She also knew now that it was Luke who had insisted his home be made available indefinitely for her, despite other family members advising him otherwise. Family members she still hadn't met.

She was determined to make Luke pleased to have offered her a roof over her head. And she'd make sure William always knew who to be grateful to.

Betty closed her eyes and conjured an image of Charlie. Of dancing in his arms, of kissing him, of lying on the grass and gazing up at the sky.

*Charlie*. She would never forget him.

There was something about Luke that was starting to remind her of Charlie, finally, after all this time. She couldn't put her finger on it, but somewhere, lurking beneath the surface, there was something. Something she hadn't seen before, but that she could see now that he was suddenly spending a lot more time at home.

He turned to face her. Smiled. Or, more accurately, gave her half of a smile. She was trying to make more of an effort to join Luke at mealtimes, especially for breakfast in the mornings, and it seemed to be working.

"What are your plans for the day, Betty?" Luke asked.

She put her cup down and turned her body to face him. He was sitting at the morning table, paper spread out in front of him, the remnants of yesterday's paper spilling across the wooden top.

"Nothing planned." She never had anything planned. Aside from the girls she'd met on her way over, she knew nobody. Had no one. So her days were filled with caring for William, talking to and helping Ivy, and making her way through the books in the library. What she needed to do was find her friends. She could use their support. But for some reason she still hadn't tried to make contact with them and neither had they found her. Maybe they were all too busy with their own lives, but they'd all promised to stay in touch and yet she hadn't heard a peep from anyone.

"I thought we'd make a trip to see my parents," he told her.

She felt slightly light-headed. *His parents?*

"I didn't know they wanted to meet me," Betty said.

He took a sip of his coffee and started to fold the paper back together. "Quite the opposite. They've been telling me how inappropriate it is to have you locked away here in the house of a bachelor, when they could accommodate for you in their home." He cleared his throat. "I've kept them away as long as I could, but now you're, well, a bit stronger, I don't think I can fend them off any longer."

He must have seen the ashen shade of her face. It was like all the blood had drained straight through her skin. In all honesty she knew it was odd that she hadn't met them yet, given that she was Charlie's widow and the mother to their only grandchild. Still, her heart was pounding and she was finding it incredibly hard to breathe.

"Relax." It was one of the few times she'd seen him direct a full smile her way. "I'm not going to drive you there and leave you. I just feel like I've neglected you, and now that I have everything under control at work, I want to spend some time with you and William."

She let out a slow breath. It had taken all her efforts to settle here, but without Ivy, she'd be a mess. Even talking to Luke sometimes took it out of her, on the rare occasions she'd actually spent a longer length of time with him. He was usually up and gone by the time she rose, and home only once she'd already taken herself off to bed.

Ivy entered the room then to clear the breakfast dishes.

"I was just telling Betty that today might be a good day to introduce her to my mother and father."

Ivy exchanged a quick glance with Betty. Luke didn't miss it.

"And I've no doubt she's heard all about them from you," he said in a dry tone.

"I haven't even mentioned them."

Ivy did a terrible job of disguising her feelings.

"They're not all bad, despite what you might have heard," Luke told Betty.

"Then why did you move away from home so quickly, Master Luke?" said Ivy, smart as a whip.

He swatted with a hand in Ivy's direction. "Enough with the Master Luke and enough with the analysis."

Betty giggled. She couldn't help it. Up until now, she'd wondered if Luke was even capable of humor.

"Enough from you, too." He pointed his finger and laughed back. "I don't need two women ganging up on me."

Ivy tutted and left the room, dishes piled in her hands.

"So?" Luke asked.

"It would be lovely to meet them." Betty smiled. "But promise you'll bring me straight back here afterward. I don't want to stay with them."

Luke rose and stopped to talk to William. That was a first too.

Her little boy was lying on the large sofa, swaddled in a soft blanket and cocooned by pillows so he wouldn't fall off. He had been busy gurgling and talking to himself the entire time they'd had breakfast.

"You want to meet your grandparents, little guy?" Luke asked him.

Betty moved to stand beside him. William had his little hands fisted, thrust into the air, and he was verging on smiling.

"Smile for your uncle, go on now?"

She leaned forward and tickled under his chin. His bottom lip started to quiver.

"Come on, William."

He swapped his gaze from Betty back to Luke. She could see Luke smiling back at him from the corner of her eye.

"Oh, look!" She laughed as William performed a series of smiles and funny expressions.

Luke laughed, too. He reached out one finger for William to grab hold of.

"I think he likes you," Betty told him.

Luke looked at her. They were standing close, both hovering over the baby. Too close.

He jerked back, releasing William's hold. The baby started to cry.

"I'm sorry, I . . ." Luke trailed off, awkward again.

Betty reached for William. He started to smile again as she pulled him into her arms.

"He's a big faker, that's all." She kissed his forehead and turned her back so he could look over her shoulder at Luke again.

"I think we should leave in an hour, if that suits you. I'll advise them we're coming," he said stiffly.

Betty turned around, only to see Luke's back. Had she said something wrong for him to be so abrupt?

Ivy appeared, her eyebrows pulled close, as if in question.

"I'm not sure if I upset Luke. I . . ."

"He's just a bit confused. You know, not used to babies," Ivy told her.

Betty shrugged, but she was hurt.

"Or women," Ivy continued.

She found that hard to believe. He wasn't Charlie, but he was handsome. Thick dark hair, brown eyes, tall. And he owned a beautiful home and what must be a successful business. Why would he not have experience with women?

Ivy read her expression.

"I'll tell you all about it one day," Ivy said, patting her on the shoulder as she passed. "Mind you, after today, you might figure it out yourself."

Betty didn't have time to interrogate her, not with only an hour until they left.

"What should I take? Do I need to get dressed up? Take an overnight bag?"

Ivy shook her head. "No to the overnight bag. Luke will be sick of them from the moment you arrive. Smart dress, but be comfortable. It'll take you well over an hour even in that fast car of his."

"And William?" Betty asked.

"Do you want to leave him here?"

"No! I mean, it's not that I don't trust you, I just . . ."

"Of course. Just be sure to take a warm blanket for the car and you'll be fine."

She felt a sudden rush of affection toward Ivy. There was something about this woman that she had grown to love over a very short span of time.

Betty walked forward and planted a kiss on Ivy's cheek.

"What was that for?"

"For just being you."

SORAYA LANE

Betty was thankful William had fallen asleep so fast. The motion of the car had seemed to lull him, and he was tucked against her, his little body rising and falling in slumber.

Luke had been quiet but pleasant company. She just wasn't sure what to talk about. Or how to start a conversation with him. Even after all this time, it felt odd not having Charlie here, too.

She watched out the window, as the landscape changed from city to country. It was pretty here, but so different from her home. She'd grown up in town, so it was lovely seeing such wide open green spaces, seeing cattle and horses grazing.

"Did many of your friends marry soldiers?"

The sound of his voice took her by surprise. She turned to face him as he glanced sideways at her.

"A few of my friends dated soldiers, Americans, but I was the only one to marry."

He nodded, eyes fixed firmly on the road.

"Charlie told me you two met at a dance," he said.

She closed her eyes for a moment, remembering Charlie watching her from across the room, then making his way over. "Yes. We did."

"He also wrote to say that he knew from the moment he saw you that he was going to marry you."

She liked that Luke was smiling as he spoke. It made it easier for her to talk to him, knowing that Charlie had shared his true feelings with him.

"I thought it was just an infatuation with a pretty girl, but he was pretty determined where you were concerned."

They fell into silence again. This time it was comfortable though. She didn't mind the quiet—it gave her time to think about Charlie, and it was nice being able to talk with Luke about him, despite the lump in her throat. Ivy was great, but Betty had desperately wanted to be accepted by Luke. For him to like her, rather than just feel she was his burden now his brother was gone.

"Betty, you never did tell me how the trip was."

The simple fact was that he'd never asked her. In fact, they'd hardly talked properly before, except for the odd exchange of pleasantries, so of course she hadn't told him.

"Ah, it was interesting," she said.

He glanced over at her again. "How so?"

"Well, the fact that I hid my pregnancy to get on the ship, then ended up having William during the voyage, made it quite a trip."

He laughed. "I'm sure it did."

"But I met some wonderful girls, and we had a lot of fun."

She was watching him and saw his smile disappear, replaced by a more tense expression. "Would you still have come, if you'd gotten my message?"

Betty stared out the window. She'd asked herself that question over and over again, so many times. Truth was, she didn't know the answer.

"Honestly, Luke, I don't know. I had nothing in London, no family, but I wouldn't have asked you to take me in. I wouldn't have expected your charity."

"It's not that I don't want you here, Betty. Please don't feel like you're a burden to me. Don't ever think that."

She nodded. Sometimes it did worry her. Often. It was hard not to think that way.

"Charlie and I were close. We had our arguments, but I loved my brother. You meant a lot to him, I know that. But I wasn't sure when you got here if it was just about the money or . . ."

"I didn't even know Charlie came from money." She wasn't going to keep quiet over the truth, not on this subject. "Other girls came here with big dreams, but I came here for Charlie and for no other reason. I loved your brother, Luke, even if that's hard for you to understand."

She saw the clamp of his jaw, the anger in his gaze. He slowed down, pulled off the road onto the shoulder, and came to a complete stop.

He kept his hands on the steering wheel, even as he looked at her.

"I thought Charlie had just fallen in love with some foreign girl, you know, taken it into his head some broad loved him as much as he supposedly loved her."

She felt anger starting to pulse deep inside her now. Until she heard Luke's voice soften.

"But after that first night, when I saw you with William, I knew that wasn't the case. And now, every day when I come home and Ivy tells me how much she's enjoying your company, I see what Charlie saw. I know you didn't come looking for a lifestyle and money. I know that you loved my brother, and that he loved you."

Relief washed through her, down every inch of her body.

He looked uncomfortable, but she was so relieved they'd had this talk.

"You'll both always be welcome in my home, Betty. I want you to know that."

"And I'm grateful, Luke. Truly I am."

He put the car in gear again, cleared his throat, and then pulled out onto the road. Conversation over.

"So tell me about these friends you made on the ship."

Betty smiled. He was as good at changing the subject as Charlie had been.

"Funny you should ask, because I might need your help," she told him.

"My help?"

It felt good, being able to talk like this. They'd gotten the heavy stuff that needed to be said out of the way, and now they could just get on with trying to be friends.

"There were four of us, all sailing for New York or thereabouts, although I think Madeline ended up a bit further away on a farm. We all found each other on our first day and we were inseparable, like sisters."

"Who were the other two?"

"June and Alice," she told him.

"Have you made plans to see them again?"

Betty would do anything to see the girls again. She'd gone for all these months on her own, living in her own little bubble, but talking about them made her miss them terribly.

"June's husband gave me his card, but I don't know where the other girls are precisely. I just know roughly where they are geographically, and their married names. I don't think any of us expected New York and the outer areas to be so vast."

"And you want me to help you find them?" Luke asked.

She wriggled in her seat, eyes lighting up at the idea. She hadn't been ready to tell anyone about Charlie, not to start with, but now she wished she'd called June straight away, instead of letting all these months pass for her to come to terms with things.

"If there's anything you can do to help me, any way we could find them, I'd appreciate it."

Luke smiled over at her.

"We said we'd stay in touch and never forget the time we shared together. But I hadn't really thought that far ahead about how to stay in contact."

"How about you call into my office on Monday morning? My secretary can spend the afternoon helping you locate them. Maybe start with calling the man whose card you already have," said Luke.

"Oh, thank you, Luke! Thank you so much."

"Thank my secretary once you find them. If she was fighting for us it mightn't have taken so long to win the war, so I've no doubt she'll track them down for you."

Betty sat back deep in the seat and couldn't help but smile. Seeing June, Madeline, and Alice again would be like a dream come true. They wouldn't believe her when she told them about Charlie. Had they faced tragedy too, or were they all living the dream lives they had imagined? She hoped so.

"Don't smile too much yet, we still have to make it through this visit," Luke said with a grimace.

Somehow, this visit seemed a lot less worrisome with the prospect of tracking her friends down the day after next.

⚭

Maybe she'd spoken too soon. Meeting her in-laws was not as easy as she'd hoped it would be. And William was not proving to be a happy distraction. He'd started crying the moment his grandmother had poked one of her long nails at him, trying to get a smile, and the look on his face still hadn't changed.

"Shall I get a maid to take him?" her mother-in-law asked.

She could see Mrs. Olliver was getting sick of his squawking. She was a larger woman, the heat clearly bothering her as she fanned her face, and the commotion William was making clearly wasn't helping her to cool down.

"I had a wet nurse for the boys." She directed her words to Luke, then Betty. "No need for a mother to amuse a child all day."

Betty bit her tongue. *If it wasn't the mother's job, then whose was it? Some poor maid who ended up with a better bond with the child than its own flesh and blood?* Not where she came from.

Was that why Luke was so close to Ivy?

"I've hardly heard William cry since they arrived, mother. He obviously doesn't like his surroundings here."

Betty tried not to laugh at Luke's dry tone.

"I can take him inside, if you'd prefer," Betty said. "I don't know what's wrong with him today."

Mrs. Olliver seemed to completely ignore her and went back to drinking her bourbon, her second since they'd arrived.

"Perhaps he'd like something to eat, you know, to keep him occupied," Mrs. Olliver said with a wave of her hand. "Lunch should be served within minutes."

Did the woman have no idea? "He's only just started on solids, as in pureed vegetables, ma'am, so just milk for him while we're here."

"Oh," she said with a disdainful sniff. "I have no idea what they need, but that's what the help is for, isn't it darling?"

She'd clearly been less than involved in the upbringing of her sons.

"Tell me, is that old Ivy any good or do you think it's time to get rid of her and find someone younger? Someone who can take the boy off your hands so you don't have to look after him."

Betty stiffened, the idea of her life without Ivy like a knife to her stomach, but she forced a smile. "Ivy is worth her weight in gold," she insisted. "I couldn't imagine not having her working in the house."

Mrs. Olliver pursed her lips and continued to fan herself.

"So Mother, any news? What's been happening in your world?" Luke asked, changing the subject and saving Betty from the conversation.

"I'd rather know about yours," his mother said. "Any special ladies?"

Betty watched anger take hold of his face, frown lines appearing around his eyes.

"Really, Mother, you must have better things to think about than my love life."

She shrugged, turning to glare at two young maids as they rushed out with plates of food.

"Where is your father?" she tutted.

Luke shrugged at his mother. She stood and marched toward the house, sending the maids scurrying forward to place the food on the table. The setting was glorious, the outdoor table tucked away from the bright sunshine, overlooking a pretty, manicured garden.

Betty jumped when he caught her by the wrist, his fingers closing over her skin.

It was the first time they'd touched, aside from the handshake the night she'd arrived and bumping into one another earlier in the morning.

"As soon as lunch is over, if I make it that far, I want you to pretend you have a headache. Feel faint or something." His words were so low they were like a quick hiss. "I'll take William, you hold my arm and we'll make a getaway."

"I thought you wanted to spend the day here?" She tried to keep the smirk off her face as she recalled Ivy's prediction.

"Play along or I'll leave you here," he told her.

Luke quickly released her wrist as his parents appeared. She nodded, trying not to laugh.

"What are you two whispering about?"

That mother of his didn't miss a thing. Betty hadn't exactly taken a liking to the woman, but it was nice to think of Luke as a friend, or at the very least a co-conspirator.

"Luke was just telling me what fun he had growing up here as a boy."

Mrs. Olliver's face lit up and she reached across to pat her son on the hand, like he was still a little boy.

"Of course he did. It's a wonder he ever wanted to leave."

Betty smiled sweetly over at Luke, who glowered back at her. She could understand precisely why he'd preferred boarding school, not to mention leaving home at such a young age. She would have run a mile, too, no matter how beautiful the surrounds.

He stood as his father approached and held out his hand.

"Father, good to see you."

"And you," his father looked less than interested, and rather vacant.

"This here is Betty," Luke told him.

She received a polite nod and smile. Maybe he didn't even know who she was?

Betty juggled William on her knee to keep him quiet.

"So, Mr. Olliver, Luke tells me you have recently retired?" Betty did her best to make conversation with him, even though talking to strangers didn't come naturally to her.

He had a kind enough face, but he looked like there was no soul behind his eyes. She guessed his wife did most of the talking and he just stayed quiet to keep the peace.

Her father-in-law didn't answer, just smiled. She was about to ask another question but a sharp kick from Luke made her gasp.

"Betty, are you all right?" Luke's face was the picture of concern.

"Oh, Mrs. Olliver, I'm dreadfully sorry, but I'm all of a sudden not feeling so good."

Her mother-in-law looked alarmed.

"I shall call someone over. Do you need to lie down?"

"I, I . . ." She put her hand to her forehead, trying to play the part.

"Mother, I think I'd best take Betty home."

"Nonsense! The best thing for the girl is to stay here a while."

Betty tried to swipe the stunned look off her face. She could almost feel her mouth drop open in horror.

"No, Betty is settled at my house. Besides, she doesn't have any of the baby's, ah, things with her."

"Richard. Richard!"

Her father-in-law woke with a start. He'd fallen asleep in his chair.

"Yes?" he muttered.

"Luke here wants to take Betty back to town. She's feeling unwell."

He looked like he couldn't care less what happened around him.

"Mrs. Olliver, please. I do think it would best for us to just . . ."

The other woman stood, hands on hips. The stance worried Betty. It looked far too, well, determined.

It seemed Luke had the same feeling.

"Mother, we're off. I need to get back to town. Betty is settled already there."

It was clear Mrs. Olliver didn't agree at all.

"Luke! Don't you dare boss me about. It's Betty's choice."

She didn't want to make a choice—they were Charlie's family and she didn't want to be difficult or cause some sort of a rift. She was starting to wish she'd never even agreed to meet them. They'd barely touched lunch, and now they were leaving already.

Luke rose from his chair and moved around the table, plucking William from her and tucking him into the crook of his arm.

"Come on, Betty."

He reached for her hand, which she placed alongside his elbow.

"Oh my, yes, I do feel awfully faint again." She was barely lying now. *Perhaps she would faint if she had to stay here.*

"I'm going to get Betty to the car. Mother? Do you care to see us off?"

She didn't look impressed, but she followed, clicking her fingers at her husband.

Betty followed beside Luke, keeping up with his long stride. She felt naughty, pretending to be ill, but she *was* feeling peculiar now. This whole meet the family business without having Charlie with her was unsettling. But at least it had brought her closer to Luke.

William stayed silent, and she found herself admiring the way he looked in the arms of his uncle.

224

He led her around the side of the house, avoiding walking through it. She was relieved. There might have been a battle again over where she should be staying if they'd gone inside. Mrs. Olliver trotted alongside them.

"Honestly, Luke. I do think it's improper, Betty staying in the home of an unmarried man."

"She has Ivy to care for her, and I am her brother-in-law." He said the words through gritted teeth. "There is nothing even close to inappropriate about that."

He opened the car door for her with his free hand, then passed her William once she was settled.

"Thank you for a lovely lunch. I'm sorry we've had to cut it short," said Betty.

Mrs. Olliver smiled tightly. Her husband gave a more enthusiastic wave.

Luke turned and kissed his mother on the cheek. Then shook his father's hand.

"Betty, did you bring anything?" Luke asked.

"Oh! My handbag. I left it in the sitting room."

He turned to get it, his mother hot on his heels. But it didn't stop Betty hearing the words she said as they walked away.

"She's a nice enough girl, Luke, I can see why Charlie was fond of her. But don't go getting any ideas," she said, her tone stern. "For all we know she's some poor gold digger, so you stay well away. We'll make sure the boy is looked after, for Charlie's sake, but that's all."

Betty found it hard to breathe. Air seemed to catch in little bubbles in her throat, allowing her just enough to keep her from choking. How could she say that! Charlie was hardly cold in the grave, and she'd loved him. She'd loved Charlie more than anything in the world and she hadn't even known he came from money!

Luke glared at his mother, his words low when he answered her. "I would never even think about Betty like that, mother, but I'll tell you right now that she's no gold digger."

Luke stormed off into the house, emerging moments later with her bag. He jumped behind the wheel, raised his hand in a wave, then hit the accelerator. Betty's heart was pounding. Mrs. Olliver's words had hurt. More confusingly, she was oddly disappointed that Luke had made it clear he wouldn't think of her as anything other than a sister. Although at least he'd stood up for her when she'd needed him, and that was what mattered.

But he never looked at her once on the way home. They didn't even talk.

Thoughts churned inside her head. She didn't want to move on. *Never.* Especially not with Charlie's brother. But had the thought of it disturbed him that much? Did he think she was that unattractive? Not good enough for him?

She shouldn't have let it worry her, but it did. On the way here, they'd seemed to develop a friendship. Now it was like the first day when they'd met. And she didn't like it one bit. Because now she was thinking about Luke in a way that had never crossed her mind before, and she felt unfaithful to Charlie's memory even considering it.

∽◦

"Well? How was it?"

Betty flopped down in the chair, holding William out for Ivy to take. She could see the woman was itching to get her hands on the baby.

"Dreadful. I need a cup of tea."

"Funny you should ask for a cup of tay."

Betty glared at her. She wasn't in the mood for being teased.

"Enough of the sour face, miss. Just so happens I finally managed to get a container of tea in for you. I went to the shop while you were out and it had arrived."

"Really?" She felt energy slowly drip back into her bones. "You mean proper English tea?"

"Come see for yourself."

She jumped to her feet and danced into the kitchen. The package stood proudly on the counter. *English breakfast tea.* Oh, yes! After the day she'd had it was exactly what she needed.

"We need a teapot."

"Check." Ivy pointed toward the far cupboard.

Betty opened it and found the most pretty teapot she'd ever seen. Made from china, it was the palest cream, with a fine spout, as if to be used for high tea.

"Ivy, it's gorgeous!"

"Just a little something I wanted to get for you."

She moved around to hug Ivy, kissed her cheek, then set the kettle to boil.

"Now you're going to have a real cuppa with me, Ivy. We can pretend we're in London."

"Did something happen today, Betty? Luke looked mighty cross when he came in, and you seem a little on edge too."

Ivy was leaning back, William lying still in her arms, gurgling up at her, fist in his mouth.

Betty spooned tea into the pot, filled it with water, and placed it on the table. Then she found two cups and saucers and popped them down too, before sitting herself.

"Betty?"

"We really need some scones with jam, or white bread sandwiches with butter and sliced cucumber."

"Betty, there's something you're not telling me."

She sighed and poured the tea, pushing one cup toward Ivy. "That woman is awful."

Ivy raised her eyebrows in question.

"Here, you need a spoon of sugar," Betty told her.

Ivy did as she was told and stirred it in.

"How so?" Ivy asked.

"Well, first of all she couldn't understand why I didn't want to let anyone else look after my baby, or that he didn't eat the same meal as we did. Then she wanted me to stay, she had a go at Luke, his father hardly said a word, and then she . . ."

"What?"

"I still can't believe she let someone else bring up her children," Betty admitted.

"I can."

"You can?" Did Ivy not believe in caring for her own babies either? Surely not?

"I can believe it because it was me who brought those babies up. It was me they called for when they were hurt, or if they were upset. I took them from little babies into boys ready for college. She wasn't interested until they were able to attend her parties and hold their own in an adult conversation."

Betty just stared at her, her tea cup suspended mid-air.

"You looked after them all those years?"

"Why else do you think it was me Charlie wrote to? I knew he'd married you before his own parents did. It's why Luke wanted me here. I love those boys like I love my own daughter."

Betty went back to sipping her own tea.

"So what was it you were going to say before?" Ivy asked her.

"When?"

Ivy gave her a look that she took as serious. Her *don't pull the wool over my eyes* look.

She sighed. "When we left, she didn't think I could hear . . ."

"By *she* you mean Mrs. Olliver?"

Betty nodded. "It was just that she suggested I'd only married Charlie for his money. That maybe I was wanting Luke in the same way and she told him to stay away from me." Betty tried not to mumble. "She didn't know I could hear, but I did, and then Luke wouldn't talk to me the entire drive home." She paused, fiddled with the hem of her skirt. "He stuck up for me in front of her, but then he never said another word."

Ivy made a noise in her throat, but didn't say anything. She sipped at her tea. Thoughtfully.

"Not bad, you know. I could get used to this," Ivy said.

"Ivy?" said Betty.

Now it was the other woman doing the avoiding, and Betty wanted to know why. Ivy set down her tea cup and sighed.

"Betty, one thing you need to know about Luke is that he's a sensitive type. Comes across all brave and strong, but his mother messed him up. Made him cautious of women." She paused. "He could have his pick, you know, but it was Charlie who we always knew would marry. His mother didn't affect him quite the same. Luke, well, maybe. But she's an old dragon at the best of times and you'd be better off not listening to a word she says."

"So you think he'll talk to me again?" Betty asked.

"Of course he will. Don't be daft. He's just annoyed with his mother. And maybe he's embarrassed because he's thought of you that way and his mother picked up on it straight away."

"Ivy!"

Betty felt her cheeks flood with burning hot color.

"You're a pretty girl, Betty. Just because you were married to his brother doesn't mean he can't look at you that way. He's a man after all. It wasn't like he knew you two as a couple."

Betty poured herself another cup of tea, desperate to change the subject.

"He did say that he'd help me find my friends. The girls from the ship I told you about. You don't think he'd go back on his word, do you? I'm so desperate to find them."

"What Luke says he'll do, he does. Now stop fussing about him and enjoy your tea. All this sitting around and talking means I'm running behind. Fancy helping me with dinner?"

"Love to."

"Maybe another cup first, though," Ivy said.

"I knew you'd love it. Who couldn't like a cuppa, huh?"

They both laughed.

Betty was a mix of emotions. Excited, worried, sad, stressed, happy. She switched from one to the other so darn fast she didn't know what she was, but right now, with Ivy, it was the latter. Hands down.

"Let's put this boy down on his tummy so he can learn to start crawling. He's getting far too heavy for us to keep lugging around," suggested Ivy. "Maybe he just needs some time on his stomach for encouragement."

# CHAPTER 23

Alice had a strange feeling she was being watched. Like eyes were travelling over her skin, even though she hadn't opened her own yet.

She kept hers shut. And listened.

This morning, for the first morning since she'd arrived, she wasn't greeted by snoring. Only silence. Something touched her face. Something feather-light and warm.

She opened her eyes.

Ralph was staring at her. Watching her.

The first thing she noticed was that he wasn't drunk. His eyes were focused on her. Alert. And his hand was hovering above her face, hesitant, like he wasn't sure whether he should have touched her or not.

Alice didn't know where to look.

"Good morning," he said.

She swallowed and just kept staring back.

"Alice." He said her name slowly, like he wasn't quite sure what came next. "Alice, I'm sorry."

*She could have died.* Could have closed her eyes and never opened them again. He was sorry? Why now? Why not before she'd committed the worst sin there was? She'd cried for hours, then bathed, over and over again, trying to rid her skin and hair of the smell of Matthew. It was like a poison that she couldn't eliminate from her body, couldn't get rid of no matter how hard she tried.

*Infidelity.* It was all she could think as she looked back at him. *She had been unfaithful. She had committed adultery.*

"Did you hear me, Alice?" he placed his hand against her face, softly cupping her cheek. "I'm so sorry. I'm so, so sorry."

Tears escaped from the corners of her eyes—tears that she had thought she'd never be able to shed in the company of her husband. Tears that stung with pain, with raw hurt. With disappointment and guilt all packaged into one.

"Don't cry, love. Please don't cry."

Ralph pulled her against him and she couldn't resist. She let him cocoon her body, just like she'd wanted all these months.

"I love you, Alice. You deserve so much better than me."

But she didn't. She didn't deserve better, not after what she'd done last night.

"Alice?"

She shook her head, slowly. "I'm sorry too, Ralph."

"You've got nothing to be sorry for."

His words were firm, almost commanding. Like they had been back in England, when he'd been someone important. When she'd fallen in love with him.

"Ralph, I . . ."

He touched his fingers to her lips.

"Ssshh."

Something deep inside told her that he'd guessed what she'd done. Maybe not the full extent of it, but he knew she'd been out with a man. That she had been drifting further and further away from him.

"I haven't been a husband to you, Alice. I've been a fool, but I haven't been able to help it. It sounds stupid but, I . . ." He paused. "I haven't been able to help it."

She tried to smile up at him but her mouth just wouldn't cooperate.

"Ralph, I've got things to be sorry for too."

He shook his head. Gave her a look she hadn't seen in all the time she'd been here with him, a look that told her the man she'd known wasn't completely lost to her. She'd done something so terrible and finally she was glimpsing the Ralph she'd fallen in love with.

"Whatever you've done, or think you've done, Alice, I forgive you." His words were strong and sincere. "If you'll give me another chance, just one chance to prove myself to you, I will forgive you anything."

Anything? She didn't know if he would still think that if he knew the truth. Could she keep it to herself? Could she really move on and pretend like nothing had happened? Forever?

"Alice?"

She made herself meet his eyes. It looked like him again. More disheveled, rumpled around the edges, but not the bleary-eyed, vacant man he'd been since she'd arrived.

"What happened to you, Ralph?" Her words came out as a whisper. "Where did you go? And why are you back *now*?"

He pulled away from her, wiped at his eyes.

He was crying. Her husband was actually crying.

"I don't know, Alice," his voice cracked as he said her name. "I don't know how everything went so wrong, but I need help." He made a choking sound, sobbing quietly. "I just want someone to stop me from feeling like this."

She stayed silent. Seeing him like this, so fragile, it nearly broke her heart.

"Will you help me?" he asked.

"I'll help you, Ralph. But you need to let me in."

He reached for her hands, squeezed them against his.

"I think you should call in sick to work." He took a deep breath but didn't let her go. "I need you today, we need to be together."

She didn't need convincing about doing that. She had no idea how she was going to face Matthew again today, anyway. Just thinking about his lunch comments made her skin flush, then chill.

"Are we going to spend the day, just the two of us, like this?" she asked.

He smiled. The real smile she'd been waiting for. The smile that told her that maybe, just maybe, she had a chance at seeing her Ralph again. That he might come back to her.

"I need you to help me talk. I've been watching you this morning, fighting the need to drink, to lose myself to that dark hole again, but I don't want to. I don't want to do that anymore."

Alice could feel emotion building in her throat again, tears pricking her eyes.

"I am here for you, Ralph. I'm here."

She just wished she'd been here for him last night. Or maybe her leaving for the evening had forced him to see what he'd become.

"I need to tell you what went wrong. What happened to me?"

Alice needed a little time to herself. She needed a chance to breathe, to tell herself it was going to be okay.

"Ralph, could you go next door and ask to use the telephone? Tell my work I'm not feeling well today, and I'll stay here."

He smiled and dropped a kiss to her forehead.

"I won't be long."

She watched as he dressed, trying not to compare watching him to how she'd felt as Matthew put his clothes on.

Alice had to get rid of the coat. Forget what she'd done and believe in her husband.

Today, she was going to make her marriage work.

If anything, what she'd done last night had made her realize how badly she wanted a future with Ralph.

If he'd let her help him, she'd suffer through anything. If her Ralph was back, it would be worth it. She just needed to find out what was wrong with him and do everything she could to help them start over again.

# CHAPTER 24

There was no longer anything about Roy that Madeline liked. Nothing she could find about him that made her want to love him.

Her fingers fell to her belly, to touch the roundness of it, to feel the soft movement of her baby. As a girl, she'd hoped that as a pregnant woman she would have a husband who would place his hand over the stretched skin, wanting to feel the life they had created as it grew inside her. But now, even the thought of Roy touching her, of his skin on hers, made her nauseous.

It had been better, in a way, when they'd moved into their own place, even if was the size of a shoebox with drafts that she could imagine would chill to the bone in winter. Had they stayed, things might have remained good. They may never have had the passion and deep romance that other couples had, but they could have worked at it, and the future may have been a bright one.

They had little, but at least what they had was theirs.

Only they wouldn't have this for much longer.

She heard footsteps on the timber deck, then the door as it creaked. Madeline went back to stirring the stew, one hand rubbing gently at her back, easing the soft ache that seemed to plague her in the evening.

"Hi."

She looked up to see Roy as he hovered at the doorway. It still shocked her, seeing him like this. Nothing like he'd been in London. But then perhaps she just hadn't looked deep enough. It had all happened so quickly. And she'd talked herself into marrying him, into believing what he told her and leaving her family. She'd reasoned her way into it, convinced that she could make a go of it, when all along she'd had her doubts. She was paying a high price for it now.

"Dinner won't be far away."

He nodded and went down the hall to change his clothes.

There were times she didn't even want to talk to him. Wanted simply to think about the baby, or lose herself in work, or day-dream of seeing her parents once again. Her father's death had been a huge blow to her. She was still numb with the shock. Sometimes, it seemed unreal, even more so because she'd kept it to herself. She'd told Lauren and sworn her to secrecy because she didn't want Roy to know yet, which meant she was struggling with it on her own. She'd have to tell him about the telegram soon, but then he'd know she was stuck here and the thought made her blood run cold.

But part of her wondered if he didn't already know, somehow. Was that why he'd been so able to stick to his guns over their move back? He wouldn't budge an inch. It was silly, but she did wonder.

But she wouldn't let herself get stuck here. She might have to go back to the farm, but it wasn't going to be for long.

Madeline only had two more days of work before she was forced to quit, but she'd been putting money away, just small amounts. And once they were down to one wage, once they were back at the farm, she was going to be as frugal as a squirrel. She'd hide what was hers and would never say a word of the money she'd tucked away.

She'd scrimp and save on spending, even on things for the baby. She'd have to be careful, with the prying eyes of her in-laws, but she knew she could do it—she was good at balancing books.

She was going to save enough to sail back to London. Even if it took her years to save up, there was no way this baby was going to live here. Not with grandparents who would try to poison the child against its own mother. Not when she could offer her child a life with cousins and aunties who would love the child in England. Even if it did mean shaming herself by leaving her husband.

She no longer cared.

Somehow, she was going to leave. Going to run from this place and never look back.

Then what would Roy say? His mother might think she had all the control, but Madeline wasn't going to stand by and let them control her, not now she had a child's needs to put first.

She almost felt sorry for him. *Almost.*

But she knew she'd never regret leaving him.

Never.

# CHAPTER 25

Betty cleared her throat.

"Luke, I'm, ah, sorry to bother you."

He looked up, placed his cup down and stared at her. She was in danger of losing her confidence. Fast.

"Is your secretary back at work yet?" she managed to blurt out.

He looked up. "Oh, yes. She's been so busy since she got back. I completely forgot."

"So the offer still stands, then? For her to assist me?"

Luke stood, folded the paper, and swallowed the last of his coffee. He studied her for a moment, cup in hand.

"She's at your disposal. Come past later today."

"Could I come with you now, instead?"

He shook his head and shrugged on the jacket that had been over the back of his chair.

"Not necessary. Have Ivy bring you past later today."

Betty nodded, then twisted her hands together, trying not to fidget. He walked toward her, smiled curtly then went straight out the door.

She let out a whoosh of air. Asking him had been harder than she'd expected. Much harder. The atmosphere between them had been strange and awkward ever since the visit to his parents.

She went through to the kitchen.

"Did you ask him?" Ivy asked.

"Yes."

"Well? What did he say?"

Betty reached for an apple and let it roll about in her palm. "He said to come past later."

Ivy threw her hands in the air and rolled her eyes.

"So why the long face?"

"He wasn't friendly." Betty slumped down at the table and let her head fall gently against the cool of the timber.

She could feel Ivy standing behind her.

"Anyone else would think you were wishing for him to be sweet on you."

Ivy said the words with kindness, but the very thought made Betty feel sick. Made her insides curdle.

"You're wrong," she insisted.

Betty sat up straight.

"I'm just saying you seem awfully worried about how he looks at you, what he says, that sort of thing. Luke takes a while to trust. Give him time."

Ivy was right. She did need to give him time.

But was she right about her feelings toward him? She still loved Charlie. Didn't she? Charlie had been the best man she'd ever met. Charlie had lit up the room that first night she'd met him. Swept her off her feet.

*But Charlie was gone.*

Betty thumped her head down on the table into her hands.

"Don't carry on like a fool," Ivy scolded. "Now go get that baby up, and I'll take him to play with my daughter and her youngest.

You can stop at the office and start searching for these friends of yours without William making a fuss and distracting you."

❧

Betty was almost as excited as the day before they'd all arrived in America. That sense of adrenalin, of anticipation. Today, she was going to find her friends.

"Is this it?"

The driver nodded. "The large grey building here on the left."

Betty suddenly realized she had no idea at all what Luke did. How had he made his money? She'd just presumed it was in a family business. Charlie had never said anything about what his brother did, except that Luke made him look like the black sheep.

"What line of work is it that Mr. Olliver is involved in?" Betty asked her driver.

The car slowed and pulled into a vacant space. The driver turned around to look at her.

"Mr. Olliver is a State Senator, Ma'am."

*Oh.* It was as if an entire fleet of bricks had landed on her shoulders. A Senator? That was important, right? Wasn't he a little young? It did explain why he'd never served though. His job was obviously important enough to keep him here. But a Senator?

"So I just go in this building here?" she asked.

"You can't miss the entrance. See the flags up there?"

She smiled and stepped out onto the pavement.

"I'll be waiting here."

"Thank you," she said.

Betty clutched her hat with one hand to battle the wind, and held her skirt with the other. She'd gone from excited about the task at hand to suddenly terrified at even setting foot in the office.

The building looked ominous, with two large doors, both of which appeared too heavy to push.

Should she just go back to the car?

A hand to the small of her back stopped her. She spun around, and straight into Luke.

"Oh! I'm sorry, I just . . ." she stuttered.

"I remember my first day working here." His hand had dropped away, but he still stood close. "I know what it's like to be afraid to walk through those doors."

She couldn't look at him. So handsome, so imposing in his tailored suit. So . . . not her Charlie, she scolded herself.

He beckoned for her to follow, and held one door open for her to pass through.

"William is with Ivy?" Luke asked.

"Yes."

"I'm glad she's able to help you. I don't keep her very busy most of the time, so having you here must be a treat."

"I don't know about a treat, but I'm very pleased to have her."

She followed Luke as he strode down the passageway. It even smelled important in here.

"Come and meet my assistant, Jean. I'm certain she'll find those friends of yours."

"I hope so," Betty said, trying not to stare around her. The oak paneling was extensive and the desk appeared to be antique, with two large paintings hanging on the far wall.

"What do you say we go out for dinner tonight?" he asked.

Luke had stopped in the doorway. He leaned against it, watching her. She didn't know what to say. Did he mean a romantic dinner or something more platonic? Her heart picked up speed, nervous but excited at the same time.

"I'm not sure I can leave William that long." She also wasn't sure she could look at him again given the confusing thoughts she was having about him.

"I'll phone Ivy and let her know. Let's make it an early dinner, just around the corner."

Betty nodded. What else could she do?

"I'd like to hear more about your family, how you met Charlie. And hopefully you'll know more about your friends' whereabouts by then."

He disappeared through the door then, and she was left to wait for Jean.

༄

Betty had found her. She'd actually found June.

Well, more correctly, she'd found June's husband. She'd nervously phoned his office, and spoken to him, relieved that he remembered her. They spoke only briefly, as he was busy, but she'd given him Luke's address and phone number to pass on to June. She tried to contain a squeal of delight as she hung up the phone.

"Good news?"

Luke was in the room. She hadn't even seen him walk in.

"The card I had, my friend's husband, well, I just got in touch."

"Good," he said.

"No luck with the others yet, but Jean said she'd try again in the morning for me, to locate Alice."

"Shall we go?"

She'd almost forgotten about dinner. She ached to hold William, to feed him, but she didn't want to be rude.

"I won't keep you away from the little man for long," Luke assured her.

Was it that obvious?

"Come on."

He held her coat out and she reached back to slip it on. For a heartbeat, he watched her, and she watched him back.

Then he turned away and offered her his arm. Betty took it.

He was so unlike Charlie. Her man would have clasped her hand, been cheeky and put his arm around her waist. Tugged her in tighter, just as he had on their very first date.

Luke wasn't like that. He never would be. He was proper, more reserved.

But now, she almost wished he had taken her hand, even though she hated herself for even thinking it.

"I can see you're anxious," Luke observed.

Betty made her hand relax as it held the glass stem.

"I'm sorry."

"You want to get back to William. I understand."

She liked that he was polite about it, but did he really understand? With a mother like the one he'd grown up with, playing the part of a doting parent probably wasn't something he thought was normal.

"I take it Ivy's filled you in on my mother. Or should I say lack of mother."

What was with him and guessing her thoughts? "I'm starting to feel like you can read me as easily as a child's book."

Luke laughed. "You're honest, Betty. You wear your heart on your sleeve. I like that."

Had he ever thought less of her? That she wasn't going to be honest?

He beckoned the waiter over. "Two steaks, cooked medium."

The waiter nodded and took the menus.

"I hope you don't mind my ordering for both of us. The steak's good here. We can eat and then get straight home."

It was years since she'd had a steak at a restaurant. The war had reduced everything in her world to coupon rations. The food since she'd arrived in America had been wonderful, but this was special.

"Betty, I wanted to bring you out for dinner to apologize," Luke told her.

"For what?" She took a nervous sip of wine.

"I know you must have heard what Mother said that day. I should have brought it up earlier."

She gulped, spluttering her mouthful. Her skin burned with embarrassment.

"I, ah . . ."

"I don't mean to upset you. It just needed to be said."

She sat still as a statue.

"I don't enjoy my mother's company at the best of times. Charlie was more patient with her, which is why I wanted you to meet them. They would have visited sooner or later, but I digress."

She glanced down and took another delicate sip of her wine. She'd never tried it before, and it was starting to make her feel mildly giddy, but it was better than staring back at Luke.

"What I'm trying to say is that my mother is desperate for me to take a wife. Quite frankly, I'd rather be alone than end up with a woman like her. I don't mean to sound rude, but she is, well, how can I put this? Everything that a woman like you is not."

Betty didn't know whether to be insulted or flattered.

"I'm not sure if you meant that as a compliment or not." Betty surprised herself by finding her lost tongue.

"Oh, a compliment. Of course it was a compliment!"

She was embarrassed all over again. And confused.

"The way you are with William, your patience, the way you enjoy Ivy's company, those are all things that Charlie would have loved to see. You're a wonderful mother, Betty. I just don't want *my* mother to lure you to their country house, to try and turn you into something you're not. Or, even worse, try and take over William's upbringing herself. That's why I want to keep you with me. You and William, well, I've grown attached to you both since you arrived. More than you could ever realize."

Now Betty had tears in her eyes. She couldn't have asked him to open up more than he had. It meant a lot to her, especially as she could tell that talking like this didn't come naturally to him.

"I won't ever want to stay with your mother, Luke. I don't mean any disrespect, but I didn't exactly warm to her."

He stopped, took a long sip of his wine, and then sat back as two plates were placed in front of them. Betty eyed the steak with delight. It was huge. A slab of beef beside tiny potatoes and mushrooms, with a sauce drizzled over everything.

"This looks incredible," she said.

Luke gestured for her to start.

"Before Ivy came to live with me, I ate here almost every night," he confessed.

Betty smiled up at him before taking her first mouthful. The meat was like marshmallow on her tongue.

"Ivy cooks wonderful meals, but this *is* good."

Luke sat back for a moment.

"You know, you've dealt with Charlie's death extremely well."

She hesitated. Was this a trick question?

"I'm not so sure about that," she said.

He raised one eyebrow before cutting into his steak again.

"If you mean the brave face I put on every day, then I guess you're right. But the real me? She's the one crying every night into her pillow, holding her baby tight and whispering his father's name, so he never forgets it."

Luke smiled sadly. Was that what he'd wanted to hear?

"I like you, Betty. Please don't take my words the wrong way. I'm prone to saying the wrong thing to women."

It was like riding a wave with this man. One minute she was attracted to him, enamored by his company, the next, he seemed to question her intentions, to artfully interrogate her.

"I loved Charlie dearly, Luke. But he's gone, and I can either live in the past and wallow, or move forward." She matched his stare. "For the record, I choose the future."

"Good." He acted as if nothing untoward had been said between them. "To friendship."

Luke raised his glass. She swallowed her mouthful and did the same.

"To family," she said.

They clinked glasses, eyes locked.

"I'm pleased you're here, Betty. Truly I am."

She wasn't sure of her exact feelings, but she was grateful to him. And pleased that she wasn't alone.

The beat in her stomach that often hit when she was close to Luke had started to thump again, but she ignored it. He wasn't interested in her like that, and neither was she in him. They shared family, and friendship. Nothing more.

"So tell me about the plan to locate the rest of your friends?" he asked her.

She smiled at his words. Finally, a safe topic.

"Well, I'm hoping to see June in a few weeks' time. She and her husband are going on vacation until then. I guess the search is still going on for the other two."

Luke finished his meal, dabbed at his mouth with a napkin, and sat back in his chair, wine glass in hand.

"I look forward to meeting this June. Perhaps we could have her over to dinner one night with her husband? After you girls have had a chance to catch up with one another."

She nodded. Perhaps. But for now, she just wanted to see June again herself. Talk with her about what had happened, confide in her, hear about her own life here in America.

Her friendship with the other girls was something she craved so much it hurt.

# CHAPTER 26

It was like she'd suddenly emerged from a dark and disastrous nightmare. Every time Alice raised her head, looked at her husband, walked into her house, her life seemed to have no resemblance to the past months since she'd arrived. The home that had once felt small, cold, and unloved now had an energy about it she relished. She rose early to fling the drapes wide open, letting sun fill the rooms with warmth. She was gathering flowers from their tiny garden for the table, baking for the joy of the aroma it sent through the house. She loved that it was the weekend, because it meant she didn't have to feel guilty about skipping work so she could stay and spend time with her husband.

And Ralph. Oh, Ralph! Her man was back and she loved him so much that it made her heart melt. It wasn't easy, and she was spending so much of her time caring for him and understanding the stress he'd endured, but he was fighting for their marriage as hard as she was and that was all that mattered to her. It made her love him more, that they were finally united, a real husband and wife. After all this time she was so pleased to have a second chance to make things work between them, and she'd realized that she didn't need to be pampered, she just needed to be loved.

There were so many things that still needed to be said, so much to do to set things right, but they would make it. She just knew they would. And Ralph was due home any moment. She checked the oven and set the timer to alert her in a few more minutes. She was making a savory pie, chicken and vegetable, like he used to love in London but couldn't get here.

"Honey, you home?"

Alice felt her heart thud as she heard Ralph's voice. In a week she'd gone from resenting his every movement to aching to hold him near.

"In the kitchen," she called back.

She turned the timer off and took the pie from the oven. If she didn't take it out now she'd have to interrupt her husband, and she wanted to hear everything about his day.

He hadn't touched alcohol since the morning they'd lain in bed together talking, but it had been hard, so hard on him to not touch the bottle again. She'd witnessed his struggle over the past ten days, had seen the physical symptoms of his withdrawal. His strength in this hard battle meant she wanted to give him all her love and undivided attention to help him through. She no longer cared about anything other than their happiness—she'd willingly go without so many things she'd once thought important if it meant seeing Ralph like this.

"Hello, sweetheart."

Ralph reached for her face and kissed her on the lips. She closed her eyes and just breathed in the smell of him. When he released her they just watched one another, before she stepped back, face flushed.

"How was your day?" she asked.

He grinned before flopping down in a chair at their tiny kitchen table.

"He's going to let me know by the end of the week."

Alice nodded. "Well, that sounds promising, right?"

Ralph smiled back at her. "He knew my father, so I think that'll help."

She didn't say anything. She still didn't know what had happened in Ralph's family and had been too scared of upsetting him to ask him further.

"I know I said I wanted to make it on my own, but if my family name helps me to get a foot in the door, I'd be a fool to turn it down." He undid his tie and put his feet up on the other chair. "His son had a similar posting to mine in Europe during the war, so who knows? That might help more than anything."

Alice held her tongue. She could see he was trying to be brave but was also worried, and they needed the money so badly. But he was doing his best, and she knew it was going to happen for him. It just had to.

"Darling, I'm not sure if this is good news for you or not, but there was a message from our neighbors that your mother phoned. She's coming to stay in a month's time."

Ralph's face was hard to read. "Oh."

Alice walked around the table to him and touched his shoulder. "I'm sorry, I didn't mean to . . ."

He grabbed her waist and made her fall into his lap.

She sighed happily at the smile on his face.

"I know you want everything to be perfect, that you're worried about me, but I'm fine, Alice. You don't have to act like I'm broken, not anymore. I guess I should be pleased that she's seeing me like this instead of how I was a couple of weeks ago."

She braved a look into his eyes. That's exactly what she feared, *that he could break if she said the wrong thing.* That this perfect little bubble could shatter as fast as it had formed.

251

"I'm not going back, Alice. I was in a bad place. I can't go back there."

"I know, Ralph, I know, it's just . . ."

"What?" he asked.

Ralph watched her and she didn't say a thing.

"What, Alice?"

"I know you've been through hard times, but I don't understand how a man like you, the man I know you to be, could have fallen like that. I mean, I just don't understand."

There, she'd said it. It was like a gust of wind had been expelled from her lungs, relieving her of keeping it captive.

He looked down at her, took a deep breath then kissed her forehead.

"Why don't you serve dinner up while I get changed, then I'll explain."

Alice felt numb. She nodded and rose, walking over on stiff legs to cut the pie.

When she looked back he'd already disappeared. He'd sounded genuine enough, like he didn't mind what she'd said, but it was the glass theory again. Had she pushed too hard and made it crack?

"Honey, this pie is fantastic."

Alice smiled up at Ralph and placed a forkful in her mouth. It was good, but the pie wasn't what she wanted to be talking about.

Maybe she needed to start things, talk about what she'd decided today. It might help him open up. Besides, if she didn't address the fact that she'd called in sick every day over the past week to work, he was going to start to wonder.

"Ralph, I've been doing a lot of thinking the past few days and . . ."

"No!" He dropped his fork with a clatter. "I know I've been difficult Alice, but I'll get a job soon. We're going to be okay—please don't go back. Not yet."

What? "Go back where, to work?"

Now he looked confused. "Home, Alice. I don't want you to leave me to go back home."

A smile lit her face. "Ralph, I'm not leaving you, silly."

Relief was clear in his eyes. "You're not?"

She picked up his fork and put it back in his hand with a chuckle. "What I was going to say was that I want to hand my notice in at work. As soon as you find out whether you have the job you applied for today, I want to leave."

He nodded. He probably would have agreed to anything right now so long as she didn't ask his permission to leave the country!

"I know you didn't ever expect to work like this, Alice. I'm sorry, I truly am. Once I'm working there's no need for you to continue."

She flapped her hand at him. "It's not that I don't want to work, Ralph, it's just that I want to enjoy what I do."

"So you want to keep working?" He looked confused.

"I want to start nursing again, Ralph." She smiled shyly. "I know it will mean retraining over here, but I want to help people. I want to do something worthwhile."

He finished his mouthful and put down his knife and fork, gently this time. "That's a great idea."

She could see in his face that he meant it.

"If you hadn't been nursing in London, I never would have met you. You were great at it then and I'm sure you'll make a great nurse here."

"Are you sure?" she asked, needing his support.

He reached for her hand and squeezed it. "You'll make a fine nurse, here, Alice. I'm so proud of you." Her heart swelled from his words but her mind betrayed her. She could see Matthew sneering at her, could see his face swirling in her thoughts. Remembering what they'd done together made her sick.

She did want to nurse again, but she also wanted to run as far from her boss as possible. And that meant handing her notice in, making up an excuse, and never looking back. Leaving that world, and her affair, behind her. Burning the fur coat or smuggling it back to him, so she didn't owe him anything, not a penny.

"Alice?"

She looked up to see Ralph watching her.

"Did I tell you about my family's publishing company before we got married?"

She couldn't remember exactly what he'd told her, but he'd mentioned bits and pieces about it. "Why don't you start at the beginning?" she suggested.

He squeezed her hand again then sat back in his chair.

"All my life we've had money. Been well off."

Alice placed her own utensils down and settled in her chair to listen. She'd been waiting a long time to hear this story and didn't want to miss a word.

"My grandfather started a publishing company here in New York, but my father never wanted to join the family business. To cut a long story short, a manager was appointed, and my family lived off a trust fund."

He leaned further back, his chair on two legs, eyes on the table. Alice wished he'd look at her, but he seemed to find it easier avoiding her eyes.

"I wasn't my father's son. My mother always said I was just like my granddad, but he died when I was a boy." He took a deep breath. "I spent all my life, right through school, wanting to join the family business. I didn't want to live off the funds, I wanted to run the place, build on what my grandfather had started. I loved books, and I loved the publishing business too."

"So what happened?"

"I spent every summer working in the company, doing anything and everything, learning whatever I could. When the manager handed in his resignation, a meeting was held, and I was given a probationary management position." Ralph paused. "I know what you're thinking, I was young, but I did well. The company did well." Alice didn't know what to say. When had things gone wrong?

"When war was declared, I thought I was going to be safe. Well, you know, that my job meant that I wouldn't be called up, but my father was having none of it. He told me that I had to fight, that choosing my job over volunteering was turning my back on my country."

It was a story Alice had heard before, from other young men when she'd been nursing, from her mother's friends. A story that usually ended up with a heartbroken wife or mother, and a dead young man.

"So I resisted to start with, then eventually gave in. The board of trustees appointed a new manager, and I went off to war."

"You seemed so confident in your position, like you were destined to be a success in the army." When she'd met him he seemed to fit the role with ease.

Ralph agreed. "I was good, I got on with the other men and I proved myself. I was the first of my age to be promoted."

Alice smiled at him.

"And I met you, so who's complaining?" he said.

The pain making his face crack told her otherwise. He'd lost a lot, something he'd wished for his entire life, because of the war. And something had gone wrong, seriously wrong, because she'd never heard him even speak about the company since her arrival. And they certainly didn't have a trust fund to live off now.

"I survived the war, Alice, and I found you, but what had kept me going was knowing what I had to come home to. I didn't blame my father. He was no different than plenty of other fathers out there."

"But?" she asked.

"But when I got home, the life I'd known, the life that had kept me going all that time, over the years, had disappeared."

They sat in silence. Alice wanted to hear more, but Ralph was just staring into space, like he was seeing it all over again in his mind.

"What happened to the business, Ralph?" she asked.

He laughed. A cold, sad laugh that gave her goose pimples.

"I came home to an empty trust fund, a business run into the ground and facing bankruptcy due to bad management, and a father on his death bed."

Alice kept her eyes down and swallowed. There was more, she could hear it in his tone.

"I did everything I could, but nothing could save the business. I was home in time to see the notice put on the door, announcing the foreclosure. There was so much debt owing that the building was sold to pay our creditors. We hadn't turned a profit in over a year, and there was nothing left in the accounts.

"The worst thing was knowing I could have prevented it. My father was a kind man, he never did me wrong, but he wasn't a businessman, that was my grandfather. When I got home, he just shook his head and blamed the recession, but he was wrong. I know I could have made it work, I could have kept the place going for my own sons. But I never got that chance." He blew out a big breath. "The entire time I'd been away, I'd hung onto the memory of coming home, of knowing I had a business and a life outside of the Army. But I never imagined how I could feel, what it would be like losing so much and coping with the things I'd seen away fighting. Maybe if I'd had you here from the start things would have been better, and I could have coped for you, but with every month that passed I got worse and it was easier just to drink and make it all go away."

"And then things got worse?" Alice's voice was soft, low. She didn't know if there was anything else left to say.

"My father died the same week the business closed, and after the funeral my mother left to live with her sister. It was like I lost my future, my family, my destiny, all in that first week home." He sighed. "I should be so grateful that I even made it home and that I have all my limbs. But the fact that I was alive just wasn't enough to help me through the darkness."

He made a fist and hit the table, enough to make a bang but restrained enough not to scare her.

"I didn't know when you were coming, where we were going to live, how I was even going to provide for you. I had it in my head that you'd take one look at me, the loser with nothing to his name, and turn around. Go back the way you'd come and I'd never see you again. That you'd think I'd lied to you, that I'd lived a lie while I was with you in London."

She didn't know what to say. All she knew was that she hadn't been able to turn her back on him, not completely, even when she'd wished she could.

"But you didn't leave me," he whispered. "I know you wanted to, I know I disappointed you, but you didn't leave me."

She reached for him across the table and smiled as his big hands clasped her wrists.

"I just wish you'd told me all this from the start. I would have understood, Ralph. I would have tried to help you."

"If I hadn't started drinking, if I'd just kept trying to get a job, kept trying to make something of myself, maybe it wouldn't have been so hard on you."

"What matters is what we do now. We can make this work," she told him.

"I know we can, Alice. Because I love you, and I'm not going to disappoint you again."

She closed her eyes for a heartbeat and smiled up at him.

"I think half my problem is not having anyone else here, no one to talk to. No friends," she confessed.

"I know how that feels. I lost touch with all my school buddies when I enlisted, and half my soldier friends either didn't make it home or live in different states." He shook his head. "I never meant for you to feel so lonely here. I never meant to drink. I . . ." He paused. "I'm so sorry, sweetheart. I never asked you how you were settling in, heck, I never helped you at all. I don't even know if you've made any friends here or not."

"Let's not talk about what we could have done, Ralph, let's just think about the future, okay? I met some great girls on the ship here, and I just need to find them."

"You're going to make a wonderful nurse again, Alice, you know that?"

"And you are going to make your granddad proud and start a publishing company of your own one day. Promise me that, Ralph Jones."

He winked at her. A kind, trusting, loving wink. Not the sleazy, knowing wink her boss and one-time lover had liked to throw her way. This one made her feel loved, like they were on the same team.

"Whatever happened in the past is going to stay there," he said. "We have a future together, a future and a family to look forward to one day."

She grinned at him.

"Are we starting over?" she asked.

"Let's just say we're going to do our best to forget the past few months. I wouldn't forget the time we spent together in London for anything."

He pulled her in for a kiss across the table, but his finger reached for her necklace before he kissed her.

"You're wearing the necklace again."

She smiled.

"You remember the day I gave this to you?"

Of course she did. That's why she'd put it on again this morning.

"I could never forget that day, Ralph. Not for as long as I live."

# CHAPTER 27

The drive to the farm was worse than Madeline had imagined, even with her tiny baby girl tucked against her chest.

The baby had arrived two weeks early, which meant she'd had three days in their old house as a mother before they'd had to pack the last of their belongings and go. She'd been in the hospital, surrounded by strangers, and all she'd thought about was how much she'd have preferred to give birth like Betty had, surrounded by people who'd genuinely cared for and loved her. The birth had been as painful as she'd imagined it would be, but she'd known what to expect from her sisters, and the overwhelming sense of love she'd felt at holding her baby for the first time had made it all worth it.

But her heart still felt shattered. Torn into a thousand pieces when she so much as thought about her father. About the funeral she'd missed, the chance to say goodbye to him alongside their family and friends, and that she'd left it too late to ask him for help.

Most of all, she regretted ever coming here. How could she have ever thought it possible to live in a foreign country, with no family, and expect to be happy?

And then she was faced with her heart mending, each piece fitting back into place, every time she looked at her child.

Charlotte's tiny hands, dark blue eyes, smattering of hair, and elfin features made her fall even deeper in love every day, with every gaze, every smile.

Only to break all over again when she thought of her child's father. *Of her husband.*

It was a vicious cycle, only made worse by the hatred she developed every day when she thought about her Roy. About what he had done, behind her back, and the life he was trying to force upon her. And now, the way he was with his daughter—like he couldn't care less for her.

"Can you make her stop fussing?" Roy said, his grumpy voice interrupting her thoughts. "I'm trying to drive here."

Madeline didn't answer, just patted Charlotte on the back to soothe her and pressed a kiss to her forehead.

Roy suddenly chuckled. "You know, I've been wishing we had a boy this whole time, but she'll still be an extra pair of hands to help out once she's bigger."

Madeline shuddered, her entire body covered in goose pimples at the thought of her darling daughter being worked on the farm.

*She hated him.*

There was no longer room for pity in her heart, for trying to understand why he'd done this. No longer even room for sadness. Only an anger that grew hour upon hour, that made her so bitter she wanted to scream from the cruelness of it all.

"Well, look who we have here."

Madeline tried to ignore the cruel taunt. There was a nasty, gleeful edge in her mother-in-law's voice that she didn't want to engage with. Not when she was still trying to hold on to the life she'd just given up and keep her morale up to plan her escape.

"Not so high and mighty now, are we?"

Madeline swallowed the lump in her throat. Why would she be so cruel? *How?* What would possess a woman to be so heartless? Madeline kept her head held high. It was obvious from his silence that Roy wasn't going to stick up for her. He'd been cold and indifferent ever since the baby was born, and she'd given up the slim thread of hope that fatherhood would change him.

She held Charlotte tight, not letting Roy's family so much as glimpse her. They hadn't met their granddaughter before, and Madeline wished they'd never been given the opportunity to.

"Did you hear me girl?" Her mother-in-law called. "Not so much better than us now, not with your Daddy dead. You'll never get back on that ship. You hear me?"

Her feet did stop then. Her shoes stuck like glue on the tatty brown grass. *How did she know?* Madeline had told no one about her father, had purposefully kept it a secret so Roy's family had no leverage over her. Despite her suspicions that Roy knew something, she had no concrete proof and he hadn't alluded to it.

Madeline turned, Charlotte still cradled firmly in her arms, as if she could somehow draw strength from her.

"I don't know what you're talking about." Her voice shook and she could feel the tremble of her lower lip, but she needed to try and call this evil woman's bluff.

Roy stood still, watching. Her mother-in-law glared at her, eyes shining, enjoying the scene, and her sister-in-law just smirked.

"Ah, that got your attention, did it?" said Sarah.

Madeline focused on the cool exhale of her breath, in and out, as her lungs worked. Just keep breathing, she told herself. Stay calm. The silly old woman couldn't know. She was just trying to taunt her, play cruel mind games.

"I read every letter, you know. Every one," she crowed. "And your sister's last letter, well that came here too."

She felt like she was being dragged beneath water. Drowning slowly, blackness all around her. It couldn't be. No. *Please, Lord, no.*

Madeline shut her eyes, tried to control her fear. Her anger. So her sister had written to her at this address, must have wanted her to know what had happened, to share her grief, and this horrible woman had taken that privacy away from her as well.

"I said I don't know what you're talking about," she repeated. Only this time she could hear the weakness of her tone, the raspy whisper of her voice that sounded like it was being dragged over gravel.

"He wrote to you. I even knew he was sick. But you missed your chance. And now he's gone." Sarah delivered this last sentence with a cruel smile.

Madeline ran. She couldn't do anything else. She ran into the house, through the kitchen, into their old bedroom. She didn't know where else to go.

The crow of laughter from outside still seemed to find her. The triumphant signal of her mother-in-law, knowing that she'd succeeded in keeping Madeline here.

She looked down at Charlotte, at her sweet, innocent face.

Had she not gotten pregnant, maybe Roy's family would have been pleased to see the back of her. They'd made their feelings about a foreigner clear. But now? She was under no illusions what they wanted. Their son and their grandchild.

Well, they could have Roy, but they weren't getting their hands on her little girl.

Not while she still had air in her lungs and fight in her body.

She wouldn't let them so much as touch her.

But she would find the letters. If the old biddy hadn't burned them yet, she was going to find them. Pour over them, remind herself of who was waiting at home for her, and then she was going to figure out just how she was going to get back there.

*Because she would.* And no one, not her husband, and certainly not her mother-in-law, was going to stop her.

All this time she'd thought her family hadn't wanted to write to her. That they'd been too busy, were annoyed at her for leaving them. She wondered if her letter telling them to use her work address had gone astray and been delayed until it was too late. She'd never even guessed her father could be sick—he'd been the picture of health when she'd left.

She'd also never considered the lengths a bitter old lady could go to ruin her daughter-in-law's life.

# CHAPTER 28

She hadn't expected there to be so many, when Sarah spitefully showed her the treasure trove she'd intercepted. Letter upon letter, all addressed to her in either her father's spidery hand, or her mother's even, perfect prose. Even her sister had written to her.

Asking why she never responded to their questions. Wondering why she acted like she'd never received mail from them, when they'd written to her week after week.

It made her feel cold. *Dead.*

Charlotte started to snuffle and make a feeble cry, but Madeline couldn't rise. How could she do anything when she now knew that her father had died, unsure if his beloved daughter was safe and happy.

And perhaps worst of all, telling her he would bring her home before he died. That if something was wrong, if she wanted to come back, for whatever reason, he would bring her. Now her family had lost her father's income, she couldn't ask her mother to spend so much to bring her home when they suddenly had so little. She'd never been the one who'd offered it anyway: it was her father who'd said he'd move heaven and earth to get her back if he had to. She was as good as on her own.

Her in-laws had known her father was on his sickbed, that he'd been unwell for months, and they hadn't bothered to tell her. *Had purposely kept it from her.*

They'd passed her the odd letter, early on, just to stop her from being suspicious, but now she realized how stupid she'd been. Between her job, the pregnancy, the stress of moving house, and then life as a mother, she'd worried herself sick but not really thought it through.

In hindsight, she should have known.

But it was all very well being able to wish on something passed.

She walked over to scoop Charlotte up in one arm, still holding one of the letters in her other hand.

This only made her more determined to go, to leave this god-forsaken place, but she just didn't have enough money. Not even close to enough, not after buying all the things they'd needed for the baby.

And it wasn't like she could go and get a job somewhere. Not living all the way out here, and with a newborn baby in tow.

It was probably one of the reasons they'd wanted her back here. To keep her under lock and key, away from the world, under their control.

It also explained why Roy had become so cold.

They'd obviously waited until the time was right. Waited until they knew she couldn't do anything about it, that she was trapped. To make sure that when they told him that his wife had the option to return home, it would hurt him the most. That he'd agree to this plan. It had to be the reason he'd been so confident that she wouldn't leave, because he'd known for weeks now that her lifeline to going back to England had disappeared.

She sat back in the old rocking chair in their room to feed Charlotte. The letter fell to the floor and she didn't bother to retrieve it. Her eyes followed it though, thinking, knowing there was something she could do.

*Betty.*

Maybe Betty could help her.

Betty had a child, she'd know the way it changed a woman, how suddenly all you cared about was the little person whose life depended on you. Surely Betty would help her?

She could go into town tomorrow, use the telephone at the post office, and find Betty.

Madeline had probably missed other get-togethers between the girls, but if she could track her down, maybe it would be her salvation.

All those girls would be there for her, would understand why she had to leave. Why hadn't she just tried to find them from the start? Instead of wishing to see them, thinking about her friends, and doing nothing about it. Lauren had been a great friend when she'd needed someone, but only another war bride, one of the girls who had come over here and gone through what she had, could ever truly understand.

She could see if Betty was able to help her arrange transportation, stay with her perhaps, and try to work out a plan. She just needed the right excuse to go into town for an excursion, perhaps to purchase something necessary for Charlotte, then there wouldn't be any fuss.

They needn't know she was going to stay with Betty, not until she'd gone. She could leave a note, disappear while no one was about, and take time to clear her head. By the time Roy realized where she was, he wouldn't be able to do anything about it.

If only Betty was prepared to help.

ᠺᢣ

Madeline's plan had been easier to execute than she'd expected. Aside from a sneer from her mother-in-law, she'd managed to slip out of the house easily enough. She'd learned to drive while helping at her father's shop, so she chugged away in the old car, making her way into town.

She hadn't considered taking the car and driving straight to Betty's with it. She could disappear with Charlotte and still technically be just a mother vacationing with a friend. Taking the car would be theft.

She parked and went into the post office, carrying Charlotte. The lady behind the counter was friendly and helped her to find the right number for an Olliver living in the city. The man's initials were wrong, but it was the only Olliver with two L's.

If it wasn't Betty, if this number didn't get her in touch with her friend, there would be nothing left for her to do. No hope. Nothing.

The phone rang five times. *Five slow, painful rings.* She was sure no one was going to answer. After driving all the way in, desperate to talk to Betty, no one was going to be there. She wouldn't even know if it was the right number if no one answered.

On the eighth ring, she'd lost hope. One more, she whispered to herself. Just one more ring . . .

"Olliver residence."

A breathless American voice rang out down the line.

*It wasn't Betty.*

Madeline started to sob. She couldn't help it.

"Hello? Who's there?"

"Madeline. It's Madeline Walker here," she managed.

"Madeline! Oh, Madeline, I've heard all about you. What's wrong?"

It didn't help her crying any to have this kind voice acknowledge her. Months of holding it all in, and now she was blubbering like a child to a complete stranger over the phone.

"My dear, I'm Ivy. I run the household here."

"Ivy, I need to talk to Betty. Please," Madeline sobbed.

"Are you sure you're all right?"

"I need Betty," she whispered.

She listened as Ivy hollered out to Betty.

"She's coming, my dear."

Ivy had a lovely, soft motherly tone, which only made Madeline want to cry more.

Then Betty's breathless voice was on the line. "Mads? Madeline, is that you? What's wrong?"

That made her cry all over again.

"Madeline, talk to me."

"I need to come and stay. Please." Her words were no more than a whisper again. "I need help, Betty."

"Of course. When? What's happened?"

"I just need to get away. Away from Roy. Away from them all." She took a deep breath. "My father died, we've moved back in with his parents. Please Betty, I need your help. I've got a baby now. I need you."

"A baby? Oh Madeline, a baby!"

She held Charlotte tight but she didn't want to talk about her, not yet. Not here.

"I need you to help me get out of here," Madeline said. "Please."

"Can you get here?" Betty asked.

Madeline shook her head, before remembering Betty couldn't see her. "No."

"I'll send a car. When can you be ready?"

"Any day," Madeline mumbled. "But it needs to be soon, I can't stand it much longer."

"The day after tomorrow, then?" Betty asked.

"It'll need to be very early in the morning, or late. I need to get out without them knowing."

"It's going to be all right, Madeline. I promise. Everything will be fine once you're here. I can do this for you. Just tell me your address and I won't let you down."

The teller was waving to her. Her time was almost up. "I have to go, Betty," she said. "I don't know what I'd have done if I hadn't got in touch with you."

Betty's tone made her want to cry all over again.

"I know what it's like, Mads. Believe me. I'm here for you. I'll have a car waiting early in the morning, day after next. Quick, give me the address."

"Okay." Relief made her shoulders sink, like she could hardly hold them up. She gave her the details.

"Oh and Madeline?"

She was still listening.

"I've found June. She might even be here before you arrive."

Then the phone line went dead, but it didn't matter. She was going to be with her friends again. They would help her.

*Help her to escape.*

She was going to take all the money from her account, just in case she needed it. Tomorrow night, she would pack her bag and hide it under the bed. She couldn't take much, they didn't have many large bags, but that was the least of her worries.

If Betty could help her, could help her figure out what she needed to do, then she might never come back here.

She hoped not.

But then she had that little problem of not having enough money.

Maybe Betty could come up with a plan to get around that.

*She hoped so.*

270

# CHAPTER 29

It was hell. Pure hell. There was no other way to describe it.

*But it was about to end.*

Charlotte was unhappy, her crying earlier had told her the baby wasn't content, but now wasn't the time for her to worry about a little unhappiness.

Now was the time to plot her escape.

She quickly put pen to paper.

*Roy.*
*Please don't be alarmed, but I had to get out of the house. My friend Betty has kindly agreed to take me to her home, for some rest and recovery.*
*I will be home within a few days.*
*Love always,*
*Madeline.*

The few days apart and the loving marked her as a liar, but she wanted him to be at ease. Yes, he'd be annoyed that she'd gone but there was no way to avoid that. If she asked his permission he would outright refuse.

It could take months, if not longer, before she could secure passage back home. She just needed some breathing space, to try and figure out what she was going to do, in a place where Roy and his family couldn't find her.

Headlights flooded the front yard.

The car was early.

Madeline reached for her single bag, slung it over her shoulder, Charlotte in the other arm, and hurried as fast as she could.

She dropped the letter on to the kitchen table and slipped quickly out of the door and across the porch.

The driver opened the door for her and went to take her bag.

"Quick! Just throw it in with me," Madeline told him urgently.

She could see a light on back at the house now. Someone was up.

The driver gave her a peculiar look but didn't argue. He thrust the bag onto the seat beside her, shut the door and got behind the wheel.

"I'm sorry, but we need to get out of here. Fast," said Madeline, panic rising in her throat.

He nodded and turned the car around.

Madeline looked back and saw a figure appear on the porch. The hanging light showed the silhouette to be a woman's.

The car surged out of the drive, and a gurgle of relief escaped from her throat as she felt tears start to fall down her cheeks.

She never, ever wanted to come back here.

She closed her eyes, held her baby tight, and prayed.

*Please God, take me home. Take me back to my family.*

# CHAPTER 30

Any minute now.

Betty couldn't stop herself, she had to keep pacing. She had her eyes locked on the window.

Any minute now and her friends would be arriving.

She hadn't spoken to June on the phone, only Madeline. But she'd received a message from June's husband saying that he'd hardly been able to contain his wife's excitement, and that she would be there before noon.

It was half past eleven already. Madeline should be here by now with June right behind her.

Nine months since she'd seen them. Nine months! How had that much time passed since they'd been together?

She heard a noise.

Then a car appeared at the end of the driveway, winding slowly up toward the house. It wasn't the car she'd sent to fetch Madeline, so it could only be one person.

June was here!

"Ivy, Ivy! She's here!" Betty called out.

"Well what are you waiting for? Get out there," Ivy said, smiling. It was good to see Betty so excited.

Betty ran through the hall and to the front door. She swung it open, desperate to set eyes upon her friend again.

"Betty!" June ran toward her, disregarding the gravel and running as fast as her heels would allow.

"Oh, Betty!"

They threw their arms around one another. June felt warm and plump.

"Look at you, huh? You look wonderful," said Betty, drawing back and taking in her friend's glowing face.

June grinned and linked arms with her. It felt so good to be shoulder-to-shoulder with a friend from the ship.

"This place is beautiful. You never told me Charlie was so well off."

Betty just turned them both around to face the door and walked her friend inside. *She'd* never known Charlie was this well off, but then she'd have given up all the money to have him here instead. A lump rose in her throat. It was going to be more difficult than she'd thought to tell them about what had happened.

"Fancy a cuppa?" she said to June, changing the subject.

June gave her a gentle push away. "Don't I wish? A real cuppa from back home."

"Ivy!" called Betty.

She appeared from the kitchen, tea towel in hand and a big smile on her face.

"Ready for your cup of tay, girls?"

Betty giggled and tugged June along.

"How did you teach an American to speak like that?" June teased.

"Ivy, meet my friend June."

Ivy grinned at them. "Pleased to finally meet you."

Betty linked arms with June again.

"We'll take it out in the garden, if that's okay with you Ivy?"

Ivy gave them a wink and disappeared again.

"You have got it good, girl," June said, hugging her tight.

Betty didn't want to burst the bubble. To tell June the truth. But she needed to confide in her, needed to talk to her about what had happened. And she wanted her tell her before Madeline arrived, now that they had a few moments together.

"How's your husband, June? He sounded lovely on the phone. So kind. And that day when we arrived and he offered to help me . . ."

"Oh, Betty, he *is* divine. So brilliant." June's eyes shone brightly. "I just love it here. I miss home, but he's just the best. His whole family are the best."

Betty led her to the little outdoor table in the garden and pulled out two seats. She knew how idyllic it must look. It almost seemed a shame to ruin the moment.

"So how about you? Could you be any happier? And where was your Charlie that day? Naughty boy keeping you waiting like that."

Betty looked down. Didn't know quite how to say it, what to say to her friend.

"June, that day, when I was waiting for Charlie . . ."

Ivy appeared then with a tray of tea and cookies.

"Here we go, girls. Tea, cookies, and even scones." Ivy laughed. "Did I say it right?"

"Oooh, can I take her home with me?" June grabbed hold of Ivy's hand like she was never going to let her go.

Ivy swatted at them and left them be, chuckling to herself as she walked away.

"Ivy has been my savior," she told June. "Seriously, I don't know what I would have done without her."

June bit into a scone and closed her eyes. "This is so good. Don't ever let her go. I can't believe you have a live-in help!"

Betty knew she had to press on, difficult as it was to break the jubilant atmosphere. "June, I had some bad news that day."

June swallowed her mouthful and leaned forward. "You mean the day we arrived, when Charlie was late? You're not still angry at him about that are you?"

Tears swam in Betty's eyes, emotion like she hadn't felt since that day when their ship had docked bubbling up in her throat, clouding her mind. Why was it so hard to say it? To admit that Charlie was gone, even after all this time?

"He wasn't late, June." She tried to keep her voice steady.

June reached out to hold her hand. "What, honey? Was it William? Where is the little man?"

"It's Charlie. He's dead, June." Her voice reduced to a whisper. "Charlie's dead. He was gone before I even arrived here."

June jumped from her chair and ran to Betty's side of the table, throwing her arms around her and bursting into tears herself.

"He can't be. Betty, no!"

She nodded as June gulped and hiccupped. Seeing her friend so upset made her stronger, made her calmer.

"He was dead before I even left London," she told him. "His family had tried to send me a message, to tell me, but I'd already left."

Betty held her, until the tears had started to ebb, and June straightened herself.

"So is this his parents' home?" she asked.

Betty shook her head. "His brother's, actually. Luke."

"Well that's nice, isn't it? I mean, it's not nice, it's awful, but, well you know what I mean."

"I think I'm falling in love with him." Betty sobbed out the words, admitting for the first time how she felt about Luke.

Her whole body started shaking. She'd said it. And didn't just like Luke, she wasn't just attracted to him, *she had fallen in love with him.*

"Oh, darling. You're just confused. With Charlie gone, and little William to care for . . ."

Betty squeezed her eyes shut and leaned deeper into June's embrace. "I'm sorry, I thought I'd be all right telling you. I guess it's just all caught up on me. I shouldn't have said it."

June stood, patted Betty's back and returned to her chair.

"I always thought you were the one who would be happy. I was so worried about my own marriage, what my new family would be like, but from your stories, I thought it was you and Charlie who would be truly happy. I'm sorry, Betty, I truly am."

When they'd been on the ship, Betty would have said the same. She'd been so confident about her marriage. If anyone was going to have a life-long love, it would have been her and Charlie. And now here she was a widow, with her mind and heart filled with love for her dead husband's brother.

What she needed was to take her mind off Luke and hear more about June. She wouldn't be able to get through the day ahead feeling so fraught, and she needed to be strong for whatever Madeline had gone through.

"As long as you're happy, June, I'm happy. Tell me Eddie's wonderful, please tell me he hasn't let you down?"

A dreamy look crossed June's face, like no matter how hard she tried her eyes had to light up just at the mention of her husband's name. "Eddie's the best. More than I could ever have hoped for. I'm so lucky."

"I'm happy for you, June, I really am." She couldn't stop the fresh flood of tears that filled her eyes though.

"Did you mean what you said before? About your brother-in-law?" June whispered.

Betty nodded, knowing it was the truth.

"Worse things could happen, Betty. Don't feel bad. You deserve to be happy, no one is going to judge you."

She suddenly didn't want to talk about it.

"I can't believe I forgot to tell you," Betty said, changing the subject.

June bent forward. "Tell me what?"

"I found Madeline." She watched as a smile lit June's face. "She's not in a good way, but she's got a baby, can you believe it?"

June's face seemed suddenly sad, but Betty wondered if she'd misread her expression.

"A baby, so soon?"

"And we're going to be seeing them both today! She was meant to get here just after you."

June clapped her hands together in delight. "What about Alice? Or do you think she's forgotten all about us by now?"

Betty sighed. "I hope not. She'll be all wrapped in furs and living in some gorgeous house. They probably go to parties all the time and have glamorous friends."

"Betty, I think your other friend is here!" Ivy called out from the house.

She jumped to her feet as her housekeeper walked toward them with William on her hip.

"Coming?" Betty asked.

June shook her head. "I'll stay here with William, I think," she said as Ivy placed him down on the rug. "He's such a darling boy, I need to soak up my time with him."

Betty watched as he crawled around. He was so fast as he moved over the lawn then tried to pull himself up to stand, so close to walking now.

"I'll be back soon," she said, and set off to welcome Madeline.

❦

Betty hadn't been prepared for being reunited with the girls. Now that she was faced with it, seeing June and then knowing she was about to see Madeline . . . she hadn't realized how much she'd missed them.

"Mads!" Betty called out, holding up her skirt so she could run to the car. "Madeline!"

Madeline turned, slowly, her body angled toward Betty. The sight made Betty stop in her tracks, her shoes skidding on the gravel, before she forced herself to walk forward again.

*It wasn't the Madeline she remembered.*

She was no longer the bossy, strong-willed girl who'd befriended her all those months ago on the ship. Not the chatty, confident young woman who'd made Betty feel like her best friend in the world when she was pregnant. *Helped to deliver William.* Been the backbone of the friendship they'd all developed. Alice might have been the life of the party, but it had been Madeline's strength that Betty had counted on.

Madeline was merely a shell of that person. A fragile, skinny shell of the woman she'd been. Her cheeks were hollow, dark, deep half-circles under her eyes creating no illusion about what she'd been through. Something dreadful had happened to her, something she was desperate to escape from.

The quiet, content baby girl in her arms was asleep. Without her, holding on to her tight, Betty wondered if Madeline could even stand upright. She was like a balloon with no air to keep her afloat.

"Oh my love, what's happened to you?"

Betty scooped the baby from her friend's arms and pulled her into a firm hug. Madeline's body was so small, but she held on, pressing into her, sobbing into her shoulder. She had known something was wrong, but she'd never imagined Madeline would look like this.

"There, there. It's okay, you're safe here."

Madeline still didn't let go, not until Betty pried her away so she could inspect the baby, worried they were going to crush her.

"Tell me who we have here? Who's this gorgeous wee girl?"

The baby was tucked tight into a fluffy pink and white checked blanket.

"Char-Charlotte," Madeline hiccupped. "This is my Charlotte."

"Well, Charlotte, let's get you and your mother inside. You can meet my William and your Aunty June."

"June's here already?" Madeline asked, her voice low, like she was scared.

Betty nodded, holding the baby in one arm and slinging her other around Madeline. Her friend tucked into her, like a child needing comfort.

"She's here. No word from Alice, but June's well. And she's looking forward to seeing you."

"And Charlie? Please tell me your Charlie is as nice as he was back home?" Madeline's eyes were pleading. "Roy, he's, he's . . ."

Tears stopped her from saying anymore.

"Shhh, now. You're okay. We don't have to talk about anything you don't want to. You're safe here."

Madeline looked up at her, still waiting for an answer about Charlie, but Betty didn't want to burden her with her own loss. Not now. She'd gotten it off her chest telling June and her focus now was on helping Madeline, even if she didn't know what needed fixing yet.

"I've got a story of my own, Madeline, but let's just get you inside and with a cup of tea in your hand first, all right?"

Madeline looked grateful, a smile slowly showing itself as her face relaxed.

"I've already discussed what I know of your circumstances with, ah, Mr. Olliver, and you're welcome here for as long as you need somewhere to stay. Our house is your house if you need it to be."

Madeline looked confused. "Mr. Olliver? That's a bit formal, isn't it? I thought his name was Charlie."

Betty hoisted the baby up and tickled her chin, smiling at her.

She wasn't going to lie, but she could avoid the topic completely. She'd tell Madeline about her circumstances soon enough. Right now, they needed to do everything they could for Madeline, because whatever had happened to her wasn't allowed to happen again.

# CHAPTER 31

Alice fought the quiver in her chin and thrust it skyward instead. There was no point in acting like a child, but turning up here was making her doubt herself all over again. She'd chosen Betty because she'd been the easiest to find, and because she'd probably be the most sympathetic. And she needed someone to confide in and just be herself around. Not that the other girls wouldn't be there for her, it was just that Betty was the one with the biggest heart. Things were so much better with Ralph, but it had been a tough few months, to say the least. She knew that if she was going to settle here, and help Ralph recover, she needed to establish a proper network of friends and support for herself.

There was only one Olliver residence listed in the public records, and she was certain it was the one. It was something she'd remembered, Betty telling her that it was Olliver with a double 'L' in the middle—it was something they probably all remembered her saying.

Alice coached herself every step of the way. Up the long driveway, toward the door and then standing on the wide porch.

The house was impressive. She tried not to let the negative thoughts creep into her head, but it was hard. This was the type of home she'd expected. The type of entrance that she thought she'd be arriving home to. The type of home that deep down, part of her still yearned to have.

But thinking like that wasn't useful. It certainly didn't do her any good moping about what should have or could have been. She and Ralph were going to make it. They were both going to succeed, make something of themselves, and they *would* have a home like this one day. Right now she had to remind herself that things like a big home and flashy cars didn't truly matter. If she had Ralph by her side then that's what counted to her.

They were going to make their marriage work, and that was the most important thing now. She also knew how fortunate she should feel not to be marked an adulteress and banished back to London.

The only other thing she cared about was finding her friends. Something she should have done months ago. *What had happened to their determined promises of staying in touch forever?* She should never have let a stupid thing like pride stop her from getting in touch with her friends.

Alice raised her hand and forced her knuckles to bang on the door. It was now or never.

No answer.

She stood, waited some more, then hit the door harder, trying to make more noise.

The door swung open.

Alice dropped her hand. It wasn't Betty.

"Can I help you?"

An older woman stood, looking her over, smiling.

"Well, yes. I hope so. I was hoping to find a Mrs. Betty Olliver and I don't know if I'm at the right house."

The woman's smile deepened.

"You've got the right house, dear. You're not one of her friends from the ship, are you?"

Alice nodded. "Yes. How did you know?"

"Oh my, Betty is going to make a fuss when she sees you. Come with me."

Alice followed the woman and shut the door behind her. The lady hadn't answered her question but she wasn't going to wait around for an answer, not if Betty was here.

"So she's home then?"

"Oh yes." This time the lady's eyes shone. "She's home, and the other girls are here too. This is your lucky day."

# CHAPTER 32

June's cup dropped from her hand like it had a mind of its own. Her ears almost fell off, the shriek from Betty was so loud.

"Betty, what the . . ."

She turned to look in the same direction as Betty. And then her mouth fell open. Oh my. It couldn't be, surely not today?

"Alice!" Betty was screaming. "Alice, it's Alice!"

June watched as Alice walked across the lawn, on tiptoe so her heels didn't get lost in the turf. Alice looked the same—blonde hair perfectly manicured, red lips painted on, but older perhaps, more mature. Or maybe she was just exhausted. Who knew what she'd been through?

"Alice Jones, what on earth are you doing here?" cried Betty.

June was surprised to see Alice blush at Betty's question. She jumped up to greet their friend, although she couldn't help but notice that Madeline stayed seated, like she lacked the energy to even move.

"I hope I'm not interrupting," Alice sounded unsure of herself, not the bold girl from the ship June remembered. "I wasn't expecting to find you all here."

She watched as Betty grabbed hold of Alice and held her tight, feet stomping in her excitement.

"You've got the best timing, Alice. June and Madeline have just arrived."

June stepped forward and hugged her too. When she pulled back she saw the confusion in Alice's eyes.

"Oh Alice, don't go thinking we've been meeting without you," June told her.

Betty looked uncertain, then seemed to realize what was going on.

"Oh gosh, no!" Betty took Alice by the hand and led her over to the table. "We only just got back in touch, this is the first time we've met since we got here, can you believe it? Nine months it's taken us."

Alice looked relieved, like she'd thought she'd been left out of whatever fun they'd been having.

"Hi Madeline," she said softly, looking down to where her friend was still sitting.

Madeline looked up, a blank look on her face, before seeming to register what was going on.

"Alice," her voice was flat but she smiled. "How are you? I'm sorry I didn't get up."

Alice swapped a look with June, but she just smiled back at her. She knew as little as Alice did. If Madeline had confided in Betty about what had happened to her, she hadn't shared it with her.

"So what's been happening, Alice? How did you find me?" asked Betty.

Alice raised her eyebrows at the tea being poured from the pretty teapot. "Something about that double L spelling."

Even Madeline laughed a little at that.

"So maybe teaching you how to spell my married name correctly wasn't so loathsome?" Betty teased.

They all nodded their heads.

"How's your man? Your Ralph?" asked June.

Alice looked up at June. "Let's just say moving here wasn't as easy as I'd expected."

June didn't know what to say to that. Was she the only one who'd found actual happiness here? Was it wrong for her to want to tell them how wonderful Eddie was?

"But please tell me your husband is a dish?" Alice asked June.

"Oh yes!" Betty answered for her. "I met him at the dock. He was divine."

June had to agree. "He's a wonderful man, I'm so lucky."

But even as she said it, knowing that she was so fortunate, she was still envious of the two children amongst them. What she wouldn't give to have one of her own here.

"And you, Betty? Is that Charlie of yours coming out to join us? Or is he scared of a group of women?"

Alice was laughing, so June gave a tight smile back, not wanting to say anything. It was Betty's place to tell them all.

Betty looked from Madeline to Alice, then to June.

"Did I say something wrong?" Alice's eyes flicked between them, aware of the shift in atmosphere.

"I don't want to ruin the mood, but I may as well just come out and tell you. Since we're all here now."

June wasn't going to let herself cry. She had to be strong for Betty. She'd been a blubbering mess before but she wasn't going to let it happen again.

"Charlie took a contract after the war, flying for a supplies company. His plane went down on his last flight, and he didn't make it home."

June heard Alice gasp. Even Madeline seemed roused from her trance, blinking furiously.

"Are you saying that Charlie's dead?" Alice asked.

Betty nodded, hands folded tightly together on her lap. "I only found out after I arrived. His brother Luke took me in, this is his home." She paused. "He's a lovely man and I'm very fortunate."

June kept her eyes downcast. She guessed Betty wasn't planning on sharing *everything* with the others.

"Oh sweetheart, I'm so sorry." Alice moved her chair closer so she could put her arm around Betty's shoulders.

They all froze when Madeline started snuffling.

"I'm sorry Betty, I'm sorry. You don't need me here with my problems too."

Madeline stood with Charlotte in her arms, eyes wild, filled with terror.

June jumped to her feet first. "Mads? What are you saying? Don't be silly. We're all here for one another."

Madeline looked like she was about to run—to take flight and get as far away as she could. Something had happened to their friend, something serious, something that she needed to get off of her chest.

June walked slowly over to her, taking her on the arm and walking her back over to her seat. She hoped her touch would help to calm her, to let her know she didn't have to run, didn't have to keep her problems bottled up inside like a disease.

"Tell us what happened to you, Madeline. Tell us what's wrong."

It was like they were all holding their breath, waiting to hear. Wanting to know what had traumatized Madeline so badly. They were all waiting to see how they could help, what they could do for her.

"I hate it here. I hate it. I want to go home."

Madeline's words were so low, spoken so softly they were barely audible. But June heard them; heard them for what they were. This wasn't just a case of not liking it here, of pining for home and missing family. Madeline was desperate.

"Has he hurt you? Did your husband do something?" June lowered her voice. "You can tell us, Madeline, you're safe here. We're not going to let anyone hurt you or your baby."

Madeline's response was to shut her eyes, tight. Like she was trying to force the memories away.

Betty and Alice fell to their knees in front of her, leaning into her, holding Madeline's hands. June reached for the baby and put her over her shoulder.

She tried to ignore the feeling of the soft, tiny child in her arms. The pang in her chest wasn't fair. She needed to help Madeline. Nothing else mattered right now.

"What did he do, honey? Is your husband okay?"

Madeline looked up, her eyes like glass. It was as if she'd died behind them, like she wasn't there anymore. "My father died. My husband's family kept every letter from me, and now they want me prisoner in their house again. I have to go home, please. *Please* help me get home. I can't stand another day of it, let alone a lifetime."

They all looked at Madeline and then at one another.

"Please, Betty. June. Alice. Please." Madeline started to sob. "I need to go home. Help me go home."

Madeline felt like a fool. It wasn't that she wished she'd kept it to herself, but she now felt like an idiot for putting up with her new family for so long.

She'd thought that maybe she wasn't being strong enough. That she needed to try toughening up. That maybe she was doing something wrong. But the look on her friends' faces had told her she was right, that she should have trusted her instincts from day one.

"Why did we take so long to find each other?"

Madeline's voice was hoarse from crying and her eyes were burning, but she felt happier than she had in a long time after talking everything through.

"We're fools, all of us."

They laughed a little at Alice's dramatic comment.

"So am I the only one whose marriage was a failure?" Madeline asked.

Betty smiled and Madeline's heart dropped.

"Oh, Betty, I'm sorry! I didn't mean . . ."

Betty raised her hand. "Don't apologize, no offense taken. You don't need to walk on eggshells around me."

Madeline bit her tongue. She wasn't saying another word.

They were quiet, all sitting on the blanket now, spread out on the grass. Charlotte was asleep in June's arms, and William was curled up against a cushion like an exhausted puppy; he'd been crawling one moment and fallen over asleep the next.

"Marriage has had its ups and downs for me."

Madeline looked up at Alice when she spoke. Saw the tired expression on her face as she stared up at the blue sky.

"How so?"

Alice sighed.

"My Ralph wasn't exactly how I remembered him, but we're getting there now."

No one asked any questions. Alice would speak when she was ready, they all knew that.

Madeline, well, she was just happy to have her mind off her problems, at least for now. Tonight, she'd probably start to worry all over again, but now she just needed to shake it off and enjoy the company. It seemed like forever since she'd just relaxed and been happy.

"I had stars in my eyes, you know?" Alice went on. "Ralph was so confident and strong, gave me everything I could dream of back in London. When he came home, he lost everything, and I didn't cope very well with the man he became." She cleared her throat. "He's suffering a form of stress from the war, but I'm doing my best to nurse him through it and he's doing so well."

"But you're okay now?" June asked.

Alice stopped playing with the edge of the rug and raised her eyes. "We're going to be fine. Deep down, I know we will be."

Madeline watched June. She could sense her friend was holding something back.

"How about you, June? Tell me about your Eddie?"

The smile that broke out on her friend's face said it all before she'd even spoken a word.

"Eddie's wonderful. I'm very lucky."

That made them all look up.

"Do tell!" Betty sounded excited again, like she had been when they'd all first sat down together. "No holding back here. Especially not with good news."

June looked nervous but Betty gave her a sharp nudge with her elbow.

"I don't know what to say." June was blushing furiously.

"Just tell us what he's like," insisted Alice, rolling her eyes.

June couldn't keep her feelings to herself.

"Eddie's incredible," she finally gushed. "Like the man of my dreams. He's so kind, his family are almost as good as my own, and he built us a house. A real home, with his own hands."

Madeline leaned back, her hands out to support her weight. *Good for her.* Thank goodness one of them was living the life she'd expected as a married woman.

"You're head over heels in love, aren't you?" It was Betty prodding again.

"In love would be an understatement."

June was bright red, the flush extending all the way down her neck.

"Is anything about your life here *not* perfect?" Alice sounded like she was joking, but it made Madeline feel awkward for June.

"I wouldn't say it's perfect, but I'm happy with my husband, if that's what you're asking. Life here is even better than I'd ever imagined it to be."

"More tea?" asked Betty, jumping to her feet. "Anyone hungry?"

Madeline shook her head, then wished that she said yes. Betty was trying to change the subject and she hadn't realized until too late. It wasn't fair to interrogate June like this, not when they'd all had trauma. They couldn't make her feel uncomfortable just because she'd had everything turn out well for her.

"Oh my," exclaimed Alice, her hand flying to her mouth.

Madeline turned. What was the fuss was about? Alice looked like she'd seen a ghost.

*Oh.* An attractive ghost.

"I'm guessing that's your brother-in-law?"

Madeline heard June's words but she couldn't tear her eyes away from the figure walking toward them. He had dark hair falling ever so slightly over his forehead. He was tall, strong, confident as he moved toward them—the kind of man any single woman would want to fall for.

"No wonder you're in love with him," June whispered.

"What!" squealed Alice.

"June!" Betty hissed. "Quiet!"

Madeline forced herself to turn away. The others were less demure—more like the American ladies they had once claimed to be so different from.

"Hello ladies."

Even his voice was divine, smooth, and commanding all at once.

"Luke, I'd like you to meet my friends." Betty's composure had returned. "This is Alice Jones, June West, and Madeline Parker. Oh, and little Charlotte here, too."

He nodded, arms crossed as he stood before them. His eyes swept over William, asleep, but Madeline saw something there. *Love.* There was no other word for it. He was like a father looking out for his son.

"Well, it's lovely to meet you all," Luke said.

The others all smiled up at him. Like love-sick puppies, thought Madeline, as she watched Betty's handsome brother-in-law.

"Madeline?"

She looked up at her name being called, then realized Luke was speaking to her.

"Madeline, Betty has told me you might be in need of somewhere to stay."

She gulped. What did she say to him? What would he think of her? Did he want to know why?

"Please feel free to stay here with Betty for as long as you need. I'm sure she'll enjoy your company. Our home is your home."

She could see even more why Betty liked the man. To invite her to stay with no questions asked? He obviously trusted his sister-in-law.

"Thank you Luke, thank you so much," she said quietly.

"No need to thank me. Enjoy your afternoon, ladies."

He smiled at them all, but Madeline didn't miss the way his eyes hovered a little too long over Betty. Like there was something more between them than a bachelor and a young widow.

All Madeline wanted was to get home, back to London. But she hoped for her sake that Betty could find happiness here with Luke. That she could stay here and make something of her life. Losing Charlie must have been hard on her, but she had a chance to make a life here, with another man, and she deserved it. She'd lost her family before the war, hadn't she? Happiness here was the least she could ask for.

"Luke, I'll come in with you. I think we might need some more sustenance out here," Betty said to him.

That made Madeline giggle. It was Betty who'd always needed sustenance on the ship. She'd always claimed that it was eating for two that made her so ravenous, but maybe she just liked her food.

Madeline watched them walk off. Close, but not touching. They had their heads bent in toward one another, like they didn't even know they were doing it.

"They'd make a gorgeous couple," June said with a sigh.

"Is she seriously in love with him?" Alice asked.

Madeline rolled her eyes. "Do you even need to ask? Look at them."

# CHAPTER 33

Thanks for being so understanding, Luke."

Betty kept her eyes on the path ahead. Now that she'd admitted it to June, it was all she could think about. Seeing him, walking with him, hearing his voice, watching how at ease he was talking with her friends—it all made her more in love with him by the moment.

It was no longer something she could control. Like a beast with its own mind, taking her over and not letting her think of anything else.

"I don't want to get caught up in any personal problems, Betty, but if she's having trouble you do what you need to do to help her."

Betty sighed.

"It's pretty bad for her. She wants to get back home."

He slowed his stride. Without even looking at him she knew his brows would be knotted. She'd watched his face, studied his expressions, so many times that she knew what every sigh and movement meant.

"Do you mean to say she wants to run away with her child, back to London?"

Betty chewed at the inside of her mouth. Did that mean he didn't agree?

"I'll tell you all the details once I've spoken to her alone, later." She wasn't lying. Whatever Madeline told her would have to be repeated to Luke if he was going to assist her in any way. "I promise I'll keep you informed."

He relaxed, she could sense his body loosening.

"I know you will."

Betty went to look up at him but her eyes froze. His hand skimmed hers, ever so gently, a brush of his skin against hers, pushing against the palm of her hand with his fingers.

Betty held her breath. Then slowly let her eyes travel toward his.

He was watching her, waiting for her reaction, and she slowly clasped her hand around his fingers, just for a moment, before she let go.

They kept walking, not saying anything. But Betty's heart sung like a bird calling out to the world, chirping so frantically she was sure Luke would hear it where it stood.

"Come and see me later, once Madeline's settled."

She liked how his voice had softened as he spoke to her this time.

"I'll see you soon," Luke said.

When he turned away to walk to his office, she could have squealed. But she didn't. Betty skipped into the kitchen and almost bowled straight into Ivy.

"Betty! What on earth are you doing?"

She shrugged, trying to be nonchalant. "Just looking for more cookies."

"And what's put that silly smile on your face?"

Betty pulled her lips down, trying to keep her mouth straight.

"Nothing. Just having my friends here, that's all."

Ivy looked suspicious but she didn't question her further.

"I've made a cherry pie for you girls. You take the cream and plates, and I'll be out in a moment with it."

It took all Betty's composure to walk demurely from the kitchen. Her heart was still fluttering, banging in her chest like it was about to explode.

She loved Charlie. She always would. But this was different.

Charlie was gone, and the way she felt about Luke was real. It hadn't been the head over heels, love at first sight kind of attraction that it had been with Charlie, but this was every bit as good. She trusted Luke, she admired him, and she respected him.

It might have been a slow-burn attraction, but the way she felt for him now was more love than she could ever have imagined feeling again. Ever.

∽

Madeline was calm. She felt safe. Relaxed, when she'd been on edge for so long.

She'd been unhappy and upset for such a long time that she hardly remembered feeling good, but she knew it hadn't been that long ago. It was less than a year ago that they were all sailing here, full of anticipation.

She looked around at the three women seated in a half-circle. It was like heaven being here with them. Knowing she could just be herself, not worrying about what she was meant to be doing, how she would be judged, working out what she could do to get away.

Madeline still didn't know quite how she was going to get back home, but she would find a way. It seemed possible now.

"I guess I'd better be on my way home," said June.

Madeline looked over at her. She didn't want to say goodbye to her friends, but the air was becoming cool, the sun disappearing for the day behind a bank of night-time cloud.

Alice stood and gave June a tug to her feet.

"How are you getting home?" Alice asked.

June laughed. "Would you believe Eddie's taught me to drive? I've got his car out the front if you trust me to get you home safely."

Alice shook her head. "You? Driving a car?"

Madeline tried to ignore the tears in her eyes as her friends chatted. Betty was looking on, too, but she seemed happy. It was different for Madeline.

She had a feeling that this would be the last time she'd ever see June and Alice again. The last time she'd ever be in their company.

If Betty was prepared to help her, she might be home before they ever met up again.

"Madeline?"

June was standing in front of her.

"Daydreaming," she confessed. "Sorry, what did I miss?"

"I was just saying that I'd love you all to come and visit me. We could have lunch? Eddie is dying to meet you and I could show you our home."

Madeline smiled. It was all she could do. She wasn't going to go making promises when she wasn't going to be here. She didn't know how long it would take, but she wanted to leave as soon as possible. "I'm going to miss you, girls." She had tears in her eyes again. "I'd love to see your house, June, if I can. We'll just have to see."

Alice stepped forward and threw her arms about her.

"You're serious, aren't you?" Alice looked her straight in the eyes, held out at arms' length. "You're really going home."

Madeline shut her eyes and took a deep breath. "I hate it here, Alice. I hate it. If I can get home, I'm going."

Understanding crossed Alice's face. "I wish I could help you but we're only just getting by. Things have been, well, difficult."

She was still hiding something, that much was obvious, but Madeline wasn't going to ask her. She didn't want to pry. They all had their secrets.

"I'll figure it out, Alice, you just concentrate on your own happiness. All right?"

Alice stepped back so June could hug her too.

"I know it sounds silly, especially since we haven't seen each other in so long, but I'm going to miss you, Madeline. I truly am. It's like we've finally found each other and it's too late." Alice sighed. "Maybe we could have helped you sooner if we'd known. Maybe we could all have transitioned easier if we'd actually been getting together."

Madeline doubted that they could have helped her, but she felt the same. "How can you miss someone you only knew a couple of weeks, and haven't seen in months, right?"

Betty elbowed her in the side. "That sound like anyone's marriage?"

They all laughed.

"Point taken," said June. "So it means I'm not just being all sentimental then?"

Madeline shook her head. So did the other two.

"If you don't mind I might just take Charlotte up to the house." Madeline scooped her baby up from the carry-bassinet and stroked her cheek. "I'm not great with goodbyes."

June touched her shoulder and walked past. Alice just smiled at her and Betty pointed up toward her home.

"Just call out to Ivy, she'll show you to your room. Help you settle in."

"Bye," she said, squeezing her breath in to stop herself from sobbing as they walked away.

"We'll never forget you, Madeline," June called out.

Madeline turned and headed to the house, Charlotte clutched to her chest. Tears fell down her cheeks, her breath came out in ragged sobs, but she made herself walk.

I'll miss you too, she thought.

They were the best and most real friends she'd ever had. If it wasn't for them, maybe she would have just given up and accepted her unhappy lot with Roy's family. Fighting took so much strength.

But the weight of her baby in her arms told her differently. Betty might be the one to help her escape, but she was doing this for herself and for her child.

It was time to go home.

# CHAPTER 34

Betty knocked softly on the door.

"It's open."

She pushed it open and walked in. Even after all the time she'd been living in this house, it was the first time Betty had ever stepped foot in Luke's office. An oversized antique desk looked out over the grounds, and two of the four walls were lined with shelves, books heaving to escape.

"I didn't mean to disturb you."

Luke continued scribbling, his hand moving fast as he made notes, before he put the pen down, pressed his palms to the desk, and stood.

"You're not disturbing me." He moved out and took a couple of steps toward her before leaning on the edge of the desk. "It's nice to be distracted."

She didn't know what to say. It hadn't been awkward between them like this for weeks, but this felt like a different kind of awkward—it was charged and powerful. Now she was unsure of herself, nervous of what to do and how to behave. She was unsure of her own feelings, or maybe she just didn't want to truly admit to how she felt.

"I just, ah, wanted to let you know that Madeline's settled into one of the guest rooms. She'll be staying until we can figure out exactly what to do."

Luke gazed at her solemnly. "What is it she wants to do?"

"Go back to London, for sure," Betty blurted. "She wants to take Charlotte and go back to her parents."

"I see." Luke leaned back into the desk. "And what does her husband have to say about this?"

She had to tell him the truth. She'd never been any good at lying and now didn't seem like the best time to start.

"Her husband and his family have been awful to her. It's a long story but they didn't even let her know her own father was dying. She needs to get away. It's very abusive by all accounts."

She expected Luke to rebuff her. To tell her that Madeline's duty was to her husband, that she couldn't abandon him and take off with his child. But he didn't.

"What do you think?" he asked.

"What?"

"What do you think she should do? Do you think we should help her? Assist her in returning to London?"

Betty was confused.

"You would actually help her get back to her family?"

Luke shook his head. "I asked what you thought."

Her eyes followed him as he walked to a side cabinet and reached for two small glasses. He poured a small nip of liquid into one and a larger amount into the other.

He walked back toward her, eyes meeting hers, not giving her the chance to look away.

Luke offered her the smaller glass. She wanted to say no, but the way he held it out to her, the promise in his smile, stopped her from saying anything.

"If it were you, what would you do?" His voice was soft now, like he was asking her something deeply personal.

She took the glass, the aroma of the alcohol filling her nostrils.

"If you'd heard what he'd done to her, Luke, you wouldn't think ill of her." Betty watched as he drained at least a third of his glass. "If it were me, I'd want to go, too."

He raised his glass and inclined for her to do the same. She tipped it to her mouth, letting a drop touch her tongue. Even the tiny amount burned her throat as she swallowed it. Was it whiskey? Bourbon? She didn't know, but it wasn't helping her. Just the smell was enough to make her light-headed.

"And how do you feel now?" He moved closer to her, his body too near for comfort. "Do you want to leave?"

*No.* She never wanted to leave him. But she couldn't say it, so she just let her head shake from side to side.

"Are you sure?" Luke asked.

He reached out to her, tilting her chin up toward him, forcing her to look at him.

"Yes," she breathed out the word. "I'm sure."

Betty wanted him to kiss her, was so sure he was about to, but as soon as he'd touched her he stopped, his hand falling away.

"Tell Madeline we'll offer her all the financial assistance she needs." Luke tipped back his glass and swallowed the remainder of his drink. "Make whatever arrangements you need to, get her on a ship back to London. Phone Jean at home, tell her to make the arrangements first thing in the morning."

Betty couldn't believe it—the fact that something had almost happened between them, or that he was prepared to help a friend of hers, one whom he'd never met before in his life until today.

"Thank you, Luke. Thank you so much."

He stopped, watched her, like there was something left to say that he hadn't said already. Something he wanted to tell her.

"Goodnight, Betty."

He took another step, leaned forward, and kissed her cheek. His lips hovered, slow, lingering over her skin, but it went no further. Heat burned her cheeks but she stayed still. *Wishing he would kiss her, that they could just admit to what they felt for one another.*

But Luke pulled away.

"Goodnight," she whispered.

They watched one another, until he smiled, almost sadly, before walking back around to be seated at his desk. Betty walked quickly, needing to get out of his office.

"Betty?"

She stopped and looked back at him.

"I'm glad you had a nice day with your friends."

She waited.

"Have them here as often as you like. I want this to feel like your home too."

Betty gave him a tight smile in reply.

It did feel like home to her. She just wished he understood how she felt about him, wished she was brave enough to tell him.

*But she wasn't. And she probably never would be.*

❧

Strangely enough, Betty was more worried about tapping on Madeline's door than she had been Luke's. She didn't want to say goodbye to her friend, not when they'd only just found each other, but she was going to help her.

Betty had spent so long feeling upset about her life without Charlie. She knew what it was like to lose hope. But Luke had been there for her, even when they hadn't connected. He was her ally. Her protector. And now he was going out of his way to help her friend, too.

Something inside told her he was doing it for her, because he knew what it would mean to her. But she also knew that it took a certain type of man to agree to what they were doing anyway: to aid a woman in escaping her husband. She was grateful, whatever his reasons for doing so were.

"Madeline? Are you awake?"

It wasn't late, but they'd all had a big day.

"Come in," Madeline called back.

She opened the door to find Madeline sitting on the bed, nursing her little girl.

"It's so special, don't you think?" Madeline smiled at her. "Just spending time with them alone when they're feeding."

She looked happy, content there. Earlier today she'd gone from wild-eyed to sad, and then frightened. Now she looked at peace.

"I love her so much, Betty. Is that how you feel with William? Like you couldn't love him any harder if you tried?"

Betty sat on the edge of the bed. "Like you couldn't ever have imagined loving anything or anyone like you do your baby?"

Madeline looked relieved that someone understood how she was feeling.

"I knew I wanted to go, to escape from here, but as soon as I knew I was carrying a child, it just made me even more determined."

Betty knew exactly how that felt, just in a different way.

"Without William, I wouldn't have survived losing Charlie." She admitted. "I would have had to move on, but part of me would have died, been broken, forever."

"And Luke?" Madeline lowered her voice. "Something's already happened with him, hasn't it?"

Betty didn't know what to say. "I don't know what's happened, if anything has, but I think it will." She paused, wanted to speak the truth. "I hope it will."

"If you love him, don't hold back, Betty. Promise me that, will you?" Madeline's eyes swung from her baby suckling to Betty, her expression serious. "If it will make you and William happy, if it's the right thing to do, don't make yourself feel bad about it. Just be thankful that you've been given a second chance at love. At happiness."

It had taken months of soul searching, of trying to make herself believe that she wasn't forgetting Charlie by moving on, but now she agreed with Madeline. Luke wasn't just anybody. He was Charlie's brother. He was William's uncle. She was still being true to Charlie; he'd want her to be happy, and Luke understood how much she'd loved his brother. She'd never lied to him about that.

But it was time to talk about Madeline, about what they could do to help her.

"I have good news for you, Mads. Tonight is about your second chance, not mine."

"You're not just trying to change the subject, are you?"

Madeline was trying to joke, but Betty could see the hope in her eyes.

"I've just finished speaking to Luke's secretary. She's been able to find out about a ship leaving for England in five days' time."

Madeline was holding her breath. Betty spoke quickly.

"If you want to go, we'll send you with a driver to the train station tomorrow, then you can take the short trip to just near the port and stay at a lodge there while Jean makes the arrangements for you. She thinks it will be best if you travel there as soon as possible, because we aren't sure who you'll need to see or what the visa requirements are. That will give you enough time to organize yourself and finalize the necessary paperwork before the ship sails."

She watched as Madeline's face fell. Of course. She'd omitted to tell her about Luke's aid.

"I've spoken with Luke and he will cover your fare back to England, and your accommodation, so you don't need to worry about anything."

Madeline started to cry. Her body shook, hands quivering, as she took her sleeping baby from her breast and placed her in the crib.

Betty gave her a moment before stepping forward to hold her. She stayed silent, still, her arms wrapped around her friend. Madeline's body was tiny, so thin, but there was a strength there that could not be extinguished.

"I know you feel bad about Luke helping you, but he's doing it for me as well, Madeline. I think he's trying to show me that he cares, that he trusts me."

Madeline just held her tighter.

"Don't feel like you owe us anything, except friendship. I know you would do the same for me if you had to. If you could."

Madeline pulled back, her eyes red, skin blotchy.

"I'm going to miss you so much, Betty. You're a true friend."

Betty pulled her back in for another hug.

"I was a frightened young pregnant woman once, and I met three friends who saw me through the hard times and helped to deliver my baby." She wiped away her own tears with one hand, but hers weren't tears of sadness, they were of gratitude for a memory she would never forget. "I know what a true friend is and you've already been one to me."

"Does that make it okay that I'm leaving you then?" asked Madeline.

"We've all got to leave one another to lead our own lives, but a friend understands that."

Madeline's brave little smile told her she understood.

"Now you get a good night's sleep. Tomorrow you're off and you need all the strength you have to travel with a little one."

"Thank you, Betty. Thank you so much."

"Goodnight, Madeline. Sweet dreams."

Betty pulled the door shut and stood in the hallway, back to the wall, eyes shut. Madeline was going to be okay, and so was she.

If Luke wanted to be part of her future, wanted her as a man wanted a woman, then she'd say yes. She would tell him she felt the same. Because she *did* deserve happiness. She still loved Charlie, but there was room enough in her heart for Luke too.

# CHAPTER 35

She was prepared for the worst, but it wasn't helping her nerves at all.

June sat cross-legged, waiting for the doctor to return to the room. She'd told Eddie that he had no reason to come, that it was women's business, but maybe she shouldn't have been so proud. Or maybe she should have asked Betty to come with her, just for support. She would have been the person to ask.

"Mrs. West?"

She looked up. Her stomach was in knots, if that were even possible.

"Yes, that's me."

The doctor smiled at her, but it did little to ease her nerves. He was middle-aged, wore glasses, and he hardly had a speck of hair on his head. *Not exactly the type of person she wanted inspecting her private parts, if that's what he had to do.*

She shuddered. Maybe she shouldn't have come. She should have kept it to herself and just kept on trying. Hadn't Eddie told her she was being too impatient?

"What can I help you with today?" he asked.

June squirmed in her seat.

"This is a rather, ah, delicate matter." She looked up and saw that his expression hadn't changed. "It's, well, my husband and I would like a family, and we have not had any success."

June could feel the burn in her cheeks. They must be flaming red.

"We can run a blood test and check your general health, Mrs. West, but sometimes these things just take time."

She nodded.

"I understand. It's just, I wasn't sure if . . ."

The doctor smiled and shuffled his chair closer.

"You seem like a fit, healthy young woman, and I'm sure you have nothing to worry about. How long have you been hoping for a baby?"

"I've been here ten months now. We were married in England, during the war."

He nodded. "Give it time, my dear. If you are still without a child in another year or so, then we'll look into what can be done."

*Another year.* A whole year or more? She wanted a family now. Wanted children filling the bedrooms and playing in the home, spilling out into the fields and waiting eagerly in the kitchen for baking to come out of the oven.

She wanted a baby now!

"Thank you for your time, doctor. I'll take your advice and come back if we're still having trouble."

"The blood tests, Mrs. West? We can at least conduct those now."

"No." She shook her head and gathered up her things. "I feel very healthy. I probably shouldn't have come."

He looked confused, but saw her to the door anyway.

June knew what she had to do.

If she wanted a family, she needed to act now. Being a mother was the most important thing to her in all the world, and she wasn't going to sit around and wait for it to happen. Not when, deep down, she had a feeling that something was wrong and that she wasn't going to be pregnant any time soon.

# CHAPTER 36

It had become a routine. Betty came downstairs while Luke was partway through his breakfast. He passed her a section of the paper, gave her a small flicker of a smile as he looked at her. Ivy brought her two slices of toast and a cup of coffee. She sat, pretended to read the paper, and instead secretly studied Luke.

That first time she met him, he'd come across as cold. *His gaze had seemed to judge her, question her.* Now, there was something there. Something neither of them had even come close to admitting.

Well, she'd admitted it to herself, to June too, but since her friend had left nothing had happened between them. Nothing at all.

They always sat in silence, but it was a comfortable lack of noise that didn't bother her. If William was awake, she usually had him in the playpen in the morning room. Luke would look over at his nephew, who always smiled and flapped his arms up at him, and he'd say goodbye to him when he left for work. Sometimes he'd scoop him up or ruffle his hair, or comment on how close he was to walking, but that was it.

Today when he rose, he stopped to drop a kiss to William's forehead as he sat playing with blocks. It made Betty happy, seeing William loved like that. *Especially by his father's brother.* There was a connection between them that she hoped would only grow stronger. She'd never, ever think of leaving America and depriving William of his only uncle.

"Why don't you meet me for lunch today, Betty?"

She recovered before her cup fell to the table, and tried to keep her voice casual.

"Oh, of course. That would be lovely."

He slung his jacket over one shoulder. His eyes scanned her, seemed to smile at her, before he turned away.

"Meet me at twelve?"

Betty nodded. Her tongue felt swollen, like a bee had stung it over and over.

He wanted to take her for lunch? Was there something he wanted to tell her? There was something about the way he'd looked, at how relaxed he'd been. It felt like something had changed or was about to change.

He wasn't getting married, was he? Did he have a secret sweetheart that he'd kept quiet? Was that the reason he'd never made his feelings known for her? Maybe he'd had a promotion? She chastised herself. *If he was getting a promotion the entire country would know about it.* He was already a State Senator.

She heard a shuffle and turned to find Ivy leaning against the open door to the kitchen.

"Anyone would think that boy was sweet on you."

"Ivy!"

The other woman just shrugged. "All I know is that before you arrived, he'd eat his breakfast in a flash and be out the door." She paused and threw Betty a knowing look. "Now he takes his time, waits 'till you're downstairs, then takes even longer finishing his coffee than he'd usually take on finishing an entire meal."

Betty went to pick William up. He was heavy now but she still loved lifting him. "Hello, my darling. Don't you listen to that silly Aunt Ivy."

William smiled and reached out to pull her hair. "Mama. Mama."

"Would it be so bad?" Ivy asked.

She held William tight, inhaled the sweet smell of his hair before putting him back down and looking over her shoulder at Ivy.

"I'm not ready for that, Ivy. I still love Charlie." She said it, but she was lying to herself. She did still love Charlie, but she *was* ready. Ready for something to happen with Luke.

"Charlie's gone, love, and Luke's here. What you two can't see I can, and you're perfect for each other."

Betty went to interrupt her but was stopped by a raised hand.

"I lost my husband thirty years ago. My daughter was older than your William at the time, but I know what it's like to be alone. To mourn."

Betty turned around to face her. Why had Ivy never told her this before?

"How long were you married?"

"Six years. But let me tell you, there were men I could have fancied at the time, men who would have been proud to have me, but I let my grief stop me from being happy."

Betty gulped. She didn't want to hear this, and yet she did. She needed to.

"By the time I realized I'd rather not be alone, I was too old. Past my prime."

They stood there, watching one another.

"All I'm saying is that if Luke has taken a fancy to you, and you like him back, don't let memories of Charlie stop you from being happy. Don't let yourself care a hoot what others might say, because you're both good people. You would make a lovely family."

Betty walked across the room and put her arms around Ivy. She hugged her back, her deep bosom pressed against her, just like she remembered her mother doing. *Comforting her.* All those years ago, before her parents had passed away, hugs like this had meant the world to her.

She only pulled away because William started calling her.

"Mama! Mama!"

"Come on, little one, time for your nap."

William was reaching his arms up, ready for a cuddle.

"Just enjoy yourself, Betty. That's all you need to do. And if something happens, let it. You are allowed to want happiness, you know?"

She nodded but didn't look back. She didn't want Ivy to see the confusion in her eyes.

She did love Luke. She'd been ready to admit it when something had almost happened between them, that night in his office, but now she was scared.

Could she love both of them? Could she still love Charlie and give Luke her heart too? Not to mention risking her heart again when it had been so completely broken.

Her eyes fell on her son, looking back up at her so innocently.

William deserved to have a father, and Luke adored him.

She wasn't sure she could love anyone like she'd loved Charlie, much less his own brother. Or maybe that's what scared her . . . *that she'd already fallen into that same kind of love with Luke.*

# CHAPTER 37

Madeline sat on the deck with Charlotte in her arms and let the breeze brush past her bare skin. It was cool, but the fresh air was divine.

"We're almost there, darling. We're almost home."

Charlotte gazed up at her. She hardly ever made a noise, besides the odd gurgle or half-hearted cry. An angel of a child, even at sea.

Madeline came up here every day, sitting on the deck so long as it wasn't raining, but it wasn't the same as last time. On her way here she'd always had someone to talk to, a friend to lean on.

There were plenty of people aboard this ship, but she wasn't interested in talking or making friends. She didn't want to explain why she was travelling home, or be truthful about what she had thought of America, or discuss why she was without a husband accompanying her. Madeline was content to hold her baby and sing her lullabies, close her eyes and dream of her family, and think about what Betty had done for her. How she'd helped her. And the words in the letter she'd written to Roy and his family kept running through her mind, making her reflect on what she'd been through and how brave she'd been to leave.

But it was the picture of her family home with its tiny lounge and roaring fire, the mantelpiece covered in her mother's little figurines and the hustle and bustle of her nieces, that filled most of her thoughts and really made her smile. She wanted to mourn her father with her family, to be surrounded by people she loved.

Madeline pulled the letter from her pocket and read the words one last time. She was going to send it the moment she arrived back in England, once there was no way anyone could stop her from fulfilling her plans. And after that she wasn't going to waste another moment thinking about her husband ever again.

*Dear Roy,*

*It seems like a lifetime ago that we first met. From our first walk together, to you telling me of your farmhouse and family back home, to the night you proposed—they are memories that seem made many, many years ago. I still don't fully understand what happened to you between our time in England and when I saw you again in America. Maybe you never thought you'd survive the war, that we'd never actually be together in your home country, but we were, and the time I spent with you and your family are months I can only hope to one day forget.*

*I arrived in America with love in my heart, having left so much behind. But instead of welcoming me with the same love, I hardly recognized the man waiting for me. Your family looked down upon me, but for what? Why? I come from a good family, a kind family, and if I'm brutally honest, they are the type of family who would have welcomed anyone with love—especially a stranger in a new country—unlike your rude, unmannered parents. Your home was cold, there was no love there, and you should be ashamed for the cruel way your mother and sister treated me.*

*I had hoped that we could move past all of that, that once we had our own home and family things would have been different.*

*But while Charlotte filled my heart with love and warmth, she didn't seem to make even a dent in yours. And then as a final devastating blow, I learned that your family stole from me the last chance to communicate with my father before he died. I can never forgive them for that, nor you for your indifference to my misery.*

*So this is goodbye, Roy. Goodbye to you and your family both. You will never see me again, and you will never see your daughter. Don't try to write to me or find us, because we are lost to you forever.*

*May God forgive you for your behavior one day, once you are finally man enough to understand the pain and hurt you have caused me.*

*Madeline*

She wiped away the tears that had gathered on her lashes and put the letter back in her pocket, holding her baby tight.

"We are really going home, Charlotte. To your grandma and your aunties and a home where you will be loved and prodded and squeezed every day by a family who will love you."

Charlotte just kept gazing back up at her. Madeline thought her heart might actually break from watching her, the love she felt for her so strong it hurt.

Her marriage had been a complete failure. But she was a great mother.

And she finally knew what true love was.

# CHAPTER 38

Today was the third day she'd met Luke for lunch. Betty sat in an over-size leather chair, hands clasped in her lap as she waited. There was a newspaper on the stand but she didn't want to read.

"Are you sure I can't get you something to drink?"

Betty smiled at Luke's assistant. "I'll be fine, thank you for asking, Jean."

"He shouldn't be long."

Betty went back to waiting. It was silly to have nerves, to want to run out the door one moment and jump up and down the next with excitement. But she didn't know what to think. What it meant, him asking her to meet him like this, and so many times.

Was it just a friendly gesture? Wanting to make her feel comfortable?

He hadn't touched her again like that night in his office, not once. She was starting to wonder if she'd imagined it.

"Betty, I'm so sorry."

She looked up. *Luke.*

His hair was disheveled, probably from running his hand through it like he did when he was stressed. He looked tired, and his tie was slightly too loose and off center.

She rose and reached to adjust it, pushing the knot higher and wriggling it into place.

"That's better." She spoke the words low, more to herself than to him.

Then she looked up. Betty hadn't realized how close she was standing to him. Her hands dropped from his tie and her eyes fell to the ground as she stumbled a step backward.

Luke caught her around the elbow with his hand.

They stared at one another, like two deer caught in the headlights of the other's gaze.

"Shall we go?" he said, his voice low.

It was as if no one else existed, as if they were the only two people in the room.

"Betty?"

His voice was gruff, gravelly, different than usual.

"Yes," she snapped out of it. "Lunch, yes, of course."

She spun around, but as his hand touched the small of her back to guide her, she wondered if everything had changed all over again. As if the rules had been altered, or maybe they were now playing a new game entirely.

Luke escorted her out the door and onto the street. The restaurant they went to was the one they'd first dined at together, and it was only a short walk away.

Betty had a feeling that something was about to change forever between them today.

Today, maybe she'd know what it was between them. Maybe they'd both find out.

# CHAPTER 39

Her feet were aching, the wool stockings rough against her skin, but Alice couldn't recall smiling so much in a single day. She'd finally gotten back into the swing of nursing, finished her two-day course, and now she was walking home from her shift.

When she'd arrived here, all she'd wanted was a life that involved parties and lunches and money. Now, she just wanted to be happy. *And she was.*

There was also the added bonus of knowing her husband was waiting for her at home. Probably anxiously waiting for her, desperate to show her the new offices.

Alice rounded the corner and started walking more briskly. Her eyes strained until she could make out their house, and then her husband. Ralph was standing on the veranda, waving.

She started to run, desperate to see him. Desperate to make sure this was real, that the way she'd looked forward to seeing him all day was actually going to be reciprocated.

"Hi, darling."

Ralph jumped down the three steps and opened his arms for her. She fell into them, face raised for the kiss she'd been waiting for.

"Hi." She bent to collect her bag from the sidewalk as he released her.

"Shall we go?" he asked.

Alice skipped up the steps and called over her shoulder. "Let me change. I'll be two minutes."

She went into their bedroom, inhaled the smell of her husband's cologne, and slipped from her uniform. Alice reached for a pair of slacks, then a blouse, and dressed quickly.

"Come on, honey, we need to get there before dark."

She spritzed herself with perfume and hurried back out.

"Ready."

Ralph offered her his arm and she looped hers through.

"So this is really happening?" she asked, looking up at him.

"Yes, Alice, it's really happening."

He looked so happy. She was so pleased for him, so excited about their future, about what was going to happen for them both.

"Did you sign the lease on the office today?"

He grinned at her. "It's ours."

She squeezed his arm tighter.

"The finances were approved today, too. The bank was very forthcoming and they're fully supportive of the business."

Alice grinned.

"Of course, they were always going to say yes, you know, given the contract I secured with the *New York Post* and a new book publisher."

Alice stopped in the middle of the street. Ralph spun around to face her, smiling.

"What?" Had she heard him correctly?

He scooped her up and twirled her around.

"It's happening, Alice, we're going to be a great success, I just know it."

She couldn't believe it. "You got the contracts? The ones you told me were on your dream list?"

He put her down and pulled her along.

"You'll have to keep nursing for a while, until the business is more established, but we're going to make it. I just know it."

They walked along in silence. Happy silence. She didn't know what to say, and it didn't matter. They didn't need to talk. They were both happy, their marriage was going to work, and their future was bright.

"We're almost here."

"Where is it?"

Ralph held her back, leaned in close and pointed across the street.

"The building with the striped awning out front."

Alice's pulse started to race. It was beautiful. It needed new paint, and the inside was probably run down, but she loved it anyway.

It signaled their future. Their success.

"I love it." The words sighed from her mouth like a breath of wind.

There was nowhere else she wanted to be. Nowhere else in the world.

The very thought struck her like a bolt of lightning to her skin.

She was happy. Truly, incredibly, without doubt happy. *Maybe for the first time in her life.*

# CHAPTER 40

Betty placed her knife and fork together on the plate and used her napkin to dab at the corners of her mouth. They had eaten fast, not talking a great deal, other than to cover the weather and talk about an important policy that Luke was putting together.

She wasn't quite sure what was going on, why he'd asked her for yet another lunch.

"Do you care for dessert?"

Betty patted her stomach. "Oh no, I couldn't fit another thing in here."

She smiled as he laughed, like the ice had finally broken. They'd both been awkward since that moment earlier in his office, but the barrier was finally starting to fall away again.

"We could always share something," he suggested, pushing his chair back from the table slightly. "Or coffee, perhaps?"

Betty shook her head again. "Lunch was lovely, but no sweets for me. Just coffee, if you're having one."

He raised his hand to beckon the waiter. "Two coffees with cream please."

Betty studied him as his face was turned: the profile of his jaw, the thickness of his hair. *Everything about him.*

She dropped her eyes as he looked back. He'd known she was watching him, of course he had, but she didn't care. She was feeling brave, braver than normal at least, and it was empowering.

"Betty, I've been meaning to say this for the last few days, but we always get so busy talking that I never get around to it."

She pressed her lips together. What was it? What did he have to tell her? That first time they'd had lunch, she thought he might have ulterior motives, but he'd never said. Now she was sure he was worried about something, had words he needed to get off his chest.

"It's been so wonderful having you and William to stay. Having you in my life."

*Oh no.* This was his way of telling her it was time to move on. He'd brought her to lunch more than once, to tell her, and he hadn't known how to say it.

"Luke please, there's no need for you to continue. If you want your home to yourself again, I'll arrange somewhere else to go."

He looked confused, then angry.

"Want you *gone*?"

There was no point in kidding herself. Just because she had certain feelings didn't mean he shared them.

"Isn't that what you wanted to tell me?"

"No." He looked dejected. Deflated even. "No, it wasn't."

She waited, confused.

"This is very difficult to say. In fact I'm not entirely sure what I'm saying, but . . ."

She held her breath.

"I feel like something inappropriate is developing between us. Something that I'm not comfortable with." He pulled at his tie, the same tie she'd so carefully put into place for him, and loosened the knot. Like he couldn't breathe. "I want you and William to feel at home in my house, but to jeopardize our relationship would be, well, foolish and irresponsible of me."

What did that mean? Was he trying to tell her he had feelings for her? Or was he trying to let her down gently?

Betty forced her chin up, made herself look him straight in the eye. She might as well be honest now.

"I, ah, think I feel the same. I mean, I know it wasn't long ago that I lost Charlie, but the way I feel for you, well . . ."

He pushed his chair back with such force the table shuddered, cutting her off.

"I have to go."

Betty looked up at him, humiliated. The look on his face said it all. That he was disgusted in her. That she should have kept her words to herself. That he'd known how she felt and he didn't feel the same.

"Luke." She reached out her hand but he pulled away. "Luke, please," she whispered, "I'm sorry, I thought you felt the same."

She didn't know what his face was telling her, but his eyes were flashing wildly.

"I'll be away on business for the next week or so. Take the car home. I'm going back to the office."

*No.* No! What had she done? What had just happened?

The waiter arrived at their table and placed her coffee in front of her, but she couldn't even bring herself to acknowledge it. Instead she turned to watch Luke hurry through the restaurant, pausing only to pay the check.

He didn't even look over his shoulder.

She'd just ruined any chance she'd had of something developing between them.

It was over. For good.

Now she might not even have a home to live in.

*He was gone.*

Betty stood, squared her shoulders and left her coffee untouched. Her heart might have been broken twice now, but she still had her dignity, not to mention the love of a child who was waiting for her. Wasn't that all that mattered? She'd obviously misread his signals, didn't understand him at all, but all she could do now was forget how she felt about him. Nothing was going to happen between them and that was the end of it.

# CHAPTER 41

June had never felt so exhilarated. All these months of learning to ride a horse and now she knew what all the fuss was about. She loved animals, all animals, but actually climbing on the back of one had never seemed that appealing to her. Riding here in America was something else entirely. She'd finally mastered the art of cantering, and she'd ridden alongside Eddie all the way down the valley, and then high up into the hills.

Now they were looking down over the farm, their house a speck in the distance.

"This is beautiful," she said out loud.

It truly was. So beautiful that it almost stole her breath away.

"Almost as beautiful as you."

Eddie rode up beside her and reached for her hand. Even after all this time his words made her blush. She didn't believe him, she never did. Not when he told her how lovely she looked or how much he loved her, because for some reason it still seemed too good to be true. Especially after everything her friends had gone through. Why was she the lucky one? Why had her new life here turned out so wonderfully?

"Are you happy here, June? Truly happy?"

She adjusted her weight in the saddle so she could face her husband.

"Eddie, I love it here, you know I do."

He lifted her hand to kiss it. "Good. I want you to be happy here, darlin.'"

She wanted so desperately to talk about children, to bring up the fact that she still wasn't pregnant, but she didn't want to ruin this moment. He was so patient with her, each month that she hadn't gotten pregnant he'd been there for her, but she didn't want to ruin this.

And she wasn't going to bring up adoption. Not yet. Not until she'd found out more about it.

"When I was at war, I thought about this view," he told her, looking down over the land. "And when I married you, I couldn't wait for you to be here, to see this with me."

"Imagine our children growing up here, Eddie. Riding over the land, running up to see their grandparents every day."

He took her hand again, his smile making his eyes crinkle in the corners.

"Speaking of family, I have a surprise for you."

"What is it?"

He made a face at her. "If I told you, how would it be a secret?"

She hated secrets. And what could it have to do with family?

"When do I get to find out?"

He gathered up his reins and his horse backed up a few steps before turning around.

"It's waiting for you at home. Let's go."

June's legs were killing her. Her calves were already starting to ache and her backside was numb, but she was desperate to find out what this surprise was about.

"Slow down!"

She looked back. Eddie was running behind her. He pushed her to the side and stood in front of the door.

"Wait here a minute," he said.

June stomped her foot, but she was finding it difficult to act angry.

He dropped a kiss to her protesting lips, and she kissed him back hungrily. But he wasn't falling for her seduction. Eddie placed his hand on her chest and gently pushed her back an inch.

"Wait here."

"Fine," she mumbled.

June waited. And grumbled to herself.

Then she heard a shuffle of feet and a noise that she couldn't place—a high-pitched noise and then a curse from Eddie.

"Honey, what's going on?" she called out.

Eddie reappeared, a blanket in his arms.

"What the . . . oh my gosh!"

Eddie's arms were moving and the blanket half fell away. In his arms, wriggling with all its might, was a pint-sized puppy. A ball of golden fluff that was itching to escape.

"Eddie!"

Her husband had a grin on his face that stretched from ear to ear.

"I know you want a family, June, and I thought this was a great place to start."

Her eyes filled with tears. She reached forward to take the puppy, its wet nose stroking her cheek, tongue flapping to lick her chin.

"I love him. Oh, I love him!"

She cuddled the puppy tight against her and leaned forward to kiss Eddie. The puppy clambered between them, trying to nip them as their lips met.

"*He* is actually a *she*. A golden retriever."

Betty snuggled the puppy against her face again, inhaling its sweet baby smell.

"A girl," she said aloud, more to the puppy than to Eddie. "A wee girl." Eddie put his arm around her shoulders.

"I thought we'd call her Ruby."

"Ruby," she repeated, holding the pup up so she could inspect her. "I think Ruby suits you just fine."

*She still wanted a baby, desperately, but a puppy was a good place to start. She could deal with a puppy.*

# CHAPTER 42

Betty pushed aside the heavy drape and let her fingers curl around the fabric. The glass was ever so slightly fogged over, and she rubbed her hand in a circular motion to better see outside.

It was a surreal experience, being here in this house. The dread that had descended over her when she'd been told of Charlie's death—it still sent a spasm of pain down her spine. But the insistent throb of grief had slowly started to fade, replaced by a longing that she couldn't quite describe. A longing she hadn't even felt that first night she'd spent with her husband. A longing that she didn't want to admit to, but one that was still there, constantly reminding her of what she'd lost.

Every time she thought of Luke, she wanted to be closer to him. To hold him. For him to admit that he felt it too.

But Luke was gone. As if it was her fault that something was happening between them. As if he was never coming back.

A tiny gurgle was replaced by a cry, and Betty turned to see William wriggling in the cot. She let the drape fall back into place and pulled her nightdress tighter around her body, trying to warm a chill that she knew wasn't caused by the cold. She was trying to pretend she wasn't waiting for him, but the truth was she was anxious for him to return. She had thought of little else since he'd left. Where had he gone? He'd told her it was a business trip, told Ivy he could be gone for a week or two. But she wasn't so sure. It felt like he'd gone and he wasn't coming back.

*Maybe he was waiting for her to leave.*

William cried again, more insistently this time.

"I'm coming," she cooed, eyes on her little boy. "Mama's coming."

He was sitting up, ruffled from bed and flushed in the face. He smiled as he saw her, his mouth breaking into a grin that warmed her heart every time she looked at him.

"Hello, wee man." Betty scooped him up and cradled him against her, even though he was getting heavy. "Hello."

He smiled up at her and she felt a familiar flutter of happiness.

"Mama." He kept smiling. "Ma-ma." He touched her face and giggled.

She smiled back. "What are you doing awake, mister?" The pleasure he brought her was indescribable—unimaginable to anyone who hadn't yet been blessed with a child, but real to her every single day.

Without her son, she would never have travelled here, would never have met Luke. And even though she still felt a touch of guilt, at the thoughts and feelings she had for him, there was no way she could forget them. No way she could ignore them any longer or push away the longing within her that beat like a constant drum, even though he'd already turned her down.

Betty heard the crunch of gravel as footfalls echoed outside. She dared not hope it was Luke home already, but the way the door shut, with such a thud, made her sure it was. Had he come home to be with her? Returned early because he couldn't wait to be back in her company?

Or had he returned to tell her to leave? That she'd outstayed her welcome? Maybe he couldn't forgive her for what she'd said at lunch the other day.

The slam of an internal door made her jump. She looked down at the alarmed eyes of her son and held him tighter.

From what she'd heard so far, it was definitely Luke; no one else had the authority to slam a door in this house. Ivy certainly wouldn't and neither would one of the maids.

*And who else would be arriving at this time of night?*

Betty heard feet stomping up the stairs. She quickly rose and turned the key in her door, locking it.

"Ssshh, baby. Shoosh now." She sat him on her bed, pressed against her pillows, and passed William the stuffed rabbit June had given him when she'd been to visit.

William started to jump the toy about, smiling, and she scooted over to the mirror. She was a mess. Luke couldn't see her looking like this.

*If it was actually Luke, and not an intruder.*

There was a knock at her door. Followed by a few more. Then the handle turned.

The lock stopped it from being opened.

"Betty? Betty, open this door now."

It was Luke. *Oh my.*

It was Luke!

His voice was urgent.

"Just a moment," she called back.

Betty brushed her hair up and pinned it off her neck, pulled it softly off her face.

"Betty!"

She was nervous. Her hands were shaking and a cool bead of sweat had broken out across her forehead. She powdered it away.

"One minute, Luke."

"Now!"

He growled out the word.

She had wanted to get changed first, to be presentable when she opened the door, but if she didn't comply he was going to have the entire household coming up to see what was going on, or possibly bash the door down.

She stood up. Color flushed her neck, curling gently up to her face. She turned from the mirror and crossed the room. William was starting to whimper, his bottom lip quivering.

"It's okay, darling," she whispered to him.

When she unlocked the door, it was pushed open with such force that it almost knocked her over.

"Luke!"

His eyes stopped her. They looked hungry, wild, far from their usual calm brown. His cheeks were covered with stubble, not freshly shaved like she was used to seeing.

"If you'd just let me finish dressing we could have been a little more civilized." She was trying to be strong but her words, her voice, were weak.

Luke took two strides, two long slow strides, until he was standing close enough to push her over with his chest. So close that she could have fallen into him just to feel his body against hers.

He reached for the back of her head then. Betty couldn't breathe, couldn't think. He cupped his hand to her hair and bent slowly, so slowly, until his lips touched hers.

She wanted to resist. To pull away and tell him no. After the way he'd run, the way he'd turned her down when she'd tried to be honest with him, he had some explaining to do. But she couldn't. Instead she responded the only way she could—kissing him back, arching into him as he pulled her even closer.

William began to gurgle, but she forced the sound away. All she wanted was to stay like this, tucked into Luke's frame, lost to the feeling of his lips touching hers. Knowing that he felt the same way she did, and that they could ignore it no longer.

He pulled away. Left her feeling confused. Cold. Upset. *Alone.*

"Betty, I'm sorry. I'm so sorry."

She scanned Luke's face. Gone was the fury, the wildness of before. The wild man who'd been pounding on her door was replaced with the Luke she'd come to love. With the kind, tortured man who only wanted to do the right thing. Who wanted her but was afraid what it would mean to admit it.

And he'd kissed her! Kissed her like she'd never imagined he ever would.

"I thought you were going to tell me to leave," she admitted.

He took a step to the side, then another, before dropping to the bed. His long legs folded as he sat on the edge of it.

"I didn't know what to do. I . . . I never should have run out on you like that."

She moved closer to him, reaching past to pull William into her arms as he flapped his hands at her.

"Can I?"

She passed him to Luke, tucked him into his outstretched arms. He wriggled to sit up on his Uncle's lap, hands on his jacket, pulling at his buttons.

"I've missed you, little man," Luke told him.

William smiled.

"I've been a fool, Betty. A bloody fool."

Luke transferred William to one arm and reached into his trouser pocket.

Betty sat down beside them, her eyes on William. She was too scared to look at Luke. Too worried about what they'd done. How she'd responded. What it meant.

Now he knew exactly how she felt. There was no going back from that.

"Luke, we missed you too. Both of us." Her voice was so quiet, so low, that she barely recognized it.

He pulled out a ring from his pocket and held it toward her.

Betty nearly fell off the bed. Her head was starting to pound like she'd just run up a flight of stairs. Why did he have a ring? What was he doing?

"Betty, this was my grandmother's ring. If Charlie had still been alive when you'd arrived, he would have given it to you."

"No." She couldn't stop it, the word just came out. "No, no, no."

"*Yes.*" Now it was Luke's voice that had dropped. "Charlie's not here anymore, I know that, but I still want you to have it."

She didn't understand. What was he saying?

"Betty?" He passed William to her and knelt beside the bed, in front of her. "Betty, will you marry me?"

# PART THREE

# CHAPTER 43
## APRIL 1947

The sun shone from high above, without a cloud to hinder the rays as they fell over the long stretch of lawn. The grass had been mowed in stripes, falling away toward the white flowers adorning the magnolia trees.

Betty had never felt so happy. *So nostalgic.* So at peace with her life.

"Are you ready, darling?"

She turned from the upstairs window to face Luke. He slid his arms around her waist, pulling her in tight.

"Is he here?"

Luke dropped a kiss to her forehead, eyes crinkled at the corners as he smiled down at her.

"He will be soon."

Betty watched as he walked away. There was nothing about him she didn't love. He wasn't Charlie, but that's why she loved him. Because even though he was different, so different from his brother, he was a strong enough man to let her love Charlie, too. No one could ever take away how she'd felt for her first husband, and she saw him in their son every day, but Luke meant the world to her as well.

She stole one last look out the window, down toward the white rose they had planted at the base of the garden. A simple white cross stood behind it, for the rose to grow up and around—a marker to ensure they never forgot Charlie.

And the exact spot she and Luke were to be married.

Betty took a deep breath and squared her shoulders. She stopped only to look at her silhouette in the full-length mirror. Her dress was simple. A dusky-pink chiffon that fell just below her calf. She had pinned her hair up, a flower pulling it gently off her forehead.

Today was her wedding day, and she felt wonderful. Pretty, confident, and happy. *So happy.*

Betty had expected her nerves to start fluttering as she walked toward Luke, but her only problem was trying to stop smiling. The priest stood, bible in hand, waiting for her, standing beside her husband-to-be.

"Are you ready?"

Betty nodded. "Yes."

Luke took her hands in his. She was vaguely aware of Ivy and their gardener standing nearby, their only witnesses to the ceremony, but she was barely conscious of anything other than Luke before her.

They hadn't wanted a fuss, nor any guests, because this was about them. This was about pledging their love for one another before God, with Charlie still in their memories.

*This was about the future.*

"I love you, Betty."

She blinked away her tears. "And I love you, Luke. More than you'll ever know."

# CHAPTER 44

The only emotion in Betty's body right now was happiness. She squeezed Luke's hand as it lay on her knee beneath the table. *It was unreal.* After making her think they were going out for a simple dinner he'd turned their wedding evening into a night she'd never forget.

Fairy lights hung from the branches above them, sending spidery shadows over the table, with paper lanterns swinging softly in the breeze. They had only a handful of guests, despite the extravagance, but there was no one else Betty would have invited.

Laughter filled the night air.

"Betty?"

She turned to face June. Her friend sat beside her husband, with Ivy at the head of the table and Alice and Ralph on the other side.

"Do you remember how much you ate on the ship? Seriously? I don't think I had even one conversation with you that didn't include the word chocolate," said June.

"Or chip!" announced Alice with a laugh. "As in chocolate chip."

Betty laughed along with them. "Well, I was eating for two then. It wasn't like I was obsessed with food without good reason."

Luke touched her cheek and she turned her face into his palm. It felt right, being here with him in the company of her friends. *So right.*

"I would like to propose a toast," announced Luke, taking his eyes off her to face the table.

He stood, one hand extending his glass in the air, the other pulling her up beside him.

"No one is more surprised than me that I managed to convince Betty to become my wife." They all laughed, Betty included. "I saw something in Betty the day she walked into my home, and although I didn't want to admit it, I loved her for a long time before I managed to say it out loud."

Everyone was quiet now. Listening. Waiting to hear what Luke was going to say.

"You girls all came a long way to get here, put faith in the men you loved about the life that was waiting for you." He paused, holding her hand tighter. "I guess what I'm trying to say is that I'm so pleased Betty came here. I'm so pleased she married my brother, that he was able to bring this wonderful woman into my life. Today I became a husband *and* a father, and I couldn't be happier." He cleared his throat. "And I'd like to make a special mention of Charlie." He smiled over at Betty. "I'd do anything to have him back, but I'd also like him to know that since he can't be here, I'll look after Betty for the rest of my life. I'll never let her forget you, and I'll make sure your son knows all about his brave pilot father." Luke had tears in his eyes and Betty looked away as she wiped her own cheeks.

"To the newly married couple," declared Ralph, glass high in the air.

"And to Madeline," said Betty, holding her own glass before her. "For the friend we made at sea."

They all clinked glasses and took a sip. A waiter appeared from inside with dessert, and they all took their seats. *All except for Betty*. She'd been waiting for the right moment, and it felt like now.

"Before we tuck into the sweet treats," she said, "I have a letter from Madeline that she wanted me to read today. She said she hoped we'd all be together to celebrate."

She glanced at Alice then June. They were both nodding, desperate to have news of her.

Betty reached beneath her napkin where the folded letter lay, and held it up to the closest light. She had read it so many times over herself that she almost knew it by heart, but she didn't want to miss a word.

*'To my darling friends, and to Betty, on your wedding day. Well, I couldn't say a bad word about your choice in husband, Betty, even if I tried. Not many men would offer the assistance that your good husband gave me, although I have my suspicions that he was only trying to impress you.'*

Betty smiled and looked at Luke. He just shrugged, still grinning.

*'But what I can say with all my heart is that I want you to be happy, and darling William too, even though I can't be there with you. I am so pleased that I came home. It's like I was asleep for a year and now I'm awake. The sound of my mother's voice, the smell of tea brewing on the stove, even walking down our street. It is everything I missed while I was in America. I may never come to terms with my father's passing, but I feel close to him here and that is what matters.'*

*'I don't know how I ever thought I could live away from here, but at least I tried. What I don't regret is meeting you girls, though, and of course I would be lost without my beautiful daughter. I tell*

*her often of the special aunties she has living on the other side of the world in big sky country.'*

Betty dabbed at her eyes. She didn't dare look at her friends for fear of seeing them crying, too. It was hard enough reading Madeline's words without seeing their reaction.

*'Have a wonderful wedding day, my love. I wish I could be there, and I want you to promise never to forget me, because I will never forget you. My love and kisses, Madeline.'*

Luke put his arm around her shoulders as she sat back down. Even Ivy looked teary when Betty finally braved a look around the table.

"To Madeline," said Alice, standing with her glass raised, toasting their friend again, only with more gusto this time.

"To Madeline," affirmed June, catching Betty's eye with her smile as she rose.

"And to us girls, for surviving that God-awful trip here," said Alice.

❧

The music swirled around them like it had a personality of its own. Luke was fiddling with the sound as Ralph swung Alice to her feet and started twirling her around. They'd all kicked their shoes off to dance on the lawn, and June was waiting for Eddie to untie his shoelaces to join her.

"I still don't see why I have to take mine off, too," he grumbled.

June gave him a playful shove. "You could break my little toes with those big clod-hoppers."

"Clod what?"

She shook her head. "Never mind, come on!"

She might have liked teasing him, but June would have danced with Eddie even if she had to stand on stilts to do so. There was nothing she liked better than being in his arms.

"So have you told them yet?" Eddie asked.

She shrugged. "Told them what?"

"About the baby?"

June pulled him closer. "This is Betty's big day. We can tell them about the adoption another time. Besides, until I have the baby in my arms it doesn't feel real."

They'd signed the adoption papers only yesterday. The young girl had been so excited they'd found her, when they'd offered her unborn child the kind of home and family that any mother would dream of for their baby.

"Can you believe we'll have a baby in our home in less than a month?"

June grinned as he squeezed her. "We might need to make two nurseries though."

Eddie stopped, his feet immobile. "You think she could be having twins?"

That made June laugh. She had known he wouldn't guess, but she hadn't thought of that possibility.

"I don't think so."

She tried to keep a straight face.

"Then what?"

June leaned in to her husband, mouth hovering over his ear.

"We're going to need two nurseries because I'm pregnant, Eddie," she whispered.

He still didn't move.

"Did you hear me?" she spoke louder this time.

"Pregnant?"

June pulled him around in a circle, laughing at the look on his face.

"Pregnant," June affirmed. "We're going to have two babies, Eddie. Two babies!"

He shook his head, in disbelief, but she saw the smirk of his mouth as he watched her.

"What?"

Eddie laughed. "I thought I was going to be the one surprising you tonight."

This time it was she who stopped moving.

"Edward West, you tell me right this minute what you're hiding from me."

"Your parents arrive tomorrow. It was supposed to be a secret but it turns out I'm not that good at keeping things from you."

"Tomorrow!" she squealed.

He laughed and scooped her up into his arms.

"Tomorrow. They'll be waiting at the house by the time we arrive home."

ᕙᕗ

Alice let her head fall on Ralph's shoulder as they walked up the steps to Betty and Luke's house, where they were staying over. It had been a long night, but an enjoyable one. Being around Betty and June again had been good for her. They shared a bond that could never be broken, something that would keep pulling them together forever.

"Are you happy, Alice?" Ralph asked.

She stopped and took her husband's hands. There was nothing she could say in answer to his question other than *yes*. They'd had their share of hard times, they'd struggled through a time that she hadn't thought would be possible to survive, and she'd acted in a way that was unforgivable. *But they'd survived it. They'd made it.* They had a future, and a happy one at that.

"I don't know how to tell you how happy I am, Ralph. But yes, the answer is yes."

He bent to kiss her.

"Even after you've had my mother staying for another two weeks?"

She kissed him back, lips not leaving his.

"Mmm-hmm," she murmured.

"We'll see. She might drive you back home across the ocean yet."

"Never," said Alice, wrapping her arms tight around her man. "I'll never, ever leave you Ralph. I promise."

# CHAPTER 45

Madeline surveyed the room. She did her best to inhale a quiet lungful of air but worried it came out more as a gasp.

She wasn't used to crowds. Especially not crowds gathered to see her.

The room was alive. Voices mingled to an almost deafening level, assaulting her ears as she did her best to push them out. She wished for her own home. To be back with her family, tucked up in her chair by the fire, shawl about her arms, instead of preparing to speak. At least now home was only a train ride away—there was no longer an ocean to separate her from where she wanted to be.

She felt a tap on her shoulder.

"Mrs. Parker, it's time."

Her pulse started racing again. Her face flooded with heat, burning a fiery flush down her neck.

"Mrs. Parker?"

She nodded, perhaps a little too vigorously. "Yes. Yes, of course."

"Come this way then."

She cleared her throat and tried to avoid looking at anyone's face in particular. Madeline focused on a spot on the back wall, trying to keep the nerves from rearing into her mind again.

The flash of a camera bulb made her blink, but she kept her focus. She had a speech to read, just like she'd rehearsed. If she lost her way she could just read her notes. *If her wet, sweaty palms didn't let the paper slip away first.*

They were all waiting for her to speak.

"My time as a foreign bride in America taught me many things." Madeline took another gulp of air and tried to settle into a rhythm. "First of all, it made me realize that to live without your family, in a foreign country, is almost impossible. Or at least it is when your new family, the one you have sacrificed so much to be with, considers you a foreign alien."

Madeline tried to slow herself down. She needed to be calm, to portray what it had been like for her over there. *She needed to speak from her heart.*

The crowd was silent, even as she took a sip of water, but she didn't make eye contact still. Not yet. She wasn't confident enough to do that yet. A cough made her jump, but she forced herself to continue.

"I left my country with a heart full of love, prepared to give everything up for my husband, but now I find myself asking what the sacrifice of a woman should be. Should a new wife accept being lied to? Should she accept a home with no love, a home where she is treated like a slave?"

A murmur started amongst the women then, but she didn't stop, only paused enough to catch her breath and let her eyes trace the words on the page. If she faltered now she wouldn't be able to start over again.

"Many of you may be wondering how bad it could be. How I could leave my husband behind? But my answer is to look at me and put yourself in my position. I married a man who told me he loved me, who promised me things that I had no reason to doubt. I ask you, would your child deserve to live in a home with no love, when a family who could provide that love were waiting here in London? Could you imagine what it's like to be a stranger, a foreigner, and be alone?"

Madeline knew that would get the crowd going, but then this was what they wanted. The newspaper publisher had wanted controversy, and she needed the money, so it was worth it. And besides, she wanted to tell her story. This was the truth, not some fabricated novel. It was the truth and she wanted to tell it.

"I don't regret my time in America. Despite the hardships I faced, I have a beautiful child whom I will treasure forever, and I made friends who will be in my heart until my dying days. It was an experience I will never forget, a time in my life that I will treasure but that will also haunt me, but it is something I'm pleased to say I lived through."

Her voice choked but she pushed through. *Had to.* She could cry later, but right now she needed to tell the last of her story. Every time she thought of how she'd left, what had made her finally give up, it made her angry. But losing her father was something she couldn't ever recover from, and something she couldn't ever forget.

"The women I met on my way to America became my closest friends. Their stories are different, although not without their own hardships, but those women got me through the hard times and made me see a way to escape my unhappiness. To them, I will be eternally grateful."

"If I had the opportunity to live the life I dreamed of, I wouldn't have hesitated when my husband asked for my hand in marriage. Maybe if I had had the husband I deserved, then it would have been worth it. But all I know now, all I can think, is that walking away from your own family for a chance at love, is a chance that has too many risks to take." She paused. "Thank you."

Madeline missed her friends so much. She would do anything to see Betty, June, and Alice again, but she knew she'd never see them. Not unless one of them took a trip home. For now, she had to be content with writing letters and receiving them. And telling her story.

"If you would like to know more about Mrs. Parker's time in America, I encourage you to buy her memoir, which she will sign for you should you wish. We will also be publishing a series of articles starting Monday of next week in the *Herald*."

"Mrs. Parker!"

"Madeline!"

"Mrs. Parker will not be taking questions."

"But is it true? What they say about our English girls and their unrealistic dreams?"

Madeline stopped. Her heart started to race.

She didn't have to answer. She didn't have to.

*But she wanted to.*

Madeline turned around and walked back to the makeshift stage, ready to speak to the crowd again.

"I am well aware that there have been many reports in newspapers here and in America, about disillusioned war brides." She let out a nervous chuckle. "My own mother cut out many such pieces and I've looked over every one since my return."

The room was quiet except for the odd laugh.

"I'm sure there were many disillusioned brides, or maybe there weren't, but all I can say for sure is that I wasn't one of them. When my husband told me he lived on a farm and had a family who would love me, I believed him. I didn't dream of money and a lavish lifestyle, all I wanted was a home and love. This wasn't about reality falling short of some romantic notion I never held, or rebelling against working hard alongside my man. This was about my

353

being a woman and expecting a real husband, a real family, and a real chance at a happy life."

Madeline stepped aside as her publisher took center stage. Her eyes did rove then, over the many faces, and she saw a mixed result. Sadness in some, understanding in others, and disgust in the remainder, or perhaps they just couldn't understand what she'd gone through.

But right now, all she cared about was the opinion of her family. Of her child. Of the friends who'd helped her escape. The people that mattered were the ones who would understand, and if telling her story helped just one other girl find the courage to walk away from a similar situation, it would be worth it.

"Mrs. Parker will take a moment to refresh herself, then she will see you all in the lobby for any questions and to sign your books."

She let herself be led away.

For the first time since she'd left, she truly wished she were back in America. Just for an afternoon. So she could sit in the sun at Betty's place again, all four of them, and talk. Laugh. Cry. They were the only women in the world who'd truly understand what she'd been through and why she'd had to leave.

She'd never forget their little war bride club. And she bet they'd never forget her either.

Madeline looked back at the crowd milling about, still unsure of how she felt about sharing her story. It meant a degree of financial security for their little family of two, so it was worth it, but . . . There was always a *but* when it came to divulging one's personal life.

She shut her eyes for a second and imagined her friends; June, Betty, and Alice all standing there, the only people in the room. That she was about to talk candidly with them about what had happened instead of with strangers.

When she opened her eyes it was with a smile on her face. No matter what she'd been through, how awful her experience had been, it had been worth it. Because she had her daughter, and because she had met the best friends of her life.

# ACKNOWLEDGEMENTS

I feel incredibly fortunate to have a career that I genuinely love. Even when I'm tired and the computer screen is the last thing I want to stare at, I always remind myself how amazing it is that I can write stories for a living! But I couldn't do what I love without my amazing support crew—being a mum to two darling little boys is a full-time job in itself, and I am so thankful to have an amazing mother who helps me on a daily basis. Without her I'd be lost, so I would like to say special thanks to her for being the best "granny nanny," for all the chats about my latest project, and the great meals that come our way, especially when I'm on deadline. I'd also like to acknowledge my equally fantastic dad, or as he's affectionately known by my boys as "Ganga."

I'm also fortunate to have a husband who doesn't think it's odd at all when I stare off into space thinking about characters! Hamish, you are truly my real-life hero, and I appreciate all the brainstorming sessions I make you endure, the times you spend sitting up late just so I'm not working into the night on my own, and for being so supportive of my career (even in the long years before I was published!).

I also have a great network of author friends, and they all need special mentions. Natalie, you are my rock and you have been for years. Nicola, where would I be without your advice and support? And Yvonne, thank you for being the best "writing sprint buddy" in the world. I would hate to be on this journey without the three of you!

I'd also like to say thanks to my agent extraordinaire, Laura Bradford. Your support, advice, and assistance over the past couple of years has been invaluable. I appreciate you more than you'll probably ever realize. Thank you!

My fantastic editor, Sophie Wilson, also needs a special mention. It was an amazing experience working with you, and the book is so much stronger thanks to your input.

And finally to Emilie Marneur, acquiring editor at Amazon Publishing. Thank you for reading my book and loving it! I still smile when I think of all the lovely things you and your colleagues had to say about this story.

# ABOUT THE AUTHOR

*Photo © 2014 Carys Monteath*

As a child, Soraya Lane dreamed of becoming an author. Fast forward a few years, and Soraya is now living her dream! She describes being an author as "the best job in the world." She lives with her own real-life hero and two young sons on a small farm in New Zealand, surrounded by animals, with an office overlooking a field where their horses graze.

For more information about Soraya, her books, and her writing life, visit sorayalane.com or www.facebook.com/SorayaLaneAuthor, or follow her on Twitter @Soraya_Lane.